D1636748

THE
BEACON STREET
BOOKSHOP

Center Point
Large Print

Also by Carla Laureano and available from Center Point Large Print:

Brunch at Bittersweet Café
The Solid Grounds Coffee Company
Provenance
The Broken Hearts Bakery

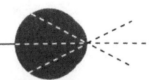

**This Large Print Book carries the
Seal of Approval of N.A.V.H.**

THE BEACON STREET BOOKSHOP

A HAVEN RIDGE NOVEL

CARLA LAUREANO

CENTER POINT LARGE PRINT
THORNDIKE, MAINE

ACKNOWLEDGMENTS

Some books come together by magic, some have to be coaxed into existence, and others have to be wrestled into submission. *The Beacon Street Bookshop* was definitely the latter—I loved these characters so much that I just kept writing . . . and writing . . . and writing . . . until the book was longer and more involved than anyone really wanted to read in a single volume!

I owe a long list of people gratitude for their encouragement and wisdom in helping me transform the behemoth of a first draft into the lean (kinda) romance machine it is now. First of all, thanks to my Facebook Reader Room: your encouragement and enthusiasm kept me going as the first draft stretched way beyond my initial deadline. Second, to my amazing Haven Ridge Beta Team—Meaghan Ahlbrand, Jessica Baker, Elisabeth Callahan, Leslie Florea, Mindy Houng, Amy Parrish, and Hope Thacker—you guys are the most astute, intelligent group of readers I've had the privilege of working with, and your insight is so, so appreciated!

Special thanks to my copyeditor, Denise Harmer, who makes me look smart and stuff, and my proofreader, Sarah Stears. This final book wouldn't be so pretty or this correct without you! I'm so appreciative.

And last, to my awesome family and friends who cheered me on, told me I was pretty and that my book didn't stink, and kept me going to the end: my husband, Rey; my sons, Nathan and Preston; and my BFFs Lori Twichell and Amber Lynn Perry. You're the best!

CHAPTER ONE

For the first time in her adult life, she was unemployed.

It was the first thing that popped into Olivia Quinn's head when she opened her eyes, just as it had been for the last month since she quit her job—or rather, been forced to leave. She'd been supporting herself since college, even if that had just meant an unbroken line of office jobs and internships and entry-level positions, until she landed her dream job.

Senior editor for a children's and young adult book line with Altea Press.

Each morning, Liv had woken up with excitement and anticipation pressing in her chest . . . no matter what was on the schedule for the day, whether it was editing a new author, presenting a property she wanted to acquire to the publishing board, or just sorting through her full inbox for the next great book. It had been her childhood dream. She was good at it. And every day she'd been grateful to sit down at the computer in her living room, look out onto the sweep of native Colorado trees and grasses outside her window, and do what she loved most in the world.

Until now.

Liv pushed back the covers on her bed and

swung her bare feet to the cool wood floor, shoving down the negative thoughts that threatened to crowd in. Once she started down this road, she knew it was a short slide to all the other worries that came along with being unemployed: like how she was going to pay her bills and what she was going to do with her life.

"It will all be okay," she told herself brightly, willing herself to believe it. She stood up straight, stretched her hands overhead, and then bent to place her palms on the floor, breathing into the stretch in her back and hamstrings. Thanks to her twice-weekly Pilates sessions, her body didn't feel nearly as old as her weary brain. Unfortunately, those workouts had been the first things to disappear along with her job. Another thing she couldn't dwell on this morning.

Instead, she threw on a lightweight cardigan over her shorts and tank top and padded down the hallway into her partially-finished kitchen, letting her eyes glide over the particle board countertops and the chipped wallboard as she went about her morning coffee routine. The remodel was supposed to have been finished sometime last year, but she'd run out of money—thanks to a flaky contractor who had gouged her and then never finished—long before the specter of unemployment had reared its ugly head.

"Living the dream," she murmured as she

poured herself a cup of coffee and raised it in silent salute.

"Do I smell coffee?"

Liv started at the voice, sloshing liquid over the rim of her cup. She grabbed some paper towels and dabbed the cup before she knelt to wipe the floor. "Taylor! What are you doing up this early?"

Liv's sixteen-year-old stepdaughter stumbled into the kitchen, sliding past her to the coffee pot, where she poured herself her own cup before doctoring it heavily with cream and sugar. "We're going hiking this morning."

Liv lifted an eyebrow. "Hiking?"

It wasn't exactly strange for her stepdaughter to do something outside on her summer break, but hiking? She wasn't sure that the girl owned footwear other than Doc Martens, and her all-black wardrobe was certainly going to be unpleasant out in the blinding Colorado sunshine. Liv could tell from the temperature in the house this morning that it was going to be a hot one.

Taylor wrapped her hands around the mug and cocked a hip against the counter. "Don't sound so surprised. I like hiking."

"Mmm-hmm. And who exactly can I thank for this newfound love of the outdoors?"

Color rose in the girl's cheeks and she buried herself in her coffee mug so she didn't have to look at Liv. That was answer enough, even before she said, "Dylan."

Liv turned away to refill her now half-full mug so Taylor wouldn't see her smile. Dylan had been Taylor's date for the Valentine's Day dance earlier this year, and though it had taken a while for them to work up to it, he'd become her first real boyfriend. Ugh. Boyfriend. She was guardian to a girl who had a *boyfriend*. She'd always teased Jason about the fact he was going to have to deal with his teenage daughter dating, but now she was the one who got to experience the drama and the heartache and the embarrassing talks. If she didn't know better, she'd think he'd planned his plane crash to miss the painful teen years and stick Liv with the responsibility.

The flippant thought struck her with guilt, crushing the bit of amusement she'd felt earlier. It was one thing to resort to gallows humor to deal with her own grief, but another to suggest her late husband would have purposely abandoned his daughter.

Instead, she turned her attention to the more important matter. "Who is going on this hike?"

Now Taylor spun away. "Just the two of us."

"Taylor—"

"Liv, I'm sixteen years old. I don't need a chaperone."

"Being sixteen years old is exactly why you need a chaperone."

Taylor arched an eyebrow in her direction. "Do

you really think we're gonna . . . I don't know . . . get it on in the middle of the hiking trail where anyone could see us? Give me a break."

Liv let that one go. Taylor was right. Besides, there was nothing that she could do to control the teen's decisions. The only thing parents could do was talk to their kids, set their expectations, and pray that they made the right choices.

And no matter how much they avoided saying it, Liv wasn't Taylor's mom.

"Yeah. I know. I just . . . it's fine. Make sure your phone is on and the GPS is active. I need to know where to send Search and Rescue if you're not home by dark."

That earned an eye roll, but Taylor did shuffle around the kitchen island to give her a quick hug around the waist. "Thanks, Liv. I promise I won't be too late."

"You better not be. I was thinking about throwing steak on the barbecue and you wouldn't want to miss that. In fact, invite Dylan over. He's a boy. Boys like steak."

Taylor smirked. "Yeah. Never gonna happen. I should go get ready now."

"Yeah, you go do that." *While I drink the rest of this coffee and then sit down at the computer to look for jobs that have miraculously overnight materialized since the last time I looked.*

The teen must have heard something in her voice, though, because she paused in the kitchen doorway. "Liv? Are you all right? Do you want me to stay?"

"No!" Liv forced cheer into her tone. "Of course not. Go have fun."

Taylor didn't look convinced, but she nodded and turned away. Liv wiped a hand over her face and let out a long, steady breath. She had to get it together. If not for her own sake, then Taylor's. The girl had been through enough upheaval and change in her young life, first with her dad remarrying, then losing him two short years later and becoming a ward of the stepmom she hadn't had any hand in choosing. They got along well—Liv couldn't have loved Taylor more if she'd been her own flesh and blood—but she was always aware that even if she could offer her the world, she'd always be second best, a poor replacement for having two birth parents who were alive, engaged, and present in her life.

So Liv needed to stop feeling sorry for herself, get her stuff together, and make the best of it.

An hour later, Taylor bounded out of her room at the buzz of the gate call button. Liv stood corrected—Taylor did own a pair of hiking boots, but she'd unsurprisingly paired them with a pair of black cut-offs, a black tank top, and a black baseball cap. "Bye!" she called, heading for the door. "I'll be back tonight!"

"Take a water bottle and sunscreen," Liv called after her, but the door closed so quickly, she knew that she was just talking to dead air. Fine. She only hoped that Dylan had more experience with outdoor things than her stepdaughter.

Even though she'd barely heard a peep all morning, just knowing that she was alone in the house made the air feel silent and stale. Liv cast a mournful look at her laptop, still closed on the desk in the living room, and made an executive decision. She was going to town.

Fifteen minutes later, driving into historic downtown Haven Ridge with the windows of her SUV down and a warm breeze ruffling her hair, she took her first full, easy breath of the morning. She'd needed the reminder of why she was here, the decisions she'd made. She could have kept her job if she'd been willing to move back to New York City, where Taylor had been born and where Liv had met Jason. But every time she'd brought up the possibility, Taylor had looked like someone had kicked a puppy.

With Jason gone, there was no way Liv could take away Haven Ridge.

And now, driving down the town's main drag, Liv knew she couldn't have given up her hometown either. It was in her blood—the beautiful red brick buildings with their white plaster trim, the sweeping hills dotted with evergreens and piñon pine and wild Colorado grasses, the deep blue sky streaked with clouds. At this altitude, they were close enough that it

13

seemed impossible that she couldn't just reach up and pluck them from the sky like puffs of cotton candy.

Her saving grace was that when she looked at the various landmarks, she didn't just see places where she and Jason had talked, held hands, kissed. She also remembered the times she'd played on the swings as a child, acted as sandwich delivery person for the cafe, spent countless afternoons at a diner table eating French fries with her best friends. This place was part of her, more than ever now that those two best friends were back in town.

Instantly, her entire mood brightened. She pulled up at the curb on Dogwood Street and smiled at the neat white lettering on the front window of the building: *Broken Hearts Bakery.* The edges of the window were decorated with hand-drawn scrolls and vines, from which cracked and stitched hearts hung like clusters of grapes. It was whimsical and beautiful and made all the more special by the fact that it was the fulfillment of her best friend's dream.

Liv hopped out of the SUV, not bothering to lock it behind her, and strolled through the front door amid the jingle of harness bells. Instantly, the fragrance of sugar and butter and chocolate and vanilla enveloped her. Behind the glassed-in bakery case stood a teenager with bright red hair, wearing a white apron.

"Rebekah!" Liv greeted the girl with a smile—she was one of Taylor's best friends, so Liv had known her for years. "How's business?"

"Not bad," Rebekah said, flashing her a smile. "Are you looking for Gemma?"

"Yeah. Is she here?" Liv leaned over the counter to peek through the window in the swinging door to the back. The sound of the big industrial mixer was a sure sign that there was something in the works.

"No, I think she's upstairs in her office. That's Aunt Chelsea." Before Liv could say anything, Rebekah was across the room and pushing through the door. "Aunt Chelsea, Liv's here!"

Liv chuckled to herself. There was no reason to disturb the woman at work, but now that she had, she wasn't going to disappear. A few seconds later, the mixer shut off and a petite blonde wearing a chef's coat came through the door. "Liv!"

"Hey Chelsea. I didn't mean to interrupt you. I was actually looking for Gemma."

Chelsea wiped her floury hands on her apron. "I think she's upstairs in her office. Do you want me to call her for you?"

"No, I'll just go up. Is she with a client?"

"She came down for cookies first thing this morning, so maybe? That was a while ago, though."

Liv paused and looked over the woman.

15

She'd once been the high school mean girl, spreading rumors about Gemma and her mom, but she'd matured plenty in the ensuing years, mostly because of an abusive marriage and her subsequent divorce. "How's it going here?"

"Good!" Chelsea smiled brightly, the enthusiasm in her voice genuine. "Business is better than expected, the new menu items are a hit, Gemma seems happy with the way everything's going."

"And how are *you?*"

Chelsea's smile faltered a little and she darted a glance at Rebekah, who was busying herself by rearranging things in the case that didn't need to be rearranged. "I'm doing well, all things considered."

"If you need anything . . ."

Chelsea waved her off. "No, you did enough. I'll always be grateful you gave us a place to stay when we needed it. Speaking of . . . any luck on the apartment rental?"

Liv shook her head. "Not yet. But you know, it's not like Haven Ridge is exactly a hot spot for new residents."

"You'll find someone. It's a beautiful place."

Liv gave her a vague smile, feeling the twinges of worry seeping in at the reminder of yet another thing that wasn't going to plan. If she could rent the apartment above the garage, it would take some of the pressure off her to find a job. "I'm sorry to interrupt you at work. I'm going to go upstairs and see if Gemma's in."

"Always nice to see you. Tell Gemma the cherry Danishes were a hit this morning."

"I will." Liv flashed a smile at her and Rebekah, then slipped out the front door in another tinkle of bells, only to go through a second door into the building's stairwell.

Up she went in the dark wood-paneled hallway, until she came to a door on the landing with a sedate, professional sign that read: *Gemma Van Buren, Attorney at Law.* She hesitated for a moment before she rapped sharply.

Mere seconds later, the door opened to reveal a tall brunette wearing a pair of slacks and a silky blouse. Before she even said a word, the woman pulled her into a tight hug. "Girl, I was about to send out the National Guard to look for you. Where have you been all week?"

Gemma ushered her in, shutting and locking the door behind her. Liv smiled, her heart lightening at the sight of her lifelong best friend. "Just busy. Looking for work."

"And how is that going?" Gemma gestured for Liv to choose one of four club chairs clustered in front of the old-fashioned fireplace and seated herself across from her. An assortment of cookies sat beneath a glass cake dome on the round table in front of her. When Gemma waved toward them, she shook her head.

"Slow," Liv said, while her eyes wandered around the office space.

Gemma followed her gaze. "You know, if you wanted to change careers, I think you could make a go of it as an interior designer. This place turned out gorgeous."

Liv had to admit it was true. It had taken a fair amount of elbow grease to transform the grimy space, but now the plaster walls were painted in a calming, historic shade of sage, trimmed out with gleaming polished wood. Vintage Persian rugs marked out different seating areas—the one in front of the fireplace, the one below Gemma's big antique desk. Liv had wanted it to be a feminine take on a nineteenth-century solicitor's office, and she had to admit that she'd hit the mark. But she still shook her head. "I'm too old to change careers at this point."

"Excuse me. And which one of us decided to be a *baker* at the age of thirty-one?"

Liv made a face. "You're still a lawyer."

"Technically." Gemma relaxed against the upholstered back of her chair and threw Liv a wry grin. "Not that I do more than look over a contract now and again."

"Why are you dressed up then?"

"Reviewing trust paperwork. Did you hear Will Parker is in town?"

"No! He didn't tell me! Was he your client?"

"You know I can't tell you that," Gemma said,

but her eyes were sparkling. "But he said he was going to look you up."

"What's he doing here?"

"You'd have to ask him yourself." Gemma smiled ruefully. It might be a small town where everyone knew everyone else's business, but she took attorney-client confidentiality seriously.

"I'll do that. I have his number."

Gemma studied her carefully for a minute. "Are you okay, Liv? I know it's been a hard month . . ."

"I'm fine." She forced a smile. "Just a bit at loose ends right now. I'm not used to not having anything to do."

"No leads on freelance gigs?"

"Not yet. And no bites on the apartment either."

Gemma hesitated, a sure sign she was going to broach something Liv wouldn't want to hear. "You know, you could always take out a mortgage on the house again. Jason had life insurance for a reason."

Liv shook her head resolutely. "No. My first responsibility is Taylor."

"You already funded her college savings," Gemma said gently. "You know Jason wouldn't want you to struggle right now."

It was true, and if he could get a message to her right now from heaven, he would probably lecture her about her stubbornness. But this was non-negotiable. She'd never forgive herself for taking money that felt like it belonged to his

19

daughter. "Jason was the one who bought the house, and it should go to Taylor. Just because I was the beneficiary of his policy doesn't mean I can do whatever I want with the money."

"That's exactly what it means," Gemma said, but there wasn't much conviction behind it. Liv knew her friend thought she was being ridiculous. His policy had been large enough to cover the mortgage payment and their other expenses for at least a decade. But what happened then? What would Taylor have to show for it? No, Liv's first priority was to make sure Taylor had enough money to go to any college she wanted and that she'd always have a roof over her head.

"It'll be fine. I mean, look at you. You had no idea if this was going to work, and six months later, your businesses are thriving!"

"That's overstating it a little, but yeah, I'm making it work. If you wanted—"

"Don't you dare offer me a job."

"I'm just saying, Rebekah is going to go back to school in three weeks . . ."

"I'll keep it in mind." Liv pushed herself to her feet. "How long ago did you see Will? I want to make sure I catch him while he's still here."

"Twenty, thirty minutes, max." Gemma gave her a sad smile, but she wasn't going to push matters, even if she clearly thought that Liv was being stupidly prideful.

But that was what Gemma didn't understand. It wasn't pride driving her decisions, it was guilt. And no amount of time or money could make that go away.

CHAPTER TWO

As soon as Liv stepped out onto the sidewalk outside Gemma's building, she pulled out her phone and pressed Will's contact number. He'd been a close friend of Jason's for years—they'd graduated high school together, though neither of them had stayed in town afterward—and he'd checked in on Liv and Taylor every few months since Jason died. Which was why it was weird he hadn't called or texted her to tell her he'd be in town. What exactly was going on, and why was he going to Gemma, whom he barely knew, for legal advice?

She pressed the phone to her ear and waited as the line rang several times. Finally, it picked up and a man's voice answered. "Liv!"

"Will! I understand you're looking for me!"

"I just got back to the house. I was going to call you, actually. You have time to come out here?"

"By the house you mean . . . Larkspur House?"

"None other."

"Sure." Liv blinked. "But why?"

"I'd rather talk about it in person, if you don't mind. If you're busy, I understand. We can do it another time. I'm not going back to Chicago until Tuesday."

"No, that's okay. I'll come over now. But what are you doing up at the castle?"

Will's voice lowered, grew husky. "Our grandfather passed away."

Liv gasped. "Oh, Will. I'm so sorry. Was it sudden?"

"As sudden as it can be for an eighty-year-old. He was in good health up until the end."

Now she understood why Will hadn't wanted to talk over the phone. "Give me twenty minutes and I'll be there."

"Thanks, Liv."

Liv hung up and shoved the phone into her pocket, then strode to her SUV and climbed in, her heart heavy. Will and his sister, Erin, had been raised by their grandparents here in Haven Ridge, and the death of their grandmother years ago had been difficult enough. But Elliott Parker had been the heart of that family. Even though he'd been in a nursing home for the last several years, his passing would hit them hard.

She flipped a U-turn in the middle of the quiet street and headed back out of town, turning onto the highway in the opposite direction of her house. Less than ten minutes later, she was bumping up a rutted gravel drive beneath an unkempt allée of elm trees, the lane marked by a rickety fence held together mostly by leggy grapevines growing wild and untended. And then it opened up to a full view of the last thing anyone would have expected in this dusty little section of southern Colorado.

A genuine castle.

The three-story structure rose imposing and impressive, built of orange stone in a Tudor-revival style with arched windows and turrets and a crenelated roofline. Tucked into the intersection of two hills, it almost completely blended into the landscape, even more so now that its neglected and derelict air made it look as if it were determined to return from the earth from whence it came. Its official name was Larkspur House—so named because of the fields of blue wildflowers that spread out in all directions around it this time of year—but everyone called it Bixby Castle after its builder and the town's most illustrious citizen.

Two vehicles already stood in the wide space before the house's entrance: a black SUV with a rental company's sticker on it and a muddy white work truck with a rack and tool boxes in the bed. Liv parked beside the SUV and hopped out of her vehicle, staring up at the structure. She'd taken a field trip here when she was in grade school, and then there had been a couple of ill-advised attempts to TP it on Halloween in high school, but she hadn't been here in years.

And, it seemed, neither had anyone else.

Liv pulled out her phone and sent a quick text to Will—I'm here—while she walked up to the front door of the castle. She was about to raise her hand to knock when the door swung open beneath it.

"Hey, Will—" she began, but the person standing in the doorway was not Will.

She blinked at the unfamiliar man. He was mid-thirties, with hair a shade of brown that hovered between light and dark and fell away in barely perceptible waves from a face lightly shadowed by the beginning of a beard. He was muscular, but in a way that said *I do manual labor for a living,* not *I live in a gym,* dressed in a dark T-shirt and pair of work jeans that were being tugged slightly down by a tool belt. He could have been any number of guys on a job site or a street corner that she passed by without noticing.

Which was why the instant, hard clench of attraction in her gut, followed by the rush of heat to her cheeks, made absolutely no sense whatsoever. She caught her breath, had to keep herself from reaching out to steady herself against the stone entryway.

Meanwhile, the man seemed to have absolutely no idea what was going on in her head—and body—and instead fixed eyes an indeterminate shade of gray-blue on her. "You must be looking for Will. He's up in the library."

"Thanks," Liv squeaked as he brushed by her, giving her a whiff of soap and sweat and dust that should have been unpleasant but wasn't. She turned to watch him go before she realized what she was doing and stepped into the cool dark interior of Larkspur House.

The library was upstairs, she knew, but instead of moving deeper inside, she shut the door and leaned back against it, letting the air inside cool her inexplicably heated cheeks. What on earth had just happened there?

It's fine, she told herself. You were just surprised because you were expecting Will.

But *surprised* didn't cover it. Bowled over. Mesmerized. She wished for a second that she edited romance novels instead of children's books because then she might have the vocabulary to describe what had just happened to her.

"Liv, is that you?" Will's voice drifted, muffled, from somewhere in the house.

"Yeah!" she called back. "Where are you?"

"Third floor, second door to your right!"

Liv blew out her breath and pulled herself together before she strode down the hallway and began to climb the creaky, wooden U-shaped staircase. The interior was cool and dim; she assumed the power was turned off, because the only light came from the windows set into the high, double-height entryway. Despite what the castle-like exterior promised, though, the inside wasn't at all oppressive or medieval. Instead, light-painted plasterwork was offset by rich golden wood, while paintings and wall-hangings gave color and life to the interior.

26

As she climbed deeper and higher into the house, though, she smelled what she should have noticed earlier—mildew plus something decaying and slightly vegetal. When she moved into the library, she understood.

A tall, dark-haired man stood in the center of what had once been a gorgeous library before a pile of ruined books.

"What happened?" she gasped.

Will looked up from the mess in front of him and grimaced. "Roof leak. At least that's what I presume. I've got a guy looking at it now."

"Yeah, I saw him," she said, and the memory socked her in the stomach again. *For heaven's sake, knock it off.* "Is it all lost?"

"It's not as bad as it looks. Just the books on this one bookshelf, and they looked to be mostly old pulp novels anyway." Will tossed the paperback he was holding onto the pile and then looked at her, really looked at her. "Liv. It's so good to see you."

Liv smiled, feeling all the weirdness from moments before melting away. "Same. I'm so sorry about your grandfather."

Will smiled sadly too, then met her in the middle of the room for a brotherly hug. "Thanks. I knew it would happen eventually, but it was still a surprise."

"It's always a surprise, no matter what." Liv

looked around. "I take it you're here to assess the house for the trust then?"

"Yeah. I called Thomas yesterday, asked him if he had a recommendation for someone who could look over some paperwork. I didn't realize until I got there that it was the same Gemma you used to hang around with as a kid."

"Still do as an adult," she said, but she knew what he meant. "You thinking of selling?"

Will made a face. "I'm considering it, but Erin's adamantly opposed."

"Erin does love the house. Is she here?"

He shook his head. "Had to go back to Chicago after the funeral. Performance tonight. Between you and me, I don't know if the trust can manage the upkeep on this place. Right now, I'm just trying to secure it so there's no more damage over the winter, and then she and I can decide what to do with it."

Liv nodded. It would be a shame for the house to pass out of the Bixby family—even though the name had been lost some generations back, Will and Erin were the great-great-great-grandchildren of the man who had built it back in the early 1900s. But these old, grand houses did demand considerable upkeep. She was all too familiar with the quirks of owning and living in a historic building.

"How can I help?" she asked finally.

"Well, regardless of what we do with the house,

there's a hundred years' worth of stuff that needs to be cleared out. I was hoping you might be able to help me with the books."

Liv took a slow circuit around the library, truly assessing it for the first time. It was practically the size of her house, stretching floor to ceiling with bookshelves, most of them filled. At first glance, a lot of them were popular novels from before the early 2000s, when it had last been used as a residence, but there were a good number of first editions and leather-bound volumes that had to be worth a fair amount of money. "You're sure you don't want to keep the library intact? Some of these are quite old."

Will's face twisted in regret. "I'd love to keep it intact. But I'm afraid if we leave them, they'll just deteriorate further. And I would rather pay for the repairs the house needs by selling off the furnishings than dip into the trust for it."

"I suppose I don't blame you for that," Liv said, even though all she wanted to do right now was pull up a threadbare chair to one of the arched windows, take down an old book, and read for the rest of the afternoon. The library even had a rolling ladder! The idea that they would remove all these old books and sell them off piecemeal, leaving the shelves empty and the room without a purpose, was heartbreaking.

Or maybe she needed to stop anthropomorphizing old houses and old books. "I'm an editor, Will, not a bookseller."

"I understand. I'm sure you're really busy anyway."

"That is the one thing I am not right now," Liv said wryly. "I quit my job."

"What? Why? You loved your job! At least you said you did."

"We got bought out and the new publisher wanted me to move back into the New York office. Taylor was trying to be a good sport, but I know it was killing her. I just couldn't do that to her."

Will's expression softened. "You're a good parent. Jason would be really pleased."

"I'm not . . ." Liv began to protest, but then she stopped. That was exactly what she was. Maybe not by title, but she was doing exactly what a parent would do in this situation. "Thanks."

"Well, I would of course pay you for your help. You could decide if you'd rather be paid hourly or a flat rate or a percentage of sales . . . whatever you think would be fair to you."

"I'll think about it," she said. And she would. She'd think about how to best sell off his books to fund the repairs on the Larkspur House all the while dodging the question of payment.

Not that Will couldn't afford to pay her. He made a very nice living as a forensic accountant in Chicago—Jason always used to joke that only Will could find a way to make the most boring job in the world at least a little bit cool. But he'd already done so much for her and Taylor, especially in those early, crushing days. He'd immediately flown out to Colorado to help with funeral arrangements, and he'd stayed long enough to make sure that they were settled and able to care for themselves, going as far as figuring out their finances. He'd been so helpful that there had been speculation in town that he and Liv might start dating, but of course it had never happened. For one, she regarded him like a brother; for another, it would have felt like a betrayal of Jason's memory.

And what do you think suddenly having the hots for a stranger does for his memory? her conscience needled her gleefully. She shut down that line of thinking immediately. She had enough legitimate guilt without adding her involuntary responses. And that had most certainly been involuntary.

"I'll do it," Liv said finally. "But there's no electricity and I don't want to spend all my time here alone, so we should box up at least some of them and take them to my house. I have a spare room I'm not using right now."

"I hoped you'd say that. I've got some boxes in the back of my rental car." Will reached out and squeezed her arm. "Thanks, Liv. I really appreciate this."

31

"Don't get your hopes up," she said. "Unless there are some really valuable things in here, you're not going to get much and it's not going to be quick."

"I'll take whatever I can," Will said immediately. "No pressure. Let's go out and grab the boxes."

Liv was hoping that the other guy would be gone by the time they went out the front door, but no such luck. He started climbing down a long ladder from the roof—just looking at the height gave her vertigo—when they popped the hatch of Will's rental SUV. Liv took an armful of boxes and headed for the front door, hoping to escape the contractor, and instead nearly ran into him.

Will stepped up beside her, a current of dread in his tone when he spoke. "What's the verdict? Do I need a new roof?"

The guy wiped his arm across his forehead to catch the beads of perspiration that had formed in the already fierce sun, leaving a dirty smudge on his temple. "It's not in good shape, but I don't think it's dire. You can probably make it another year or two. Your leak is coming from the flashing between the tile and the brick on the chimneys. I can just seal that for now."

Will let out a sigh of relief. "How much will that cost?"

"A few hundred. But keep in mind that this roof will be thirty, forty thousand to replace. The square footage is substantial and tile roofs are not cheap. You'll definitely want to plan for it soon."

Liv felt Will deflate at that pronouncement. "Understood. Seal what you can and I'll worry about the rest later."

"No problem. Won't take me more than a day." His eyes flicked to Liv briefly, then focused back on Will.

Will caught the gesture. "Sorry. This is my good friend, Liv Quinn. She lives in a historic home too, so she knows all about this stuff. Liv, this is Charlie Castro."

Charlie gave her a friendly smile and held out his hand. "Nice to meet you, Liv."

Liv propped the boxes on the toe of her shoe and reached to shake his hand. The minute his strong, calloused fingers closed around hers, a rush of warmth shot up her arm, straight through her chest, and into her cheeks. She swallowed hard, once more at a total loss for words, and prayed that the sun would be enough excuse for her flush. Quickly, she withdrew her hand before the boxes could topple.

"Sorry, let me grab those for you." Charlie reached out and took the batch easily. "You want these up in the library?"

"Oh, that's not necessary—"

"Of course it is." He flashed her a quick smile. "Lead the way."

"Actually, you can go up with Will. I need to get something from my car." *Like my dignity.*

Charlie shrugged like it made no difference to him. Why would it? She was just some stranger who showed up at a job site and needed help with boxes. She was the one who was looking at him like he was an oasis in the middle of the desert. What on earth was wrong with her?

Nothing's wrong. You've just been out of the game for a while and there's something about this guy that appeals to you. Get the books, go home, and you never have to see him again.

Liv opened the door and pretended to rummage through her purse in the front seat while Will and Charlie headed for the house, their arms full of boxes. Just before they went inside, she heard Will ask, "Hey, do you think you could bring these back to Liv's and help her get them inside? I have to wait here for the appraiser."

She didn't need to hear Charlie's response to know what it was going to be. "Sure. Not a problem."

Except that was not even close to the truth. Charlie Castro was a very big problem.

CHAPTER THREE

Liv Quinn was trouble.

It was the first thought that had surfaced when Charlie Castro opened the door to find the willowy blonde standing there, and it was that thought that circulated over and over in his mind as he followed her SUV down the highway back to her house.

Actually, he should be blaming Will Parker for this, because he was the one who had asked Charlie to help Liv back to her house with what ended up being about twenty boxes of books. And it wasn't even an unreasonable request, given that each of them weighed at least forty pounds. The woman looked like she was in shape, but he wouldn't let anyone move eight hundred pounds of books by themselves.

Right. And if she didn't look like that, you would have jumped on the suggestion just as quickly.

Charlie ran a hand through his hair, annoyed when it dislodged flecks of plaster and dust he hadn't even realized were there. He needed to stop thinking this way. He needed the job at the Larkspur House, needed every single dollar he could collect before he reapplied for his contractor's license and put his handyman days behind him. It was time to get his life back.

And the fastest way of getting his butt fired and kicked out of town was to start something up with the client's girlfriend. Not that he thought every woman who caught his eye would return the sentiment; it was just that he could have sworn that in those five seconds when Liv's hand was in his, she'd felt the same thing that he did.

Lightning.

It was the only way to describe the shock that had traveled through his body, because the minute he touched her, he felt as if he'd grabbed a live power line. He'd managed to cover his shock by being brief and friendly, but had she asked him his full name, his birthday, or where he lived, he probably would have just stared at her. His mind had gone blank, every semblance of witty conversation fled, condensing only the most primitive imprint of instinct and attraction into a single word.

Mine.

Which would go over like a lead balloon, so he was going to carry in her books, go back to the Larkspur House to fix the roof, and then be on his way.

Up ahead, the SUV put on its signal and drifted into a left-turn lane. He followed as she turned down a dusty road that meandered along plots of gated land, rural and dotted with native plants and trees. When at last she slowed, it was in front of a low-slung brick and timber house, little more than a rectangle with a two-story barn next to it. Scratch that, garage. She leaned out of the car to punch the numbers into a keypad and waited for the gate to swing open before she led the way onto her property.

Charlie parked behind her SUV and hopped out of the truck as soon as he saw her circle to the back. "Let me get those. Can you open the door?"

Her gaze slid away from his. "Sure. We can go in through the front."

He hefted a box out and followed her to the front door, yanking his gaze away from the sway of her hips in her cargo shorts, keeping his eyes instead fixed in safer territory. As she held the door open for him, she said, "You can put them in the living room near the fireplace."

Charlie stepped inside, immediately surrounded by a sweet fragrance that he could only describe as female: vanilla and fabric softener and scented candles. The interior was cool despite the hot day, and as he looked around, he realized that the building was solid brick.

"Nice," he said. "I take it that this is old construction you added onto?"

Liv glanced over her shoulder at him, her expression surprised. "Yeah. It was built in the 1890s as the town's schoolhouse. My husband and I bought it a few years ago, fixed it up ourselves. Mostly."

Husband. Every secret hope he'd had came

37

crashing down. So he'd misread the situation with Will, but she was still married to another guy. Probably for the best. He brushed past her, skirted the sofa, and plopped the box down in front of the hearth where she indicated. Only when he turned and saw the half-finished kitchen did he pause.

"You're still renovating?"

Liv gave a little, awkward laugh. "For the last year."

There was something in her tone that suggested otherwise. He furrowed his brow and she admitted, "I was in the middle of the renovation and my contractor flaked on me. I couldn't get anyone else out to finish it, so I used the reno money to finish the apartment over the garage."

"Ah." It was a common story, unfortunately. In Colorado, contractors were in short supply, as were crews, and the less scrupulous ones would quit jobs midway if another, bigger one came along. Charlie never did that—he took too much pride in his work and his reputation to leave clients in the lurch. Much good that had done him in the end anyway. "I know you don't want to hear this, but the price of materials keeps going up. Especially cabinetry."

"Oh, I have the cabinets," she said. "In a back room. I just couldn't afford the countertops and I couldn't bring myself to put in something cheap just to throw it away later."

Even though he knew he would live to regret them, the words were out of his mouth before he could stop them. "You know, I have a supplier who could probably get you a good deal on stone. If you've got the cabinets, we could finish this up pretty quickly."

Liv stopped and looked at him, but he couldn't begin to guess what she was thinking. Maybe he hadn't been as successful at hiding his rush of attraction as he'd thought. Women—especially married women—didn't like getting hit on by the help. "Talk to your husband and let me know. I'll give you my card."

She glanced away and cleared her throat. "My husband died a couple of years ago. Just me now. And my stepdaughter."

Leave it to him to step in it. "I'm sorry. In that case, I guess, think about it and let me know. I'd be happy to help. I don't have anything lined up in the next week or two after I finish the roof out at Larkspur House."

"Thanks, I'll consider it," she said quickly. "Let's get the books in first."

He dipped his head and followed her back out of the house to her SUV. Not married then, but widowed. And from the tone of her voice, not nearly through grieving him. That made matters easier. Even if he were inclined to act on that sudden, fiery spark of attraction he'd felt, a recently widowed woman taking care of her stepdaughter was one hundred percent off-limits. Besides, when—if—she was ready to date, she'd be looking for something long-term, permanent. And the last thing Charlie intended was to get permanently stuck in a tiny town in the Sangre de Cristo mountains.

Liv hefted a box of books from the back of her SUV with an ease that said she was no stranger to labor, and Charlie followed suit, trailing her back into the house. Within a few minutes, they had all twenty boxes lined up in neat rows in front of her fireplace, an impenetrable cardboard wall. She dusted her hands on the sides of her shorts and flashed him a vague smile. "Thanks for your help. I'm sorry I pulled you away from your job."

"No, don't be. Happy to do it." He retrieved his wallet from his back pocket and withdrew a business card. "Consider what I said. We could get that countertop ordered and installed in a week or two if you wanted to go forward. I'll give you a good deal."

Her eyes narrowed, but she took the card from his fingers. "Why would you do that? You don't even know me."

Charlie looked around at the historic home, the evidence of so much love and care a stark contrast with the rough, half-finished kitchen space. "I know. But it just feels like you could use a break. And I have the time."

Liv licked her lips unconsciously as if she

was considering, and he glanced away so she wouldn't see his thoughts in his eyes. Finally, she gave him a little smile. "I'll let you know. But either way . . . thanks."

"You're welcome." He dipped his head in a wordless goodbye and then turned and headed for the door. Just before his foot hit the threshold, however, she called out after him.

"Charlie!"

He turned.

"If you're really looking for work around here, you should put up a flyer at the Brick House Cafe in town. Everyone checks the board when they need something done."

Their eyes locked for a long, breathless moment, and he had the sudden, wild thought that she didn't want to see him go any more than he wanted to leave. "Thanks. I'll look into that."

Liv gave him a slight smile, and he left while he could still get away with his dignity intact. Still, when he climbed into his truck, he sat there behind the wheel for several seconds before starting it.

The smart thing to do was to finish up the project for Will Parker and head back to the Springs. Pick up as many handyman jobs as he could so he could afford the bond and insurance premiums he needed to get his contractor's license back, rebuild his business. He had a crew ready to go: men who had been loyal to him for years, men with whom he'd celebrated marriages and births of children, just waiting for the word that he was once again hanging out his shingle. That would be the sensible decision.

But as Charlie put the truck in gear and made a tight turn toward the gate of the dusty, rural property, he had to face a single, unfortunate fact: when it came to Liv Quinn, it would be impossible to be sensible.

CHAPTER FOUR

Liv paced her house restlessly after Charlie left, unsettled by everything that had just happened. What was she thinking? Was she really going to take this guy up on his offer—seemingly out of the blue and from the goodness of his heart—to help her finish up her kitchen?

Of course you are, her inner monologue, the more logical part of her, replied. *You've been trying to find a contractor for almost a year with no luck. Are you really going to look a gift horse in the mouth? Turn down an actual miracle?*

Because that's what this was. Yes, there were other contractors in the area, based out of Salida and Buena Vista, but they were booked up for more than a year, working on full-scale renovations and remodels that came along with the recent population boom in surrounding towns. No one wanted to take on a simple job like this. Liv had the skills but not the muscle to finish it herself.

But if you had him get the countertops, you could do the tiling yourself. It's not like you have a job right now.

Right. And every month she didn't have a job, her savings dwindled a little more.

But that was stupid. A couple thousand dollars

wouldn't break her. She and Jason had prioritized saving when he took a pay cut to come back to Colorado, and she really hadn't had much need to spend money in the last few years, not with the mortgage paid off and Taylor's college savings funded.

No, the real reason she was hesitating was because the longer she spent in Charlie Castro's presence, the less she could think of anything but how it would feel to be pressed close to his hard, lean body . . .

"Enough!" She wiped away those thoughts with a stern shake of her head. She must be really hard up to be fantasizing about a literal stranger. And in the house that she'd shared and remodeled with her husband, the love of her life. That was a betrayal of the highest order.

No, she needed to expend her energy on figuring out what to do with this huge pile of books, not having sexy fantasies about a handsome contractor with eyes the color of a winter sky.

"Maybe I should write a romance novel," she muttered to herself. "Get it out of my system." But her few attempts at writing a book over the years had proved that wasn't her path. She was more of a midwife, coaching books into existence, helping other people create and then shaping the finished product into the best version of itself. And since that currently seemed to be out of reach, at least she could still be surrounded by books.

This was going to take forever if she didn't have a plan. Liv plopped down on her living room sofa and opened the web browser on her phone. Fifteen minutes later, she had a general idea of where she could sell the books, how to set up the accounts, and how to record them. Five minutes after that, she had downloaded a book cataloging app, complete with a bar code scanner. She went and retrieved a box cutter from the kitchen junk drawer and slit the top of the first box open.

Even with the aid of technology, however, the process was slow. She dusted each book off with a rag, scanned it in, double-checked that the app registered the correct edition, and then made a note of its condition in a custom field so she didn't have to actually look at it again until she sold it. Then she put it into one of the many piles she had designated around her: contemporary fiction, classic fiction, non-fiction, or gift books.

It wasn't long after that she realized she was going to need a lot more categories and a lot more space. And some help.

She pulled out her phone and texted Gemma. Got plans tonight?

Meeting up with Stephen after he gets back from the Springs. But probably not until 9. Why?

Want to come over and help me with a tedious book cataloging project?

Will there be wine?

Liv laughed. *I might be able to make that happen.* She didn't drink, but she always kept a few nice bottles on hand for other people.

I'll be over about 5 when I finish up here. Want me to bring dinner?

Why do you think I texted you in the first place?

Gemma replied with a string of laughing emojis and Liv smiled to herself as she flipped back over to the book scanner. She hadn't realized how much she'd missed her best friend. They'd been nearly inseparable from childhood to their junior year of high school, when Gemma's parents got divorced and she and her mom had been forced out of town by some nasty gossip—ironically, spread around by Chelsea and her friends. Despite the fact she and Gemma had managed to see each other once or twice a year—beach getaways, mountain ski trips—it wasn't the same as living in the same town, being able to get together at a moment's notice, doing everyday life things together.

She might have lost Jason, but she'd gained Gemma, and most days, that was enough to get her through.

By the time Gemma showed up at five fifteen—changed into jeans and a T-shirt instead of the business clothes she'd worn earlier that day—Liv finally had a handle on the project.

"Wow," Gemma said, tossing her handbag on the sofa. "When you said tedious, you meant it."

Liv looked around at the mess in her living room. She'd unpacked half of the boxes, forming rough piles according to genre and size, then labeled the empty boxes with Sharpies to make it easier to find them later. This was just a start—she still had to determine selling price and what the profit would be after the retailers took their cut—but at least she had a system. It was going to be a slow-moving project with paltry profits, but what else did she have to do with her time?

The familiar fragrance of chicken and soy sauce and ginger wafted from the kitchen, and Liv perked up. "Chinese?"

"Ginger chicken for you, Mongolian beef for me. You want to eat on the sofa or . . ."

Liv laughed at the mountain of books on the dining table and laughed. "Where else? I'll grab some plates."

She brought back plates and spoons from the kitchen, and they unpacked the meal on the portion of coffee table that Liv managed to clear. She flopped back onto the sofa, her bare legs crossed in front of her, and used chopsticks to lever food into her mouth, sighing with happiness.

They ate for a few minutes in relative silence, but the question that had been churning inside Liv all afternoon bubbled up. "Have you ever met someone and felt . . . an instant connection?"

Gemma put down her chopsticks and cocked her head. "How so? Like déjà vu? Like you knew them?"

"Not exactly." Liv felt her cheeks color. "Like . . . attraction."

Now Gemma's mouth widened into a smile. "Sure. Lots of times. Why? Did you meet someone?"

"No. I mean, yes. Kind of."

Gemma shoved her plate onto the table, a sure sign she was giving Liv her full attention. "Tell me. What happened?"

Now she regretted even bringing it up. Gemma had been on her for months to consider dating, and Liv had brushed her off, telling her that she had no interest. But now that Gemma knew she'd met someone who made her feel something other than indifference, she was never going to let it go. "Never mind. It doesn't matter."

Liv couldn't have said anything that would have interested Gemma more. She saw the calculating light in her best friend's eyes, the one that said she had found a particularly interesting problem and she was going to puzzle through it until she solved it. "You don't mean Will, do you? Because I couldn't blame you. He was always a little nerdy, but in the last ten years or so—"

"No," Liv said quickly. "I don't mean Will."

"Then who?"

She was almost embarrassed to say it. "There was this guy out fixing the roof at Larkspur House. And when I saw him . . ." She swallowed and broke off.

"He's that good-looking?"

"I guess? I mean, he's not *not* good-looking. On the handsome side of average. But not at all the type I go for."

"You mean he's not Jason."

Liv's cheeks heated. Jason had been objectively beautiful. Nearly-black hair, deep brown eyes, cheekbones to die for thanks to his mother's part-Korean heritage. But she'd taken time to warm up to him. It had been nothing like this instant, raw magnetism.

"I fell for Jason over time. I was attracted to him once I got to know his personality. But this guy, Charlie . . ." She forced herself to say what she was thinking, knowing Gemma wouldn't judge her. "The minute I saw him, I couldn't breathe, couldn't think. It was like getting struck by lightning. Getting hit by a train. And every time I'm in his presence, I just . . . want to touch him."

Gemma was trying valiantly to bite back her grin and failing miserably. "Exactly how many times today have you managed to see this guy?"

"Will asked him to help me get the books back over here."

"So he's been in your house?"

"Yeah." Liv winced. "And he offered to help me finish the kitchen. Said we could probably do it quickly and he'd give me a deal."

She'd thought Gemma's grin couldn't get wider, but she'd been wrong. "So he was struck by lightning too."

"No! He was just being nice, I'm sure."

"No guy is that nice. What did you say?"

"I said I'd think about it . . . and then told him if he was looking for work, he should put up a notice at the cafe."

"Oh yes. Keep him close. Very practical."

Liv stuck out her tongue, and Gemma laughed. "Okay, look at this logically. There is such a thing as pheromones. Just because you guys are attracted to each other doesn't mean anything. You can't really help if you're chemically compatible with someone."

Liv let out a long breath. She knew Gemma would be logical about this.

"On the other hand, that's kind of how I felt the first time I saw Stephen, and I spent fifteen unnecessary years trying to replicate that with someone else. Which, as you well know, was an abject failure."

Okay, not so logical. Then again, she couldn't deny the truth in her friend's words. All you had to do was spend a little time in Gemma and Stephen's presence to realize they were made for each other. Two sides to the same coin, two halves of a whole. They just made *sense*. Whereas she and this Charlie contractor guy made no sense whatsoever.

"What I want to know is, what's the harm in letting yourself touch him?"

Liv barked a surprised laugh. "Other than the fact that I have to be a good example to my sixteen-year-old stepdaughter?"

Gemma rolled her eyes. "I didn't suggest you take him to bed the next time you see him. But do you really think you're setting a good example for Taylor by suggesting that you only get to be in love once? What happens when she and Dylan break up?"

"It's not the same and you know it. I was married to her *dad*. I still hear her crying in her room sometimes. She's not ready to see me with someone else."

"Maybe not," Gemma said, "but you are not her mom. She's already had to see her dad with someone else, and she accepted you. Why do you think she would want you to stay single and alone?"

There was wisdom in Gemma's words. But it hadn't quite been three years. Let's say she actually did like Charlie, and he felt the same way. Was she even ready to have another man in her life? Was she ready to let Jason go? His imprint was everywhere in this house. She'd finally gotten rid of his clothes last year, but the wooden box holding his watches still sat on her dresser. She still slept on the right side of the bed because it felt like a betrayal to sleep in the middle. And, even though she wouldn't say it out loud, Taylor wasn't the only one who still sometimes cried in her bedroom at night.

Those thoughts must have shown on her face, because Gemma reached for her hand and squeezed hard. "I'm not trying to pressure you. If you're not ready, you're not ready. But try not to beat yourself up over being attracted to someone else. It doesn't have to mean anything. And if it does mean something? That's not a crime. You deserve to be happy. However it comes about."

It was what she needed to hear. Liv shoved her plate aside and scooted close to hug her friend tightly. "Thank you," she whispered.

"You're welcome." A mischievous look came over Gemma's face when she sat back. "For the record, I still think you need kissing. Often, and by someone who knows how."

Liv broke into startled laughter. "Thank you, Rhett Butler. I'll keep that in mind. Besides, when do you paraphrase *Gone with the Wind*?"

"Just that line. I've always loved it. The big question is, do you think this Charlie knows how?"

Liv let her memory drift back to that sudden,

fleeting flash of heat in his eyes when he'd taken her hand. "Gut instinct? Oh yeah."

Gemma let out a surprised laugh, and Liv fell into helpless giggles. Gemma was right about one thing. It felt good to be silly over a guy for the first time in years. Even if she had no intention of pursuing it—and she didn't—maybe it was time to stop holding Jason's memory in quite so much respect. He would never have wanted her to be alone forever, and even though a part of her would probably always mourn him, she was only thirty-one years old. It was unreasonable to expect her to keep all her feelings locked away forever.

"Thanks, Gemma. I needed some perspective."

"That's what I'm here for. Now, these books. What the heck were you thinking?"

Liv laughed and started to explain the situation to Gemma, her heart feeling lighter by the moment. She was making something out of nothing. So what if she felt a spark of attraction to a stranger? Now that she'd recognized it, wasn't suppressing it, surely she would have a handle on it next time she saw him. And in that case, there was no reason that she shouldn't take him up on his offer. Even Jason would say she was being stupid for not jumping on the chance.

Besides, it would give her one more thing to occupy her thoughts so she didn't dwell on the other, more serious pressures weighing her down.

CHAPTER FIVE

Even considering his morning distraction, the work on the Larkspur House was not particularly complex, and Charlie finished the necessary repairs by the time the sun started to dip toward the horizon, washing the sky in flaming shades of orange and pink. It was a good thing that he'd done plenty of roofing over the years—and that he was wearing a harness—because his mind was not fully on the gaps between the tile roof and the surrounding brick.

It was on a willowy blonde with eyes the color of melted chocolate.

When Charlie finally climbed down the ladder, Will was waiting for him, squinting up at the roof as if he could actually view the repairs from where he stood. "What's the verdict?"

"All done." Charlie pulled his cell phone out of his jeans pocket and swiped through a couple of photos, showing Will the work that had been done. "Like I said, you're going to have to look into replacement in the next couple of years, but this will keep the water out."

"Great. When can you start on the inside?"

Charlie blinked at him. "I'm sorry?"

"The plasterwork. Obviously, the finish work could probably wait, but the plaster is wet and I

don't want to risk mold growing. I have to leave on Tuesday, and I don't know when I'm going to be back."

Part of Charlie wanted to demur. He was certainly capable of fixing the damaged plaster inside, but it wasn't a particularly easy job. He'd focused more on modern renovations—drywall and joint compound—and even when he had done a historic home that required traditional plaster and stucco coatings, he'd had a guy who did it for him. It had been years since he'd picked up a trowel. Then there was the fact that he was staying at a cheap, barely acceptable motel twenty miles away since there weren't any accommodations in Haven Ridge. Two very good reasons to say *no thank you* and move on.

And one very good reason to stay.

"Okay, let's take a look," Charlie said finally. He turned back to his truck to get one of his smaller ladders and hoisted it onto his shoulder before following Will back into the house. Even with all the windows in this old house, it was getting dark inside now that the sun was down, casting everything in a dim gray twilight.

Once in the library, Charlie set up the ladder and poked the ceiling experimentally with a hammer. The plaster crumbled, dusting his hair and shoulders. "The lath is still damp under here. I'll need to scrape off the damaged plaster and let it dry. It's going to take a while."

"How long?"

"Not before Tuesday." Charlie climbed back down the ladder. "It'll take a few days to dry out the lath and then a few more to fix the plaster."

Will frowned at the ceiling, thinking. "Are you willing?"

"To wait around and do nothing for a few days while your ceiling dries out?"

"I wouldn't say do nothing. There's work around Haven Ridge. Put up a post in the Brick House Cafe and your phone will be ringing off the hook. There's always older folk that need repairs, especially before the snow starts in the fall. It can be hard to get someone out here for small jobs."

"That's exactly what Liv said." Charlie frowned. "How exactly did you hear about me again?"

"I found your card in my grandfather's things at the nursing home. I figured you'd done some work there."

Charlie shook his head slowly. "I've never worked at a nursing home. Maybe one of the employees gave it to him?"

"Maybe." Will shrugged. "In any case, now that you're here, you might as well stick around a bit, take advantage of the work."

Something in Will's voice made him wonder how much he'd guessed about his situation. "I already told Liv I'd help her finish up her kitchen if she wanted."

Now Will's expression turned cautious. "Liv's been through some hard stuff lately."

Charlie tried not to let his intense interest show. "She mentioned that her husband had died. What happened?"

"Plane crash."

"Like, an airliner?"

Will shook his head. "Private plane that he was piloting. He was an excellent, accomplished pilot and even worked as a flight instructor for a while. There's no good explanation for what happened."

Charlie grimaced. No wonder Liv still seemed a little traumatized. It was one thing to see it coming, another to have someone ripped tragically from your life. The rush of sympathy clinched it—there was no way he was going to leave her in the lurch now.

"Okay," he said. "I'll do the plasterwork. Let me write up an estimate for you, and I'll email it to you tonight. And I'll head into town and see if I can drum up some business for myself while I'm waiting."

"Try the meatloaf at the Brick House Cafe. It will make you a believer, I promise."

Charlie grinned and shook Will's hand. "Thanks for the tip. See you tomorrow." He folded up his ladder and hauled it back downstairs, secured it on the rack on his truck, and then began to pack up the rest of his tools. Will was just locking up the castle when he turned his truck around in the wide driveway, raising his hand out the window in farewell.

This was not how he'd expected to be spending the month of August, but it did solve the need to solicit business back home. Hopefully, this little detour would bring enough income to make up for the cost of the overpriced motel. Charlie found himself humming to himself as he navigated down the long lane onto the highway, back toward Haven Ridge proper.

And his sudden good mood may or may not have had anything to do with Liv Quinn.

The lights were just beginning to wink on in town as Charlie crept through the narrow streets of historic Haven Ridge, and he found himself craning his neck to get a glimpse of the tops of the red brick buildings with their gingerbread trim. He may have made his reputation from building and renovating modern houses, but there was something about the history in these old towns that he loved. It always felt like if you looked close enough, you could see the shadows of the past still clinging to them—horses and wagons, women in full dresses and men in long black coats. It was almost like going back in time.

The farther into town he got, the more crowded Dogwood Street became—crowded being a relative term—the spaces that lined the sides of the street filling with cars and trucks of all types and vintages. This must be the heart of downtown then. He pulled into the first spot that would accommodate his vehicle, put it in park, and hopped out into the rapidly cooling evening air. He gave his shirt and his hair a quick brush to remove the plaster dust and then stepped onto the cracked concrete sidewalk.

Up close, he could see that this place was almost a ghost town—windows and doors on some buildings boarded up, others standing empty. There were a few signs of life, though. He passed one building with a small dumpster in front of it, its interior swept clean, ready for a new tenant. In other places, empty buildings sported new coats of paint, their windows sparkling.

Maybe this ghost was on the verge of resurrection.

When he reached the end of the street where all the cars were parked, he recognized the building before he even saw the sign: the Brick House Cafe. Bright yellow light spilled out of the plate glass windows, back-lighting what looked like a nearly full house. The faint smell of cooking drew him toward the door, his stomach rumbling.

The minute Charlie stepped inside amid the tinkle of harness bells, he was enveloped in the scent of home-cooked food and the buzz of conversation. He'd no sooner stepped toward the register than a bearded, dark-haired man appeared with a smile, holding a stack of plastic menus. "One for dinner?" he asked pleasantly. When Charlie nodded he said, "Looks like we only have space at the counter right now, but you could wait for a table if you'd like. It should only be about fifteen minutes."

"No, counter is fine." Charlie slid onto the first available seat and accepted a menu. When the man returned with a glass of ice water, Charlie asked, "Is there a board somewhere that I can post my business card? I'm a handyman."

The guy looked at him with a flicker of curiosity. "New to town?"

"Kind of. I'm working up at Larkspur House right now."

Understanding lit the other man's features. "Ah, right. Will was in here earlier this morning, said he had someone coming to look at water damage. How bad is it?"

"Not bad. But it will take a while to dry everything out before I can start. Will thought there might be some people who could use a hand in the meantime."

"Be careful what you wish for," the guy said with a grin. "You'll probably be flooded with inquiries. Right now, everyone just helps out the best they can. You'd think being this close to bigger towns, we'd be able to get contractors out here, but it's like Haven Ridge is invisible."

Charlie smiled, though he'd been wondering

about that. Haven Ridge was less than a half hour between two larger towns, but somehow it felt like it was in the middle of nowhere. But he could already tell that this cafe was the center of town life, and if he wasn't mistaken, the man in front of him was the proprietor. He held out his hand. "Charlie Castro."

"Nice to meet you, Charlie. I'm Thomas Rivas. My wife, Mallory, and I own this place."

So he'd been right. No doubt Thomas would be a good source of information. But first things first. Dinner. He scanned the menu quickly, then said, "Will recommended the meatloaf?"

"House special. I don't think you'll be disappointed. It's my grandmother's secret recipe and she's pretty much known county-wide for it."

"Meatloaf special it is then." Charlie smiled and handed the menu back. "And an iced tea, please."

"Coming right up. The board is by the restrooms, all the way back and to the left. Just pin your card up there. I'll spread the word."

"Thanks." Charlie slid off the seat and made his way back through the restaurant, suddenly aware that all eyes were on him. Not in a judgmental way—or at least he didn't think so, though his work clothes and boots were traced with plaster dust—but in curiosity. This town was obviously small enough that a stranger in their midst wouldn't go unnoticed, especially one who looked like he was here to work.

He found the restroom easily and stopped in to wash his hands, then returned to the board just outside the door. He pulled a couple of business cards out of his wallet and pinned them to an empty patch of cork. But just as he was about to turn away, a sheet of white printer paper caught his attention. Slowly, he unpinned it and took it down to read.

Accessory unit for rent, available immediately. Monthly and yearly arrangements possible. Call Liv Quinn. Below it were several grainy photos of what looked like an updated apartment in a converted barn and Liv's phone number.

Don't be crazy, that little internal voice warned him. Except there was no denying this would be better than the motel room with the hard, lumpy bed and the cracked tile floor. He knew he should just snap a picture, but instead, he folded the listing into quarters and tucked it in his back pocket.

Fewer people watched him on his way back to his seat this time, though Thomas was talking to a couple at a table and they all kept throwing glances his way. Hopefully he was drumming up some business and not having to explain why a dirty stranger had wandered into the middle of the town watering hole. Sitting there at the counter by himself made Charlie feel awkward and exposed, so he pulled out his cell phone again. He found himself searching *motels near*

Haven Ridge, Colorado, and unsurprisingly, coming up with absolutely nothing within twenty miles. He opened up VacayAway and searched again. Nothing closer than Salida, and everything that did come up was booked or way out of his price range.

Which brought him back to the flyer in his back pocket. He drew it out and smoothed it flat on the counter. The next time Thomas passed, he stopped, a flicker of surprise on his face. "Oh, that's a good idea. She's been trying to rent the apartment for months, ever since it went vacant."

"Do you know if she'd be open to renting weekly?"

"Wouldn't hurt to ask. She's been trying to find someone to finish her kitchen for a while, too."

Charlie smiled. This really was a small town if the owner of the cafe knew about the state of Liv's kitchen. "I'll give her a call and see."

The door behind them tinkled again, and Thomas's lips lifted into a wry smile. "That was fast."

Charlie twisted to see an elderly woman walk through the door, though *elderly* didn't exactly fit either. She had to be in her eighties, judging from her wrinkled face and snow-white hair, but he'd never seen an eighty-year-old in an electric blue leather jacket and matching Air Jordans. She smiled first at Thomas before her gaze shifted to Charlie and locked like a heat-seeking missile.

She strode right over to them, slid onto the seat next to Charlie, and looked at Thomas expectantly.

Thomas laughed. "Charlie, this is my grandmother, Pearl. Granny, meet Charlie Castro. He's doing some work for Will out at the castle."

"Nice to meet you, young man." The woman stuck her hand out to shake. "Everyone calls me Granny Pearl. Welcome to Haven Ridge."

"Thank you, Granny Pearl. It's nice to be here." Charlie shook her hand and threw a glance at Thomas, who just shrugged amusedly before he moved away to answer a nearby table's summons.

"So how long will you be in town?" Pearl focused that laser-beam gaze on him, and Charlie shifted uncomfortably.

"Um, I'm not sure yet. It'll take me a few days to finish up at Larkspur House and then I may be doing some work out at Liv Quinn's place. I also put my card on the board back there."

Pearl gave a nod of satisfaction. "About time Haven Ridge had its own handyperson." She hopped off the stool and gave him a little wink. "I'll spread the word. But be careful. You might never want to leave." She gave his arm a friendly squeeze and wandered off to speak to one of the groups at a nearby table.

He was still blinking in confusion when Thomas came back. The other man laughed. "Yeah, my grandmother has that effect on people. Did she give you the third degree?"

"No. Just said she'd spread the word."

"Huh. Maybe she's losing her touch." Thomas shrugged. "Give me just a second. Your meatloaf is coming right up."

Charlie sat there, letting the buzz of the cafe circulate around him, feeling like he'd walked onto a movie set. It wasn't that this place felt fake—the warmth from the people here seemed genuine. But he hadn't thought places like this existed in real life. He might know the checkers at his grocery store and the cashier at the local gas station and the waitstaff at his favorite diner, but other than that, he could go through his daily routine for months without seeing the same people twice. Virtually no one outside of his family and clients knew his name. Being here in Haven Ridge felt like being transported into the Twilight Zone or Mayberry or any number of fictional small towns with benignly nosy citizens and a fascination with new faces.

It was not an altogether unpleasant sensation.

And neither was the food. When Thomas finally set his meatloaf special in front of him, Charlie wanted to apologize for every bad thing he'd ever thought about the dish. It was moist and juicy and delicious and perfectly seasoned. And even then, it was almost upstaged by the absolutely stellar garlic mashed potatoes. He was just finishing the last bit of his meal when Thomas returned. "Can I interest you in a slice of pecan pie? I make it myself."

"I couldn't," Charlie said with a groan. "Maybe next time."

Thomas laughed and whisked his empty plate away. Then he paused. "If you don't mind me asking—because Granny is going to regret not grilling you and come ask me later—how did you end up in Haven Ridge, anyway?"

"Chance, I guess. I'm not all that clear on it myself, to be honest."

"Ah."

"What does that mean, *ah?*"

"Nothing. We're just not real big on chance here in this town. I tell you what. I'll box up a piece of the pecan pie to go. On the house."

Charlie smiled his thanks, though inwardly he was a little unsettled. Once upon a time, he'd thought that he didn't believe in chance either, that everything happened as it was supposed to, that there was a reason for everything. But after all that had happened in the past year, the way that his life had disintegrated almost overnight, he no longer found that thought comforting. Because that meant that someone out there was pulling his strings, making all these things happen, taking away everything he loved.

He'd much rather believe in chance. Because the alternative meant that the universe wanted him miserable. Or worse yet, that he'd made himself miserable all on his own.

CHAPTER SIX

Liv and Gemma made an impressive dent in the pile of books in the living room before Gemma had to leave to meet Stephen. Liv was just finishing up her fifth box when the keypad on the front door beeped with the sound of the code being punched in.

"That you, Taylor?" Liv called, though it was a stupid question. Gemma was the only other person who had the code to her house, and she'd just left.

Taylor clomped into the living room, looking flushed and sunburned and happy. Liv twisted and smiled at her. "Did you have fun?"

"Yeah, it was great." Taylor froze when she saw the boxes spread out on the living room rug, the happy smile sliding from her face. "What's with the boxes?"

"I'm helping Will. He needs to get rid of the library in Larkspur House before it gets destroyed."

The relief that washed over Taylor's face was so stark that it took Liv a long moment to understand. A pang of sympathy pierced her. "I would never do that to you, Taylor. We make these decisions together, remember? We're staying right here."

Taylor bent to unlace her boots and toed them off in the hallway before she padded to Liv's side for a side-hug. "I didn't think you'd do that, but . . ."

Liv could practically finish the sentence for her: it never paid to assume when you were a teenager and your life was largely out of your control. She might not have experienced the same life changes that Taylor had, but she remembered what it was like to be sixteen, to have tasted a little freedom and know you were so close to becoming an adult while still having so little say about what happened to you.

"Want to help?" Liv asked, gesturing to the books.

"What are you doing exactly?"

"I'm scanning the barcodes, registering their condition, and then marking which box I put them in to make them easier to find later."

Taylor looked less than thrilled about the idea, but she shrugged. "Sure. Give me your phone and I'll scan while you sort."

Liv handed over her cell phone without question and picked up the next book on her stack, a paperback Ludlum novel with the original cover, still in mint condition. Inwardly, she wasn't so sure there was any point to all of this when the book itself was worth less than the cost to ship it. She'd left the really expensive collector's editions for last, when she had the time to do a little research on them, but the elder Parker's taste in reading material had run decidedly toward the commercial.

"Like new, box three," she told Taylor, flipping over the book to display the bar code.

"Done." Taylor dropped it into the box marked *3* and held her hand out for the next one.

"You hungry?" Liv asked. "There's still some leftover Chinese in the refrigerator. Aunt Gem brought it by."

"Nah, Dylan and I ate in town at the diner. Everyone was whispering about the new guy."

"The new guy?" Liv asked, keeping her voice level, uninflected. She handed Taylor another book, this one a hardcover with a slightly crumpled dust jacket. "Good condition, box five."

Taylor scanned that one, too, and dropped it into the box with a thud that made Liv cringe. "Yeah, a contractor or something working up at the castle."

"Oh. Right."

Liv's attempt at disinterest was apparently less than convincing, because Taylor looked closely at her, frowning. "You've met him already. Over at the house when you got the books."

"I did." The only way to play this off now was to be straightforward. Not that there was anything to play off, whatever the heat rising in her cheeks seemed to suggest. "In fact, he said he might be able to help us finish the kitchen."

Taylor's face lit up. "Really?"

"Slow down. I don't even know if we can afford it yet. He thought he might be able to get us a good deal on stone, but I still haven't found a job."

Taylor held out a hand for another book—another hardcover, like new, box five—and scanned it when she chewed her lip. "You know, if we really need money, I could probably pick up some shifts at the Koffee Kabin."

Liv stopped and turned to her stepdaughter, touched and a little pained by the offer. "Thanks, love, but you don't need to do that. We're fine for now. I just don't like shelling out big chunks of money without knowing how I'm going to replace it."

"Yeah, I understand. I just feel responsible."

"Why?"

Taylor didn't meet her eye, just held out her hand for another book. "Because you stayed here for me. You'd still have a job if it weren't for me. And you put all Dad's money into my college fund."

The words struck to Liv's heart. And here she thought the girl hadn't been paying attention. "We didn't just stay for you. We stayed for me too. This is our home. All our friends are here, our life is here. I can find a new job. It's not that easy to reproduce the community we have here."

"I know, I just—"

"It will be fine. And as far as your college fund goes . . . that was for my own peace of mind. Your dad and I always talked about how we were going to pay for your college, and it was something I wanted off my plate. Something I didn't have to worry about. Okay?"

Taylor lifted watery eyes to Liv's and nodded.

"Ah, honey." Liv put her arms around her stepdaughter and hugged her tight. "I know."

Taylor sniffled against her shoulder. "I just miss him so much, you know? It's not that you aren't great. You are. But . . ."

"But he was your dad. And no one can ever replace him." Liv squeezed Taylor even tighter. "I miss him too. I thought we were going to have a lot more time together."

Taylor nodded against her shoulder and then pulled away, wiping her tears with a furious swipe of her hand. "It just doesn't seem fair."

"No," Liv said with a little sigh. "It doesn't. But I wouldn't change it for anything. If I hadn't married him, I wouldn't have had three wonderful years of memories and I wouldn't have you. That makes it all worth it."

Taylor gave her a watery smile and visibly pulled herself together. "Just you and me now."

The words sent a pang straight through Liv that felt suspiciously like guilt. "That's right. You and me against the world."

They fell silent for a moment, going back to

71

their cataloging project, when Taylor stopped with a copy of *The Velveteen Rabbit* in her hand. "I don't understand why everyone loves this book so much. It's traumatizing. No way this should be a kids' book."

Liv smiled. "It's not just a children's book, you know. It's a story about the passage from childhood to adulthood. The things that we give up with maturity. And, of course, about the metaphysical reality of the imagination."

Taylor looked at her, and for a second, Liv thought she was going to laugh. "You know a lot about this stuff."

"Well, yeah. I have a literature degree. And I've worked in children's publishing for over a decade. Books have pretty much been my whole life."

Taylor turned the book over, like she was seeing it for the first time. "You have all these books. Why don't you open a bookstore?"

"That is an entirely different endeavor. You have no idea how difficult and expensive that would be."

Taylor's face fell, and Liv instantly regretted her hasty reply. "It would be pretty great, though, wouldn't it? I used to dream about owning a bookstore. Of course, I thought that I was going to be writing novels in the back office while my assistant sold books out front, but that idea was probably the biggest fiction of all."

Taylor crossed her arms. "You always tell me that I can do anything I want if I put my mind to it. So why can't you do anything you want?"

Because I'm a grown-up with a teenager to support and bills to pay. It wasn't just belief in imaginary playthings that one had to give up with adulthood. Liv held out her hand for the book. "Maybe someday."

Taylor handed it over with a sigh, then pushed herself to her feet. "I'm really tired after the hike. I'm going to take a shower and go to bed. I can help you with this in the morning if you want."

"Sure. Thanks. I'm glad you had fun today."

Taylor shot her a quick smile and then hurried from the room, leaving Liv surrounded by books and a melancholy silence. She propped her arms up on her knees and buried her face in them, hiding the hot tears that sprang to her eyes.

She was failing. There was no other way to describe it. Failing to be a proper mother to Taylor, failing to be a proper provider, failing to be an example of the kind of woman she wanted Taylor to be. She didn't want to raise her with a fatalistic belief that reality always trumped dreams, that you only followed your calling when it was practical and affordable and realistic. These years were the ones where her stepdaughter should be taking chances, making mistakes—within reason—and following those dreams. Not worrying about getting a job to help her stepmother pay the bills. Or even worse, feeling responsible for their financial situation because she had a fully funded college savings account.

The thought should have prompted Liv to open a job listing app and start searching for employment that had absolutely nothing to do with literature or editing or the book world in general, just so Taylor didn't have to worry about helping with household expenses. But inexplicably, she dug in her pocket and pulled out Charlie Castro's card, then opened up a text message.

Hey, it's Liv. Do you have time tomorrow to come over and talk about the kitchen?

She put the phone aside and reached for another book, but the response came through almost instantaneously. Sure. How's 10 am?

Liv paused to consider her reply, consider the whole idea, but before she could second-guess it, she replied with a single word.

Perfect.

CHAPTER SEVEN

The second-guessing followed immediately. Liv was already fretting over it by the time she climbed in bed that night, and it was the first thing she thought of when she climbed out of bed in the morning.

It didn't stop her from throwing on her favorite floaty cotton summer top, though, and she couldn't even pretend that the little makeup she was putting on was for her own benefit.

Fine. Even if she had no intention of pursuing this inexplicable attraction, that didn't mean she didn't want to look nice. That maybe she needed to see that spark of interest in Charlie's eyes again, just to remind herself that she still had an entire life ahead of her, even the chance to fall in love again.

Just not now. When Taylor went off to college, she could think about all that. Right now, her primary concern was leaving her stepdaughter with only bright, positive memories: watching movies with Liv and Gemma, rolling out sugar cookies and gingerbread at Christmas, talking over problems while a big pot of soup bubbled on the stovetop. Liv didn't want Taylor to think back about their sad, half-finished kitchen, the remodel that had been left undone because of her college fund.

She didn't want her biggest memory to be that Liv couldn't take care of her half as well as her dad had.

Taylor still wasn't out of bed—despite her talk about going to sleep early, Liv had heard YouTube videos playing in her room until well after midnight—so Liv started a pot of coffee and pulled out some leftover muffins from the pantry. While the coffee was brewing, she swiped through her phone for the gate app and punched the button to open it for Charlie. Then she returned to her desk with her morning caffeine, where her laptop sat closed and ignored since Friday afternoon.

Her heart gave a leap when her email chimed and several messages hit her inbox.

Not just any messages, but responses to the freelance editing inquires she'd sent out to several publishers she knew from her time in the industry.

" 'Dear Liv,' " she read aloud, " 'So nice to hear from you! I was sorry to learn that you'd left Altea Books. I've always thought you had impeccable taste, so much so that for years I've auto-bought any books you acquire for my own kids. Unfortunately, we're not using any freelance editors right now, but if that changes you'll be first on my list.' "

Liv let out a long, shaky breath. She opened the second one and realized it was just an out-of-office auto-responder. Disappointing.

The third wasn't from an editor, she realized, but her favorite author, Malcolm Barry. He was an older man with a kindly, grandfather-like demeanor, and he wrote the most wonderful and whimsical middle-grade books about shelter animals who broke out of captivity and had adventures while they looked for their forever homes. She'd fallen in love with the concept and writing at first read, and she'd been the one to champion him from an unknown to a solid seller.

Dear Liv,

You can probably guess that things at Altea/Tamberlane aren't the same without you. I just wanted you to know that I lobbied hard for them to bring you back freelance to finish The Wanderers series, but I was unsuccessful. I was ready to walk away to force their hand, but my agent thought they'd likely let me go. She told me that it would take time to find another home for the series, if ever . . . and you know I just couldn't do that to my readers.

The editor they've assigned me is young and capable. She doesn't have your wonderful instinct for dialogue, but I think we'll do all right together.

Thank you for all you did for me. The Wanderers wouldn't exist without your sharp eye and your belief in what the stories could be, and I will always be grateful.

Sincerely,
Your friend, Malcolm

Liv sniffled and blinked away yet another round of tears. It was sweet of him to write, even sweeter to think that he could force Tamberlane to hire her to finish the series. Would that he could. Despite the fact he was a solid seller, she'd been his sole champion in-house. She was just glad that they'd kept him on and intended to finish the series.

She sipped her coffee while she considered how to respond. She had just put fingers to the keyboard when a knock sounded at the door. Ten o'clock? Already? She was really going to need to start getting up earlier.

Liv shut the laptop without responding, smoothed a hand over her hair, and moved to the doorway in bare feet. When she opened it, Charlie was standing back, dressed in what seemed to be his uniform of T-shirt and jeans. This morning, his hair was still a little wet from the shower, curling around his ears and at the nape of his neck. Her heart gave a little hiccup at the bright smile he sent her way. "Good morning."

"Good morning." Liv stood aside for him, holding her breath as he brushed past. Despite the hiccup, today her knees stayed solid beneath her. Good. Maybe it had just been an aberration.

Still, she couldn't prevent herself from appreciating the stretch of a fresh dark T-shirt over broad shoulders or the fit of faded jeans over strong legs. *Stop it. What is wrong with you?*

"So," Charlie said, unhooking a measuring tape from his belt as he turned, "do you mind if I take a few measurements first?"

Liv shook her head and gestured toward the hall that led to the kitchen. "Not at all. Make yourself at home."

She probably should make herself scarce, but instead she followed him into the kitchen and hung back in the doorway while he pulled a small pad from his back pocket and a mechanical pencil from behind his ear. Briskly, he sketched out the rough shape of the countertops and then began to measure each side with confident movements.

"Were you thinking stone or quartz?" He didn't look at her as he added the dimensions on another page.

"Um . . . I don't know. Which is more affordable?"

He glanced up at her, meeting her eyes with his gray-blue ones, and she felt a little quiver somewhere near her center. "Granite is probably going to be the most affordable, but the less expensive slabs won't be in the fashionable colors. Quartz is more expensive, but more durable over the long term as long as you don't set hot things on it."

Liv knew all this, had once considered all the options from budget to luxury. "What would you do?"

He looked around her kitchen. "You want white?"

She nodded.

"Do the quartz. It's not as expensive as white granite, and it's going to be a lot less maintenance." He must have seen her involuntary cringe at the word *expensive,* because he added, "If you're not too picky about what pattern, we might also be able to get you a deal with remnants. The island is the only thing that needs a full slab."

"Yeah, that's a good idea."

Charlie smiled at the surprise in her voice. "I can send you to my stone supplier's website and you can give me an idea of what you like." He took another look around. "Can I see the upper cabinets?"

"Yeah, they're in the back room, but Taylor is still asleep." She held up a finger to her lips.

"Understood." He gestured for her to lead the way and she quietly moved down the hallway to the bedroom wing.

Too late she realized she'd left her door open

and her bed unmade, and her neck prickled as she imagined him seeing her private space. She didn't dare glance back to see if he was looking. But when they came to the second bedroom, adjacent to Taylor's, he merely went inside and poked around the white upper cabinets stacked on a drop cloth. He examined the hinges, looked at how they were constructed, then gave a satisfied nod. "Custom?"

"Semi." She gestured for him to follow her back to the kitchen, where once more she put a safe distance between them.

"Have you already chosen tile for your back-splash?"

"Yeah, it was in the back closet. It's just a glass subway tile."

"Okay." Charlie turned another page in his notepad, scrawled and totaled several more numbers, and then handed it over to her. "This is just a rough estimate. I can give you a more accurate number when we pick the countertop material."

Liv took the paper, and her eyes widened. It was far less than her balance with the last contractor who had bailed on her. She scanned the columns of numbers. "You forgot to include labor."

"I was actually hoping we might be able to figure out a trade."

She jerked her head up, swallowing hard as their eyes met. "A trade?"

He pulled a folded sheet of paper from his back pocket. Her ad for the apartment. "I'm staying in Salida, but it looks like I might have work in Haven Ridge for the next few weeks. I was hoping we might be able to trade board for labor? Just while I'm working here. I don't expect you to put me up indefinitely."

"Oh." Liv stared at him while she considered. She hadn't had any luck in renting the place since Chelsea moved out, and if it meant that she didn't have to pay what was probably a substantial amount of labor costs to get her kitchen done, why wouldn't she jump on it?

Because that means that he'll be twenty yards from you every night.

But that was silly. It wasn't like she intended to act on this insane attraction, regardless of proximity. And from the dispassionate way he was looking at her now, she probably didn't need to worry about it anyway.

This was the sensible solution for both of them.

"I think we could work something out," she said finally. "I still . . . that is . . . would you mind filling out the application anyway? So I can do a background check?"

His expression shifted from openness to wariness in an instant, striking another little pang—this time not the good kind—into her stomach. "What is it? Is there something I should be aware of? Do you . . . do you have a criminal record?"

Charlie laughed, but he still looked uncomfortable. "No, nothing like that. You should know, though . . . I lost my contractor license last year."

She could see what it was costing him to admit it; he wasn't quite meeting her eye. "What happened?"

Now he looked up at her, and she could see what looked like pain in his face. "I gave my business partner responsibility he shouldn't have had. He made some big mistakes." He shook his head. "No, mistakes imply that it was accidental. He made some bad choices, defrauded customers, and because it was under my license, I was on the hook for it. I tried to make it right with the clients, but they sued me for damages. Even though I could get my license back, I can't afford the insurance or bonds. I'm deemed high risk now."

There was so much shame laced in his tone that instantaneously, her heart ached for him. "But you're still able to work without a license?"

"In cities that don't require one. In ones that do, I can do anything as a handyman that doesn't require a permit or inspections. Roof repairs. Minor remodeling."

"Oh." The revelation should probably concern her, given that he was going to be working on her house. But her gut told her that Charlie was telling the truth, that his biggest crime had been trusting someone he shouldn't have. And he'd lost everything. Now he was just looking for a way to get back on track, somehow. Some way.

There was something that she related to about that in-between sort of life.

"Thanks for telling me," she said. "I don't think that's a concern. I just have a teenage girl here, and for her safety, I don't want to cut corners."

"For *your* safety, you don't want to cut corners." He held her gaze steadily. "Give me a copy. I'll fill it out now."

She had to tear herself away from that look to retrieve a copy of the application and background check agreement from her desk. She handed it to him with a pen and he immediately bent over the counter, filling it out in neat block letters. Even though she knew she should probably step away, she found herself watching him, noting the slight flex of muscles in his forearm as he wrote, the line of his broad shoulders. When he reached up to run his fingers through his hair, pushing it back out of his eyes, an involuntary little shiver skittered through her.

When he was finished, he handed the pen and the application back to her. "When do you want to get started on the kitchen?"

"As soon as possible. But don't you have to finish Will's job first?"

"I'm waiting for the ceiling to dry before I can do the repair. I thought we might pick out the stone, and I can work at Larkspur while we're waiting for the countertops to be fabricated."

"*We* can pick the stone?"

"Of course. I assume you want to see it in person. My supplier is in the Springs, but we can make it up and back in an afternoon. I need to pick up the plaster anyway."

An entire afternoon. Alone with Charlie. Her brain said *no no no* while her hormones said *yes yes yes*. This time the brain would win out. "There's not that much variation in most of the white quartz," she said. "Why don't I pick out the colors that would be acceptable to me and you can see what they have? If you're not sure or you find something else you think I'd like, you can always video call me."

He looked disappointed, but he nodded. "We can do that. I'll text you the website so you can see what they carry. I'll drive up in the morning if you can make your selections by then. And that gives you some more time to do the background check."

"That sounds like a plan. And . . . thank you. I know Taylor really wants this to be done."

"The timing just happened to work and I'd rather be busy than standing around, literally watching plaster dry." Charlie flashed her a quick smile. "Speaking of which, I need to head over to Larkspur House now and get started on the prep. Text or call when you know what you want."

Liv swallowed and nodded. "Thanks." She saw him to the door, waited until he crossed to his truck outside her house before shutting the door behind him.

Text or call when you know what you want.

She knew what she wanted, all right. The bigger problem was knowing that she couldn't—wouldn't—let herself have it.

CHAPTER EIGHT

Now that Liv had a direction, she should be filled with a sense of purpose. Pick out her countertops, get this remodel done so that Taylor didn't spend the last two years of high school in a construction zone, finish cataloging the boxes so she could begin listing the books for Will. Instead, she wandered away from the front door back to the half-finished kitchen and poured herself another cup of coffee.

She'd never had a problem with productivity, not even as a child. She'd always been focused, disciplined, determined to go after what she wanted. It was how she'd ended up as valedictorian at Haven Ridge High, how she'd gotten a full scholarship to Columbia, how she'd landed an intern position with Random House the summer between her freshman and sophomore years of college. When she knew what she wanted, she went after it with terrifying single-mindedness.

But now she faced the idea that maybe even hustle and determination and a good reputation in her industry weren't just going to drop another job in her lap. She was great at long-term goals, but not so good at figuring out what to do next when those were shown to be unachievable.

Her phone beeped, and she jerked her eyes down to the screen. Charlie. She opened the message and found a link to his countertop supplier.

Well, there was her first task. No, second. She should put in the request for the background check. She topped off her coffee mug and returned to the laptop she'd abandoned less than an hour before.

Liv logged into the background check service she'd signed up for when Chelsea had vacated the property, then sat there, staring at the blinking cursor. She was well within her rights to require one—maybe even obligated—but she still felt like a voyeur as she typed Charlie's information into the online form. Were he just some random stranger who wanted to rent the place, she wouldn't think twice. But having a personal interest in him made this feel like an invasion of privacy. Like a shortcut to intimate knowledge she shouldn't have already.

Shouldn't have *at all*.

For example, she now knew he was thirty-five years old, and his birthday was April 28th. He'd put down a Colorado Springs post office box for his mailing address, though there was a residential address in Monument that looked like it might be an apartment. She resisted the urge to put it into Google Maps to see for sure. Instead, she forced her mind back on her typing, filled in all the important details, and then clicked *submit*. A window popped up asking for a credit card payment, which she entered and sent before shutting the site down. There. In less than forty-eight hours, she would know if Charlie Castro was who and what he said he was. Or at least she would know if he was a criminal.

The boxes of books were calling her, but it was more from curiosity over what might be inside than an actual desire to finish. Instead, she checked Charlie's message again and carefully typed the web address into her browser bar. A homemade-looking website popped up, featuring photos of a stone yard with slabs of natural stone on racks. She scrolled down the page to the quartz section and clicked on the section for white.

The screen was filled with page after page of identical-looking white stone.

Liv laughed. She could probably just pick one at random and it would look fine. Still, she did her duty and enlarged each photo in turn to examine the flecks, the undertones, the artificial veining. She probably should care more about what she was picking, but it had been so long since she'd actually approached the project with enthusiasm, now she just wanted it done. She jotted down the names of the styles she liked best—all with a vague, tone-on-tone marble look in shades varying from bright white to cream—

and then carefully tapped them into a reply to Charlie. At the last minute, she added, I trust you to pick what will look the best. Err on the side of least expensive.

There. She was probably the least fussy client he'd ever had.

Less than a minute later, she got his reply. Good choices. I'll see what I can do. Heading down tomorrow.

Good. That at least gave her another day to get his background check results. She didn't want to commit to the project until she knew if their labor/board trade would work out.

Liv glanced at her watch. It was a little after eleven, and Taylor likely wouldn't be awake until lunch. She changed into her workout clothes, scrawled a quick note to Taylor, and laced up her running shoes. After a moment's consideration, she grabbed her car keys and went out to her SUV.

But instead of veering toward one of her favorite back-country paths, she found herself navigating toward town. Her mind was full of worries and concerns. The last thing she needed was the deep quiet where she'd have no choice but to face them.

Instead, she parked at the very edge of Haven Ridge and climbed out to stretch her legs before she slipped into a slow jog. She loved this part of town, its houses a pleasant jumble of historic styles, many of them kept up over the years and passed down through the generations. From the pride evident in the new plots of flowers and freshly painted fences, you'd never know the town had been slowly dwindling away.

That fact was more evident on the commercial side of town: more buildings boarded up and vacant than occupied, entire blocks devoid of any sign of life. But here, too, was some encouraging evidence of revitalization—a painter's sign taped up in the window of one peeling building, shiny glass where last week there had only been plywood.

Was it possible that they were really seeing a revival in town? Ever since Mallory had written an article about Haven Ridge for *Altitude Magazine* the summer before, they'd seen a slow trickle of tourists pass through. And now that Gemma had made a success out of the Broken Hearts Bakery, maybe others felt encouraged to try their hands at a business, too.

The very idea set a glow in the middle of her chest, lifting her spirits and speeding her pace.

But she slowed again when she approached a row of old-fashioned brick buildings on Beacon Street, now sporting identical *For Sale or Lease* signs in the window.

Liv peered into the dirty windows one by one. Some of them were empty and dark, others littered with debris. They'd been vacant for as long as she could remember, their abandoned interiors giving no hint as to what businesses they might have once housed.

Liv stopped in front of the one in the middle, then stepped back to view the entire building. It was the only three-story in a row of mismatched facades, its white paint peeling, the carved scroll ornaments above the second- and third-story windows chipped and cracked by time and weather. The main floor had a bump-out bay window with the original wooden frames and a charming wood door set with a big pane of glass.

Liv moved to the window again and cupped her hands around her eyes as she peeked inside. Boxes and papers scattered the floor, and what looked like old wooden shelving had collapsed into a pile of boards. But beyond the disaster, a curved wooden staircase led to a second-floor loft that left most of the first floor open to the level above. Something in her chest caught in recognition, like a longing that she'd always had but until now had never recognized.

Why don't you open a bookstore? You always tell me that I can do anything I want if I put my mind to it. So why can't you do anything you want?

"Because it's a ridiculous idea, that's why." Liv had worked in publishing far too long to think that a bookstore was a money-making opportunity or anything besides a massive cash sink. Reluctantly, she dropped her hands and moved back the way she had come, that momentary bloom of hope fading to something that felt like resignation. By the time she reached Gemma's bakery, she was sweaty and out of breath and mostly in control of her wild fantasies.

There was a line in front of the bakery, snaking out the door, and Liv smiled as she dodged an exiting couple holding Styrofoam cups of coffee and warm cinnamon rolls on paper plates as she fell into line. It hadn't taken long for the Broken Hearts Bakery to become a Sunday-morning destination, and not just because the Brick House Cafe filled up by eleven o'clock. Only on Sunday did Gemma and her staff make their huge sheet pans of cinnamon rolls, twice the size of a man's fist and dripping with caramel sauce, pecans, or cream cheese icing, and it wasn't unusual for customers to buy a dozen on Sunday to eat all week long.

When Liv finally made it to the counter, Gemma was looking a little frazzled, but her cheeks were pink and her eyes glowed with happiness. "Best Sunday yet," she said to Liv with a grin. "What can I get you?"

"Do you really have to ask?"

Gemma laughed and turned to the counter on the back wall to cut out another roll and transfer it to a paper plate. Liv reached for her phone to pay, but Gemma waved her off as she always did. "Your money's no good here. But I'll send you home with a dozen if you come back when you're finished and help me."

Liv twisted to see the line, which had formed up even longer behind her, and only then did she realize that Gemma was the only one behind the counter. "Where are Chelsea and Rebekah?"

"Chelsea called in because the twins are sick, and Rebekah went to Denver with her dad."

Liv stepped aside as Gemma smiled at Mrs. Walters, one of the town's oldest and most devoted residents—she'd been their history teacher in high school. "What can I get for you, Mrs. Walters?"

"Two of those cinnamon rolls, two coffees, and a dozen chocolate chip cookies."

"Great-grandkids coming over today?" Gemma asked, sliding away to the glass-fronted pastry case to get the cookies.

"Oh yes, they'll be with us the entire week while their parents are in Seattle. Anniversary, you know."

"That's nice." Gemma produced the cinnamon rolls, poured the coffees from the commercial brewer, and pushed them across the counter before she tallied the order on the register. She glanced at Liv with a smile that looked like a thinly-veiled cry for help.

Liv laughed, held up her breakfast, and then mouthed that she would be back. She had to pick

her way through the crowd in the small space before she broke into the sunshine. Gemma might pretend like she was overwhelmed, but Liv had never seen her friend this happy. Despite her successful practice as an LA divorce lawyer and all the trappings that life afforded, Gemma had always had this shadow in her eye. As if she was just holding on, waiting for the next shoe to drop. Now she looked happy and light, even if she was sometimes stressed, and it was clear that she was where she was meant to be. In a short time, both she and the Broken Hearts Bakery had become essential to the town.

If that's true for her, why couldn't it be true for you?

Liv wandered down the street to the park, where she found an empty bench and plopped down on it to eat her cinnamon roll. She couldn't deny that the idea of going to work every day in her own shop, surrounded by that coffee-and-chocolate smell that came from the lignin and cellulose of old paper, sounded undeniably appealing. And not just because she secretly wanted one of those rolling ladders. It was the idea of being able to curate titles, make recommendations to her community, help cultivate a love of reading in her young customers.

No, it wasn't a lack of interest that was holding her back. It was the simple, ugly lack of funds.

Liv exhaled and forked the last bite of cinnamon

roll into her mouth, though it didn't taste as good as it had the moment before. Everything came down to money. Even if she could negotiate an affordable lease, there was no guarantee she could even turn a profit, let alone support herself and Taylor.

Liv's steps were a little heavier as she moved back down the street, tossing her plate in a green metal trash can as she passed. There was still a line at the bakery, but it no longer stretched outside—looked like she'd taken too long to eat. Even so, she slid behind the counter, washed her hands, and tied on a Broken Hearts Bakery apron, ready to bag and serve the orders as Gemma took care of the money.

Within minutes, they had served the entire line, and the trickle of customers slowly diminished until the bakery was empty. Gemma leaned back against the counter and pushed a stray piece of hair from her eyes. "That was crazy. I swear everyone and their mother has guests this weekend."

"Good for you, though," Liv said.

"Good for me," Gemma agreed. She took one look at Liv and said, "What's wrong?"

"Nothing's wrong. Why would you say that?"

Gemma cocked her head and gave her a reproving look.

Liv sighed. "Really, nothing is wrong. I just have a lot on my mind."

Gemma's eyes lit up. "About Charlie?"

Oh. Well, that was the advantage of her current angst—she'd momentarily forgotten about Charlie Castro. "No, actually. Assuming his background check comes back clean, he's going to handle my countertops and install everything. And in return . . . he's going to stay in the apartment for free."

A slow, sly smile crept across Gemma's lips.

Liv pointed a finger directly at her. "No. Don't look at me that way. There is nothing personal about this. It was a strictly practical decision."

"Right. Has nothing to do with the fact he's got you so hot and bothered you couldn't even think about saying no."

Liv widened her eyes in warning and looked around her, though there was no one to overhear. "I will kill you if you start any rumors."

"Relax. You know I'm not going to start any rumors. And it will be nice to finally have your kitchen done. You've lived in a construction zone long enough."

"It actually is perfect timing," Liv admitted. "I've felt bad that this is what Taylor is going to remember about the house when she goes off to college. At least she'll have two good years in a finished space."

Something must have shown on her face, because Gemma reached out and took her hand. "Is that what this is all about? Taylor?"

Liv shook her head. "No, it's just . . . this is not what I had in mind for her. For us."

"You think this is what I had in mind for me?" Gemma asked. "Tell me a year ago that this would be my life and I would have thought you were absolutely crazy."

"I know, I know. It's the next step to new adventures, blah blah blah."

"Well, I don't think I would have said anything that saccharine. Probably something more about opportunities and bootstraps."

"Taylor thinks I'm a sellout."

"No, she doesn't!"

"She asked me why I didn't buy all the books from Will and open a bookstore—"

Gemma gasped. "That's a great idea!"

"Not you, too? Do you have any idea how much money it costs to open a bookstore?"

"Yeah. Probably close to what it costs to open a bakery."

"Exactly." Liv drilled Gemma with a severe look. "You had the money for it. I don't."

"You could have the money for it . . ."

"Not going to mortgage the house, Gemma. You know why I did what I did. Even if I have to get a cashier's job at Walmart, I'm going to launch Taylor into college and make sure she has something to inherit from her dad."

Liv could tell from the look in her friend's eyes that she thought she was being ridiculous. And maybe she was. After all, a bookstore would be a dream come true. But if she gambled their future security on an uncertain venture like this, what would she do if she failed? Liv owed it to Taylor to be practical, to put her needs first.

"You know," Gemma said softly, "it's okay to move on."

Liv jerked her head up. "You think that's what I'm doing? Refusing to move on?"

Gemma paused as if she was weighing her words carefully. "I think that you're trying very hard to make sure that nothing changes. Not your job, not the plan you and Jason had for the house, not your vision for Taylor. But Liv, everything has already changed. And no matter how hard you try to hold onto the past, there's nothing you can do about it." She placed a gentle hand on Liv's shoulder. "The life you envisioned is gone. Don't you think it's time to get a new one?"

Liv blinked back tears, pierced by the words, but she couldn't be angry at Gemma for speaking the truth. There was simply one thing that Gemma didn't seem to understand, couldn't possibly understand unless she'd experienced that sort of loss.

The pieces of the life that Jason had left behind were the only part that remained of him. And as much as she wanted to be able to move on, she just wasn't ready to let go.

CHAPTER NINE

As Liv jogged back to her SUV, Gemma's words nagged at her: *The life you envisioned is gone. Don't you think it's time to get a new one?* Gemma meant well, but she could be blunt to a fault, especially when she thought her friends were being foolish.

But Liv wasn't being foolish. She was being the exact opposite. Opening a bookstore in this town was a terrible idea. For one thing, Haven Ridge was tiny, so there was no guarantee she'd sell enough books to even pay for the rent. For another, even if she were to open the bookstore, she wouldn't do it on that lonely stretch of Beacon Street, surrounded by buildings that had been boarded up for almost as long as she'd been alive. She'd never be able to count on passing traffic to help with sales, and she'd have to be completely reliant on advertising, something which she most certainly did not have the money for.

Except both the Brick House Cafe and the Broken Hearts Bakery are surrounded by empty buildings, her inner voice reminded her. In fact, the cafe had been on the verge of shutting down before Thomas moved home and decided to take it over. And the Broken Hearts Bakery had only started as a joke between Taylor and her friends, a hashtag in response to some snarky conversation heart cookies Gemma had made her. Looking at the bakery now, it was impossible to imagine that it hadn't always been a fixture in the community.

Just like a bookstore could be, if only someone would take a risk and open one.

That doesn't mean that someone has to be you.

When she got back to the house, the dozen promised cinnamon rolls in hand, it was still and quiet and Taylor's door was closed. Liv knocked gently on the door. "Taylor? Time to get up. It's almost noon."

There was a mumbling inside that sounded only vaguely human, but she heard things shifting around as proof of life. By the time Taylor emerged, sleepy, hair in disarray and wearing paint-splattered sweat shorts, Liv had a new pot of coffee made and a cinnamon roll waiting on a plate on the kitchen counter.

Taylor squinted at her and looked suspiciously at the cinnamon roll. "What's wrong?"

"Why do you think there's something wrong?"

She gestured to the pastry like it was a serpent. "You never get cinnamon rolls on Sunday."

"I do, sometimes, and it doesn't mean any-thing's wrong. But I did want to talk to you."

Taylor paused in pouring her coffee. "And there it is."

Liv let the tone go. Taylor was like a bear

emerging from hibernation when she woke up, even though Gemma swore she had been a perfect ray of sunshine when she stayed with her last. The difference between being the fun aunt and the stepmother, Liv supposed.

"It's nothing bad, I promise."

Taylor just nodded and took her cup of coffee and the cinnamon roll to the sofa. Liv poured herself what might be her tenth cup of coffee for the day and puttered around the kitchen, putting a few glasses in the dishwasher and straightening up a messy shelf in the pantry. Finally, Taylor returned with an empty plate and a half-drained cup, looking far more alert and pleasant than she had ten minutes before.

"Okay. So what did you want to talk about?"

Liv leaned back against the counter, bracing her palms before a splinter dug into them and she jerked upright again. Taylor smirked and she stuck her tongue out in response. "I've made a deal with that handyman to come finish our kitchen. And in return, he's going to stay in the apartment."

Taylor's expression shifted into one of suspicion. "Okaaay. That's good, I guess. Especially if we're getting real counters."

"We're getting real counters. He's going to the Springs tomorrow to see what they have in our price range."

"Okay, then. Was that it?"

Liv opened her mouth to mention the space she'd found today, then snapped it shut. What good would it do to get her excited when she had no intention of going through with this mad idea? It would be just one more thing for Taylor to be upset with her about, and she didn't need any more of those right now. Instead, Liv just nodded. "Yeah, that's it. I just didn't want you to worry if you see a guy you don't know around the property. I'll introduce you two once everything's finalized."

"Cool." Taylor turned and shambled back down the hall. "I'm going out with Meghan and Jada today, okay?"

"Okay," Liv said absently. "I'll probably just clean the apartment. Let me know if you need a ride."

Taylor mumbled a response, but when she emerged twenty minutes later, dressed and made-up for the day, she actually paused to give Liv a half-hug goodbye. "Jada's here. I'll be back for dinner."

That little bit of connection, that peek of softness, was all Liv needed to tell her she was right. Taylor was the important thing here. Everything else was just a distraction.

Liv grabbed a bucket of cleaning supplies and carried them over to the garage apartment, where she scrubbed until her only worries were the strain in her arms and the kink in her back.

By the time the sun went down, the place was spotless: the new wood floors she'd laid clean and glowing, the kitchen fresh and lemon-scented, the bathroom gleaming. She'd worked hard on this space, doing everything from painting the walls to refinishing wood trim to installing new flooring herself, and seeing it sparkling clean always filled her with a feeling of accomplishment. It was proof that she could do hard things if she put her mind to it.

It might have been that feeling of accomplishment that had her pulling out her phone and typing in *321 Beacon Street* into the county assessor's property search. She nibbled her nail while the outdated website spun up its results. She was just looking. Probably it was owned by some developer who had bought up the property before deciding that Haven Ridge was a poor risk. At least she wouldn't have that nagging feeling of *what if* hanging over her head. After all, it wasn't simply the idea of a bookstore she was daydreaming about—it was that particular building, with its curved staircase, second-floor loft, and impossibly high ceilings.

So her jaw dropped open when the search returned the last result she would have expected.

Owner(s): Bixby Trust, The

Liv blinked. That was impossible. She must have put in the address wrong. Still, just to check, she typed in a range: *300-400 Beacon Street.*

And came back with a list of six buildings, every single one of them owned by the Bixby Trust.

Liv sank down on the edge of her sofa, simultaneously filled with elation and terror. She'd been preparing herself to hear it was some big property investment group out of Denver or Boulder, and instead, the owner was a trust run by her dead husband's best friend.

She started to laugh.

It was all too much. Taylor pushing her on her dreams. Gemma nudging her to get a new vision for her life. Even her, thinking that she wasn't ready to move on and eliminate the image that she'd had of her life when she'd gotten married, become a stepmom, and moved back to Haven Ridge.

But now that her dream was potentially in the hands of the one person who was especially inclined to help her? It felt like Jason had reached down from heaven to give her a little nudge. To tell her that she needed to let go of those rigid expectations and embrace what was in front of her. And whether that was just fanciful imagining or if that was even possible, it felt like something that she couldn't ignore.

Before she could think better of it, Liv opened her messaging app and tapped out a text to Will: Are you available tomorrow? I need to talk to you about something.

Almost immediately, his response came back. Uh oh. Sounds serious. Should I be worried?

She started typing back a reply, assuring him there was nothing to worry about, then deleted it and started over. Depends. I need a favor.

There was no hesitation from Will. I've always meant what I said. Anything I can do to help.

Brick House Cafe at 9? I'm buying.

Sure. And I'M buying. See you then.

Liv's stomach leaped in response. There was always the possibility that Will wouldn't lease the place to her, that he would want too much for it. After all, he'd probably listed them because he needed the money to fix up the castle. But even if it wasn't true, she knew Will would find a way to make it work for her.

And then, like it or not, she would be committed.

On a Monday morning before ten, Dogwood Street was quiet, only a few cars parked along the curbs with a larger cluster in front of the Brick House Cafe. Liv took a spot beside Will's rental SUV, put her car into park, and grabbed her purse as she hopped out of the driver's seat. Her stomach did a back flip the minute her sandaled foot hit the pavement.

Inside, she raised a hand of greeting to Thomas behind the counter while she scanned for Will, who she quickly found in the last booth on the corner. He stood when he saw her coming and pressed her into a quick hug. "Hey. Good to see you. I'm sorry I was busy when you came over."

Liv stepped back and gave him a smile before she slid into the booth across from him. "Not at all. I know you've got a lot to do before you go back to Chicago."

Will took his seat as well. "Yeah, but I'm never too busy to see you. You have me curious, I admit."

"We'll get to that soon enough. First, breakfast. And *I'm* buying." Liv threw him an amused look and then signaled for Thomas to come over and take their order. Will only ordered a cup of coffee and a slice of coffee cake—despite Liv's disapproving look, he was no doubt trying to keep the tab low—and Liv ordered the summer special pancakes with cinnamon chips and strawberry sauce.

As soon as Thomas had disappeared to the kitchen to put in their order, Will folded his hands on the table and said, "Spill it."

Liv laughed. No point in beating around the bush. "I'm thinking of opening a bookstore."

Will's eyebrows raised. "Oh?"

"Yes. And I was wondering how much it would cost for me to buy that whole lot of books from you, to give me a head start on my stock."

"I hadn't really thought about it," Will said slowly, "but if you need them—"

"Don't you dare say you'll give them to me."

He chuckled. "Okay. Well, I was just hoping to cover the cost of the roof repairs and plasterwork. If you're willing to match that, we'll consider it done."

Now Liv's eyebrows raised at the figure he quoted. It was less than half of what he could get if he was willing to be patient and sell them all individually. But then, that would take months, maybe even years. A bird in the hand, she supposed. Slowly, she nodded. "I think I could do that."

"Good." Will smiled. "Now where are you thinking this bookshop is going to be located?"

Liv grimaced. "Well, there happens to be that entire block of buildings owned by the trust on Beacon Street . . . 321 in particular."

Will shook his head. "I'm sorry. I can't help you there."

Liv blinked, taken aback. "Why?"

"Terms of the trust. There are some odd provisions that are meant to keep all the Bixby properties together. Which means that unless you wanted to buy the entire block—which I hardly think you do—I couldn't split them up."

"I understand. I hadn't really considered buying anyway. I can't afford it."

Will looked surprised. "Oh. In that case, I could lease it to you. I'm sorry, I just assumed . . . What were you thinking in terms of rent?"

"Um, as little as possible?" Liv felt heat rise to her cheeks. "That's not fair to ask of you, I know. I would pay market rate if I could, but I can't."

Will's eyes sparkled as he regarded her. "You know, I seem to be making a lot of ill-advised financial decisions today because of you. It's not a good look for an accountant."

"Will, I'm sorry. I shouldn't have asked. You've already done so much for Taylor and me, I shouldn't be asking you for any more favors—"

"No, actually, I've done precious little for you and Taylor, and I regret it." His expression was serious, his voice solemn.

"You're not responsible for us, Will."

"Kind of feels like it though." He threw her a wry smile, and then took a deep breath. "What about this? If you cover the cost of the property taxes and insurance so my net investment in that building is zero, we'll call it even."

Liv stared. "Are you serious?" She'd seen the taxes on the property when she'd looked at the assessor's site and it was only a few hundred dollars a year. The insurance would be double or triple that . . . which still made her monthly cost barely more than a slot at a farmer's market. "I couldn't possibly do that."

"Why not? The place is vacant. If you occupy 321, that can only have a good effect on the potential sale or lease of the other properties on the block. All the improvements will be your responsibility, of course."

She stared at him in disbelief. Or perhaps it was just shock. Yesterday, she'd been adamant that this was never going to happen. Today, she was making arrangements for a retail space and purchase of stock. She actually felt a little faint.

"Liv? Do we have a deal?"

She blinked and refocused on Will's kind expression, directed toward her. He really was a better friend than she deserved, no matter what he might say about his duties to Jason's memory. Slowly, she nodded.

"We have a deal."

CHAPTER TEN

The best part of the two-hour drive to Colorado Springs was that it gave Charlie time to think. The worst part of the nearly two-hour drive to Colorado Springs was that it gave Charlie *too much* time to think.

Especially when those thoughts largely revolved around Liv.

He had no business thinking about her. Liv was his new client and potential future landlord. That automatically made her off-limits, even without the fact she was a widow with a teen stepdaughter. No way was he anything but a complication for her, especially when the last thing he was in the market for was a serious relationship.

Not after the way his last one ended.

Charlie's hands tightened on the steering wheel as they always did when he poked the old-but-not-so-healed wound. It was bad enough that his best friend and business partner had cheated him, cheated his clients. He might have been able to forgive that; people made stupid, desperate mistakes, especially when they were in financial trouble. He might have even been able to forgive the fact that his girlfriend had slept with his best friend and business partner—though that one was more of a stretch. But the fact that Kyra had been carrying on behind his back *and* she knew what Dan was doing to Charlie's business . . . and she'd kept both of those from him for almost a year?

The broken relationship he could have survived. He might even have endured the betrayal of a friend. But in one fell swoop, Kyra and Dan had decimated every single area of his life, leaving him nothing but rubble. No girlfriend, no friend, no business, no money, no house, no livelihood. And the path to reclaiming it felt steeper and rockier every day.

Even worse, the wounds of this betrayal would probably last longer than his current financial predicament. And no spark of interest or inexplicable pull toward another woman would change that. Especially when no woman in her right mind would want to get wrapped up in the unmitigated disaster that was his life. What did he have to offer besides a ruined reputation, a steadily draining bank account, and a lot of baggage?

No, better that he put both Kyra and Liv out of his mind and focus on the things he could control. Doing these jobs to the best of his ability, banking as much cash as he could, and starting over from scratch. He'd built a life from the ground up once. He could do it again.

But by the time he navigated the I-25 traffic and pulled into a pot-holed lot outside a warehouse on the south side of Colorado Springs, his mood had taken a decidedly negative turn. He hopped out of his truck, slammed the door hard enough that the window rattled, and made his way into the building.

The interior was stark and industrial: bare concrete floors, steel frame, and an air conditioner that could barely keep up with the heat radiating from the metal roof overhead. An L-shaped counter floated in the middle of the space, and Charlie made his way over to the end where a middle-aged man with shocking red hair stood, talking on the phone in front of a computer. He looked up, his expression brightening when he saw Charlie, and held up one finger.

Charlie waited as his friend finished up the call, then set down the receiver and circled the end of the counter. The man slapped his hand into a tight grip, and then hauled Charlie in for a hug. "Nice to see you, man. It's been a while."

"Too long. How have you been?" He'd known Brock his entire adult life; the man was about a decade older than him and had already taken over the family's stone yard when Charlie started in this business the summer he turned nineteen.

"Not bad, all things considered. I should be asking you that."

Charlie made a face. "Just passing time. I'm doing some small jobs up in Chaffee County and then I'll be getting my license back. Hopefully."

Brock nodded thoughtfully, his face twisted

into that same concerned, yet cautious expression all Charlie's business acquaintances used. "I was really sorry to hear what happened. That was a rough break. I can't believe it."

"Yeah, you and me both."

Brock gave a little laugh. "Well, as good as it is to see you, you didn't come in to say hi. What can I do for you today?"

Charlie pulled out the notepad from his back pocket and swiveled so Brock could see his measurements. "I've got a client in Haven Ridge who needs countertops, but she's on a really tight budget. If we can piece it together from remnants, I think that would be best."

"Color?"

"Shades of white."

"We could probably do that. But you're looking at a full slab for the island and that's going to cost her, no matter what material she chooses. Sure she wouldn't go for butcher block?"

"Talking yourself out of business?"

"Just trying to be realistic. Forty square feet of anything isn't budget-friendly."

"I was hoping you could give me the friends-and-family discount."

Brock indicated with his head that Charlie should follow, leading him down aisles between slabs of rock that were, in some cases, two or three times their height. "Calling in favors? She must be pretty."

"She's gorgeous," Charlie said immediately, earning a surprised laugh from Brock. He'd expected Charlie to deny it. "That's not the point, though. I feel bad for her. Lost her husband, lost her job, raising a teen stepdaughter, contractor flaked on her halfway, and they've been living in a construction zone for over a year. I'd just like to do something nice for her. She deserves it, you know? There's only so many losses you can take before you need a win."

Brock flicked him a look, as if he realized Charlie wasn't just talking about his client. "I'll see what I can do. I still owe you for that mention in that design magazine a couple of years ago." He held up a finger. "I can cut you a deal on the fabrication but not on the material. Costs are costs."

"Gotcha. I'll take whatever we can get."

As Brock led Charlie to a section filled with rack after rack of white quartz, he couldn't deny that he missed this. He'd been working with the same suppliers for decades. But when he'd lost his business, he'd pulled back from all that out of shame. No matter how understanding or sympathetic they were, he knew they were wondering how he could have been so blind, so trusting. They would never let anything like that happen to them. They would be smarter than that. So either he was incredibly stupid or he'd been involved in the fraud. Those thoughts seeped into their words and their gestures, just like Brock's unconsciously careful demeanor right now.

"I really didn't know," Charlie said quietly as they perused a slab of speckled white granite.

Brock looked at him, surprised. "Of course you didn't. Of all the people I've ever known, you're among the most honest."

"Well, you're one of the few who believe that. Even my brothers have their suspicions."

"Your brothers have always been idiots, so I'm not surprised." Brock clapped a hand on Charlie's shoulder. "Anyone who truly knows you knows that you would never cheat customers. Especially when those cut corners compromise safety."

"Planning and Community Development doesn't truly know me. They just know they yanked my license."

"Then don't be a contractor in Colorado Springs," Brock said. "There are other cities in this state. It's not like you have a house to worry about here."

"Thanks, man."

Brock winced. "You know what I mean."

"I do." He nodded toward a gray-and-white granite slab. "What about that one?"

"Out of your price range."

"Really?" Charlie fixed a pointed stare at him.

Brock sighed. "Fine. I'll see what I can do. It's been there a while anyway."

"See?" Charlie clapped him on the shoulder. "That wasn't too hard, was it?"

"You're a sneaky son of a gun, you know that?"

"One who made you a lot of money, so yeah."

Brock chuckled and shook his head. "Let's go write this up and you can see if your girlfriend will go for it."

Charlie huffed out a surprised laugh, but he didn't bother to correct him. Because secretly, deep down, he liked the sound of it.

CHAPTER ELEVEN

When Liv got home from town just after ten thirty, Taylor was already up, leaning against the kitchen island and staring into space with a half-finished cup of coffee in hand.

Liv threw her a tentative smile while she dropped her keys and purse on the countertop. "Did you accidentally make decaf again?"

Slowly, Taylor swiveled her head toward her. "What?"

"Because you're . . . never mind." Liv shook her head. "Go get dressed. I have a surprise for you."

The slow blink her stepdaughter gave her didn't seem promising, but at least she answered somewhat coherently. "A surprise? What kind of surprise?"

"If I told you that, it wouldn't be a surprise." Liv nudged her. "Now go."

"Fine." Taylor heaved a sigh and pushed away from the counter, then paused mid-step and swung by the pantry to grab one of yesterday's leftover cinnamon rolls before she stumbled back down the hallway into her room.

Liv just rubbed her forehead wearily. Was it too much to ask for at least a little show of faith here?

Taylor emerged twenty minutes later, properly

dressed in jeans and a tank top, her hair pulled into a smooth ponytail and her usual dark eyeliner carefully applied. Liv wasted no time grabbing her purse. "Come on. Let's go."

The teen stifled a yawn and followed her to the car, where she stared blankly out the window the whole drive back into town. But when Liv pulled up at the curb in front of the block of vacant buildings, Taylor sat up straighter. "What are we doing here?"

"You'll see." Liv hopped out of the car, digging in her pocket for the key that Will had given her and gestured for Taylor to follow her. She stopped in front of number 321. "This is it."

Taylor looked doubtfully at the ramshackle building. "This is what, exactly?"

"Our bookstore."

The look on Taylor's face was just as satisfying as she'd hoped. "Wait, what? Our *bookstore. Our* bookstore? Since when do we have a bookstore?"

"Since now," Liv said. "If we want it."

"But I don't understand. You said—"

"I know what I said. And I know what *you* said. You were right. If I'm going to tell you that you can do anything you want, I should try living it. And I've always wanted to own a bookstore."

A small smile raised the corners of Taylor's lips, but she clamped down on it almost as quickly. "Well, you could have picked a place that wasn't a wreck. Let's see it then."

Liv shook her head and put the key in the lock. Nothing happened. She tried again, jiggling it a little. This time, the sticky cylinder swiveled and she put some weight into the door hoping it would break free from the aging frame.

A jingle sounded from the tarnished sleigh bell mounted on the inside of the door, and a musty smell enveloped them. Liv wrinkled her nose and stepped aside for Taylor. There was no question this place had been shut up for years, if not decades, and if the state of the first floor was any indication, vacated in a hurry. There was a thick layer of dust over everything, a fine coating of trash, paper, and cardboard across the floor, and what looked like oak shelving that had pulled away from their mounts in the brick walls to collapse in heaps along the perimeter.

"Well, it's um, old." Taylor picked her way through the litter scattered across the expanse of stained green carpet. "What did this used to be?"

Liv picked up an envelope that surely had to be from the early 1980s from the look of the stamp. "Appears to have been a five-and-dime."

"What's a five-and-dime?"

"Kind of like a dollar store or a mercantile." Liv turned in a circle, taking it all in. The exposed brick walls still had patches of white clinging in places, as if they had once been plastered or limewashed. The thud of their footsteps on the floor suggested hardwoods beneath the stained carpet, and the ceiling stretched two stories above them to a plastered, medallion-adorned ceiling that held a huge, cloudy crystal chandelier. A winding staircase—with a smooth, ornate oak banister—curved up to a second-floor loft that looked over a railing to the floor below.

"It's beautiful," Liv breathed.

Taylor slanted her a doubtful look.

"No, really. Try to look past the trash. It's got great bones. This ceiling alone . . . and the chandelier . . . and the staircase . . ." Liv carefully picked her way across the floor and climbed the stairs to the second-story loft. The boards creaked slightly beneath her feet, but they still felt solid.

Despite her fears, the loft was completely empty and much larger than it had looked from below—probably about the same square footage as the retail space on the first floor. But unlike the bottom floor, the wood was in much worse shape—even from the top of the stairs she could see the splintered and rotted boards. Slowly, she took a step back before turning and descending again. She wasn't going to take a chance of falling through up here. Not until she was able to get someone to come check it out.

Charlie popped into her mind, and she immediately shoved him aside. Time enough for that. He was already working on her kitchen. She didn't need to drag him into this. At least not yet.

Downstairs, Taylor was staring blankly, her

arms crossed tightly over her chest, her expression unreadable. "So," Liv asked carefully, "what do you think?"

Taylor snapped back to the present and Liv braced herself. Then the girl's face blossomed into a grin. "I love it."

"You do?" Until now, Liv hadn't realized how much she wanted—needed—her stepdaughter's buy-in. "So what do you think? Should we do it? Will you . . . do it with me?"

Taylor gave her an arch look. "Oh, you need me. This place has moody academia written all over it, and who is moodier and more academic than me?"

She did have a point.

Taylor was walking around the perimeter now. "We absolutely have to have solid wood bookcases. Metal is never going to work in here. Maybe some wingback chairs here by the window where people can sit and flip through books while they're deciding—or better yet, a real reading room in the loft up there. Maybe a double-height bookshelf going all the way up with a rolling ladder, though then we'd constantly be chasing kids off it . . ." There was a gleam in Taylor's eye that was entirely new. "I'm thinking an old English library vibe, like you'd find in a huge manor. Dark wood and rich colors and fabrics, maybe some antique rugs. You can find all sorts of vintage textiles on eBay . . ."

Taylor sounded so confident that Liv found herself gaping. "Since when do you know about any of this?"

Hurt flashed through Taylor's expression. "I've been thinking about studying design in college."

Liv blinked. This was the first she was hearing about this. "Really? What kind?"

"I don't know. Industrial, maybe? Architecture?" Taylor frowned at Liv. "You've seriously never seen any of my drawings?"

"I didn't want to snoop!"

"Or pay attention," Taylor mumbled as she turned away.

She couldn't have said anything that would have struck deeper to the heart. Blood drained from Liv's face, leaving only the chill of dread on her skin. "You think I don't pay attention?"

"Never mind," Taylor said, heading for the door. "It doesn't matter."

"No, it does matter. You think I don't pay attention to you?"

Taylor spun. "Well, you don't. I mean, you make sure I eat and I get my homework done and stuff. But you have no idea what I like. You barely know anything about my friends. I mean, even Aunt Gemma got to know them in February and she was only here for a week."

Liv's stomach clenched. "Taylor, I . . . I don't know what to say. I really thought . . ." She had been trying hard not to get too involved, not to pressure her, not to snoop. She'd thought that was what you were supposed to do with teenagers who were becoming independent. Who wanted parents knowing every detail of their lives when they were sixteen?

But justifying her actions wouldn't fix this. Liv swallowed down all her defensive, instinctive responses and instead said, "I'm sorry. I never meant to make you feel like I didn't care. I just didn't want you thinking that I was trying to replace your parents."

Taylor's face shifted through so many emotions Liv couldn't follow them all, passing through stricken on the way to stony. "Well, mission accomplished then." And before Liv could say a word, Taylor turned and left the shop.

Liv stared at Taylor's departing back, frozen in shock while the tinkle of bells lingered in the silence. She'd misjudged everything. It was just that Taylor was so put together, minus the occasional friend drama or school meltdown, that Liv hadn't felt like she needed to micromanage her. It would have been different if she'd seen her heading down the wrong path. But Taylor had a good group of friends, a seemingly respectful boyfriend, and excellent grades. She had already started doing her own college research—Liv realized now that she shouldn't have simply assumed Taylor still wanted to study history like she had when she was younger—and pretty much lived her life like an adult.

But inside there was still a kid who just wanted to be seen.

And that was where she had gone wrong: thinking that the only thing Taylor needed from her was financial support and a steady routine, an open-door policy, when maybe she had wanted Liv to push and prod and take an interest—even an overly specific one—in her life. Like a real mom.

Liv buried her face in her hands and took several long calming breaths until she got her emotions under control. "I screwed up, Jason," she whispered in the silence. "I'll fix this. I promise."

Taylor was standing on the curb beneath a tree when Liv made her way back out. She didn't look away from the street when Liv came up behind her.

"I'm sorry," she said softly.

Taylor shrugged. "It doesn't matter. You didn't do anything wrong."

"I did, though. I thought you needed me to support your independence. When you just wanted me to be interested in you."

Taylor didn't say anything, but the little shift in her shoulders said she was listening.

"The thing is, when I married your dad, I felt like I didn't fit. You two were so close. He knew everything about you, and it had been just the two of you for so long, I felt like I was intruding. The last thing I wanted to be was this person who tried to barge in and change things. Act like your mom when I didn't have the benefit of all those years with you."

That seemed to get through, because Taylor shifted to face her. "It wasn't like that. I wanted a mom."

"I know," Liv said softly. "But I was just never very good at it. I mean, I could braid your hair and make your lunch and pick you up from school . . ."

"But that's what a mom is," Taylor said. "You were there. You were my room mom in sixth grade, for heaven's sake. That has *mom* right in the title!"

Liv huffed out a little chuckle. "But that's what you needed from me then. And now that you're older . . ."

"I still need you." Taylor's voice was disbelieving. "My dad died. Why would you think I would need you less? But it was like as soon as he was gone, you . . . disappeared. I mean, yeah, you made sure that I was doing okay in school and gave me a curfew and things, but . . . you're always on your computer. Or working on the apartment. Or trying to finish the house."

"Because I've been trying to provide for you. Trying to give you everything your dad could have . . ."

"The only thing I want from my dad is my dad!" Taylor yelled, tears forming in her eyes. "I don't care that he was going to pay for my college or leave me the house or any of those things you think are important. I just don't want him to be dead. And since that's not going to happen, the least you could do is be *here!*"

The tears spilled over Taylor's lower lashes, bringing a trail of mascara on their slow slide down her cheeks. Liv's own eyes filled at the hurt in her stepdaughter's voice, the full understanding of how badly she'd failed. "Taylor, I'm so, so sorry."

The girl didn't resist when she put her arms around her, though she hesitated for a long moment before she slid her own arms around Liv's waist and held on tight. Her shoulders shook with sobs, her tears wetting the shoulder of Liv's blouse, and Liv sniffed back her own emotions before they could overwhelm her too. Finally, when the torrent subsided and Taylor pulled back, Liv gripped her arms hard and forced her to stand before her.

"I may have messed this all up, but you should know one thing. I love you like you were my own blood. I am incredibly proud of you in so many ways. And anything I may or may not have done was because of my own failures as a parent, not because of any lack in you."

Taylor's bottom lip wobbled, her eyes filling

with tears again, and she bit down on her bottom lip. "You mean that?"

"Of course I mean that. Why do you think I fought so hard to be your guardian?"

"There was nowhere else for me to go."

"There *were* other places for you to go. But there was no way I was going to send you off to relatives you barely know when I was here and willing. Okay? Never doubt that. I made the choice. It wasn't forced on me."

Taylor blew out a long breath and gave a watery nod. Even with the wrecked black makeup, she looked younger and more innocent than Liv could remember in a long time. She should have addressed this long before Taylor could draw her own conclusions about the situation.

"It's just you and me. By choice." Liv stared into Taylor's eyes. "So what do you think? Are we going to do this thing?"

Taylor sniffed hard and wiped her hand across her cheeks, collecting the smear of makeup on her fingertips. But her smile was hopeful. "Let's do this. Together."

Liv wanted to believe that things were fine, that the drive back home would be looser, freer between them. But the truth was, the ghost of her failures still hung between them. It was one thing to apologize, to realize what she was doing wrong. It was another thing to prove that she meant it by actively fixing things. By trying to do better. And even though she'd meant every word that she said, her insides twisted at how much was at stake. What did she know about being a parent anyway? She'd missed the first eleven years of Taylor's life. She didn't have the history with her, the trust, that a mom would have. All they had was their shared grief and Liv's willingness to try harder, whatever that meant.

And the bookstore.

After they'd driven all the way back to the highway in silence, Liv said, "So I was thinking. I have a bunch of things to work out before we can really get started. What if you started on design ideas while I get a business plan together?"

Taylor nodded thoughtfully. "Sure. But I'd need some supplies and things. Like I need a laser measure so I can get dimensions. It's too big for a tape measure."

Inwardly, Liv was impressed. She'd been thinking the girl would dive in with sketches, not architectural renderings. "I think that could be arranged. We can order one when we get home."

"Cool. Because I was thinking, since we already have that loft . . ."

As Taylor rattled on, her quick mind already working through the details with the logic and vision of a much older person, Liv felt the warmth of pride building in her chest. It was easy to think Taylor's single personality trait was *quirky* because of her fashion sense, but listening to her detail all the steps for their new bookstore, Liv realized once more that she really hadn't seen her as a whole person. Maybe that was a realization all parents had at this age, when their children went from dependent on them to becoming their own fully-formed human beings.

"What?" Taylor broke off when she realized Liv was staring. "You don't agree?"

"Oh no, I agree. I was just sitting here thinking how impressive you are and how lucky I am to have a smart business partner."

Taylor flushed, but it was pride and not embarrassment shining in her eyes. It made Liv feel even worse to realize that she'd been unintentionally starving Taylor of the attention she really needed. The girl returned to her monologue, and Liv hoped that her stepdaughter would remember it all later, because she certainly wouldn't.

When they finally pulled through the gate of their property, it felt like the rift between them had been repaired, at least for now. Liv put the SUV into park and turned to look at Taylor. "Well, I suppose we've got a space now. And we've got a plan. What's next, future business mogul?"

Taylor threw her a smirk. "How should I know? I'm just working on the design. You're the grown-up."

Liv rolled her eyes and shoved her with her elbow, earning a laugh. She supposed there was nothing left to do but get started on all the boring details of forming a business. With a little help from Gemma and a lot of internet research, she had no doubt they could bring it together fairly quickly.

Then there was the little matter of talking Charlie into working on the place.

Almost as if the thought had summoned him, her phone rang in her pocket, his name flashing up on her screen. Video call. Liv tilted the screen toward Taylor so she could see who was calling, then punched the button to accept and held the phone out at arm's length. "Hey!"

"Hey!" Charlie's voice was muffled, a little echoey, but it still gave her a little hitch in her stomach. Stupid. "I'm here at the stone yard and I wanted to show you what I found."

Liv flicked a glance at Taylor who gave an enthusiastic nod. "Oh yeah? Let's see."

The picture shook wildly before it stabilized to show huge slabs of stone tilted up on their edges on racks. Charlie's disembodied voice came through the screen. "So we've got this pure white right here. This is the full slab, but they have a bunch of remnants. If you don't mind a seam beside the sink and at a couple of corners, I can piece it together at about forty percent of the slab cost."

"Wow, really?" She threw a quick look at Taylor, who just shrugged. The seams on white wouldn't be that noticeable, and besides, it was loads better than the particle board they had now. "What about the island?"

"Well, here's what I was thinking. It's a little bit more than you wanted to spend, but . . ." He angled the camera to show a gorgeous slab of white-and-gray granite. "You can't see it very well on the camera, but it's got some charcoal and tan in it as well. So it won't be quite as stark."

Liv grimaced. "How much?"

Charlie flipped the camera around so she was looking at his face again. When he named the figure, she could tell he was holding his breath.

"For the whole island?"

He nodded.

"That's not bad. What is it all together?"

When he named the total, Liv almost felt faint. It was half of what she'd been quoted last and less than her original budget. "I don't understand. How did you manage that?"

"Owner of the company is a friend of mine and he owes me. I didn't mind calling in a favor since you're doing me a favor with the apartment."

"Yeah, but that's because you're giving me a break on labor. I can't . . ." She broke off. She most certainly could. She was not going to turn down a favor because of pride. "Thank you. You have no idea how much I appreciate this."

His face cracked into a smile, his eyes crinkling at the corner in a way she found much too appealing. "You're welcome. So I can tell them to move forward?"

"Yes, you can tell them to get started. If you send me the contact info, I'll call with my credit card number for the deposit."

"I'll text you," he said. "I'm glad we could find something that will work for you. It's going to be beautiful."

"I think so, too." Liv hesitated. "If you have time, could you come by my house when you're back in town tonight? Or tomorrow if that's better. I want to talk to you about some things."

The ease vanished from his expression. "Problems?"

"Oh, no, nothing like that. New project. I am . . . potentially altering the scope of your work."

Charlie laughed. "I like the sound of that. I'll be back in Haven Ridge about seven tonight. I'll swing by then if that's okay."

"Sure. That's fine. Thanks again."

"You got it." He grinned and clicked off the call before Liv could.

She shoved her phone back into her pocket, and when she turned, Taylor was eyeing her closely. "You didn't tell me that your contractor was hot."

Liv laughed. "Why would I? He's my contractor. Well . . . I guess he's also our tenant, as soon as I get the background check."

133

"Mmm," Taylor said, but she wasn't smiling.

"What? I thought you didn't mind him staying there."

Taylor just slanted her a dubious glance.

"Taylor, whatever you're thinking, it isn't true."

"I'm not thinking anything," she said, and Liv knew she wasn't going to get anything else out of Taylor now. For all her laid-back demeanor 80 percent of the time, she was unexpectedly prickly the other 20. Liv just wished that she knew if this was typical teenage temperament or if it was because of her.

And she wished that she could be 100 percent truthful when she said that whatever vibe Taylor was picking up between her and Charlie was in her imagination.

Liv cleared her throat. "So. I get started on business plans, you work on design?"

"Sure." Taylor shot Liv a look, the suspicions of moments before fading. "I'm glad we're doing this. I'm glad I get to help."

Liv smiled, her rush of relief so strong she nearly had to blink back tears. "Yeah, me too. Why don't you go in? I'll be along in a second."

"Okay." Taylor reached for the door handle and hopped out, leaving Liv ensconced in the quiet car. She tipped her head back against the headrest, taking a long, deep breath.

She didn't know who or what to thank for the pieces falling into place here, whether it was

town magic or coincidence or just well-meaning friends giving her the nudge she needed. But she knew a second chance when she saw one.

And she wasn't going to squander it.

CHAPTER TWELVE

Liv and Taylor hunkered down at the dining room table for the rest of the afternoon, a companionable silence surrounding them while summer rain tapped at the windows, a counterpoint to the click of their laptop keys. But despite the fact that Liv knew she really needed to work on the business plan for the bookshop, her eyes continually wandered to the teenage girl, her mind replaying what Taylor had thrown at her.

Just because Taylor had been angry and hurt didn't make the words untrue. Liv had withdrawn. She hadn't meant to, of course, but taking on the mantle of parent had altered her relationship with Taylor. When Jason had been around to do the "real parenting," she'd painted with Taylor on the patio and made snowmen on winter days and played Dance Dance Revolution in front of the living room TV.

No wonder Taylor thought that Liv had forgotten about her, even though the teen was at the forefront of every decision she made and every worry she had. She'd lost the Liv she knew and gotten a pod parent in her place. And now Liv couldn't help but regret the nearly three years that she'd lost. There was a huge difference between thirteen and sixteen—those carefree days where she might have been a best friend were past.

But they had this bookstore. It was an idea they both loved, something they could do together.

Finally, Taylor sighed and closed the screen of her laptop. "Why do you keep staring at me?"

Liv flushed; here she'd thought she was being discreet. "Just thinking how much you've changed since I met you. And how proud of you I am."

Taylor rolled her eyes, but her little smile hinted that she was secretly pleased. "Well, thanks. But can you, like, not do that? It's making me nervous."

"Sorry," Liv said, hiding her smile. "How's it going over there?"

"Good," Taylor said. "I put together a mood board so you could see what I'm thinking." She opened her laptop again and swiveled it so Liv could see all the photos she'd pinned onto a digital inspiration board: photos of spiral staircases and old libraries with a few industrial touches that gave it a slightly funky, steampunk vibe. Through it all, though, there was a unifying thread, a defining style. Taylor indeed had a good eye for design.

"What are you calling it?"

Taylor thought for a minute. "How about industrial academia?"

Liv grinned. "I love it."

"Do we have a budget yet? Do we even have any idea how much it's going to cost to renovate the place?"

"Not remotely. But when Charlie comes over tonight, I'll ask him to go take a look."

Fortunately, the mention of Charlie passed without comment this time, but whether it was because Taylor believed her when she said nothing was going on or because she was too busy working, she didn't know. Instead, Liv turned back to her computer and forced her mind onto the work in front of her. Daydreaming about what this meant for them as a family didn't really help her accomplish it.

By the time six thirty rolled around, they'd already finished two pots of coffee and all the cookies in the pantry, and still the rumbles of their stomachs punctuated the room. As if on cue, a knock came at the door.

"I'll get it!" Taylor popped up from her chair and hustled for the front door.

From the hallway, she heard the door scrape open, followed by cheery greetings from two familiar voices, one male, one female. Stephen and Gemma.

"Hey, Taylor. Is Liv home?" she heard Gemma say.

"In here," Liv called.

Gemma breezed into the room, wearing neither her lawyer clothes nor her baker clothes, but rather a sundress and a pair of strappy sandals. Her handsome boyfriend, Stephen—tall, sandy-haired, well-built—followed, holding a large paper bag.

Gemma went immediately to Liv's side to give her a quick hug. "We heard you had something to celebrate, so we brought dinner."

"Wow, that was fast. We barely just decided."

Stephen followed and set the bag down on the table before he leaned over to give Liv a quick hug as well. "You know how news travels in Haven Ridge. Will talked to Thomas, Thomas talked to his grandmother, and the rest is history. The whole town knows by now."

Liv rolled her eyes, but she couldn't help but chuckle. Granny Pearl was the grand dame of the town—descendant of the original founder, general well-meaning busybody, and self-proclaimed mystic. Now that she thought about it, it would be weird if Pearl *wasn't* already in the middle of everything.

Taylor had bypassed the niceties and was already opening the bag. "What did you bring?"

"Spaghetti and meatballs and garlic bread from Mario's," Gemma answered, already moving into the kitchen to find plates and utensils. She'd spent so much time at Liv's house since moving back to Haven Ridge that she was as familiar with it as Liv. When she came back, Liv and Taylor had moved their laptops to the living room to make room for the table settings, Taylor already unpacking the plastic containers onto the table.

"Bless you," the girl breathed when she took the lid off a container. "I have a severe garlic bread deficiency today."

Gemma grinned at her and took a seat directly across from Liv, Stephen claiming the seat next to his girlfriend. Taylor filled in the gap, and Gemma wasted no time dishing out food onto each plate. Liv just sat back, her heart swelling with sudden gratitude. Yes, she was being a sentimental sap today. But a little over a year ago, she would never have thought that the three most important people in her life would be sitting around her table, eating a casual spaghetti dinner on an ordinary weeknight. She, Gemma, and Stephen had been a tight trio in high school, but until last summer, they'd been scattered across the western US and she'd about given up hope on them ever living in the same place again. Another way Haven Ridge worked in mysterious ways, she supposed, though the fact that Gemma and Stephen had never gotten over their high school romance and were just secretly waiting to reconnect probably had something to do with it too.

"She's been like this all day," Taylor said with a wry grin, gesturing toward Liv, who was indeed still beaming.

"Don't mind her," Gemma said. "She's been doing this for months, ever since I moved back to town."

That snapped her out of it. "I have not!"

"You have too." Gemma grinned and reached over to pat Liv's hand. "It's okay. We've always known you were the mushy one out of the three of us."

"Really? I thought that was Stephen."

Gemma made a considering face, but Stephen just grinned at Liv. "How are the business plans coming?"

"Slowly. Even considering that we're getting the place for the cost of the taxes and insurance and Will gave me a jump start on the inventory, I'm not sure where I'm going to come up with the money for the renovations. A loan, I guess? But I haven't even started to look into what that would involve and what I'd have to put up as collateral."

Gemma propped her chin on her clasped hands, thinking. "Why don't you crowdfund it?"

"What?"

"Let the community determine whether or not they're going to make it a success. If people put in enough money for you to open it, you get your seed money and they get—I don't know. A book-of-the-month membership or something, plus their name on a founder's wall, or . . . we can come up with something creative. And if you don't raise enough, it tells you it wasn't going to be successful and everyone gets their money back. Win-win."

Liv stared at Gemma. "That's brilliant."

"I do have my moments, you know."

"You have more than your moments," Stephen said, nudging his girlfriend. "Cinnamon rolls on Sunday only? Genius."

Gemma laughed. "Scarcity/FOMO. Works every time. But seriously, Liv, this is a big thing for the town. Have them get involved."

"That's not a bad idea," Liv said slowly. "But I feel weird asking people to essentially support us. I do need to draw a salary to pay bills."

"Then make it a B-Corp," Taylor mumbled around a mouth full of garlic bread. "Or a nonprofit."

All three adult heads turned toward her.

Taylor held up a finger while she chewed and swallowed. "We learned all about them in business class last year. B-Corps make a positive impact on society while pursuing profits. And nonprofits—well, you know what they do."

"That's an idea," Liv said slowly. "I've already been mulling how to incorporate community outreach. We don't have a public library in town to fill that need and the ESL programs at the high school got shut down a couple of years ago."

Taylor perked up. "Maybe we could do something like Dolly Parton's Imagination

Library, where kids could get a free book once a year—maybe for summer reading—if we can get donations and sponsorships from local businesses. We wouldn't even have to do it all at once. We could make each level a different goal, then people would be motivated to donate to reach the next level."

Liv turned to find Gemma and Stephen both watching them with benevolent expressions of amusement. "What?"

"It's like watching you with your Mini-Me," Gemma said with a grin.

"You don't think this is a good idea?"

"Oh, I think it's a *great* idea," Gemma said. "And I think you two will make perfect business partners. Once word gets out, you'll probably be flooded with help. In fact, I'd be surprised if it wasn't already lined up."

Liv frowned. "What do you mean?"

Gemma and Stephen exchanged a long look. Stephen seemed to have drawn the silent short straw, because he said, "Granny Pearl has been talking about a bookstore ever since word got around you were going to have to quit your job."

"What?"

Taylor grinned at her across the table. "There you have it. Destiny."

Liv shoved down the sudden flutter in her stomach. "Not destiny. Just . . . a good, logical extrapolation. I mean, if anyone was going to open a bookstore in town, it would be me, right? Or Stephen, but he's too busy as it is."

"That's why Will put the place up for rent!" Taylor said. "Because the universe knew we were going to need it."

Liv just rolled her eyes and took a bite of garlic bread so she didn't have to answer. Yes, there were all sorts of legends about the town founder and how her descendants possessed some sort of preternatural intuition. A direct line to God, Pearl sometimes said in reference to her great-grandmother with a knowing sort of nod. But to say that Pearl had known this was all going to happen and helped nudge it along . . .

"It is coming together rather quickly," Gemma said. "You have the books, you have the contractor . . ."

"Both of which happened because Elliot Parker died, and we're not going to say that's destiny, are we? Speaking of which, Charlie's actually supposed to drop by at seven." Liv pulled out her phone and quickly checked her email. "Oh good, his background check is back."

"And?" Stephen prompted, tone serious.

Liv opened the document and scanned it quickly. "Clean. No flags."

Gemma twirled spaghetti on her fork. "That's good then. Right?"

"Absolutely. Especially since he found me a

deal on our countertops today. Finished, grown-up kitchen, here we come."

"Are you going to ask him about the shop too?" Stephen asked.

Liv had been thinking about that. "I think it depends on the scope of the work. He's technically a handyman right now because he doesn't have a contractor's license and I don't know if we'll need permits."

Stephen's demeanor shifted. "Why doesn't he have a license?"

"It's not really my story to tell, but I guess his business partner was shady and left him on the hook for some things he had nothing to do with."

Stephen lifted an eyebrow.

"Don't look at me like that. You know I'm a good judge of when someone's lying."

"I know you *think* you're a good judge of when someone is lying," Stephen said.

Outside, she heard the rumble of a diesel engine, moments before a notification popped up on her phone screen. She pressed the button to open the gate and pushed herself away from the table. "Well, judge for yourself, because I think he just pulled up now." Liv moved to the front door, surprised by the sudden surge of protectiveness she felt over Charlie. Stephen was just looking out for her. If she were in his position, she would be suspicious too. But nothing in any interaction she'd had with Charlie said he was lying to her.

She pulled open the front door just as he was stepping up onto the porch. He blinked at her in surprise. "Hi."

"Hey. Come on in."

She stood aside for him to enter, not letting her eyes linger on any part of him, though she registered that today he was wearing a nicer pair of jeans and an actual button-down shirt with his dusty, steel-toed work boots.

Charlie looked alarmed when he saw the gathering around the table. "I didn't mean to interrupt dinner. I can come back tomorrow."

"No, we were just finishing up," Liv said. "In fact, have a seat. There's plenty."

If it were possible, Charlie looked even more uncomfortable. "Thanks, but I just ate." His eyes flicked to Stephen, who had risen and was standing a little in front of Gemma.

Liv looked Stephen over from an outsider's perspective for the first time in ages, and she had to admit that between his height and his physique, he could be a little intimidating. But his smile was friendly when he stepped forward and offered his hand. "Hi, I'm Stephen Osborne."

"Pleasure. Charlie Castro."

Gemma scooted out from behind her boyfriend, touching Stephen's arm briefly as if in warning before she offered her hand as well. "Gemma Van Buren. Nice to finally meet you."

"Likewise."

Charlie's eyes flicked past her friends to Taylor, who had remained seated at the table.

"That's my stepdaughter, Taylor," Liv said quickly.

Charlie raised a hand in a casual wave. "Hey Taylor."

"Hey." Taylor's tone clearly said that the jury was still out on him.

Liv took a breath and shoved down the flutter in her stomach that warned of impending danger. She hurried to complete the introductions. "Gemma owns the bakery in town, as well as the lone law office, and Stephen teaches literature and coaches track at the high school. Charlie's going to be renting the apartment while he works on some projects around town."

"Oh? The check came back already?" Charlie asked.

The focused gaze from those beautiful eyes short-circuited her brain and she had to wait for it to reboot itself before she could answer. "Yeah. All clear. You can move in whenever you want."

"Wonderful. I was getting tired of that drive from Salida. Is tomorrow morning okay? I have to be over at the Larkspur House first thing, and I don't want to wake you up with the truck."

Liv waved her hand. "Don't worry about us. We can sleep through anything. Let me give you the codes and you can let yourself in." Liv bustled into the kitchen, where she rummaged in the junk drawer for a sticky note and jotted down both the gate code and the apartment's door lock combination, which she'd reset after Chelsea had moved out. She returned and held it out to him.

He took it slowly, his eyes still fixed on her face. "Thanks. I appreciate this, Liv." He glanced around at the others, his demeanor just as polite as ever. "Nice to meet all of you. I'm sure I'll see you around."

"I'll walk you out," Liv said quickly. "I have some questions for you before you go."

Charlie headed for the door, and Gemma grinned at her behind his back. Liv shot her a *don't you dare* look and then followed Charlie out the front door and into the rapidly cooling night.

"So, I'm not sure how to say this, but it looks like I might be opening a bookstore in downtown Haven Ridge."

Charlie swiveled to her, his breath catching on a laugh. "And this just . . . happened?"

Liv laughed, too, realizing how crazy it sounded. Two days ago, she didn't have the money for countertops and now she was opening a bookstore? "You'll find that's just kind of how things go around here. I don't even know if it's feasible yet. It's going to be a nonprofit, so we're going to try to crowdfund it, but I need to know what my budget should be . . ."

". . . and you need me to work up an estimate for you for the build-out."

Liv exhaled in relief. "Yes, exactly. Do you mind?"

"Not at all. I'm starting on the plaster at Larkspur tomorrow, and then I'll be here on Wednesday to hang your cabinets. I should be able to go take a look at the shop later this week. Would that work?"

"That would be great, thank you."

Charlie dipped his head, but his eyes sought hers again. "It's my pleasure."

The moment stretched into awkwardness until Liv looked away. Charlie cleared his throat. "I'll be going then. Sorry again for interrupting dinner."

"No apologies necessary. I'll see you tomorrow."

Another awkward, lingering look, and both of them swiveled on their heels at the same time, Charlie heading for his truck, Liv heading for her front door. She could really use a moment to herself, but on both sides of that door there were people scrutinizing her reaction. So she took a deep breath, turned the knob, and stepped inside.

Stephen and Gemma were back at the table, but Taylor's place was empty, her plate already cleared. "Where'd she go?"

"Phone call," Gemma said. "Boyfriend, I think. She certainly didn't want us to overhear the conversation."

"Ah, yes." Liv reseated herself. "I know we're

not supposed to like the boyfriend, but Dylan strikes me as a good kid. I can't be too upset."

"He is a good kid," Stephen said. "For a teenage boy."

Liv laughed, but Gemma was looking at her expectantly. "What?"

"So that's the guy?"

"Yeah . . . why?"

Gemma folded her arms and grinned. "No wonder you can barely keep your hands to yourself. He's hot."

Stephen flicked her a bemused look. "I'm right here."

Gemma smiled and pressed a quick kiss to her boyfriend's lips. "So? You're hot too. His hotness does not diminish yours."

Stephen chuckled in response. "Thank you. My ego remains intact."

Gemma waved him off. "You just didn't tell me that he's totally into you."

"Wait, what? You can tell from the whole thirty seconds he was standing here?"

"Oh yeah," Stephen said.

Liv blinked. "How?"

"For one thing, he was as polite as if he was meeting your parents for the first time."

"He was being professional!"

"You didn't see the relief on his face when he realized Gemma and I were together."

The idea that Charlie might have been jealous

of Stephen brought a sudden flush of pleasure she couldn't altogether quell. Just so she didn't have to look at her friends directly, she picked up her half-empty plate and took it into the kitchen.

But Gemma wasn't going to be put off. "So, what are you going to do?"

"About what?"

A lifted eyebrow was her friend's only response.

Liv sighed and paused in her work scraping the plate over the trash can. "I don't think there's anything to do. You saw Taylor's face. She did not look pleased."

"Well, she's probably afraid a man would take you away from her," Stephen said from the dining room. "I know it's not logical, but trust me, teenagers are rarely logical."

It was more logical than he thought. Losing Jason had taken her away from Taylor, and she couldn't blame her for not trusting Liv to handle another person in their life well. "Logical or not, it just wouldn't be fair to her. She's only with me for another two years. That's not too much to ask. Besides, it's not as if I have room in my life for romance anyway. If this bookstore really happens, it's going to be all-consuming."

Gemma and Stephen exchanged a look—either they thought *she* was being illogical or just in denial—but they didn't press. "None of our business," Gemma said finally. "But if you're trying to stick to that plan, maybe it's best not to

151

start a big multi-month construction project with the guy. You're not even touching and you can practically smell ozone from all the sparks."

Liv flushed at that very astute description of what it felt like to be around Charlie Castro. And she had to admit that Gemma gave sensible advice. It would make her life so much easier to not spend any time with a guy who made her feel like a fourteen-year-old with her first crush.

But given her limited options, she didn't see how that was going to work. They would just have to be grown-ups about the whole thing and keep their relationship strictly professional.

Surely they could manage that. Couldn't they?

Liv didn't sleep at all that night. Her mind whirled and snagged on all the tasks that she still had to do to make this off-the-wall dream a reality, all the things that she hadn't researched, the possible pitfalls involved in starting a brand-new venture. She'd always known she was a planner—after all, with the exception of being widowed at twenty-nine, her life had pretty much unfolded as she'd envisioned it. But now, facing down a big stack of unknowns, she realized how much she'd relied on those plans to feel safe and secure. To keep the fear at bay.

She couldn't deny that Charlie created a little part of that fear. No matter what you thought about the town and its tendency to bring people together when they were needed, she couldn't deny the fact that his appearance was well-timed. Almost as if it had been arranged, fated. She wasn't stupid enough to turn down that kind of fortune when it landed in her lap. And yet every time she thought she had talked herself out of her feelings towards him, all it took was a text from him on her cell phone or a video call or a visit to her doorstep to shatter those illusions.

Feelings for him. She rolled her eyes at her dramatic thoughts. Feelings implied that she actually knew the man, liked him. Well, okay, she did like him, at least what she knew of him. He was laid back and kind, and she suspected he would probably be fun to be around. But that wasn't what had her tied up in knots. It was that uncontrollable live-wire sensation she felt in his presence.

The fact it was nothing more than pure chemical attraction, a perfectly explainable alignment of pheromones, didn't make her feel better. In fact, it felt even more like a betrayal of Jason, considering her attraction toward her husband hadn't come on instantly like it had for Charlie. In fact, she'd been determined never to see him again.

They wouldn't have even met if it hadn't been for the Haven Ridge telegraph. She'd been working as a copyeditor at a publishing house in

Manhattan at the time. Jason had just transferred to New York with his software firm . . . and his mom just happened to be Liv's mom's Bunco partner in New Mexico where they spent most of the year. Somehow the two ladies had fancied themselves matchmakers and convinced them to meet up for coffee. Liv had only vaguely remembered him, having been five years behind him in school, but she'd thought it might be nice to see a familiar face, so she'd accepted an invitation for lunch in the East Village. Where she waited . . . and waited . . . and waited . . . for a date who never showed.

Liv, of course, had been furious and hurt. Then she'd gotten a call—not a text message—from Jason begging her forgiveness. He'd gotten stuck on a stopped subway train and been unable to call or text to let her know what had happened. She'd been tempted to blow him off, but just imagining her mom scolding her for not giving him another chance had her setting a coffee date down the street from her office the next day.

And when Jason had shown up, holding a bunch of flowers and a cheerily wrapped apology gift, she couldn't help softening toward him. He turned out to be funny and intelligent, if a little quirky and literal, but it wasn't until he kissed her on their third date that everything else had locked into place. It was like she'd needed to get to know him in order to be attracted to him.

Which was why that instant, knee-weakening pull toward Charlie felt like such a betrayal.

Liv rolled over in her bed and clamped her pillow over her head in frustration. She needed to stop thinking about it. About *him*. Clearly she wasn't ready to start dating yet, and Taylor most definitely wasn't ready for her to start dating yet. Jason had been gone for less than three years. And while they might have only been married for two years before that, she'd fully believed he was her one and only, the man she'd spend the rest of her life with. She hadn't expected that her wedding vows—*'til death do us part*—would come so quickly.

It was only two years until Taylor went off to college, started having her own life. Chances were good she wouldn't come home for longer than the summer. And when that final bond was broken, when she no longer considered Haven Ridge her home, then Liv would be free to do what she wanted. To follow her heart.

And in those two years, maybe her heart would catch up with her hormones.

Somewhere around four a.m., her swirling thoughts finally exhausted themselves and she drifted into a light and disturbed sleep, only to snap her eyes open at six thirty when the light glowing around the edges of her bedroom blinds got too bright to ignore. She dragged herself up, eyes gritty and head pounding, threw on a pair of jogging shorts and a tank top, and stumbled into the kitchen in search of coffee.

Come to think of it, her difficulty sleeping might have had less to do with all the worries on her mind than the two entire pots of coffee she and Taylor had consumed yesterday afternoon. She gave a helpless little sob as she waited for the dark brew to drip down into the pot. Maybe she'd forget the jog and go back to bed instead.

But no sooner than that thought crossed her mind—and the final drop of coffee landed in the pot—the now-familiar rumble of a diesel engine had her looking out the window. Sure enough, Charlie's work truck was creeping through the slowly-opening gate onto the property, its big tires crunching on gravel. He must have still been concerned about waking her up, because the minute he pulled onto the concrete pad in front of the garage, he cut the engine, leaving an echoing silence in its wake.

She poured herself a cup of coffee and watched at the window as he climbed out of the cab and then hauled a battered duffel bag out of the bed of the truck. It really was a little unfair that the guy was so attractive with his mussed, too-long hair and plaster-splattered jeans. She'd never really gone for the rugged, overtly masculine, *I work with my hands* type, but now, looking at Charlie Castro, she could definitely understand the appeal.

She should probably go out to greet him, but somehow, she knew this was a defining moment. She could follow her instincts, go say hello, establish a friendly rhythm that would persist for as long as he occupied the apartment, where they chatted in the yard and he borrowed sugar or she asked him to help fix a sink.

Or she could stay in the house, making it clear that their relationship was strictly client/ contractor, landlord/tenant.

She knew which one she wanted, just as she knew what the right answer was.

She moved away from the window and sat down at her desk with her laptop.

CHAPTER THIRTEEN

Helped along by most of the coffee in the pot but hampered by the knowledge of Charlie's presence a mere hundred feet away, Liv powered through the rest of the simplified business plan and had already moved on to researching the IRS nonprofit application by the time Taylor woke up. From what she could tell, they didn't need it to get started, but it would be easier to solicit donations and support for their crowdfunding campaign once their nonprofit status was approved.

"What do you think about making part of the back space a library?" Liv asked, not looking up from her laptop when the girl stumbled into the living area.

Taylor shot her a disbelieving look, then turned to the coffee pot without answering. When she returned with a full mug in her hands, looking only marginally more awake, she plopped herself down in the chair across from Liv. "Like a legitimate library? Check things out, bring things back?"

"Yeah." Liv leaned back in her chair. "I mean, it's not like we could have everything a regular library does . . . but if we're really going to make this part of the community, we should have

spaces where people can come and hang out without being expected to spend money."

Taylor thought for a moment. "I like it."

"Really?" From the unimpressed look, Liv had been expecting the teen to shoot it down. Or maybe that was just Taylor's general unhappiness about being awake before noon.

"Yeah. Maybe we can make that top part the fiction loft. Kids can come in and read without having to check things out, or they can check them out and take them home. The school library is pretty good, but the librarians don't like you to linger."

Liv remembered. It wasn't that the librarians were unfriendly . . . It was just that the space was small and there were very few places to sit without having people stepping over them to get to the books. "Yeah. It was like that when I was in school too."

"To start, we can stock it with the books that are too messed up to sell," Taylor said thoughtfully. "I mean, it would be nice to have new books, but this is better than throwing them away, right?" Her eyes lit up, a sure sign the caffeine had taken effect. "We can have a whole rack of books by the checkout for people to buy in order to donate to the library. Maybe let kids make wish lists for what they want to see on the shelves."

Liv blinked. "That's brilliant."

"I know, isn't it?" Taylor grinned, pleased with

the idea. "That makes money for the bookstore and funds the library."

"You do realize that this is probably all insane, right?"

Taylor shrugged. "Just because no one has ever done it quite like this before doesn't mean we can't. I mean, who's gonna stop us?"

The words sparked an idea in Liv's brain, and she grabbed for her notebook, scribbling down a few lines of garbled notes before she could forget them. Then she opened up her business plan again and started another section for their lending library. This project was growing in scope by the minute, but they had a ton of space to fill and the more value they could offer to their community, the better. Especially if they were expecting the town to rally around them.

For the first time since they started this idea, something clicked into place inside Liv. Yes, she'd been excited about the idea. Yes, she loved that this was something that she and Taylor could work on together—though she had to admit it was more ambitious than the typical mother-daughter craft project. And yes, it played to both their strengths—Liv's love of books and Taylor's love of design, their love for Haven Ridge, which had caused them to stay even though it might have been more practical to go.

But until now, it really hadn't connected in her heart.

So much of her life had been built around books, even her friendship with Stephen and Gemma, who were both book-lovers in different ways. The idea that she could have a bookstore that catered to both buyers and borrowers, the people who could support it and the people who needed support, engaging both her professional experience and her latent crunchy tendencies . . . somehow it felt like this had just been waiting for her, all this time.

And in that moment, Granny Pearl's prognostication didn't feel all that far-fetched at all.

"Uh oh. You've got that look."

"What look?"

"The same look you got when you decided we were going to grow our own vegetables and make hemp milk."

"Hey, you loved the hemp milk!"

Taylor made a face. "It was okay. But all the vegetables died."

"Yeah, I'm not a gardener. But you know what I am good at? Books."

Taylor looked at her for a minute, then her own smile grew. "Yes. You are."

"I need to go into town this morning. You want to go with me?"

Taylor drained the rest of her coffee cup. "Nah. Some people are coming over here today to help me with design ideas. I'm still waiting for that laser measure, but at least we can do some concept sketches and things. You should see Dylan's drawings. He's amazing. He does all these cityscapes and things."

"Wow. An artist and a drummer?" Now that Taylor was talking about her friends, Liv wasn't going to waste this chance to learn more. "Is he going to study music or art in college?"

"Nah, I think he's going dual sociology and language. He wants to work for the CIA."

"Okay then." Liv never would have thought shaggy-haired Dylan was so interested in geopolitics. Then again, Taylor had pointed out that Liv hadn't really made the effort to get to know her friends. "Well, how about I fire up the barbecue and cook hamburgers for lunch when I come back?"

Taylor looked a little surprised, but she quickly hid the expression. "Yeah. That would be cool. Thanks."

"Not a problem." Liv saved her file, hit print—sending the printer over on her desk whirring before it spit out the pages of her forms—and then shut the screen on her laptop. "I'm glad we're doing this, Taylor."

Again that flicker of surprise, which softened into a smile. "Yeah, me too."

Liv drove to town on auto-pilot, her mind turning over the beginnings of her plan. She had the framework of the business figured out, at least as much as the IRS required, and the printed copy of her business plan lay inside a manila envelope on the passenger seat beside her to show Gemma. Taylor was hard at work on design ideas, though how feasible they turned out to be still remained to be seen. Now all she needed was to start rallying support from the town.

And she knew exactly where to start.

Liv cruised down Dogwood Street and pulled into an empty spot in front of the Brick House Cafe. Even odds as to which one of the Rivases was working today; but it didn't much matter, because both of them would serve different parts of her plan.

The bell welcomed her when she walked in, and she scanned the place automatically. She knew everyone scattered through the cafe today, but fortunately not well enough to do more than give a wave in greeting. She exhaled and made her way toward the register.

Almost immediately, Thomas appeared behind the swinging door to the kitchen. Perfect.

"Liv!" Thomas flashed her a genuine smile. "Can I get you a table?"

"Can I grab a stool and a cup of coffee?"

He put back the menu he'd pulled from behind the counter and gestured toward the long line of unoccupied diner stools. "Make yourself at home."

Liv picked one halfway down and hopped

onto it, the vinyl seat sticking to the back of her thighs. Thomas returned quickly with her mug of coffee and set it down in front of her. Before he could move away, she said, "Actually, I came to talk to you."

Thomas paused, a smile surfacing again. "This wouldn't have anything to do with a certain bookstore, would it?"

She shouldn't have been surprised. Will had told Thomas first, after all. "Who all knows about this?"

"Conservative estimate? Everyone in town. You can't blame us, though. This is the most exciting year we've had in decades. First Mallory's article, then Gemma's bakery and law office—and now your bookstore. You can feel it in the air."

"Feel what in the air, exactly?"

Thomas smiled at her. "Change. Optimism. Hope that Haven Ridge might be coming back to life."

"How much did Will tell you about our plans?"

"Surprisingly, not much. Just that he was practically donating the building in the hopes it will improve the whole block."

"That's true. But what Will doesn't know is that we're making it a nonprofit. We want to offer community literacy programs and a lending library. And we're crowdfunding it."

"I love it," he said immediately. "How can I help?"

"Funny you should ask. Can I get on the agenda for the town council meeting on Friday?"

"Of course you can. I think right now, the only things on the agenda are an appeal to fix the pothole on Zoo Street and what is most likely going to turn into a rant by Mrs. Marshall on the unfairness of disallowing backyard chickens within town limits."

Liv's brow furrowed. "I thought chickens were allowed within town limits."

"They are." Thomas gave her a *what are you going to do?* shrug. "She saw something on Facebook about it and feels the need to air her grievances."

Liv chuckled. This was why Thomas was the perfect mayor for this town. He'd grown up here, so he'd known the quirkiest inhabitants his whole life; he knew it was just easier to indulge them for five minutes than have them chase him for the entirety of his term.

"Can I go on before the chicken rant?"

"I will put you up first, while everyone is still there and awake."

"Thank you." Liv smiled. "How are things going, by the way?"

Thomas seemed to know what she was referring to without her needing to spell it out. "They're going. The overflow from Salida's summer events has helped us quite a bit. Having Gemma supplying us with baked goods has *definitely* helped the bottom line. But you know, restaurants are expensive."

"So are bookstores," Liv said wryly.

Thomas winked at her. "We're all in this together. We'll make it."

"Speaking of which, I'm not quite ready for it yet, but once our crowdfunding campaign is underway, would you be willing to act as a collection point? Some of our older and less tech-savvy citizens might just prefer to drop money in a jar."

"Sure. Actually, once you get approval for your nonprofit, I think I can probably collect money as part of the actual bill. Let me look into it."

"You would do that?"

"Of course. I meant what I said. We're all in this together. If Haven Ridge is going to come back to its former glory, we all have to pull together. What kind of mayor would I be if I weren't the first to help?"

"Honestly, you'd still be a better mayor than the last one." Liv's voice turned sour. No one had ever really liked Doug Meinke as mayor, but he'd run unopposed, so they'd gotten stuck with him. Fortunately, when Chelsea had left his abusive household, his true nature had come to light and he'd been summarily recalled. For a while, there had been a concerted effort to get Stephen into office, but he'd ultimately thrown his support behind his friend. Which made sense. Thomas

166

was a direct descendant of the original founder of the town, and he'd grown up on stories of Elizabeth Strong's vision for Haven Ridge. He was the most logical choice, even though she wondered how he managed to run a restaurant and a town at the same time.

Thomas moved away to retrieve an order from the pass-through and take it to one of the waiting tables, leaving Liv to sip her coffee in silence, thinking. Things were happening so fast, it was almost hard to wrap her head around them. Maybe it was good that she didn't know what she didn't know. If she had a full picture of what she was getting herself into with this venture, she probably wouldn't do it.

She drained the rest of her coffee and slid a five-dollar bill beneath the cup, then swiped her envelope off the counter as she hopped off the seat. Outside, she bypassed her vehicle and opted to walk the two-and-a-half blocks to Gemma's building, where she found her best friend elbow deep in bread dough with Chelsea. She just gave them both a cheery wave and dropped her business plan on the back counter. It was time to get home to Taylor and her friends for their promised barbecue anyway.

She already had pre-shaped hamburgers in the freezer for just this kind of emergency, but by the time she got through a quick run at the superstore for fixings, chips, and sodas, it was already well past noon. Liv lugged her reusable grocery bags through the front door, expecting to find a bunch of teens sprawled on the sofa, playing video games while music blasted. The throb of some sort of experimental metal proved that last part right, at least. But instead of being scattered around the room, Taylor and her friends were clustered at the dining room table, their heads bent over laptops and notebooks.

"What's going on?" Liv asked cautiously, plunking the bags down on the kitchen island.

"We're working on stuff for the store." Taylor looked up from her computer screen, but her fingers continued typing, an unsettling effect. Liv moved over to the table.

Jada—whom Liv knew from the vast amount of time the girl had spent at her house—had her head bent together with Rebekah's, whispering and clicking through a web page. They offered cheery hellos before going back to the computer. Next to Taylor sat Dylan, sporting a skater-style undercut haircut and dressed in a black band T-shirt and skinny black jeans. He looked up and gave her a confident smile. "Hi, Mrs. Quinn. Thanks for having us over."

"It's no problem, Dylan. You're welcome any time. What are you guys working on?"

This time Taylor did stop typing. "I'm working on a book list. I texted a form to pretty much the entire high school asking them what books they wanted us to carry. Dylan is working on some design ideas for the loft—"

"Just a rough sketch," he put in with a smile, throwing a doting look at his girlfriend. They really were cute together.

"And Jada and I are working on putting together a Read-A-Thon for the elementary school to raise money," Rebekah said. "You know, where they get pledges for reading a certain number of books?"

Liv's eyebrows lifted. "That's a really good idea. Where did you come up with that?"

"Aunt Chelsea is friends with the school principal, and I was there when Mrs. Martin came over last night. She said she'd approve it if we did all the work on planning and organizing it. And since we need our service hours for school anyway . . ."

"Wow," Liv said, impressed. "Maybe the shop could give away a gift certificate to the winner for every grade level." It was money going out, of course, but she'd been involved in too many of these " 'thons" to not know how much money they raked in when people were sufficiently motivated to win. Especially at the elementary school level, when kids still loved to read and participate in school events.

"I'll put that in here. They'll love it." Rebekah bent her head over her laptop and started typing again, and Liv couldn't help but smile.

This was part of the reason she'd never been motivated to grill Taylor's friends. They were good kids, kids who would give up a summer day helping their friend and their town—and yes, getting service hours out of the way before school started was also a motivating factor.

"So, I'm going to put the burgers on. Anyone have any allergies I need to be concerned with?"

Dylan glanced up. "I'm gluten-free, but I just won't eat the bun."

"Okay then, great." Since Liv was completely extraneous to this project, she started preparing the burgers and turned on the grill on the back patio. While the burgers were cooking, she sliced tomatoes and onions, washed lettuce, set out all the condiments on the island. Thank goodness she was going to have new countertops soon. Every time she had to set something on the sheets of particle board, she dreaded spilling anything that might stain it.

Which brought her back to thinking about Charlie, which brought her back to thinking about anything *but* Charlie.

She was flipping burgers on the grill when her phone rang from her back pocket. She closed the barbecue's lid and pulled it out. Gemma. "Hey! What's up?"

"I just looked at the business plan you dropped off for me. It looks good. Kind of light on the details though."

"Yeah. If you hadn't guessed, I don't exactly know what I'm doing here."

Gemma laughed. "You'll figure it out. Just make sure you understand nonprofit accounting and you'll be good."

"Wait, there's a different method?" To be fair, Liv had only had a little bit of experience with accounting in general.

This time, Gemma sounded a little worried. "Yeah, it's called fund accounting. You might want to buy a book on it."

"Fund accounting," Liv repeated, while the anxiety rose up inside her. How had she ever thought she was going to be able to do this? She wasn't a businessperson by nature, not like Gemma was. She was an editor. She knew books, she loved books, but she'd never actually tried to *sell* books.

"Okay, now you're freaking out. I can tell you're freaking out. It's going to be fine, okay? And also, maybe you can get an accountant to donate their time to get you up and running. We've got to have a few of them here, don't we?"

"Well, there's Will, but he's leaving today or tomorrow, so I couldn't really ask him."

"You do realize he doesn't have to physically be in town to help you, right?"

"Oh. Right." Liv pressed a hand against her warm forehead. This whole thing was turning her into a basket case. There was nothing like putting a capable person into an unfamiliar situation to make her realize how much she really did not know.

A sudden sizzle drew her attention back to the grill, and she lifted the lid to find the burger in the corner getting scorched by a gigantic plume of flame. "Uh, gotta go, Gemma. Burger emergency."

"I'll be over later to help you figure it all out, okay? Also, Stephen had some ideas he wanted to run by you."

"Sounds great, thanks." Liv clicked off the phone, grabbed the spatula, and rescued the burning burger before it could turn into a charcoal hockey puck. She quickly moved them all onto a plate, twisted off the burners, and balanced her armload of burgers and supplies as she slipped in through the back door. Hopefully the kids liked their beef flame-broiled.

She needn't have worried, though. They descended on the food like a swarm of locusts, and by the time they were done making their plates, there was one lone patty left—clearly surrendered to her—and a sad scattering of fixings. She laughed and fixed herself a burger, grabbed a handful of potato chips from the decimated bag, and brought her plate back out to the patio to give the kids their space.

Outside, she took a bite of the crispy burger— they'd left the burned patty for her—and pulled out her phone again. To Will, she tapped out: Are you still in town?

Almost immediately, the reply came back: For a few more hours. Flight at 7. At the castle now.

Perfect. She could catch him in person before she left. Can I come over? I have something to ask you.

Does it have something to do with your bookstore?

Yes, she truly was underestimating this town. She typed back: Maybe. Depending on how generous with your time you're feeling?

Do you even need to ask?

Can you give me a crash course on good accounting practices or whatever it's called when you get back to Chicago?

GAAP. Yes, I can give you a crash course. And he ended it with a smiley face.

Well, that was easy. She was about to type her thanks when another message came through.

Are you still coming over? Charlie's here.

She didn't know if that was supposed to be a warning or an inducement, but either way, a personal appearance seemed unnecessary. Only if you need me to throw myself on your mercy in person.

Ha. No need. I'll call you later this week when I get back into the office.

Done. Liv sat back in her chair, the worry in her chest easing a little. Every time she ran up against a road block, someone appeared with the expertise she needed. Gemma, Charlie, Will. That had to be a sign, wasn't it? This plan of theirs was meant to be.

At least she hoped so. Because somewhere along the line, this project had taken on a life of its own. And if she failed at this, she wasn't just failing herself or her stepdaughter but the entire town.

CHAPTER FOURTEEN

Thanks to a late-night planning session with Gemma and Stephen, Liv managed to do a respectable job of ignoring Charlie's existence, but the minute her eyes snapped open the next morning, nervousness and anticipation flooded in.

It was simply because today was the day her upper cabinets were getting hung, she told herself, but even she didn't believe that. If she did, she wouldn't be in the shower at six thirty, shaving her legs and washing her hair.

By the time the knock came at the front door precisely at seven a.m., she was dressed in shorts and a T-shirt, her wet hair tied up in a knot on her head, and the barest coat of tinted sunblock, lip balm, and mascara standing in for actual alertness. She walked across the creaky wood floor in her bare feet and opened the door, still holding her coffee mug.

"Good morning," she said brightly, standing aside for him to enter.

His smile made her heart do a little leap. He was dressed for work in his usual T-shirt and jeans, his tool belt around his hips—why on earth did she find that, of all things, sexy?—and a host of other tools in a large white bucket dangling from one hand. "Good morning. Are we ready? Is everything cleared out of the kitchen or do you need more time?"

"Oh, yeah." Liv flushed. She hadn't thought about the fact she needed to clear off the countertops. "Let me go do that now."

While Liv removed all the things from her kitchen surfaces, Charlie brought in several two by fours and another bucket full of what looked like boxes of bolts and screws.

"You want some coffee?"

"Ah, no thanks. I already had mine." He smiled and looked her over in what she thought was appreciation, until his gaze snagged on her bare feet. "You'll probably want to wear shoes until I'm done here. Don't want you stepping on a nail or a screw."

"Oh." She glanced down at her pink pedicure, suddenly embarrassed by her assumption. "Probably a good idea. I'll get out of your way then. The cabinets are in the spare room, so let me know if you need help with anything."

"Thanks, I will."

Liv turned and retreated down the hall to her bedroom, getting halfway there before she realized she'd left her laptop and she had to go back for it. "Forgot my laptop," she said awkwardly, holding it up as evidence.

He just kept smiling and she beat it back to her bedroom.

She wasn't usually this much of an idiot. It wasn't like she wasn't used to having people work here. But all she could focus on was how much *space* Charlie took up with his presence. How incongruent it was to be thinking sexy things about a different man in the house that she and her late husband had worked on together. How the fact that any time she was alone with him, it felt like the oxygen had been sucked out of the room.

But they weren't alone, she reminded herself. Taylor was still asleep down the hall. So that was fine. Everything was perfectly fine.

But an hour later, she had to admit that everything was not perfectly fine.

Her curiosity got the better of her and she popped back into the kitchen—her feet thrust into trainers this time—to see the progress. Charlie had screwed in ledger boards horizontally around the kitchen for support, and he'd already hung the corner cabinets. Seeing something where there had been nothing for such a long time took her aback. As did the flex of muscle in Charlie's arms and shoulders as he held another cabinet in place and screwed it into the studs on the wall.

"Wow." She wasn't sure which sight exactly she was referring to.

Charlie threw her a grin over his shoulder as he reached into his tool belt for another screw. "It makes a difference, doesn't it? Even without the backsplash, it's starting to feel finished."

Liv watched him for a minute as he finished fastening the cabinet to the wall and then climbed down the stepladder. "You love this, don't you?"

"Yeah, I do. I did other things related to construction over the years, but I always came back to home building. I love seeing the finished product come together."

"It was beginning to feel like it would never be done," she admitted.

"And yet by the end of next week, you'll have a fully functional kitchen."

"You're a lifesaver."

Charlie glanced up at her, something shifting in his expression, but he didn't comment. He just hefted another one of the cabinets and carried it across the room to rest it on the ledger. And God help her, she enjoyed every second of the view.

Apparently, she hadn't quite escaped that primal programming that found capable men with muscles appealing.

"You want to help?" he mumbled around the screw between his lips. "You don't have to . . ."

It felt like a challenge. "Sure. What do you want me to do?"

"Just come here and hold this steady. It will go faster."

Liv went to his side, scooted beneath his arms to keep the cabinet from tipping forward, then realized her mistake. Not because it took any strength or much effort at all. But because this close to Charlie, she could feel the heat off his body, smell the scent of his laundry detergent and soap and something that was uniquely him. A shiver rippled down her spine.

Charlie didn't seem to notice as he drove four screws into the back of the large cabinet. He set down the screwdriver and climbed off the stepladder, then paused for a second. "It's not going anywhere now."

"Oh, right." Liv let go and turned, found herself standing face-to-face with him. He froze, his muscles seizing in place, but his gaze held her eyes. Then it drifted down to land on her mouth.

Involuntarily, she licked her lips and saw his Adam's apple bob as he swallowed. He cleared his throat. "Three down, six more to go."

Liv blinked and stepped back, yanking herself out of that heated moment. Right. She was supposed to be helping. Thinking about kissing him was definitely not helping anything.

She kept her eyes to herself while they hung the rest of the cabinets and tried to keep as much distance as she could—a losing battle considering he had to reach over her. But before she knew it, all the boxes were up and it looked like . . .

"A real kitchen," she said.

"Almost." He grinned at the stack of doors that were leaning up against the wall in the hallway. "How are you with a screwdriver?"

"I can handle a screwdriver," she said. "Why?"

"You want to put on the hinges and I'll install the doors?"

Something that let her help without having to be six inches from his body? "Done."

Despite her wandering attention, she had to admit they made a good team. Liv set each door in turn on the towel-cushioned island and affixed the door hinges before handing it off to Charlie, who screwed in the other half of the hinges and adjusted them so the doors lined up evenly with the faces. It wasn't even lunch by the time they stepped back and looked at their work.

"It looks great," Liv said. "Thank you."

"Oh, I can't take credit. It was your design and layout. Sure you shouldn't go into kitchen design for a living instead?"

Liv laughed. "Hardly. It took me ages to figure out what I wanted. And honestly, I might have procrastinated on this part because I was afraid to see what it was going to look like."

"You want to figure out the tile layout? I won't do the tiling until the countertops go in, but at least we can start thinking about what you want."

Which was how Taylor found them half an hour later, poring over subway tile laid out in several different patterns. "What's going on?" she asked suspiciously.

Inexplicably, Liv flushed again. Not because she had anything to be embarrassed about—they were a full foot apart—but because Taylor's tone made her immediately revisit thoughts she didn't want Charlie to guess. "We're figuring out the backsplash layout. What do you think?"

Taylor moved toward them before she noticed the full spread of upper cabinets. "Whoa."

"I know, right? Looks different."

"It almost looks finished," she said in amazement. She turned her attention to the tile, taking a station opposite them at the island. "I like these two the best." She pointed to the two most modern ones, a vertical running bond and a horizontal stacked configuration.

"Vertical running bond it is," Liv said, throwing Charlie a look. "It's the only one all three of us agree on."

Charlie picked up the tiles and moved them over to the countertop, pressing them against the wall, his fingers spread to hold them in place. "That's what it's going to look like."

"Perfect," Taylor and Liv said in unison.

"In that case, I need to get going. I'm looking at Mrs. Marshall's sprinkler system today. I'll be back to do the tile after the countertops are installed."

"Thanks, Charlie. We really appreciate it."

"No trouble." He smiled at the two of them, then started to pack his tools into the buckets. "Let me know if you need anything else in here."

"Will do, thanks again."

He smiled at both of them, but his gaze

definitely lingered on Liv. As soon as he carried out the buckets and the two by fours, Taylor turned to her with raised eyebrows.

"What?" Liv asked innocently.

Taylor opened her mouth, then shut it firmly with a shake of her head. "Never mind. I don't want to know." She went to the coffee pot, which was now plugged in on Liv's desk, and poured herself a cup. "Can I get the keys to the bookstore? Dylan's going to meet me there to help do the measurements. We need accurate dimensions for the drawings."

"Sure," Liv said, relieved that Taylor wasn't going to press the issue. "Just stay on the ground floor for now. We need to have the loft inspected before you go up there."

Taylor made a face, but she nodded and pocketed the keys before once more leaving Liv alone with her thoughts. She should be fleshing out the business plan—Gemma was right about it being a little skimpy—but instead, she was thinking back on the morning, how Charlie's chest had pressed up against her shoulder as he reached past her, that heated moment when she could have sworn both their minds had shifted to something decidedly unprofessional.

And yet they'd both pulled away because they were adults who realized how bad of an idea this would be. Just because Charlie had arrived in town when she needed him, reeling from his own tragic backstory, didn't mean there should be more to this tale. Yes, he was attractive and patient, willing to do whatever she needed, and he made her feel pretty by the way he looked at her. It was a classic Prince Charming scenario.

If Prince Charming was a bit rough around the edges with calloused hands and defined muscles that brought to mind the attractive handyman trope from her (secretly) favorite smutty romance novels.

Liv groaned and buried her head in her hands. She needed to get her stupid, overactive imagination under control. Because that was all this was—fantasy. Probably the instant she acted on these feelings, the illusion would be gone. Charlie would be just another guy, and she'd realize she'd just wanted someone in her life after feeling so alone for the past three years.

Whether or not that was all true, it was a reasonable enough explanation that Liv was able to sit down at her desk and focus on the business plan for the bookstore. It involved a lot more internet searching than actual writing—she knew even less about community outreach and nonprofits than she did about bookselling—but by the time Taylor came back with her notebook full of dimensions, the paltry one-page plan had expanded to six times the size, brimming with ideas to make them not just a successful business, but a valuable, contributing part of the community.

"Wow," Taylor said, reading over her shoulder. "You think we can actually do all this?"

Liv's stomach jumped in response, but she gave an emphatic nod. "Stretch goals, remember?"

"Yeah, but we're going to have to do better than 'Haven Ridge Bookstore,'" Taylor pointed out, referring to the document title. "What about Cover Stories?"

Liv laughed. It was creative. "Sounds like we'd only sell mysteries and thrillers. What about Between the Lines?"

Taylor wrinkled her nose. "The Paper Trail?"

"Okay, now you've got me worried since everything you think up somehow has a crime angle."

Taylor grinned. Liv was about to float Words on the Street as an idea when an email popped up from Will. The subject line read, *Lease Agreement for Beacon Street Bookshop*.

They looked at each other for a long moment.

"It's a little on the nose," Liv said slowly.

Taylor cocked her head, considering. "But it has a nice ring to it. Especially since we want the place to be a beacon of knowledge and community for the town."

"The Beacon Street Bookshop." Liv tried it out, liked the way it sounded on her tongue. "I could be persuaded."

"Yeah," Taylor said. "It fits. Just hope that we never have to move locations or that's going to be a big hassle."

Liv chuckled. She guessed that just meant they needed to work extra hard to be successful so there was no reason to leave.

"Now we just need to figure out a business name," Liv said.

"Oat Endeavors," Taylor said.

"Oat?"

"O.A.T. Olivia and Taylor."

Liv laughed. "That's what you want it to be called?"

"Sure. Why not?"

It was goofy. But no one was ever going to see this name anyway, and the fact that Taylor wanted their names melded in a company name set off warm fuzzies inside her. "Okay. OAT Endeavors, DBA the Beacon Street Bookshop it is."

And somehow, saying that made it all seem real for the first time.

Taylor disappeared, leaving Liv space and quiet to finish the pile of paperwork that was still required to make this a reality. She filed her charitable organization with the state of Colorado, as well as the bookstore DBA. She filled in all the company information—the only thing left on her IRS application—and emailed a copy to Gemma to look over. At last, she opened the lease agreement that Will had sent her.

And froze in shock. Not only had Will written the lease to be automatically renewed at the end of the term should she not give notice otherwise, he'd also written in a clause requiring a five-year notice for termination by the lessor.

No, surely that must be a mistake. He probably meant five months. But she couldn't sign this until she knew for sure. She reached for her phone, and instead of sending her usual text message, dialed his number.

Will picked up immediately. "Liv! Hello." His deep voice was laced with warmth. "Did you get the lease?"

"That's why I'm calling, actually. There's a clause that says the owner needs to give me five years' notice?"

"That's right."

She paused, taken aback. "I don't understand."

"It's a fail-safe for you. In the event that I sell the buildings, even if the new owner wanted to evict you, he couldn't do it for five years. I figure that gives you enough time to build up a clientele and establish the business."

"But Will, won't that make it harder to sell? The new owner will want to review the lease and I doubt anyone wants to be obligated to a tenant for five years."

"And what about my obligation to you? I promised you I'd help however I could. So let me help."

I promised you I'd help however I could. Liv, not Jason. Her heart began to pound as she thought over their interactions the last time he was in Haven Ridge. How Will had offered her this job with the books and left compensation up to her, then sold them for a song. The casual way he always managed to touch her. His words and the sparkle in his eye when he'd cut her the lease deal in the bakery: *I seem to be making a lot of ill-advised decisions today because of you. It's not a good look for an accountant.*

"Will . . ." she began.

He must have heard the dawning realization in her voice, because his turned low, rough, pained. "Liv, please don't. I know. I understand."

She took a deep breath and let it out slowly so he wouldn't know how much the realization shook her. Will Parker had feelings for her? How long had this been going on?

And more importantly, did this change anything?

Almost immediately, she had her answer: no, it didn't. She'd come to love him since Jason's death, but like a brother, a treasured friend. Maybe there had been a moment when she could have looked at him another way, but she'd been too mired in grief to recognize it, and now that moment had passed.

That chance had vanished the instant she met Charlie and realized she was still capable of feeling passion and attraction and curiosity, none of which she felt toward Will, however kind and handsome he might be.

"I can't let you do this," she said quietly. "Not knowing . . ."

"Please." Will's voice sounded almost desperate. "Let me help you this one last time."

The words caught her off-guard, shock rippling through her. "Can't we just . . ."

"Pretend?" He gave a little laugh, but it sounded sad. "Not anymore, I don't think. I know I missed my chance, Liv. You weren't ready back then . . . and now that you are, I'm not there. But I can't lie and say that I didn't hope that maybe someday . . ." Will paused to clear his throat. "I'll always be here if you need me, I owe that much to Jason."

Tears pricked her eyes. "Will—"

"Sign the lease, Liv. And have a happy life."

The line went silent before she realized what was happening and she lowered the phone slowly, surprised by her sudden sense of loss. She might not have loved Will the way he wanted her to, but he'd been an important part of her life for almost three years. A safety net. A pillar of strength and assurance. In fact, she *should* have feelings for him, and the fact she didn't just seemed unfair.

But not as unfair as knowingly stringing him along.

"Liv?" Taylor paused in front of the open fridge. "Are you okay?"

Liv swiped away the tears caught in her lower

lashes. "I'm fine. I think we're going to have to hire an accountant, though."

"Okaaay," Taylor said, staring at her as if she'd begun speaking a foreign language. She grabbed a bottle of water and then disappeared back into her room, leaving Liv alone with the lease agreement staring at her from her computer screen, just waiting for her signature.

She took a deep breath and typed her name into the box, followed by *OAT Endeavors, DBA The Beacon Street Bookshop*.

A fresh start.

CHAPTER FIFTEEN

The awkward conversation with Will and the nerve-wracking experience of committing herself to a lease without any means of paying for it seemed to be the motivation that Liv needed to make this long-held dream a reality. She approached the Friday town hall meeting like a determined general going into battle—it might be ugly, but one way or another, she was going to prevail.

Which was silly, she realized, considering this was her town. Her people. Thanks to Granny Pearl—and most likely Thomas and Mallory—working behind the scenes, she was sure to find support for the venture. After all, she couldn't be the only one who thought a bookshop was integral to a thriving town. A place that valued knowledge also valued progress, and progress was definitely what Haven Ridge needed at the moment.

She worked out her nerves by running her favorite full loop through the foothills, and by the time she reached her car once more, Liv was feeling much more optimistic about her chances of success tonight. She hopped in and rolled down the windows, embracing the breeze and the dusty smell of high desert foliage, and turned back toward home. She had enough time this morning to bake a batch of muffins for brunch and make Gemma's suggested changes to the nonprofit application before she had to start getting ready for the town council meeting.

But all that hard-won peace came to a screeching halt when she pulled into her driveway and saw that, unlike the last couple of days, Charlie's muddy truck was still on the parking pad. Even worse, Charlie himself was bending into the cab of the truck.

No way to avoid him now. Liv pulled up beside him and hopped out of her vehicle. "Good morning," she called, venturing a wave in his direction.

Charlie slammed the door and turned toward her, a bright smile on his face. "Good morning. I have good news."

"Oh? I'll always take good news."

He chuckled, and she had to resist the happy vibration that it put into her chest. "I just heard from Brock at the stone yard. Your countertops are being fabricated today and they're going to drive them up here on Tuesday. If all goes well, you'll have a finished kitchen by the end of next week."

Liv forgot all about the fact she was avoiding him. "Really?"

"Really. It will take them a good chunk of the day to install them, but it won't take me more than two to do the backsplash. We should be completely done by next Friday."

She exhaled in relief. "You have no idea how happy that makes me."

"I think I do." Charlie was still smiling. "What are you up to today?"

"Not much. Just got back from a run. I'm presenting about the bookshop to the town council this evening."

"Oh? Do they have to approve it?"

"No, but there are a lot of old-timers who attend these meetings, and Thomas has agreed to give me the floor. I'm counting on the support of some of the town's retirees to volunteer for our various ventures. Getting their buy-in will go a long way to making this work."

"That's great," Charlie said, and there was genuine admiration in his voice. "Can anyone come?"

"I suppose. Why?"

"Well, if it's okay with you, I thought maybe I'd tag along. For moral support."

Now her stomach did a back flip. "You don't need to do that."

"I know I don't. But I'm finished out at Larkspur—you need to inspect my work for Will, by the way—so my afternoon is free. Of course, if you don't want me there . . ."

Seeing him staring at her from the audience was only going to make the butterflies in her stomach multiply, but what could she say? If she flat out refused, she'd hurt his feelings *and* look like a jerk. And if she told him that she didn't want him there because he made her nervous, well, that revealed far too much.

"No, that's fine. Taylor and I are going to go over a little early, but if you want to meet us there . . ."

"Love to." Charlie smiled, holding her gaze for a long moment, then gestured to his truck. "I was going to ask you, is it okay if I use your hose to wash my truck? I can't stand when it gets this dirty."

"Sure. There's soap and rags on one of the shelves in the garage. Help yourself." Liv grimaced at her own vehicle, where a layer of pale dust lay over the dark blue paint. "I should wash mine too. If I were smart, I'd park in the garage, but it always feels like too much work in the summer."

Charlie just smiled noncommittally and she realized she was on the verge of babbling. "Okay then. I'll see you this afternoon." She gave a little wave and hurried into her house before she could become even more awkward in his presence.

Anyone who thought she was put together had obviously never seen her around a guy she liked.

And she did like him. Why wouldn't she? Charlie was friendly and handsome and undemanding. But it was more than that. She'd

193

never met anyone who seemed more comfortable in their own skin, and that kind of calm was catching. Like when she was with him, she didn't need to be thinking about the image she was projecting, she could just be herself.

Clearly, after that little bit of awkwardness, that might not entirely be a good thing.

No. No more thinking about Charlie. She had a plan for today and she was going to stick with it.

Liv took a shower and dressed in shorts and a tank top, which she'd trade for more appropriate clothes later this afternoon. Then she made a batch of blueberry muffins—Gemma's recipe, which Taylor had begged for the last time she was here—and brewed a pot of coffee. It only took a few minutes for the fragrance of fresh-baked muffins and coffee to lure Taylor out of her room.

"What's the occasion?" Taylor asked, stumbling sleepily into the kitchen.

"Getting myself psyched up for the town hall meeting," Liv said. "Today, the Beacon Street Bookshop goes official."

"Cool. What time should I be ready to go tonight?"

"Four thirty, maybe?"

Taylor snagged a muffin, saluted her with it, and then disappeared back into her room. Just as well. Liv still had plenty of tasks left, and her list felt like a multi-headed hydra—every time she checked one off, two more popped up in its place.

Somehow, despite the slow start, the day slipped away without Liv noticing, and when she glanced at the clock, she realized she had just enough time to do hair and makeup and change before they had to head into town for the meeting. Haven Ridge wasn't a dressy place, but she still needed to look professional, so she chose a pair of dark jeans, a blousy, flowered tank, and a black blazer. She thrust her feet into peep-toe booties that she rarely got to wear outside New York City and put her hair up into a simple French twist. After a quick swipe of lip gloss and mascara, she stood back and studied the effect.

She still looked like she belonged in Haven Ridge, but now she projected a confidence that she wasn't sure she actually felt.

Liv pushed small hoop earrings through her piercings as she left her room. "Taylor, we have to go. Are you ready?"

Taylor popped out of her bedroom immediately. Liv's eyebrows rose. Instead of her regular goth/Japanese schoolgirl mash-up, she actually looked kind of . . . professional. Taylor had paired the black pantsuit she'd worn for a speech meet earlier this year with a white band tee, her hair brushed back into a high ponytail, and her usual dark makeup traded for something that looked more glam than goth.

"Wow," Liv said, looking her over. "Who's the young professional business owner now?"

Liv fully expected an eye roll, but Taylor just laughed. "OAT gotta represent."

"I'm going to regret going with that name, aren't I?"

"If you don't, I'm not doing my job." Taylor ducked back in to grab her handbag—black leather studded with silver spikes—and then gestured for Liv to lead the way. "Let's go kill this thing."

Liv winked at her, warmed by the solidarity. But as she walked out their front door headed for the SUV, now alone on the concrete pad, she stopped.

"What's wrong?" Taylor asked.

"My car. It's . . . clean." The layer of dust that had covered it earlier was gone, and the tires and wheels gleamed. Had Charlie done this? This had to have taken him hours.

"About time," Taylor said, circling to climb into the passenger's seat. "It was filthy."

"Yeah." Liv slowly got into the driver's side, sluggish with surprise. It was a very kind thing to do. But it was not a very tenant/contractor thing to do.

She didn't have time to think about it. She had quite enough butterflies without wondering what he meant by this gesture. The fact that Charlie's truck was already gone made her wonder if he was even going to show up. Maybe he had found something better to do.

But no, when they pulled up to the town hall—a historic brick building flying both American and Colorado flags—she immediately caught sight of Charlie's truck in the parking lot. He'd just beaten them there.

Liv parked and sat in the driver's seat for a long moment, calming herself with deep breaths. Taylor gave her a strange look. "You okay?"

"Yeah, I'm fine. Just a little nervous."

"Why?"

Liv grimaced. "I'm not overly fond of public speaking."

Taylor just stared at her, uncomprehending. "What do you mean? You're involved with all sorts of town things."

"Yeah. In the background. It's easy to be a room mom or a PTO member or help organize a festival. That's all one-on-one. But the entire town is going to be here. Looking at me."

Taylor looked at her with amusement. "You've known almost every single one of these people your whole life. Some of them probably changed your diapers."

"Not helping, Taylor."

"Look. You know I wasn't super keen on public speaking myself, and I ended up on speech team. Mr. Osborne told me something that was very helpful. Do you want to know what that is?"

"Yes, I very much would right now."

"Play a role. Like, regular Taylor was terrified of speaking in front of people. But Boss Taylor knew she was smarter and better than everyone in the room and was going to go in and crush this. So, Liv might be nervous, but *Olivia* is a bad—"

"Taylor—"

"—fine, *business owner* who everyone is going to admire and want to help. Just think what *Olivia* would do and play that role and you'll be fine."

It sounded ridiculous, but at this point, Liv was willing to give anything a try. She'd never gotten involved with theater or dance or anything that required her to be in the public eye. She hadn't even tried to get her early attempts at novels published because the idea of people reading her words and knowing how she thought was almost sickening in its vulnerability. It was why she loved being the one behind the curtain, the person who amplified other voices.

But now she had no choice. She was a business owner, a nonprofit head, and if she was going to continue to amplify voices—both writers and those with needs in the community—she was going to have to get over herself. Become Olivia instead of Liv. She took a deep breath and imagined a transformation coming over her, like she was being infused with liquid iron. When she finally stepped out of the car, her back was straighter and her head higher.

Taylor threw her an approving look. "Now that's what I'm talking about."

Her confidence lasted for exactly as long as it took to walk into the building and seek out the council chambers, which was really a large room with a long table and a bunch of interlocking chairs.

Almost every single one of those chairs were filled.

Her stomach crashed into her feet. "Why are there so many people? There are never this many people."

"Mallory and I may have put out the word earlier this week," Taylor admitted. "But it's fine. You've got this. Right, *Olivia?*"

No, Olivia does not *have this,* she thought, swallowing hard as she moved up toward the front of the room, where the seats reserved for scheduled speakers were located. Her eyes scanned the crowd as she and Taylor moved to snag two empty chairs near the aisle, registering and returning friendly smiles. And then her eyes landed on the row behind the empty seats where Charlie sat, his gaze fixed on her.

Great. Not only did she feel sick about speaking, but now she had to contend with Charlie's proximity. Taylor took the seat directly in front of him, unaware of Liv's turmoil.

As soon as she sat, Charlie leaned forward, his eyes bright with anticipation. "You ready for this?"

"Not remotely," she whispered back.

He took in her deer-in-the-headlights look and reached out, his big hand settling on her elbow where it rested on the back of the chair. Her muscles tensed, skin tingling from the contact. But he held her gaze steadily. "You're going to be great. You know why? Because you care about this town. You're not asking them for anything. You're telling them what you want to do for them. This is for their benefit. Right?"

She blinked. "Right."

He gave her a little wink and sat back in his chair, dropping his hand. "Go get 'em."

Liv twisted around and settled back into her own seat. Taylor had suggested being someone else, which she couldn't deny was good advice. But somehow Charlie had picked up on who she actually was and reminded her that this was just an extension of everything she already did in and for this town. By the time the meeting was underway and it was her turn to speak, the terror had sloughed away, leaving in its place only excitement.

And when her gaze landed on Charlie's smiling face as she began to speak, she didn't feel nervousness or butterflies or resistance.

Surprisingly, all she felt was comfort.

Charlie had never thought people could be an actual shade of green, but Liv's complexion when she walked through the door proved otherwise. He saw Taylor's worried glance, the way Liv fidgeted with the button on her coat jacket. Was it possible that the utterly self-composed Liv Quinn was afraid of public speaking?

She didn't need to be. Liv was part of the fabric of this town. He could see it from the way people looked at her when she walked into the room, the way people smiled when she passed. They loved her.

But they also pitied her, and he hoped that she didn't pick up that part. He had a feeling that Liv didn't do pity any better than she accepted help.

Which was why he ignored his better judgment and whispered advice to her over the back of her chair, dared to reach out and touch her even though that contact made his insides clench. Slowly, he saw the terror drain from her eyes as she realized that she could, in fact, do this.

And she was magnificent. When she spoke, her voice was confident, compassionate, intelligent. Even Taylor, standing up beside her looking calm and hip and collected, seemed surprised. Liv's passion for helping people came through with every detail she shared of her nonprofit, her vision for creating a community space, her desire to have it be a place for learning and tutoring and growth. A safe place for kids and adults alike, where everyone was welcome whether they could afford to buy a book or not.

In that minute, Charlie fell a little bit in love with her.

Her vision for her bookstore wasn't that far off from why he built houses. It wasn't just the technical aspects of steel and timber and tile he enjoyed. It was that he knew he was making a place where people would spend their lives. Hopefully, it would be a place of comfort and acceptance and safety; a home like he'd always wished he'd had as a kid. It was as if Liv was trying to make a place for the child he'd been, where if someone had paid attention to his struggles, they would have learned of his learning disability way before his sophomore year of high school. And in that moment, everything he'd been trying to resist, all the reasons he'd found to talk himself out of his pursuit, they all vanished in an instant.

Because now he knew he wasn't just attracted to what she looked like, but who she was. That they were essentially similar at their cores, the way they looked at the world, how they wanted to leave their mark.

And now that he'd realized that, all the reasons he shouldn't pursue her seemed unimportant.

When her presentation was over, the hall burst into a round of spontaneous applause. Liv flushed with pleasure, surprise on her face, and clasped her hands together with a little bow of acknowledgment. Hurriedly, she retook her seat, and he saw the elated way that she and Taylor gripped hands between their chairs.

Charlie leaned forward to whisper in her ear. "That was amazing. I want to help and I don't even live here."

Liv threw him a grateful smile. "Thank you," she mouthed, before she turned forward again for the Q&A part of the town meeting.

Charlie didn't pay much attention to the rest of the meeting. He didn't much care who was letting their dog poop on Mr. Anderson's lawn, even though Mr. Anderson certainly did; Charlie did see the sense in the repeated petition to put in a stop sign on Acorn and Florida to stop speeding into the residential part of town. Thomas presided over the event with an ease and aplomb that belied the fact he had apparently only been in office for six months, but when it was all over, the overwhelming flood of attention went back to Liv.

Charlie hovered in the periphery while various people offered their congratulations or their intention to volunteer time or books or money. He lost track of the actual conversations, his focus fixed instead on Liv, the way she greeted everyone with genuine warmth and enthusiasm, the way she laughed at jokes and smiled at children and made everyone feel like her attention was a precious gift.

But he couldn't help but be just as impressed

with Taylor. Beside Liv, the teen made notes in her cell phone like an attentive executive assistant, drawing people off to get their contact information when Liv was done talking to them.

When at last the crush of people had moved on and it was just Taylor and Liv standing in the front of the room, Charlie approached carefully. "Well, I would say that was a resounding success."

"You're not kidding," Taylor said. "I think I have . . ." She opened her app and counted. "Ten people who want to help run the shop, five potential tutors, and too many offers of book donations to count. It's going to take the next two weeks just to call and organize all this stuff."

"It's going to take longer than that," Liv said. "We haven't even started on our space yet."

"I think this calls for a celebration then," Charlie said. "Why don't you let me take you two ladies out?"

Liv smiled at him, but it was reluctant. "That's very nice of you, but . . . honestly, I might be all peopled out. If we go anywhere in town, everyone is going to want to talk to me."

"Well," he said slowly. "Then why don't we all go home and I'll make you dinner?"

"You cook?" Taylor asked doubtfully.

His immediate response was indignity, but she was sort of right. "That might be overstating it. Let's say I can prepare many recipes in a mediocre fashion, but I am excellent at a few. And it is one of those excellent few that I propose cooking tonight." His gaze flicked back to Liv. "I actually managed to get to the store this afternoon."

"After you washed my car?" she asked, her lips tipping up. "You didn't have to do that."

"I did, actually, because I accidentally sprayed yours and turned it into a mud bath. So I had no choice."

"Mmm." Liv clearly didn't believe him—and she shouldn't. "Thank you then. It was nice of you."

"So . . ." he prompted. "Dinner? I guarantee you won't regret it."

Liv glanced at Taylor, who didn't look thrilled, but finally shrugged assent. "Okay then. Just let us know when."

"It'll take me an hour," he said. "I'll text you when it's ready."

"Okay, that sounds nice. Thanks." Liv threw him a quick smile. "See you back at the house?"

"I'll be right behind you." He watched them leave the building thoughtfully. Taylor was going to be the deciding factor here. He wasn't sure if Taylor didn't like the idea of any man around her stepmom so soon after her dad's death or she just didn't like *Charlie,* but just from those few seconds, he could see that Taylor was going to have to approve of him before he had any shot with Liv.

Hopefully, tonight would go part of the way toward that. Because while he had been truthful about his mediocre cooking skills, it was more from lack of interest than lack of skill.

His grandmother's recipes never went wrong.

CHAPTER SIXTEEN

Liv and Taylor drove back home, the teenage girl chattering the whole way. Liv couldn't blame her for her excitement: the meeting had gone extraordinarily well. She only realized now that it was all over how much she'd doubted the town's enthusiasm. Yes, she'd stayed here for the community, but she still remembered a time when things were more fractured, when the townspeople might have just tutted about how far their beloved Haven Ridge had slipped and then gone on with their lives.

But Taylor had never doubted and neither had her friends. Somehow they knew the value of what they had, and they were determined to build the kind of town they wanted to live in. If anyone had any concerns about what the younger generation could do if they put their minds to it— and banded together—she need only bring them here and introduce them to Taylor and her crew.

That thought buoyed Liv's spirit even more than the successful town meeting. She found herself stealing looks at Taylor as the girl rambled, smiling at the enthusiasm flushing her pale cheeks.

Taylor caught her and stuttered to a stop. "What?"

Liv smiled. "I was just sitting here thinking how much I love you and how happy I am you're working on this with me."

Taylor's eyes grew wide for a second before she turned to look out the window, the flush in her cheeks deepening. "I'm glad we're doing this together too. And um, I love you too."

Liv's smile widened into a legitimate grin. She knew that her stepdaughter loved her, but for some reason she found it much easier to say the words to Gemma than she did to Liv. It was a dynamic that Liv didn't wholly understand, but she wasn't going to push.

"In any case," Liv said, "I think you're going to have a very busy two weeks before school starts. Because I am putting you and your squad in charge of tracking down and collecting all of those donations and putting together a spreadsheet of volunteers."

Rather than groan at being given the task, Taylor's eyes lit up. "Done. What are you going to be doing?"

"*I* am going to be doing everything else." Liv smiled through the sudden rush of anxiety. There was a lot of *everything else*. She needed to take Charlie to see the bookstore space and get an estimate on renovations. Actually begin the cleaning and repairs. Start their crowdfunding campaign—and quickly—so she could afford to do all those things. And then there were all the small details that immediately leaped to mind—credit card processing, inventory and point-of-sale software, not to mention all the things that she didn't yet know she needed.

"Liv, you're hyperventilating."

Liv glanced at Taylor and made herself take a long, steady breath. It would be okay. After all, she'd helped Gemma sort through these same considerations only a couple of months ago, though she was ashamed to say that she'd been more moral support than any kind of practical help. She'd known her employment was coming to an end, so she had been focused on finishing all her outstanding projects. And even then, she hadn't gotten to see some of her recent acquisitions come to fruition.

But she was moving on to something almost as exciting. She had to focus on that and not how much work it would be or how much she'd had to give up to stay here.

Because the teenage girl next to her, now bursting with enthusiasm over the "dream job," was worth it.

They pulled into their driveway a minute later, and after a moment's consideration of the storm clouds mounding on the horizon, pulled into the empty garage. Charlie had gone to the trouble of washing her car for her, so she wasn't going to mess it up this soon. Taylor shot her a questioning look, but didn't say anything, only jumped out of the SUV and headed for the house. Liv lingered, wandering around the back of the garage while Charlie pulled in directly behind her and took his spot on the parking pad. He hopped out of his own vehicle and slammed the door, then stopped when his gaze rested on her.

"Everything okay?" he asked cautiously.

So her anxiety wasn't obvious to only Taylor. "A little freaked out, to be honest."

Now his expression turned even more careful. "About dinner? I promise, I'm not that bad of a cook."

The joke, even delivered deadpan, made her laugh. "No, not about dinner. It just hit me that the bookstore is official. We're really doing this. And there's so much that I don't know about running a business."

Charlie jingled his keys in his hand as he moved toward her. "It's a lot," he agreed. "It can be daunting. Trust me, I know. But just take it one step at a time. Focus on the things that absolutely have to happen now and figure out the rest as you go along."

"If you think I'm a 'figure it out as I go along' sort, you obviously don't know me that well."

His gaze never wavered. "No, I don't. But I'd like to."

In an instant, all her worries about the bookshop disappeared in a rush of squirmy feelings—unfamiliar but not altogether unpleasant. She felt heat rush to her face and searched quickly for a reply. She'd known she hadn't misread his interest in her, but now it seemed like he wasn't even trying to hide it. Her mind began to race and her breath sped at the merest inkling of what that might mean.

But he saved her. "I'm going to head up and get dinner started. I'll text you when it's ready. Unless you want to eat at your house."

"No, we can come there, it's fine." Liv smiled, her awkwardness eased a little by his composure—and his graceful change of subject. "Thanks again."

He gave her a knowing smile and a little salute before he turned toward his apartment. She closed the garage and walked back across the yard to the front door, cursing the jitters that had settled into her stomach at the prospect of having dinner with him tonight. She needed to get a grip. It was only dinner, for heaven's sake, not a marriage proposal.

Liv half-expected Taylor to be sitting at the dining room table on her laptop, getting a jump on the spreadsheet idea, but her stepdaughter was nowhere to be seen. Slowly, she walked down the hall toward their bedrooms, following the barest echo of Taylor's voice. And even though she knew it was an invasion of privacy, she stopped outside Taylor's door for a moment to listen.

". . . went really well, but it's going to be a lot of work . . ."

Liv smiled. Taylor was talking to a friend.

"Yeah, I can't wait to see you too."

No, from the excitement in her voice, she had to be talking to Dylan. Liv turned toward her own room. She might have been a little cautious about the idea of Taylor having a boyfriend—what parent wouldn't be?—but so far he seemed to be good for her. If the worst thing she caught them talking about was plans for the bookstore, she would consider herself the luckiest mom on the planet.

Liv moved into her bathroom and fussed with her makeup a little bit, fluffed her hair. She was aware that she was just killing time until she got Charlie's text, and equally aware that she was spending it making sure she looked fabulous. She rolled her eyes at herself in the mirror and turned away. If she really wanted to distract herself, she had plenty of work to keep her busy. After all, she'd meant what she'd said to Charlie about her list-making tendencies.

Which is why when the text came from him telling her that dinner would be ready in ten minutes—a very thoughtful warning—she had already filled fifteen pages of a yellow legal pad with notes, each page a different aspect of the business that she'd have to research or complete. It should have made the project feel more daunting, but in reality, now that she saw how the parts fit together, it seemed much more doable. And if Gemma and Thomas—and Charlie—were willing to give her the benefit of their experiences, she should be able to figure it out.

She put aside the notebook and walked back down the hall to Taylor's room, where she knocked on the door. When there was no response, she carefully turned the knob and poked her head in. Taylor was sitting at her desk, wearing a pair of headphones, typing intently on her laptop.

"Taylor? Dinner is ready."

Taylor started and slammed the laptop lid before she twisted, a look somewhat akin to guilt on her face. "I'll be right there."

Liv's eyes narrowed. "What were you doing?"

"Just chatting with a couple of friends on Discord," she said with a forced smile.

Just lying to me about Discord, Liv thought. Maybe she wasn't as internet savvy as her stepdaughter, but she knew what the chat on a Discord server looked like, and that had not been it. But why would she have lied? Embarrassed to have her find out that she actually had a Facebook account at the age of sixteen, after she'd told Liv that only boomers used it?

"Taylor," she said slowly, trying to keep her voice light, "do we need to have a conversation about not talking to strangers on the internet?"

Taylor's face cleared. "I wasn't chatting with strangers, Liv, I promise."

That Liv believed. Taylor might be evasive and private, but she was a terrible liar. She nodded slowly. "Okay. I believe you. Charlie texted. Dinner is ready."

"Great. I'll be right out."

Liv lingered for just a second before she turned and left, weighing her need to keep Taylor's trust with her desire to make sure she wasn't doing anything stupid on the internet. At least she was sure that she'd just seen text on the screen, not photos.

When Taylor came out a few minutes later, she'd ditched the suit jacket she'd worn earlier in favor of her favorite black Haven Ridge HS sweatshirt, swapping her heeled boots for a pair of skate shoes that rarely got seen out in public. Liv didn't say anything more about the computer, and she could tell that Taylor was relieved, since the tension drained out of her with each step they took toward the apartment.

Liv rapped on the apartment door and stood back on the concrete pad. A moment later, Charlie opened the door, a kitchen towel slung over one shoulder. "Come in. I'm just about to take the food out of the oven."

A delicious savory smell wafted toward them as they stepped inside, and Charlie shut the door behind them before leading them up the stairs to the second floor. Liv surreptitiously looked around as he led them into the combination kitchen/eating/living area at the back. Even though she'd decorated it herself, it looked homier with the signs that someone was actually *living* here instead of just staying temporarily. Several coats had hung on the hooks downstairs above his work boots; here in the living room, there was a stack of paperback books and a glass of water on the side table.

He'd set the table with three of her plain white plates and cutlery, and a large water glass sat in the center stuffed with spiky flower stalks in a shade of dark purple. Liv bent and sniffed the larkspur, inhaling a fragrance that was more herbal than floral. "Did you get these from the castle?"

He looked abashed. "They're everywhere. I figured it wouldn't matter."

"It doesn't," Liv said, throwing him a smile. "They're wildflowers. Our altitude is a little too low for them, which is why it's so notable they grow at the castle. It has its own microclimate, a special little ecosystem."

"You seem to know a lot about Larkspur House." Charlie turned away to the oven and pulled open the door, taking out a baking sheet upon which rested a beautifully golden chicken, spatchcocked flat. He set it on the grates of the range top and then bent to take a second sheet, which looked like crispy potato wedges.

Liv resisted the urge to comment on the food until he was ready, seating herself at the island table beside Taylor, where the girl was tapping away at her cell phone. "It's a Haven Ridge landmark," Liv said. "We used to go on field trips there when we were in elementary school, back when Mr. Parker lived there."

"That's why you know Will and his sister?" Charlie asked casually.

"I know Will because he was my husband's best friend. They were both older than me, so we didn't really run in the same circles."

Charlie murmured wordless acknowledgment as he took a knife out of the block and started expertly carving the chicken into quarters. "Is there a platter somewhere in here?"

"Yeah, there's one in the cabinet above the fridge. Let me get it." She hopped off her seat, retrieved the white stoneware platter from the top shelf, and then set it on the counter beside Charlie.

"Thanks." He turned his head just enough to meet her eyes, and despite her best efforts, her breath caught.

"No problem." She hurried back to her place at the table. A minute later, Charlie brought them a platter arranged with chicken pieces, crispy potato wedges nestled in beside it.

"Piri-piri chicken with chips," he announced, swapping it with the vase of larkspur. "Help yourself."

Taylor had looked up interestedly when the food arrived, and now she shoved her phone into the kangaroo pocket of her hoodie. She wasted no time stabbing a chicken breast and putting it on her plate, then helping herself to some of the chips.

Charlie nodded to Liv. "Please."

Liv took one of the leg quarters—not because she preferred dark meat, but she wanted to leave Charlie with a choice—and his smile said that he knew exactly what she was doing. How could he read her that well when they'd known each other for days? Was she really that transparent? Were her thoughts written across her forehead in bold serif type?

She forgot to be worried about it when she took her first bite of the chicken. It was savory and garlicky and spicy at the same time, with a subtle hit of lemon. Her eyes widened as she chewed. "This is delicious! What kind of food is it?" The words *piri-piri* hit in her mind, but the only thing she could think of was a British fast food place she'd eaten at while in London for the book fair.

"Portuguese by way of Angola," he said.

"Is that what you are?" Taylor asked bluntly. "Portuguese, I mean."

"I'm a little bit of everything," he said, unperturbed. "Portuguese, Spanish, English, and Irish with a bit of German mixed in for good measure. My dad's mom was born here, but she

217

lived in Portugal for a while. So it's mostly her recipes that I know."

"Well, thank goodness for the Portuguese grandmother," Liv said, going in for another bite. "This is really excellent."

"Thank you. I'm glad you're enjoying it. Depending on where in Portugal you're from, you might eat it with rice instead of chips, but when I was a kid, I always thought it was junk food because we ate it with French fries."

Liv laughed. The meal was as wholesome and homey as it got, and he'd done a good job on it, yet the amount of time he'd spent at the diner this week made her think this had been arranged for her—their—benefit. However casual he'd been about the invitation, had he planned this all along, to impress them with his grandmother's recipe?

Watching Taylor devour her food and go back in for seconds, Liv decided she didn't much care about his motivations. If he'd intended to make them like him a little more—or prove that he could do more than hang shelves and plaster ceilings—she had no problem with that.

She only realized that she was staring at him thoughtfully when she noticed the small, amused smile that tugged at his lips. She shook herself and looked away, going back to her food, but the heat crept up the back of her neck anyway. She might as well have told him out loud that she was interested.

Because despite every attempt she'd made to ignore it, she *was* interested.

When the platter was clean and everyone had stuffed themselves with delicious chicken, Charlie hopped off his seat and began clearing the table. "I hope everyone left room for dessert."

"Dessert?" Taylor perked up again, while inwardly, Liv groaned. "You can bake too?"

Charlie laughed. "That is way above my pay grade. Fortunately, I was told that the Broken Hearts Bakery makes the best cinnamon coffee cake on the planet. And I do happen to make good coffee to go with it."

He brought a pink pastry box to the table and then went back to retrieve small plates and forks from the drawers.

"Gemma does make a killer coffee cake." Liv opened the box and carefully removed the cake on its cardboard circle. "She supplies the cafe now."

"How do you think I heard about it? I had a piece of the almond one, and Mallory told me the cinnamon was even better, so I picked one up down the street." Charlie bustled around making coffee—pouring from a bag marked *Solid Grounds Coffee Company*, an expensive local brand he probably picked up from the Koffee Kabin—and soon the kitchen was filled with the delicious scent of freshly brewed coffee.

Taylor's phone trilled, making them all startle. "Sorry, this is Dylan. Do you mind?"

Charlie shook his head. "Not at all."

Taylor flashed him a smile. "Save me a piece." And then she was rushing down the hall, her hushed greeting fading as she hurried down the stairs and out into the evening's dying light.

"To be sixteen again," Charlie said.

"You couldn't pay me enough."

Charlie laughed. "Surely it wasn't that bad."

Liv sighed. "No. I mean, I was popular and I was a good student. But I was about Taylor's age when Gemma left—she was my best friend even back then—and then there was a lot of drama around town that spilled over onto me, especially because I remained friends with her ex-boyfriend. At that point, I just decided to focus on school. I wanted to get out of this town, go to New York, become this big-time editor."

"And?"

"I went to New York and became a *small-time* editor."

Charlie laughed. "Close enough. How did you end up back in Haven Ridge then?"

"Sort of by accident. Jason and I reconnected in New York when our mothers set us up. He was working in quantitative data analysis on Wall Street."

"Opposites attract?" he asked.

"More like opposites hate each other at first sight." Liv knew that she shouldn't be telling this story to another man, but he looked interested, not put off, and some part of her had to get it out, had to make him understand her reluctance to date again. "He stood me up when he was supposed to take me out to lunch. I was never going to speak to him again. But it turned out he had a good excuse, and I agreed to meet him for coffee the next day. He apologized with flowers and a copy of my favorite book."

"Which was?"

Liv smiled. "*The Velveteen Rabbit.*"

"Which is how I know that you have a dark side."

Liv laughed. "Taylor would agree with you. She thinks it's traumatizing."

"It is!"

"You're that familiar with it?"

Charlie smiled. "My niece made me read it to her every time I saw her because her mother couldn't stand to."

Liv smiled. "Took one for the team."

"Well, if you met my niece back then, you'd know she had everyone wrapped around her little finger." He flashed a smile. "But back to Jason. You obviously gave him another chance."

Liv smiled, overtaken by nostalgia. "He grew on me. And he was persistent. So despite the fact that we had nothing in common—maybe because of it—we ended up married after a year. And not long after that, we decided to move back to Haven Ridge."

"For Taylor."

"Mostly," Liv agreed. "And partly because we both had fond memories of the town, and we could have a life here that we'd never be able to have if we stayed in New York. The luxury of time. So yeah, we bought the crazy falling-down historic home and started renovating . . . and the rest is history."

Charlie seemed to understand what she wasn't saying. "I'm sorry."

"Yeah. Me too. There's no way to really prepare yourself for something like that. I mean, when someone has cancer, it's awful, but you know it's coming. But this . . . If I had just . . ." She shook her head. "Anyway. You don't want to hear about all that."

"I want to hear about it if you want to talk about it," he said softly, holding her gaze.

"I really don't."

"Then coffee it is. How do you take it?"

"Uh, black is fine." She really preferred cream and sugar but at the moment, she couldn't find the words. Suddenly didn't know how she felt. It was kind of Charlie to let her talk about Jason. Some men, when they were interested in a woman, didn't want to hear about the past, especially the bits that involved other guys. But he seemed to understand that Jason would always be a part of her. How could he not be, when she had a constant reminder of him in Taylor?

Charlie set a mug full of fresh coffee in front of her, then came back with a knife to cut the coffee cake. "What do you think the chances are that Taylor is actually coming back?"

"Slim to none."

He laughed. "That's what I thought. I'll send some of this back with you. Notice I did not say that I would send the whole thing back with you."

Liv laughed, too, grateful for him lightening the mood. "I would never dream of depriving you of it. Gemma is a pretty fantastic baker. For a lawyer."

Charlie served them both a piece and then took a bite of his, nodding in agreement. "She is. How did that happen anyway?"

"That is a long story for another day. Let's just say that Haven Ridge has a way of sucking people in and not letting them go."

"I've noticed that," Charlie said wryly. "I ran into Granny Pearl yesterday and she gave me the rundown on all the available properties I might be interested in buying when I moved to Haven Ridge."

"Ah yes, she will not give up until she has you permanently settled here."

"There are worse things, I suppose. Though I still have doubts that there's enough work for me here."

"Well, I know about one project. Are you still interested in the bookstore?"

"Of course. I was actually just going to mention that. I have something planned tomorrow afternoon, but I could take a look in the morning. Say nine?"

"Thank you. I appreciate it. I realize I'm asking a lot of you."

"You really aren't," Charlie said, holding her gaze. "But whatever you need, I'm here for it."

And she realized in that moment that he wasn't just talking about the shop.

CHAPTER SEVENTEEN

Charlie was pushing his luck with Liv.

He knew it, and he just couldn't get himself to stop it. It wasn't just because now that he'd decided to pursue her for real, every minute that he was in her presence and couldn't touch her felt like an eternity. It was that every time Liv brought up Will and Jason so casually, it reminded him of what he was up against, how many other men would kill to even catch her eye. Men who could offer her much more than he could. Will owned what seemed like half the town. Jason had been a quant—a financial engineer at an investment bank—and he knew the salary that would have been attached. Meanwhile, Charlie was just a blue-collar guy with no money, business, or future, who hung her cabinets and rented an apartment above her garage. How could he possibly compete?

And yet she flushed and stammered when he flirted, which was all it took to stoke the wild hope in his chest.

At least she'd finally asked him about the bookstore. She'd been dancing around the idea for ages, but she'd never actually asked him if he'd be interested in doing the work. Technically, she hadn't done that yet either, but she'd made it sound like he had the job if he wanted it.

And he wanted it, even without seeing it, because it meant being close to her.

He went to sleep too late that night, and when he finally did drift off, his dreams were filled with Liv. All those things that he tried to repress in her presence during the day seemed to find free rein at night when they weren't restrained by his better judgment. Which was why he woke up the next morning—Saturday morning—feeling stretched thin and exhausted.

That feeling went away the minute he saw her waiting. Like him, she was dressed for a construction zone in jeans and boots, which hinted at the mess they'd be walking into.

He smiled at her as he approached. "Good morning. You look prepared."

Liv smiled back brightly, her enthusiasm undiminished by her next words. "Just wait until you see it. It's at least a two-dumpster project."

"That good, huh? What did it used to be before?"

"A five-and-dime. It's a wreck." Liv grimaced. "I'm hoping it's not actually as bad as it looks."

Charlie chuckled. "I will give you my honest opinion. You ready to go? I can drive if you'd like."

"We're waiting on Taylor," Liv said. "She and I can drive over together. I know you have plans after this."

He knew he shouldn't have mentioned his

job this afternoon. It was just assembling and securing bookshelves for one of the older ladies in town, a widow that had been given his number by Granny Pearl. It did seem like the town was in serious need of a handyman; word had spread quickly through the older set that he was willing to do small jobs like fixing sprinklers or assembling furniture and not just the big ones like remodeling a bathroom. Part of him figured he should regard these sixty-dollar jobs as beneath him, but he enjoyed being of use. He liked dealing with problems that seemed insurmountable to an elderly lady but were an easy fix for him. Compared to the kind of large-scale management he was used to, it was refreshing to be posed with a challenge that could be overcome in an afternoon. And his clients were so appreciative, they made him out to be a hero when anyone with the slightest bit of mechanical understanding could have done the same. They simply didn't have anyone like that in their lives.

Taylor chose that moment to emerge, dressed similarly to Liv but in all black. He smiled warmly at her and then switched his attention back to Liv. "I'll meet you over there?"

"Beacon Street and Delaware."

"I'll follow you then."

And he did, all the way off their property, onto the highway, and into town on a winding course he realized was designed to avoid stop signs and potholes. A route only a native would choose.

At last, Liv parallel-parked at the curb in front of one in a long row of mismatched buildings, two and three stories with the graceful brick and trim that he would expect in a late-nineteenth-century mountain town. He could see why she liked this street. Compared to other parts of Haven Ridge, Beacon Street had a quieter, more elegant feel. The buildings were almost European in style, graceful and ornamented, compared to the harsher, straighter lines on Dogwood. He pulled in behind her and climbed out of his truck, taking his notebook and laser measure with him.

"It's cute," he said when he joined Liv and Taylor in front of the building. The ladies exchanged a look. "What?"

Liv dangled a key. "Let's see what you say about it in a minute." She moved forward, shoved the key in the lock, and with an extended jiggle, pushed the door open.

Charlie followed Liv in amid the tinkle of harness bells. And stopped.

Liv dared a glance at him. "You're rethinking this, aren't you?"

Charlie looked it over critically. It was a mess, no question—the place was strewn with wood debris and there was no identifying the original color of the thin carpet underfoot. He turned slowly, taking in the double-height ceilings, exposed brick, second-story windows. Not even the air of neglect could hide the character oozing from every inch.

"This is amazing."

Liv and Taylor looked at him as if he'd lost his mind.

"Come on, obviously you thought so or you wouldn't have been interested in it. It's got such potential." He picked his way through the mess and tried to lift one of the oak bookshelves that had collapsed. "These might even be salvageable."

Taylor blinked at him. "Well, yeah, we thought it was great, but we figured you'd probably run screaming."

"From a challenge? Never." He grinned at her. "This is a good pick, ladies. At least architecturally."

Structurally, he wasn't so sure, though the brick would probably stand another two centuries with proper care. Though like the Larkspur House, it had been vacant for at least twenty years, so everything else seemed to be in some stage of decay.

But Liv had asked him here for a quote, not for pessimism. So he brought out his laser measure and began to sketch out a floor plan, marking down the distances in the one large downstairs room. Then he carefully moved past the staircase into the hall.

Back here was just an office and a lavatory, both of which were spare and simple and last updated sometime in the eighties. He noted copper plumbing beneath the pedestal sink and hoped that meant the pipes had been updated all the way to the street.

The luck just kept coming when he found the fuse box with an upgraded panel and modern fuses with room to expand. Which was good, because the old-fashioned radiators in each room suggested it lacked central air and heating.

He moved upstairs to the second-floor loft, which was considerably bigger than it looked. It was also cleaner up here, which made it easy to identify floorboards that needed to be replaced. He debated a second before grabbing hold of one of them and pulling it free. It let loose with a loud crack.

"Um, Charlie, what was that?" Boots thundered up the stairs.

"Rotted board," he said when Liv and Taylor came into view. He pulled a small flashlight from his belt and shone it into the cavity the board had just revealed. "The joists look okay, though. Come look at this."

Liv gave him a funny look, but she knelt beside the hole and bent to peer inside. "Whoa," she breathed. "What kind of beams did they use?"

Charlie grinned at her when she straightened

up. "I think they were railroad ties. Probably surplus from when they built the rail line."

"Is that good?"

"I don't think this place is going anywhere for the next five centuries," he said with a laugh. "So yeah, it's good." He climbed to his feet and offered Liv a hand. "Let's go see the third floor."

After a moment of hesitation, she put her hand in his and he gripped it tight, pulling her up off the floor. But he didn't immediately let it go once she was standing, and she didn't try to pull it away. Instead, they just stared at each other for a long moment, the room around them narrowing to a pinprick.

"Uh guys? Are we going to go upstairs or what?" Taylor's disembodied voice drifted from the stairwell. Abruptly, Charlie released Liv's hand just as she yanked it back.

"Coming right now," she called, and she followed her stepdaughter without another look at Charlie.

The top floor was empty and in good shape, more of an attic than any kind of usable space. But Liv looked around approvingly while Charlie checked out the floor and the ceiling and what bits of the walls he could see behind the bad 1970s paneling.

"This could be a sorting station," she said. "We could bring the donated books up here and volunteers could catalog them and prep them for sale or borrow. A table and a few chairs and we're in business."

"Yes, we are," Charlie said, pulling open a gap between two ugly sheets of faux paneling. "This is MC cable. New commercial-grade wiring. Someone redid this fairly recently. You're lucky, Liv. The vast majority of the work here is cosmetic."

"What's the verdict then? Do you think it's a good risk?"

"I think by the time we're done with it, it's going to be perfect." Charlie smiled at her. "I'll put together a quote for you tonight. I just need to know what kind of upgrades you're thinking."

"Refinished floors and woodwork," Taylor said immediately. "A fresh coat of paint. New or repaired wooden bookshelves on both floors. Better lighting everywhere. Get the chandelier cleaned and working . . ."

Charlie glanced at Liv, who gave him an amused smile. "You heard the girl."

"Yes, ma'am. Ma'ams. I think that could all be done."

"How long?" Liv asked.

"Assuming we don't hit anything unexpected, like a roof leak or old plumbing, maybe a month."

"So does that mean that you're accepting the job?"

Charlie looked at Liv. There was no question that he was accepting the job. Except as much as he'd love to do it for her as a favor, he still had to make a living. "I guess that would be your decision. Why don't I write up an estimate and you can decide if you want me to work on it?"

Liv flushed as if she'd forgotten that was the way things worked. True, their relationship had gotten a little murky when it came to contractor/client status, and he hated to be the one to remind her. "Thank you," she said, holding his gaze for a second. "For everything."

And even though he wasn't entirely sure what the *everything* encompassed, he knew she was more than welcome.

Liv had to get outside and it wasn't just because of the smell that hinted at rodent activity in the recent past. It was the threads of connection that were swiftly forming between her and Charlie and strengthening with every minute they spent in each other's company.

She led the way down the staircase from the third floor, noting the creaks under her boots and filing them away for future repair. Behind her, Taylor and Charlie chatted about the teen's vision for the space, but Liv barely registered it. When she finally broke free into the warm breeze outside on the sidewalk, she took a long deep breath and steadied her nerves. There was no reason to feel this way. Nervous. Spooked.

Guilty.

Taylor and Charlie followed a moment later, and she locked the door behind them. "So," she said, clapping her hands together too loudly and earning startled looks from the other two. "I guess we should let Charlie get on with his estimate, and Taylor, you and I have some planning to do."

"Okay," Taylor said, a little bewildered, but she threw a faint smile at Charlie. Apparently he had won her over with his enthusiasm for her design vision. She went to the SUV and climbed in, leaving the adults standing on the sidewalk.

"I need to make a few calls," he said, "get clear on what's required in this county." He frowned and looked at her more closely. "You okay? You feeling faint? It was a little stuffy in there."

"I'm fine," Liv said brightly. "Just over-whelmed by it all. I see all that work and I think of everything that still has to be done to make it a workable business and . . ."

"Hey." Charlie reached out and gripped her upper arms gently, looking straight into her eyes. "You've got this. And you have a ton of support in this town. Everyone wants to see you succeed. So maybe just have a little faith in yourself."

Liv glanced back at the SUV, saw Taylor watching them with interest. Charlie followed her gaze and then dropped his hands. "Thanks," she said quietly. "I appreciate it. Really. I'll see you back at the house tonight." Without waiting for an answer, she circled her vehicle and climbed in the driver's seat.

"What was that all about?" Taylor asked as soon as Liv shut the door, indicating Charlie—who was still standing on the sidewalk—with her head.

"Nothing," Liv said brightly. "He was just telling me it's not as daunting as it looks."

Taylor didn't seem convinced, but she didn't press the issue, launching instead into her thoughts on how to convert the second floor to a reading room.

Liv listened with half a mind and inserted responses where appropriate, even though Taylor didn't seem to register her silence. When her stepdaughter finally took a breath, Liv said, "So I take it that we're doing this? Full speed ahead?"

"Oh yeah. The Beacon Street Bookshop is in business."

Liv glanced at her stepdaughter, saw the excitement in Taylor's face that had been notably absent since Jason's death, and all her complicated feelings vanished.

For the first time since this wild idea had surfaced, she had absolutely no doubts about what they were going to do.

CHAPTER EIGHTEEN

Liv could hand it to herself: she might not be able to shut off her feelings like a switch, but she had absolutely no problem distracting herself by burying herself in work.

Or rather, a dry book on Generally Accepted Accounting Principles she'd overnighted as soon as she realized she could no longer ask for Will's help. Even with a mug of coffee within reach, she couldn't make it more than five pages without her eyes drifting closed.

When Charlie knocked on Liv's door later that night, she practically ran for the door. She ushered him into the kitchen, where he laid a sheet of paper out between them. "This is what I have so far. Keep in mind this is just a rough estimate."

Liv's eyebrows flew up. It was not an insignificant amount of money, but it was still less than she'd feared. "Is this labor estimate accurate?"

He nodded. "Since this is going to be a non-profit and you're crowdfunding it, I thought it made more sense to pay you rent directly than deduct it from the project. Assuming you're still okay with me living here."

Liv didn't look at him, even though the

knowledge that he'd still be staying on her property prickled the back of her neck like an impending lightning strike. "Of course. You're welcome to rent the place for as long as you'd like."

"The good news is that neither the county nor the town of Haven Ridge requires a contractor's license to do the work. Which means that unless we find unexpected plumbing or electrical problems, which would require a license, we're clear to begin."

"Wow. Okay. So we're really doing this."

"We're really doing this. We can get started just as soon as your kitchen is done."

"Good. I should get to work on the crowd-funding appeal, now that I know how much we need to raise."

"Happy to help," he said, straightening beside her. "I'll see you on Tuesday morning then, if not before."

"Great, thanks." Liv walked him to the door, feeling the whole time that she should be asking him if he wanted a cup of tea, if he wanted to stay and chat for a while. After all, he had become more than her contractor or tenant at this point, particularly after he'd cooked them dinner. But she wasn't entirely sure that she could call him a friend.

She wasn't entirely sure if she wanted to put that label on him in case it stuck.

"See you later," she said lamely as he stepped out onto the porch. She shut the door behind him and sagged back against it. What was she doing here? It was like she was constantly making resolutions about Charlie and then immediately breaking them the minute he was near. She banged her head against the solid wood a couple of times.

"Liv?" came Charlie's voice from outside. "Are you okay?"

"Uh fine!" she called back through the door. "Just bumped into something." She scurried out of the entryway, cursing her own awkwardness. Work. She needed to focus on work. Not on Charlie. She needed to stop acting like a lovesick fourteen-year-old and start acting like the capable adult she actually was.

By the time Tuesday morning rolled around, Liv had convinced herself that she really did have things under control. With Taylor's help, Liv had set up the crowdfunding campaign and turned it live. After a long debate with Taylor—and a few phone calls to Gemma—they'd decided on their stages. The first goal was to get the bookstore open and running—pay for the building, the repairs, and the initial stock. The second part was the library upstairs, which would require money to build out and also to stock, though Taylor once again requested that they start with fiction. And then the third stage would be the tutoring and the community outreach. Taylor reasonably pointed out that people would be more likely to give generously to get to the later stages they deemed more important. Liv wasn't sure if that was true or not, but it was a rather astute observation of human nature. Once more, she realized how badly she'd underestimated the teen.

And for the first time since the whole thing had begun, Liv rolled out of bed feeling optimistic.

Liv stifled a yawn and stumbled into the bathroom to wash her face and brush her hair. The countertop guys were supposed to be here in an hour—she suspected that Charlie had had to do some sweet talking to get them to bring it all the way up here—and the least she could do was look halfway presentable. It had absolutely nothing to do with the fact Charlie would be here supervising.

She pulled on a pair of shorts and a cute top—again, totally for her own benefit—and then wandered down the hallway to the kitchen to get the coffee started. While she was waiting for the slow drip of liquid consciousness to fill the pot, she pulled her phone out of her pocket and opened the crowdfunding app to see if she'd gotten any new questions or comments.

And nearly dropped the phone on the floor.

When she'd gone to bed, the total at the top center of the screen had been $0. Now it read nearly five thousand dollars.

Liv just gaped at the figure, hardly able to

239

process what she was seeing. Surely that had to be a mistake. She'd just put it up ten hours ago! And while that was just a drop in the bucket of their overall needs, she could hardly believe that they'd gotten such a quick start. She scrolled down to the bottom of the page, where it listed the contributors. Several of them were labeled anonymous, with donations of $50 or $100. But there was one that clearly stated *Pearl Anderson* with the staggering figure of $1500, and another with the initials *W.P.* for $500.

Will Parker.

Guilt hit her again and she had to shove it down. She hadn't asked for him to feel that way about her. Even though they'd been friends, even though she owed him so much for his support, she didn't owe him *this*. Still, she couldn't let his generosity pass without acknowledgment. She opened her text app and a message.

You didn't have to do that, but thank you.

He didn't immediately reply, so she poured herself a cup of coffee and took it to the sofa where she'd left her laptop and notes last night. She was just booting the device up when his reply came through.

You're welcome. I'm rooting for your success. Haven Ridge needs this.

Haven Ridge. Not Liv. She supposed she couldn't blame him for pulling back a little, given the awkwardness of their last discussion.

The little dancing dots below his message suggested he had more to say, but then they disappeared and never returned. Liv shoved the phone into her pocket just as a knock came at the door. She skimmed across the floor in bare feet to throw it open. Charlie.

"Morning. Ready for the big day?"

"More than ready. You want some coffee?"

"I'd love some coffee." His smile never left his face as he followed her into the kitchen, where she found him a mug and poured him his own cup. When she handed it over, their fingers brushed. Not by accident, if the way that Charlie held her gaze meant anything. She swallowed, licked her lips, and glanced away.

"I got a text that they're on their way." Charlie took a sip and then nodded his approval. "Just wanted to make sure that you had everything cleared off so they can bring them right in."

Liv swept her hand toward the bare countertops. "Just need to move the coffee pot. Left that until the last minute for obvious reasons."

"No problem, I'll move it. Listen, if you want to leave, I can handle everything here. You don't need to supervise. I know you have a ton of work to do."

She started to say that she didn't mind, but he was right. She did have a ton of work to do, and she was only going to be in the way if she hovered to watch them secure big sheets of stone into place. She and Taylor had talked about going to the Springs that afternoon to price out some furniture and fixtures for the shop so they could get a better handle on the budget, but before she could do that, she had a substantial to-do list to finish.

"That would be great, actually. Thank you." Liv gave him a quick smile and turned back down the hall, where she knocked at Taylor's door. It opened almost immediately to reveal a groggy but fully-dressed Taylor. "The installers will be here in a few. What do you say we take our laptops and get breakfast in town before we head to Colorado Springs?"

Taylor perked up at the idea of a Brick House Cafe breakfast. "Give me twenty minutes."

Forty minutes later, they were on their way to town, their laptops and notebooks on the back seat of Liv's SUV, Taylor already tapping away at her phone.

"Who are you talking to?" Liv asked, more curious than concerned.

Taylor quickly shut off the screen and shoved the device in her pocket. "No one. Just a friend."

Liv bit her lip to keep from prying. This was the second time she'd caught Taylor chatting with someone she didn't want Liv to know about. Little alarm bells sounded in the back of her head, but she prevented herself from asking any of the questions flitting through her mind. She knew from experience that trying to get information out of Taylor when she was already defensive was impossible. Best to broach the subject in a roundabout way once her guard was down.

Just thinking that way made her feel slightly bad. It was probably simply that she was talking to a boy who was not Dylan and she didn't want to answer questions about her relationship status or have Liv think she was cheating. But in case it wasn't . . .

Liv pulled into a space in front of the Brick House Cafe and turned off the ignition. "Okay. Liège waffles, here we come."

Taylor grinned and reached back for her laptop before she hopped out of the vehicle. She beat Liv into the cafe, then ground to a halt in front of the register so quickly that Liv nearly ran into her. "Taylor!" she scolded automatically. But Taylor just pointed.

A big glass cookie jar sat at the side of the register with a hand-lettered sign that said *Support our new town bookstore and library.* And the bottom of it was already littered with cash. Not just coins and one-dollar bills either. Even from where she stood, she glimpsed several twenties and a fifty.

What in the world?

Thomas appeared before them with menus, grinning broadly. "Surprise."

Liv blinked at him. "I don't understand. I literally just put up the campaign last night."

Thomas laughed. "And you thought that Mallory wouldn't immediately jump all over it? There's nothing she loves better than an arts and crafts project that benefits the town. I mean, it's not much yet, but given that's just from the morning rush . . ."

Liv blinked away sudden tears. "Thomas, I don't know what to say—"

"Oh no, here comes the waterworks," Taylor muttered under her breath, but Liv thought she saw her hide a smile.

She ignored her stepdaughter and focused instead on the cafe owner. "Thank you. And thank Mallory as well. I can't believe people are giving money already, and we don't even have our nonprofit status yet."

"It'll come," Thomas said, gesturing for them to follow him. As they moved through the restaurant, Liv was suddenly aware of all the people who were staring at them, many of them smiling, others looking on with what she could only describe as approval. All of this because of a bookstore and reading room? Liv slid onto the bench in the corner booth, aware she was on display.

"Don't let it get to you," Thomas murmured as he set down the menus in front of them. "It was the same when I took over the cafe. People are just happy we're investing in our hometown."

Liv smiled up at him and nodded. Before he

could flit off to another table, they ordered coffee and Liège waffles. When Thomas took back the menus from Liv, she realized that Taylor was looking at her.

"I'm really glad we didn't leave," Taylor said quietly, a little smile on her lips.

Liv reached across the table and squeezed the girl's hand. "Yeah. Me too."

CHAPTER NINETEEN

The trip to Colorado Springs turned out to be the most fun Liv had had in a long time. She loved Haven Ridge, but as she and Taylor walked through home furnishing outlets and antique stores, she realized how small her world had become. When Jason was still alive, they used to take day and weekend trips all over Colorado; before that, they'd explored New England by car and train. Taylor had been young enough to still be enthusiastic about road trips and naive enough to be charmed by chain candy shops, simply because they didn't have them back home.

But in the last couple of years, every suggestion that she'd made to Taylor to venture farther than nearby Salida had been met with an eye roll or an outright refusal. And Liv, thinking that she was doing the right thing by not pressing it, had just let it go. Let the couple square miles that defined their tiny town enclose her life as well. It made her wonder if she'd used Taylor as an excuse to stay in Haven Ridge. She hadn't wanted to be taken out of her comfort zone. She hadn't wanted to face an outside world where she constantly had to explain that no, she hadn't given birth to Taylor as a teen, she was actually her stepmom and sole guardian. It had seemed easier that way.

Now, she wondered if she hadn't done them both a disservice.

They were leaving an antique shop, where they'd dithered over an art deco sideboard that they thought might make a good checkout counter for the shop, when Liv turned to Taylor. "I'm sorry."

Taylor glanced at her, her brow furrowing even as an uncertain smile touched her lips. "What do you mean? Sorry for what?"

Liv cleared her throat as they walked down the sidewalk side by side. "Sorry that I haven't pushed you to get out more. I've kind of let you just hang out in Haven Ridge, and I'm not sure it was the best thing for you. We should have done this a long time ago."

"We should have," Taylor agreed, and Liv automatically stiffened, waiting for the hard words to come. "But honestly, I don't think I would have thanked you for forcing me."

"Here I thought you were mad at me for not being involved enough."

"I was," Taylor said. "But I don't think you could have won either way."

Liv heaved a sigh and shook her head. "This hasn't been the easiest on either of us, has it?"

"No. But my dad died. Your husband died. I don't know if there's an easy way to deal with that. You just kind of have to deal."

It was a surprising bit of insight from a teen. "How did you get so smart?"

Taylor gave a little self-conscious shrug. "I might have talked to Mrs. Landry, the psychology teacher, a little."

"Wait. Haven Ridge High has a psychology teacher?"

"She teaches social studies," Taylor said with a smile. "But she does have a psychology degree. And she's pretty smart."

"Sounds like it." It was just another way that Taylor's generation differed from Liv's, for all that they were only fifteen years apart in age. When Liv was young, going to see a therapist—or even talking to a teacher about your problems—was taboo. But Taylor just threw it out there like it was nothing. "So, tell me some stuff."

"Like what kind of stuff?"

"I don't know. I feel bad that you thought I wasn't paying attention—and I wasn't not paying attention—so tell me what I missed. You've been talking about studying design. Got any schools in mind?"

"I'm not really sure," Taylor said slowly. "I haven't even decided what kind. But I was thinking . . . maybe Parsons?"

Liv's eyebrows flew up. "In New York?"

Taylor suddenly seemed nervous. "Yeah. The school is in Manhattan. On Fifth Avenue."

"I know where it is," Liv said. "I used to work down the street from it. Half of the publishers in New York are on Fifth Avenue."

Taylor seemed surprised at that. She had been pretty young when they'd left, and she hadn't spent as much time in Manhattan as Liv and Jason, considering they'd lived in Brooklyn. "It seems like a good option since they have majors in every possible area of design I might want to study. Product design, fashion, architecture, whatever."

"Are you sorry we didn't move there this summer?"

"No! Of course not. I wanted to graduate with all my friends. I mean, we're all going to be leaving in two years. So this might be the last time we're all together."

Don't be so sure, Liv thought. She'd assumed the same thing when she, Gemma, and Stephen had all gone their separate ways, studying in different states. She'd been sure the only time they would see one another was on planned visits. And then over the course of about four years, they'd all come back to Haven Ridge.

But that was the last thing that Taylor wanted to hear. Unlike her friends who had been born in Haven Ridge, Taylor knew both the benefits and drawbacks of small-town living, and she'd make her own decision about where she wanted to live. It still caused a pang in Liv's chest when she realized that her responsibility and influence over Taylor would soon be diminishing. Not coming to an end—Taylor was family, regardless of whether they were bound by law or blood. But it wasn't the same as if she was her real mom. There might come a time when Liv only saw her every couple of years, if she was the one to make the trip.

She would be well and truly alone then.

No, not alone. She had her friends and she had her town, and soon she would have her bookstore.

But it hadn't really struck her until now that this part of her life, the family life, would be coming to an end.

"Liv, you okay?"

Liv blinked herself back to the present and glanced at the girl. "Yeah, I'm fine. Just a little sad at the idea of you going off to college. When I met you, that seemed incredibly far away. But time has gone a lot faster than I expected."

Taylor threw her a reproving look. "It's not like I'll never come back. I mean, I'm still coming home for holidays and summers."

Liv put an arm around Taylor. "Of course you will." She squeezed her against her side for a second—and Taylor actually let her—not saying what she was thinking: Taylor thought she'd come back, but there would be boyfriends and summer jobs to consider. She'd build a life away from Colorado, maybe even decide to stay in New York, and Liv would be like a distant relative.

"I mean," Liv continued, as if her thoughts

hadn't spiraled out to an entire future without Taylor, "we'll have the bookshop. So I'm fully expecting you to come home in the summer and work there. It's as much yours as it is mine."

"Of course I will. But first, we need to actually raise the money to get it going."

"True. Speaking of which, let's check." Liv pulled out her phone and opened the app. "Hey! Fifty-six hundred. Not bad." The extra six hundred was listed as from *Anonymous,* so she had no way of knowing who it was from.

"This is actually going to work, isn't it?" Taylor said, a little bit of wonder in her voice. "We're actually going to do this."

"Don't sound so surprised! You've been the one who's believed in this from the start!"

"Well, yeah, but it's one thing to think it could happen and another to actually *see* it happening."

Liv knew what she meant, didn't tell her that most of life unfolded that way. That you started getting so used to unexpected detours you were surprised when something went to plan. Instead, she steered Taylor toward a pub ahead that she happened to know served an excellent cheeseburger and even better fish and chips.

By the time they turned back toward home, hot and tired from walking around Old Colorado City all day, the light was already taking on the warm yellow glow of late afternoon. They'd barely joined the highway into the mountains before

Taylor's eyes drifted closed and her head lolled against the window.

It had been a good day. A necessary day. Liv had been foolish for wasting the last three years trying to parent the "right" way when really she should have just been spending time getting to know Taylor without her father between them. Liv vowed that she wasn't going to pass those chances up anymore. She was being given a gift, the opportunity to create something lasting with Taylor, something that would bond them together in a way that even loss hadn't.

Liv was feeling thoroughly sentimental by the time she pulled through the gate at their house. The installer's truck was gone, but Charlie's still stood where they'd left it. She parked right beside it and reached over to gently shake Taylor's arm. "Tay, we're home."

Taylor started awake, blinking groggily around her. "Already?"

"Yeah, you slept the whole way. You sure you're getting enough sleep?"

"Mmmph," she mumbled, rubbing her eyes automatically and then scowling when her fist came away smeared with black. "I'm fine. It was just hot today." She grabbed her studded handbag and half-fell out of the passenger door before stumbling sleepily up the walkway.

Liv grinned to herself. She grabbed her own purse, retrieved their laptops from their hiding place in the cargo area, and then crossed the yard to their front door.

"Tay, I have your laptop," she called as she kicked off her shoes and rounded the corner. And then stopped short.

Charlie looked up from where he was working, a trowel in hand, his arms dotted with white. "You're back! I was hoping to finish before you got home."

Liv opened and closed her mouth like a fish a few times. The countertops had been installed and they were even more beautiful than she'd expected: gleaming white around the perimeter, gorgeous natural stone on the big island. And on the far side of the kitchen, starting at the pantry and wrapping its way around to the exterior wall was a swath of dove gray glass tile in a vertical running bond pattern.

"Charlie, this is . . . I don't know what to say."

Taylor dropped her purse and bent over the island, spreading her arms wide as if she could span the entire run of stone. "It's so pretty I just want to hug it."

Liv laughed. "I think that says it all."

"You're happy then?"

"So pretty," Taylor mumbled. Then her phone buzzed in her pocket and she straightened abruptly. "Gotta take this. Thanks, Charlie! It looks great!" And before they could say another word, she was down the hall, her phone pressed to her ear.

Charlie looked at her. "How about you? Are you happy?"

Unexpectedly, tears came to her eyes, and Liv had to swallow down a lump in her throat. "Yeah, I'm very happy. It felt like it was never going to happen."

Charlie cocked his head to study her, then set aside the trowel and peeled off his gloves. "What's wrong? I hope those are happy tears."

Liv bit her lip and swallowed. "Don't worry, they are."

But Charlie didn't seem to buy it. He crossed the space between them without hesitation and enfolded her in his arms. "Somehow I don't believe that. Tell me."

She was so surprised that she didn't move for a second. And then her arms went around his waist, her cheek pressed against his chest. He was warm and strong, and he smelled of fresh laundry detergent and faintly chemical mastic and a pleasant scent that she had come to realize was just him. And in that moment, she felt suddenly, inexplicably safe.

Which was probably why the tears began sliding down her cheeks and a sob slipped from her lips.

Charlie brought up a hand to stroke her hair, the other one holding her more tightly against him as she cried. In the moment, it didn't strike her as strange when he pressed a kiss to her hair, whispered in her ear. "It's okay. This has probably been a long time in coming."

It was only seconds later—when she realized that she was crying on a virtual stranger for reasons that she couldn't even define—that she tried to pull back. Charlie didn't try to keep her, just let her slip away. She focused on the damp spot she'd left on his dark T-shirt. "I'm sorry. I got you all wet."

He didn't look down. "It's okay. You want to talk about it?"

"I . . ." She shook her head. "I don't even know why I did that. It's just been . . . a lot lately."

"Come on." Charlie reached out a hand, and without thinking, she took it. "Let's talk outside."

In the shadow of the house, the air had begun to cool, even though the day's warmth still lingered. He led her around to the bistro table and chairs on the little cement pad outside his apartment door, pulled out a chair for her before he took the one opposite. And then he just waited.

Liv wasn't even sure what to say. Wasn't sure how to articulate the swirling, complicated feelings in her. For well over a year, she'd stared at that stupid unfinished kitchen, feeling like a failure. The house was a project that she and Jason had started, had intended to finish together. She'd continued it as a sign that she and Taylor could get along without him. And then it had gotten stalled, and as time passed, it had become like a festering wound, something that would never quite heal. A reminder that she really wasn't up to this job that she'd been left with, that she was failing on every count. And then to walk into the room and see it almost finished, just as she and her husband had discussed, only he wasn't there to share it with her? How did she put something like that into words?

Except it seemed like she didn't need to. Charlie watched her silently for a long moment, then said softly, "I hope I haven't overstepped."

She jerked her eyes to his face. "Why would you say that?"

"Because it wasn't supposed to be me doing this."

Liv shook her head. "It wasn't. But that's hardly your fault. I really appreciate you stepping in. I didn't realize how much it nagged at me every time I walked through the house."

"But . . . ?"

She shook her head. "There is no but."

"Then why the tears? I may not be the most sensitive guy on the planet, but I can tell the difference between happy and sad tears."

In her book, that did make him the most sensitive guy on the planet, or maybe she just wasn't used to it because Jason had always regarded her tears as a puzzle to be worked out. Hadn't understood half the time why she reacted the way she did. She took a deep breath and let it out in a huff. "It isn't about the kitchen, not really. It's just been a lot lately. I gave up a job I loved to stay here with Taylor to give her some stability. And I don't regret it. But my late husband's stamp is all over this place. It was his idea to buy it and renovate it. His dream, really. And all the unfinished stuff is just a reminder that I shouldn't be doing this without him. I shouldn't be raising his daughter without him, and quite frankly, doing a pretty terrible job of it."

She expected him to jump in, contradict her words, but he just watched her silently, letting her talk.

"But it's still been okay. Because Taylor was my priority. Making a good life for her, making sure she's okay. And then we started talking about college today and I realized in less than two years, she'll be gone. And I will be completely, utterly alone." She drew in a long breath and let it out in a shuddering stream. "Sometimes I feel like I've already lived my entire life. Married, widowed, raised a teenager, sent her off to college, only to find myself alone again."

Charlie seemed to be taking it in, thinking about it. "I can't imagine what that's like. You have Taylor, but in some ways that's even more lonely, because she's a responsibility and not a companion."

"Yeah," Liv said softly. "That's exactly it."

"But I do know what it's like to be alone."

Liv studied him for a second, really looked at him without the lens of attraction or resistance. Beyond looks, beyond his aura of capability, there was a warmth to him, something that somehow signaled that he was a good, reliable person. Even if she couldn't quantify it, she'd known it the minute she met him. She wouldn't have let him stay in her apartment, spend time around Taylor, if she hadn't known that he was trustworthy. Which made the fact he was single all the more confusing.

"You've never been married?" she asked.

He shook his head slowly. "No. Came close a couple of times."

"What happened?"

"First time was in my twenties. My college girlfriend, Fiona, and I talked about it, thought we might do it. But in the end, she wanted to travel and I wanted to start my life here. We came to an agreement that she would spend six months in Europe while I built my business. And then she'd come back, we'd get married, start a family."

"And?"

Charlie threw her a wry look. "She never came back. Met some guy in France, got a work visa. Last I heard, she's still there, raising a couple of French babies."

Liv grimaced. "Ouch. Were you crushed?"

"Not as much as I should have been. It wouldn't have lasted anyway. I'm not sure she would have been happy with me long term." He threw her

258

another self-deprecating look. "I'm a simple man with simple desires, and that would never have been enough for her."

When Liv was in her twenties, that statement would have been a red flag for her, too. Simple was never what she wanted for herself. But at thirty-one, living in a tiny town with a small life, she could understand why that would appeal to someone. "You said 'a couple of times.' "

"Yeah. Dated another woman after Fiona for about two years. She'd been divorced already at the age of twenty-five. Wasn't really sure she wanted to settle down again. I thought that would be enough for me—a committed long-term relationship, regardless of what a piece of paper said—but it turned out that it wasn't." He shrugged, though a bit of humor lit his eyes. "This simple man wanted the piece of paper."

She smiled a little, saw the answering lift of his mouth. "Was that it?"

"Oh no. Relationship disasters come in threes. I was seriously involved with a woman last year. Her name was Kyra. I'd started looking at rings, planning a proposal. Turns out the whole time my best friend and business partner was defrauding my clients, he was also having an affair with my girlfriend. Last I heard, they were living the good life in Ecuador, on my money." He smiled, but there was pain in his eyes. Of all the three, that one had hurt the most.

Liv lifted her hand to her mouth. "I'm so sorry. That's awful." She straightened. "But if you don't mind me saying, none of the three seemed worth your time."

"That's what everyone says." He shrugged. "I suppose I'd rather them decide that they didn't want the life I could give them up front than figure it out after we got married."

There was wisdom in those words, but something about it ruffled her feathers, made her forget about her own pain. "Yeah, but how is it your responsibility to *give* them a life? Isn't that the point of marriage? To build something together? I mean, they should be happy that you're the kind of man who stands by his word, that you're not the vindictive sort. I'd be tempted to hunt them down in Ecuador and . . ." She shook her head, words failing her. "I don't know what I'd do, but you're being kinder than they deserve."

"Trust me, I spent plenty of time on revenge fantasies. Swore that I'd never get close enough to anyone to be hurt again. But I've realized that only punishes me, not them. If you live your life always trying to protect yourself from pain, you miss out on all the joy, too."

Liv studied him silently, inwardly marveling at the strength it must take to maintain that outlook. To even consider trusting her after he'd been so badly betrayed. But the words also somehow eased a bit of the ever-present ache inside her.

Jason hadn't been perfect; he'd driven her crazy at times, and if she was being fully honest, part of her was still angry that he'd gotten into the plane that day. That he'd made a choice that had brought about his own death. But she didn't regret a minute of the time they'd had together. He'd loved her, wholly and sweetly, and she was better for having known him.

Charlie deserved to have that same experience. It was hard to believe that three women could get to know the man that she was sitting across from and not know, without a doubt, that he was one of the good ones. One of the ones worth struggling with and for.

Right now, he seemed to be expecting an answer to his comment. She pushed herself back in her chair and stood. "Thank you. I think I needed to hear that."

"What are friends for?" he quipped.

But that made her pause. "Is that what we are? Friends?"

She expected him to say something like, *Of course*. Or, *if you'd like to be*. But instead, he looked at her with those sky-gray eyes, dead serious, his voice a little huskier than usual when he said, "I'll be whatever you'll let me be."

The words hit her in the gut like a shotgun slug, mentally staggering her back. There was no mistaking the intention in those words, the offer. He wasn't pulling punches anymore. And even though she could barely breathe, didn't know how to feel about what he had just implied, she managed to keep herself from brushing off the offer. The invitation.

Instead, she held his eyes and gave a slow nod. Her voice came out a touch too breathy. "Noted."

And then she turned and walked back into the house.

CHAPTER TWENTY

Liv barely slept that night and it was all Charlie's fault.

She kept replaying that last moment with him over and over in her mind. The serious, intent way he had fixed his attention on her when he'd said, *I'll be whatever you'll let me be.* His voice warm and hoarse and filled with promise. A promise that kept bringing to mind all the delicious scenarios that would be possible should she decide she could be something more to him than just a client or a landlord.

It was those scenarios that had her tossing and turning in her bed, fluttery and overheated in a way that even the lack of air conditioning in the old brick house couldn't explain.

She could no longer run from the truth. She'd gone from powerfully attracted to infatuated in a little over a week, and it was not one-sided. All it would take was a single signal to him that she was willing and interested to take their acquaintance to the next level and there would be no stopping them.

And she wanted to. Oh, how she wanted to. It wasn't just because she found him attractive—his capability and intelligence, his rough edges. It was how kind he was, how patient. The fact that he'd openly shared his past relationship failures with her, explained without shame why he was still single, trusting her to understand. The way he seemed to get her guilt and her hesitation. Part of the reason she'd been so hesitant to date—besides the fact she wasn't ready—was because she felt the pressure to assure someone else that she no longer loved her husband, no longer missed him.

She wasn't sure she'd ever be able to say that. Jason would always be a part of her life. Unlike people whose relationships ended in divorce, who had some sort of closure, who could point to the reasons it had ended, all she had was bad luck and fate. If only one of them had done something different. If only Jason had decided to go hiking that day instead of flying.

If only she hadn't been consumed with the manuscript she was editing and agreed to go to Salida for the day with him and Taylor. If only she hadn't suggested that he take Taylor up in the plane with him so she could have a little peace and quiet.

Those last words more than anything else haunted her. It was bad enough that her husband had died because she was too busy for him. Even worse that, had he listened to her, she would have sent her stepdaughter to her death as well.

Hot tears slid from the corners of Liv's eyes to wet her pillow, the whiplash from longing to guilt almost painful in its sharp crack.

Rationally, she knew she wasn't responsible for any of it. Jason often took up his Piper on the weekend when she was busy and sometimes when she wasn't. Many days she came along. More than a few times, he took Taylor with him. She'd had no way of knowing that this time wouldn't be like all those other times. That when she'd absently kissed him goodbye and then turned back to her computer, it was the last time that she'd ever see him.

It just didn't stop her from replaying the memories in her mind, going over every detail, as if by analyzing them, she could convince herself that she couldn't have done anything different. Every innocent decision she made each day could have disastrous consequences. Letting Taylor drive herself to school instead of making her ride the school bus. Letting her go to town with a friend's parent instead of driving her herself.

She knew that. So why was she constantly torturing herself with the past?

Liv rolled over onto her side and dragged Jason's pillow against her, wrapping her arms around it as she hugged it to her middle. It had long since stopped smelling like him, but she still kept it there, even though it was flat and old and made the bed look lopsided next to her fluffy new one.

"I miss you," she whispered out loud. "And yet I feel guilty that I don't miss you as much as I should."

They'd had three years together. One dating, two married. A tenth of her life. *Only* a tenth of her life. Sometimes, she had to look at pictures to remember exactly what his smile looked like. Or watch old videos on her phone to recall the exact cadence of his speech or the way his laugh always seemed like it was cut off at the end. And sometimes, she caught herself feeling glad that she didn't have to pick up the workout clothes that he always left on the tile floor of the bathroom or that she could watch a movie without him explaining all the ways that the writers had gotten the tech aspects wrong. That she could cook with as much spice as she wanted without being concerned it was going to give him indigestion.

Jason was fading with each day and she was helping it along by reminding herself of the small things that she didn't miss about him.

She would never think that she was better off without him, but remembering that he wasn't perfect made it easier to face each day alone. Allowed her to pretend sometimes that it was preferable to be alone, even though that belief never truly made it past her head into her heart.

She didn't want to be alone. But she didn't want to fill the space with just anyone, either.

She wanted to roll over in bed and see the man she loved smiling at her, to have him reach for her, still sleepy and warm from their blankets.

To drink coffee silently at the table and let their eyes speak for them, testament to an easy companionship that only people who were completely secure in their love for each other could share. And she definitely didn't want to give up sex for good—she was way too young to flip that switch.

But in order to ever have any of that again, she had to take a chance.

She just couldn't yet tell if Charlie was the one she needed to take a chance *on*.

She finally fell asleep just before dawn, when the sky started to lighten from midnight blue to dusty gray, the bare shimmer of dawn sliding around the edges of her bedroom blinds. She slept deeply, and if not dreamlessly, without the nightmares that sometimes plagued her when she thought too much about the past. So much so that when she woke up, she had no idea where she was or what day it was.

Slowly, Liv pushed herself up in bed, blinking at the pillow crumpled beside her, her eyes gritty and swollen. She didn't think she'd been crying, but it had been a long, strange night, the thoughts she'd wrestled with for hours already fading in the face of daylight.

Coffee. She needed coffee. Groggily, she swung her feet over the side of the bed, thrust them into her slippers, and nearly buckled when she stood up. Apparently her legs had forgotten how to work. Still bleary, she shuffled down the hallway, shoving her messy hair out of her eyes.

And found herself face to face with Charlie.

Liv stumbled back, startled, one foot coming out of her slipper in her shock. He reached out to steady her, set her back on her feet. He was dressed in his usual jeans and T-shirt, though his hair was still a bit damp from the shower and the smell of fresh soap and shampoo wafted off him. It was all she could do, even through her shock, not to fill her lungs with his scent.

"What are you doing here?" she finally managed. "How did you get in?"

"Taylor let me in. She's in her room now. I hope I didn't wake you up. I figured you needed your sleep."

"What time is it anyway?"

"Ten."

Ten. No wonder Taylor had let him in. He was supposed to be finishing the backsplash today. "Is there any coffee?"

"Over on the table." He gestured with his head to the dining room table, where the coffee maker was indeed plugged into an extension cord, an almost-full pot on the warmer. When his eyes flicked back to her, doing a quick, involuntary once-over before returning to her face, she looked down.

And realized that she was clad only in silky shorts and a camisole top that showed much more of her skin than she would ever display in public.

Liv barely kept from crossing her arms over her chest, which would only draw attention to the display. To his credit, he was doing a respectable job of keeping his eyes on her face.

"Clothes first," she said, trying her best to act like her cheeks were not burning in embarrassment. "Then coffee."

"Probably a good idea." The corner of his mouth twisted, a sure sign that he was trying not to laugh.

With as much dignity as she could summon, she turned and walked back to her room, trying not to focus on the possibility that he was watching her butt and the full expanse of leg displayed by her shorts as she left.

No, scratch that. Trying not to enjoy the fact that she *knew* he was staring.

She shut and locked her door—unnecessarily— while she searched for something to throw on, then realized that she hadn't yet done laundry this week. Workout wear then. A sports bra contained the girls without emphasizing them, the shorts and performance fabric T-shirt were anything but seductive. She quickly gathered her hair into a ponytail, splashed water on her face, and brushed her teeth. She had herself almost fooled into casualness before she caught a glimpse of her own face in the mirror—color high, eyes sparkling.

The woman who stared back at her looked more alive than she had in the past three years.

She went out in bare feet, where Charlie was back to work, leaning across the countertop as he used a float to force grout between the tiles. She let herself appreciate the view for a moment—turnabout was fair play, and besides, he did have a very nice butt—before she brushed past him to get a coffee mug out of the cabinet.

He didn't turn to look at her. "Pastries on the table."

"Pastries?"

Now he did look, and his eyes were sparkling in a way that made her think he had very much enjoyed that earlier encounter. "Chocolate croissants."

"My favorite."

"I know." He grinned at her and troweled another dollop of grout onto the float. "Gemma told me."

"She did, did she?" Liv didn't even try to quash the hint of flirtation in her voice. "What else did she tell you?"

Now he turned and leaned against the counter, hands braced against the stone top. "She told me that you were the best person she'd ever met, and if I hurt you, she'd make sure that I regretted it."

Liv snorted with laughter. "That would be Gemma for you. She's very protective."

"I've noticed. But I told her that she had

nothing to worry about. If there was anyone at risk of getting hurt in this equation, it was me."

Liv's breath stilled in her chest for a long second. It took her even longer to find her words. "Charlie—"

"It's okay," he said, turning back to his grouting. "You don't need to say anything. I've made it very clear where I stand on this subject. But don't worry. I can be patient."

He didn't seem to expect an answer, so she went to the coffee pot and poured herself a cup, then flipped open the pastry box behind it. She wondered if Gemma was sending a message with these croissants, that she approved of Charlie's interest in Liv. She didn't just give away personal information—not even pastry preferences—for no reason.

Liv seated herself at the table and ripped a piece off one of the croissants, sighing in pleasure at the first taste of bittersweet chocolate and flaky pastry, crackling sweet with caramelized sugar. After a few sips of coffee, she felt coherent enough to ask questions. "So what's the timeline here?"

"I'm going to be finished with the tile this morning. I'll come back tomorrow to finish the caulking in the corners and next to the cabinets."

"What about the bookstore?"

"If you're ready to start tomorrow, I can schedule a dumpster."

"Let me make sure Will countersigned the lease." It was a convenient excuse to stay in the room without just sitting there and staring at Charlie while he finished tiling the back wall, which was going shockingly fast. She booted up her computer and opened her email. There was indeed a message, but it was the automated one telling her he'd signed the document. Nothing else. No personal note, no good luck message.

Their friendship, if he'd ever truly thought of it that way, was over.

The realization came with a fleeting sense of disappointment, but as she looked at Charlie, she knew it had been the right decision. "It's official. The place is mine. Let's get started."

He might be the stupidest man alive.

That was the only thing Charlie could think of as he swiftly finished grouting the backsplash, knowing that the minute he was done, he'd have no excuse to be in Liv's presence for the rest of the day. Even from across the room where she was buried in her computer, he swore he could pick up the slightly floral scent of her shampoo, making him want to move nearer. It had been bad enough when he'd had only the suspicion that there was not an inch of her that wasn't beautiful; today's confirmation only made him want to touch her that much more. He'd already been daydreaming about kissing her. If he wasn't careful, that daydream would turn into thoughts of a lot more, and then the pleasure of being in her presence would be more like torture.

No, scratch that, it was already torture. And one that he'd willingly signed up for. Rather than giving himself the opportunity to pursue her, to woo her, he'd just stated his intentions. And she'd barely responded. The ball now was so far in her court that he wasn't sure he'd ever be able to find it again.

Except he was pretty sure that she was stealing covert looks at him from across the room when his back was turned.

Still, when he finished grouting the last stretch of tile, it wasn't without a sense of regret. "Finished," he said, straightening and pulling off his gloves. He took a wet rag and wiped up an errant smear of grout from her new countertops and stepped back to admire his work. The tile really was beautiful, the traditional shape and material taking on a fresh look from the modern pattern they'd chosen. Liv pushed away from the table and came to stand beside him, cocking her head while she considered.

It was everything he could do not to touch her. Instead, he settled for inhaling her scent, his skin prickling with her nearness.

"It looks great," she said finally, smiling up at him. "Really beautiful. Thank you."

That smile hit straight to his heart, and he

glanced away before she could read it in his eyes. "You're welcome."

"I almost can't believe this is my house," she murmured. "It felt like it was never going to get finished."

"Lucky I came along then," he said, just for something to say.

But her tone was thoughtful. "Yeah. Lucky." She cleared her throat and took a step away from him. "So tomorrow? We're going to start cleaning out the inside of the bookstore?"

"Yeah. That's the plan." Now everything had started to feel awkward. "I have another job this afternoon in town, but I was wondering—"

"Did you leave me any croissants?" Taylor strode into the kitchen, then stopped when she saw the two of them standing close. "Am I interrupting something?"

"No, not at all," Liv said hurriedly, putting some space between them. "And yes, there are plenty of croissants. I only ate one." She narrowed her eyes at her stepdaughter and pointed a finger at her, mock-severe. "But you better not eat them all. Last time I brought them home, you ate the entire box."

"I promise." Taylor gave her a sunny smile and crossed her chest with her finger. "I did kind of want to talk to you about something . . ." Her eyes flicked to Charlie, a sure sign that he'd overstayed his welcome.

"Let me just get my things and I'll get out of your way." He took his trowels and sponges and dropped them into an empty bucket, along with the mostly-empty pail of grout. "I'll see you in the morning."

"I will try to be conscious before noon," Liv said wryly, but the smile she gave him was open and appreciative. "Thank you again, Charlie."

He dipped his head, picked up his stuff, and made his way to the door. Of course Taylor would have interrupted him when he was about to ask her to dinner, but maybe that was for the best. He'd already put himself out there and she hadn't responded with anything but a smile. Clearly, Liv wasn't ready for him to actually pursue her. And Taylor might be tolerating him, but he had no way of knowing what she would say if he started dating her stepmother. All it would take is some disquiet from the teen and Liv would run so far and fast from him that he'd be lucky to glimpse her as he left his apartment, let alone ever be in the same room with her again.

He let himself out of the house and started the walk across the yard to his apartment. But as he did, the crunch of gravel beneath tires drew his attention to the gate at the end of the drive, where a nondescript white sedan had come to rest. A jitter began in his stomach, a warning he didn't quite understand. Slowly, he returned to the house and poked his head in through the front door.

"Liv?" he called. "There's someone at your gate."

A moment later, the door jerked wide open and Liv stepped out, Taylor following her. Liv frowned in confusion, but it was the look of anticipation on Taylor's face that inexplicably filled him with dread. Liv looked at her stepdaughter. "Are you expecting someone?"

"Yeah. That was kind of what I was trying to tell you."

Beyond the gate, a thin, dark-haired woman climbed out of the driver's seat and peered at them.

Taylor's gaze flicked to Charlie before they landed on Liv again. "That's my mom."

CHAPTER TWENTY-ONE

Liv must have heard Taylor wrong. "Your mom," she repeated, her voice flat. "I don't understand."

The woman lifted a hand and waved. "Hi! Am I in the right place? I'm looking for Taylor Quinn."

Taylor shifted from foot to foot, her face a picture of excitement. "Are you going to let her in?"

Liv's thoughts came slow as molasses, barely flowing with her confusion. "I don't understand. What is your mom doing here? When . . . how?"

Taylor sighed, obviously impatient with how slowly Liv was catching on to this situation and marched down the drive toward the car, where she stopped and punched the code into the inside keypad. Slowly, the gate swung open. As Liv watched, Taylor slipped through, approaching the visitor tentatively. They exchanged a few words and then the woman enfolded her in a tight, fierce hug.

Liv felt like the ground had shifted beneath her feet.

"Whoa." Charlie reached out and steadied her, and when she didn't immediately respond, slipped an arm around her waist. "Are you okay?"

"No," she whispered while her mind spun

through all the things that Jason had told her about Taylor's birth mom, Maggie. The drug addiction. The frequent absences. The failed treatment programs. And eventually, the abandonment of her husband and daughter. They hadn't heard from Maggie in so long that Liv had started to wonder if she'd died of a drug overdose. Or even started over with a new family, leaving her old one behind.

"Breathe," Charlie murmured in her ear, and the reminder made her suck in a lungful of air. It steadied her a little, but she didn't try to pull away from him. Right now, she needed all the support she could get.

Maggie was climbing into her car, and Taylor was running back up the drive like a little girl, so excited it was painful to watch. As she neared, Charlie said, "I'm going to leave you alone now. But you know where I am if you need me."

"No." Liv's hand shot out of its own accord to grip Charlie's arm, her fingernails leaving little half-moon indentations on his tanned skin. "Please. Stay. I can't give you the whole background right now, but I don't know what to expect from her. She is—was—a heroin addict."

Charlie's expression flashed through surprise to determination, and he placed his hand over hers and squeezed. "I'll stay then. But I'll keep out of the way."

The white car—a rental, it seemed, from the

fleet plates—pulled to a stop right in front of the house's entry, off the parking pad. The woman stepped out, a tentative smile on her face. Slowly, she approached Liv with her hand outstretched. "Hi. I'm Maggie Quinn."

Hearing Jason's surname attached to this woman who had abandoned her family brought an equal pang of sickness and anger to Liv's gut, but she responded automatically, taking the woman's offered hand. She'd always pictured Maggie as a strung-out junkie, but she'd never actually stopped to think what Jason might have seen in her when he married her.

Maggie Quinn was beautiful, and Liv could instantly see the resemblance to Taylor. High cheekbones, pale skin, glossy dark brown hair. She was still thin, but in a chic, healthy way, like someone who took care of her body and ran marathons for fun, not someone who would rather consume drugs than food.

All this must have flashed over her face in those few seconds, because Maggie grimaced as Liv withdrew her hand. "I take it this is all a surprise to you. I'm really sorry to just show up. Taylor had said she was going to talk to you beforehand."

"I was," Taylor said in a rush, beaming at her mother, her expression something just short of worship. "You just got here a little earlier than I expected. And Liv got up late."

It was an innocent comment, but the quick glance that Maggie gave her struck her to the core, as if she was assessing Liv's fitness as a guardian. Liv's face flamed.

"Why don't we go inside?" Charlie suggested. "I can put a new pot of coffee on."

Maggie focused on him and gave him a cautious smile. "And you are?"

"Oh." Charlie held out his hand and shook Maggie's. "I'm Charlie Castro. I'm a friend of the family."

"I see." Another appraising glance at Liv—this time probably wondering if she had a live-in boyfriend. Liv's stomach sank even further. She really couldn't blame Charlie for stepping in, given how she was gaping at the virtual stranger in their midst rather than acting like a proper hostess. But part of her resented the fact that he'd invited this *woman* into her house without asking her.

Calm down, she told herself. Taylor obviously has been in contact with her for a while. She invited her. You need to be cordial and accepting, if only for Taylor's sake.

"Come in," Taylor said, pushing the door open and gesturing to Maggie. "We're just finishing up the kitchen."

Liv and Charlie trailed behind the other two, Taylor's excited chatter about the house drifting to them from the inside. Just before they stepped in, Charlie held her back, put a comforting hand on her shoulder.

"I'm going to stay out of this. But I'm here if you need me. Okay?"

In that moment, she was grateful for his steady presence. He slid his hand down her arm and squeezed her fingers, then moved it to her lower back to steady her as she walked into what now felt like a war zone.

But as soon as she made it into the kitchen, Liv put on her game face, hoping that she didn't look as rigid as she felt. "Would you like to take a seat in the living room?"

"Sure, thank you." Maggie smiled at Liv and moved into the attached living space, taking the nearest spot—Liv's spot—and seating herself gracefully. Liv circled around and sank down onto the edge of the other sofa while Taylor sat near her mom.

"So, as you can probably tell, this is quite a surprise. How did you and Taylor get back in touch?"

"Facebook, actually," Maggie said. Her voice was perfectly calm, but she was twisting the edge of her shirt between two fingers—the first sign that she felt as awkward as Liv did. "It was kind of strange. Taylor popped up as a suggested friend. At first, I couldn't believe it was her. But then I saw her location was Haven Ridge and I knew it had to be her. So I sent her a friend request."

Liv nodded, even though every word felt like a knife to her chest. She couldn't even think coherently with all the feelings coursing through her. So her only reply was completely inane, and a lie as well. "I didn't know you were on Facebook, Taylor."

"Yeah, I made a profile so I could set up a business page for the bookstore, remember? I only have a few friends, because let's face it, it's for old people."

Maggie and Liv's eyes met above Taylor's head in unison, a shared moment of amusement before Liv could shut down any feeling of commiseration with this woman. It all made sense now, though. Taylor's secrecy, her even more constant attachment to her phone than usual, the way that she slipped out of the room to take secret calls. Now Liv wished she'd pressed her stepdaughter more. She would have at least had a heads-up that this was coming, instead of being steamrolled by Maggie's appearance.

"I . . ." Liv shook her head and decided to speak plainly. "I can't lie to you, Maggie. This is a shock. And not a pleasant one."

Taylor gave Liv a fierce look that clearly said *don't embarrass me*.

"You gave up your parental rights a long time before I came along. I didn't even know you were still alive. And now you've showed up, I'm assuming to be part of Taylor's life? You're going to have to give me a minute to adjust to this. Because frankly, you can't blame me for being taken aback, if not outright suspicious."

Liv braced herself for Maggie's retort, but the woman only looked at her sadly. "I deserve that and more. Frankly, I'm grateful you even invited me in. I wouldn't have blamed you—and Taylor—for telling me to go away. I just want you to know that I'm not trying to mess things up here. Taylor has told me that she's happy living in Haven Ridge. She told me about the bookstore, which sounds like a dream come true. Really, I just want to get to know her. I am her mother."

You lost your right to call yourself that when you left her, Liv wanted to say, but she held it back. Because despite her possessiveness and her fear, Maggie was right. She was Taylor's mother. She had a bond with the teen that Liv could never reproduce, one of blood and not of law. And even though she wasn't inclined to think charitably about Maggie, Liv also knew that the addiction wasn't entirely her fault. Jason had told her about the car accident and subsequent spinal fusion that had caused Maggie so much pain that she was on heavy opiate painkillers for months. And when the doctors had abruptly withdrawn the pills, she'd had to go elsewhere for them. First to friends with pills left over from dental procedures and surgeries, then high schoolers selling them in the playground, and when those sources dried up, heroin from street hustlers. Liv was not without her sympathy for the situation. But she was also not prepared to hand Taylor over to someone who had chosen drugs over her own kid.

"You understand why I'm cautious," Liv said quietly. "My first responsibility is Taylor's well-being."

Maggie clasped her hands in front of her earnestly. "And I would hope for nothing less. You have every right to be suspicious. But I will tell you that I've been clean for six years. I am an office manager for a company that rents heavy machinery in Wichita. All I want is the chance to spend a little time with my daughter."

Taylor beamed at her mother, then turned to Liv with pleading eyes. "Please, Liv."

What was she going to say? Taylor had obviously timed this one so Liv had no choice but to relent. They'd have a conversation about that bit of manipulation later. But timing aside, would Liv really have refused Taylor the opportunity to see her mother? Did she really have the *right* to deny her access to the woman that gave her birth?

"Of course you can spend some time with your daughter," Liv said, and both Maggie and Taylor heaved a sigh of relief. "In fact, why don't we all have lunch together, so we can get to know each other?"

"Oh, well, I—" Taylor began, but as soon

as she saw the look that Liv leveled at her, she broke off.

Maggie seemed to pick up on where Liv was going with this and gave her a tentative smile. "That would be wonderful. Taylor has told me a lot about Haven Ridge. Maybe you could show me around? I'd love to see this bookstore space that you're going to be working on, too."

"Of course. We'd be delighted to show you." Liv stood and wiped her sweaty palms on her shorts. "Are you staying nearby?"

Maggie got to her feet as well, and Taylor followed a moment later. "I have a vacation rental in Salida for the week."

"Oh, but we have room—" Taylor began.

Maggie immediately shook her head. "No, Liv's right, Taylor. We should get to know each other first. Besides, I've already paid for the place and I would hate for a hot tub to go to waste."

Taylor's eyes lit up at the mention of the hot tub, even though there was one outside on their patio that never got used. Liv gave her a quick shake of the head before she could even ask the question. "We'll talk about everything later, Taylor."

"Okay." Taylor grabbed Maggie's hand like a little girl. "Before we go, I want to show you my room. I designed it myself."

Maggie glanced quickly at Liv for permission— which she grudgingly appreciated—and she nodded. The woman allowed her daughter to pull her down the hall to show off her room.

Liv took a long, deep breath and closed her eyes. When she opened them, Charlie was standing next to her, rubbing gentle circles on her back. "Are you okay?"

Liv started to say *yes,* but she reversed course. "No. Not even remotely. I don't like the fact she thought it was okay to come out here without even talking to me. I don't trust her."

She expected Charlie to tell her that she was just being jealous, but he nodded slowly. "Go with your instincts then. Even if you can't do anything but supervise and watch for warning signs. Can you do a background check?"

The thought had already crossed her mind, but without a social security number, there was nothing Liv could do with her resources. But she thought she knew someone who could. "No. But we have connections in the sheriff's department. I'll see what I can do."

"Good. And in the meantime, I'm here if you need me."

"Thank you," she whispered. He smiled sadly into her face and trailed his thumb across her cheekbone. Any other time, it probably would have sent a shiver through her, but now she felt so numb she was just glad for the warmth of his touch, any touch. "Are you going to come to lunch with us?"

"Can't," he said. "But I can make a quick stop at the bakery and let Gemma know what's going on if you want."

Voices reached them again as Maggie and Taylor returned from the bedroom. She would rather text Gemma herself but there was no way to do it without being conspicuous. She gave Charlie a quick nod and squeezed his hand before she moved out to meet them.

"So," she said brightly to Taylor. "What do you think? Should we introduce Maggie to the Brick House Cafe?"

Half an hour later, they walked into the Brick House Cafe, and Liv immediately regretted having chosen the location. She'd done it because it *wasn't* neutral—it was a place that she and Taylor frequented often, so it felt like home turf—but she'd underestimated the heads that would turn in their direction when they walked in with an unfamiliar woman.

An unfamiliar woman whom Taylor resembled so strongly it was almost impossible not to know that it was her real mother.

It was Thomas behind the counter this morning with one of his teen employees, Madeline, for which Liv was grateful. Not because she didn't love Mallory, but because the woman would immediately start giving Liv sympathetic looks and she was barely keeping it together as it was.

The ride to town in Liv's SUV had been torture, listening to Taylor catch Maggie up on the last ten years she'd missed as if it had been an accident that she'd been a ghost in her daughter's life. By the time they drove down Dogwood Street and found a spot in front of the cafe, Liv's nerves were strung so tightly that someone could have played a sonata on them.

So when Thomas just gave a neutral smile and asked pleasantly, "Three?" she was immeasurably grateful she didn't have to answer any questions.

Until Taylor chirped, "Hey Thomas. This is my real mom, Maggie. She's here from Kansas for a visit."

Thomas smiled and dipped his head in greeting. "Nice to meet you, Maggie. You can all follow me."

The man led them to the back through a gauntlet of curious looks and seated them in the booth that Liv and Taylor had occupied the day before. Not surprisingly, Taylor slid into the booth next to Maggie, their backs to the window, leaving the bench opposite for Liv. She sat down and accepted the menu from Thomas, who was maintaining his neutral formality. But just before he walked away to get their drinks, he gave her a slightly wide-eyed, lifted-eyebrow look that told her he knew exactly what was going on and was sorry for it.

"So what's good here?" Maggie asked, her

voice conspicuously light, as if she were as determined as Liv to pretend that this was all normal and fine.

"Pretty much everything," Liv said, before Taylor cut in. "The cheeseburger is amazing. Best burger you'll ever have."

They were pretty good, but Liv recognized the almost manic tinge to Taylor's voice, filed away the warning that said the girl was desperate to make this work. Liv needed the reminder that this situation wasn't about her. It affected her, sure, but no matter how much Taylor tried to pretend that it was an everyday occurrence to reconnect with the woman that had given birth to her, been largely absent through her addiction, and then disappeared for a decade, it was anything but. No doubt the girl thought if she was interesting and entertaining enough, Maggie would stick around.

And if Maggie did stick around, if that was truly what Taylor wanted, Liv would have to be okay with it.

She really wanted to bury her head in her arms at the table, but instead, she maintained her pleasant demeanor and perused the menu. A few minutes later, when Thomas came back to take their orders—a cheeseburger for Maggie and Taylor and a chef salad for Liv, who knew she wouldn't be able to choke down more than a few bites—she decided that she was going to make an effort. She folded her arms in front of her and made her expression open. "So, Maggie, you said you lived in Kansas. That's a long way from New York. How did you end up there?"

Maggie shifted uncomfortably, sending a quick look at Taylor. "That's kind of a long and involved story. I actually lived in Milwaukee for a few years, and I worked as a customer service rep for a company in the same industry. They bought this other company, whose headquarters was located in Wichita, and I moved there when this job opened." She grimaced, as if she didn't want to continue, but to her credit, she looked Liv straight in the eye. "Milwaukee was expensive for me, especially given my history. It was hard to get a well-paying job at most companies, so I was grateful for this position. I've been there for about three years now."

Liv nodded slowly, wondering if she was properly understanding the subtext. Maggie probably had a felony drug conviction—or more than one—that made it difficult for her to pass the background checks required by higher-paying jobs. Liv seemed to remember Jason telling her that before the whole drug thing, Maggie had been a legal secretary with aspirations of law school. Clearly those dreams had never come to pass.

The thought sent a pang of sympathy into Liv, which she immediately resented.

"And you're just here to visit for the week? Did

you have plans while you were here?" Might as well get straight to the point.

"Well, I was kind of hoping that I could spend the week with Taylor. Assuming you didn't already have plans."

Liv opened her mouth, but Taylor beat her to it. "We're going to start cleaning out the bookstore to begin the renovations. You could help if you want. There's a lot of work, and we could use another pair of hands."

This time, the words were like a blow to Liv's chest. The bookstore was their project, hers and Taylor's, a way for them to bond, to solidify their shaky relationship. And now she wanted to bring her real mom into it?

Maggie's eyes flicked to Liv's. "Are you sure that's okay? I don't want to get in the way."

Liv gritted her teeth in order to smile. What was she going to say? That Taylor couldn't spend time with her mom because it would ruin Liv's idealistic hopes for what the bookshop would mean to them? Besides, they'd just be shoveling out trash. It wasn't as if she hadn't already expected other people from town to pitch in at some point. What was the difference?

But there was a difference. Because this was for Haven Ridge, and they were part of the community. Maggie was a virtual stranger who expected them to just accept her by virtue of her name on a birth certificate.

Somehow, Liv managed to keep her tone level. "Of course it's fine. Like Taylor said, the more hands, the better. It's not a huge job but it's not a quick one either. The place has been vacant for quite a while."

"Well, I think it sounds amazing," Maggie said, smiling down at her daughter. They had the same smile, Liv noticed, though Taylor didn't tend to smile so wide unless she was really caught up in the moment. Like now. "Everything you and your friends have planned to raise money is really impressive. I'm proud of you."

Taylor beamed, and Liv struggled to keep her own smile from faltering.

Which turned out to be the theme of the entire lunch. Maggie and Taylor talked while Liv picked at her salad, answering only when Maggie double-checked with her that the plans or the questions or her involvement was okay. At first Liv thought it was just the woman's insecurity, her attempt at inclusivity. But as the lunch wore on and Liv saw the quick way that Maggie made sure Taylor was watching before she asked, she began to wonder if her motives weren't quite so benign. After all, could Liv actually say no without hurting Taylor and driving her closer to Maggie? The minute the teen thought that Liv was trying to stand between her and her real mom was the moment that she withdrew from Liv completely. And as uncharitable as Liv felt for even having the thought, she wondered if that wasn't the whole point.

After over an hour of torture, Maggie's and Taylor's plates were clean and Liv's was barely touched. Maggie insisted on paying for their meal and slid out of the booth to walk up to the register, leaving her and Taylor alone at the table.

Taylor turned to her with shining eyes. "Isn't she great?"

"She seems really nice," Liv said carefully. "I do wish that you had given me some warning, though. It's a lot to take in at once."

Taylor's expression faltered for a second before something resembling rebellion surfaced. "I figured you wouldn't let her come if you knew."

"Taylor, when have I *ever* given you the impression that I wouldn't want your family in your life? I asked you if you wanted to visit Maggie's family and you said no."

That struck, but Taylor clearly wasn't going to give. "Yeah, but you're not happy she's here. I can tell."

"I'm not thrilled to have this sprung on me before I could prepare myself," Liv countered. "I just want you to be happy. And safe. If that's spending time with your birth mom, that's fine with me. But I do want to get to know her first. It's my responsibility as your parent."

"As my *guardian*," Taylor emphasized, and she couldn't have said anything that would have cut her deeper. Before Liv could react, Maggie was back at the edge of the table, smiling brightly.

"Ready to go?"

"Sure." Liv tossed her paper napkin onto the table next to her plate. "Let me just use the restroom and then we can walk over and see the bookstore."

She'd just entered the restroom and checked to make sure both stalls were empty when her phone buzzed in her purse. She pulled it out, saw Gemma's name on the lock screen, swiped to read the message.

Charlie told me. I'm on it. Call me when you're free.

Liv braced herself against the cold porcelain of the pedestal sink for a long moment before she twisted on the tap and splashed cold water on her face. She took several deep breaths, willing them to calm the roiling anxiety in her gut. Nothing in her experience could have prepared her for this . . . fear. This gut-deep, bone-chilling certainty that nothing good would come of Maggie's appearance. The visceral, irrational knowledge that if she wasn't careful, she was going to lose the thing most precious to her.

Her daughter.

CHAPTER TWENTY-TWO

It was the longest day that Liv could remember since the phone call that told her that her husband was dead.

After lunch, she and Taylor walked Maggie up the street and over to the future site of the Beacon Street Bookshop. The other woman walked around the interior, oohing and aahing over the original features that had made them fall in love with the space, throwing out some non-committal decorating ideas that Taylor hung on as if she was in the presence of Frank Lloyd Wright. Then they drove back to the house, where Maggie and Taylor sat at the dining room table, talking, while Liv puttered around cleaning and pretending not to be straining her ears to catch every word.

By the time that Maggie finally left, promising to meet them at the shop tomorrow to help with the clean-out, Liv felt as wrung out and worn thin as the old T-shirt she was using to unnecessarily polish the wood trim. The effort of pretending she was fine for Taylor's sake—a losing battle, from the way the girl had reacted earlier that day—made her body ache all the way down to the bones. She ordered pizza for delivery, hoping that maybe she and her daughter could flop down on the sofa and watch something on Netflix, regain some of the closeness that she couldn't help but feel had been fractured by the appearance of the "real mom" in the middle of their normal lives.

But instead, Taylor just scarfed down a single piece and retreated to her room, claiming to be tired from the day. And maybe it was true. As much as it might feel like it, Liv didn't have as much riding on this visit as Taylor did. Yes, part of Liv's fear was that Maggie might try to take Taylor away from her, or at least fill Liv's place in her life. But the bigger part of it was knowing how long it had taken for Taylor to get over her abandonment. She'd been young enough not to understand, to build a life without a mother figure before Liv came along. But now? What would a second abandonment do to her at sixteen? If Maggie wasn't the reformed, recovering, concerned parent that she was portraying herself to be, what kind of mess would she leave behind for Liv to clean up?

One thing was for certain: Whatever Gemma had threatened Charlie with was nothing compared to what Liv would do if Maggie hurt Taylor.

Liv flopped down on the sofa, leaning her head back against the cushions. She should call Gemma and get an update. So far her best friend had already checked in on her twice, restraining her own curiosity when Liv just texted back things like, *Ugh, call you later and tell you all about it.* But now that it was later, she found that she didn't have the heart to rehash it with Gemma.

Oddly enough, the person she wanted to talk to was Charlie.

But she couldn't have that either. He'd take it to mean that she was ready for a relationship with him, when really all she wanted was a comforting shoulder to cry on. And though she had no doubt that he'd gladly provide it, it wasn't fair to him.

So instead she sat like a puddle of goo on her down-filled sofa cushions and stared at the wood-paneled ceiling, feeling sorry for herself.

Liv's phone buzzed on the cushion beside her. Gemma.

Are you just sitting there feeling sorry for yourself instead of calling me?

Liv laughed. How did she do that exactly? She tapped in, Summoning the energy.

It went that well, huh?

Oh, it was brilliant. Maggie is SO smart. Maggie is SO interesting. Liv knew her sarcasm was immature, but she was too hurt and wrung out to care.

Ouch. Yeah. That couldn't have been fun. Want me to come over?

Yes. But we couldn't speak freely here. Taylor's in her room.

Fine, then come over here.

Liv closed her eyes and groaned, waiting until

she could manage to tap out a reply. That would require me driving. And putting on shoes.

Okay, then. I'm coming to get you. No arguments.

Liv was about to refuse, but she backspaced the words and put down her phone. Why shouldn't she go over to Gemma's tonight? Taylor was in for the night and she probably wasn't going anywhere. Maggie wouldn't be coming back if she knew what was good for her. And Liv had a camera on the front gate, so she would know if anyone came or went while she was gone. That would have to be good enough.

It was, admittedly, the first time she had really worried about the prospect of Taylor sneaking out or having someone over who wasn't supposed to be here. That was the kind of person that Maggie's appearance had made her, and she didn't particularly like it. Then again, her daughter had been carrying on an internet conversation with her birth mom for who knows how long without giving her an inkling of what was coming. Maybe she had reason to be a little suspicious.

About fifteen minutes later, Gemma's message buzzed through: Outside. Liv heaved herself up off the sofa and ambled down the hallway to Taylor's room, where she knocked before opening the door. "I'm going to run into town for a bit with Gemma. Stay here, okay? And if you decide to go out, you need to call me first."

Taylor looked up from her phone where she was texting away. "Okay. I don't think I'm going to go anywhere."

Liv nodded, barely resisting the urge to ask who she was texting, then closed the door softly. She shoved on her flip flops, grabbed her purse, and ran outside to Gemma's waiting red Audi.

As soon as she climbed into the passenger's seat, Gemma took one look at her and pronounced, "You look awful."

"Ha. Thanks. I can guarantee however bad I look, it's better than I feel."

Gemma nodded thoughtfully as she made a three-point turn and headed back for the gate. "I don't blame you. A bit of a kick in the teeth today, wasn't it?"

"You can say that again. I go back and forth between being sympathetic for what Maggie went through and hating her for coming and disrupting our life. And at the same time, doesn't Taylor deserve the chance to get to know her mom if she wants to?"

Gemma paused to wait for the gate to open. "It's a hard one. On one hand, she gave up any right to call herself a mother when she left them and signed away her parental rights. On the other, Taylor's always going to feel the hole that she left. Whether or not that's going to be healed at all by her showing up now is hard to tell."

Gemma was so reasonable about the whole

thing, it reminded Liv that she'd spent almost her entire career in family law dealing with these kinds of dynamics: broken families and hurting children. At least there weren't feuding spouses involved here. Just a jealous and suspicious stepmom.

Once they were out on the dark highway, the bright white beams cutting through the night, Gemma said delicately, "I did some digging today."

Liv immediately knew what she meant. "Did you find out anything useful?"

"Well, it's pretty much what you thought. I only have access to public records, court filings, and such. A bunch of arrests between six and twelve years ago. Most of them drug-related. One for solicitation."

Liv grimaced, though she shouldn't be surprised. Most heavy drug users ended up involved in prostitution one way or another. She had to concentrate to make sure it was the sympathy and not the judgment that took the upper hand, though.

"Then not a lot for a while. An arrest for driving under the influence about six-and-a-half years ago in Wisconsin. By some miracle, she got a sympathetic judge who ordered her to rehab instead of jail. And by all indications, that was it."

It all lined up with what she'd told them—six

years sober. How sad that it had taken Maggie that many years of addiction to get there though. If she'd gotten help sooner, or maybe gotten a judge that forced her to get help sooner, she might have been reunited with her family.

And Liv wouldn't even be in the picture.

"I don't suppose you talked to Andrew?"

"Chelsea was there when Charlie came in. She said she'd ask him tonight."

Liv smiled to herself. Andrew was better known as Deputy Dixon, the sheriff's deputy who had initially taken Chelsea's statement when she left her abusive husband. It hadn't taken long for them to develop a . . . fondness . . . for each other, though to Liv's knowledge they weren't officially dating. But given that Chelsea worked for Liv's best friend and Andrew happened to be Thomas Rivas's uncle, there was no way that he wouldn't dig into Maggie's past if he were able.

"How are you doing really?" Gemma asked when Liv didn't say anything for several long moments.

"Honestly? I'm devastated. And scared. And mad. And I feel guilty for all of it. I feel like I should be supportive, and all I do is swing between resenting Maggie's presence and being afraid that she's going to crush Taylor's spirit."

"All reasonable."

"Is it, though? I mean, I'm not actually Taylor's mom."

"Oh, shush. You are Taylor's mom in every way that matters. You have been the only mom she's known for most of her life. When her dad died, you stepped up and took responsibility for her. You guys are opening a business together. Maggie showing up is not going to change any of that."

"I wish I could be sure."

"Well, I am. That's not to say that it won't be hard and scary and probably difficult to manage at times. But Taylor loves you. She's not going to just cut you out of her life because her mom— who will never *really* have the day-to-day responsibility of motherhood—decided to show up."

Gemma was right. Liv knew that Gemma was right, but it didn't loosen the vice on her heart or ease the knot in her stomach. She was looking for a guarantee, but she knew all too well that there were no guarantees in life. Pain, the possibility of loss—it was all part of loving someone and being loved in return. She just wished it didn't have to hurt quite so much.

They were finally back in town, and Gemma pulled into the alley behind her building, parking in one of two parallel spots. Gemma locked her car and they went in through the back door, which connected to the lower-floor hallway that led up old-fashioned stairs—past the law office and to the top floor that Gemma had made into her apartment. Her friend unlocked the door and led the way in.

Despite herself, Liv smiled when she walked into Gemma's flat. It was hard to believe that this was the hoarder's nightmare she'd initially purchased. Through a lot of hard work, elbow grease, and a little help from the town, it had been transformed from a dirty, dingy apartment to a beautiful, eclectic blend of turn-of-the-century charm and modern aesthetic. The plaster walls sported a new coat of cream paint, the oak floors and moldings refinished and polished to a shine. The fireplace in the front room had been scrubbed free of its soot, a comfortable-looking dove gray sofa and a clean-lined coffee table settled in front of it. Gemma tossed her keys onto the end table and hung her purse on a coat tree near the entrance before moving toward the one unrenovated space in the place—the 1970s kitchen.

"I was thinking about asking Charlie to help with the kitchen," she called as she clattered around, undoubtedly putting water on for tea. "I know he's busy with the bookshop right now, but assuming he's looking for a reason to stay in town . . ."

Liv had been so absorbed in the many moving parts of her life that she had almost forgotten Charlie hadn't come to Haven Ridge to stay. "Did he say something to you?"

Gemma poked her head out of the kitchen. "He didn't have to."

Liv wandered around the living room for a second before she seated herself in the arm chair by the sofa. "Why do you say that?"

Gemma came out a moment later with a plate of cookies from the bakery and set them on the table in front of Liv. "Because he was genuinely worried and concerned for you when he came to see me today. The second time. The first time, he just wanted to know what your favorite breakfast pastry was."

Liv smiled despite herself. She couldn't believe that had just been this morning. It felt like a lifetime had passed since she'd bumped into him half-dressed in her hallway. "He's a good guy."

Gemma lifted her eyebrows. "Did I actually hear you say something positive about a man? Who likes you?"

Liv rolled her eyes. "Come on. You make me sound like some man-hating spinster."

"No. Not man-hating. Man-fearing maybe."

Liv gaped at her. "I do not!"

"So why haven't you gone out with him when he's obviously head-over-heels for you and you dig him too?"

"Because I don't know if Taylor is ready for that."

Gemma sat down beside her on the sofa. "I don't think Taylor gets to make that decision,

Liv. She didn't consult you when she started communicating with her mother. If she's allowed to have a second mom, why aren't you allowed to have a boyfriend?"

Boyfriend. The word felt foreign to Liv's ears. She'd been a wife and a widow, but *girlfriend* seemed like a long time ago, a different life ago. "I don't know if I can."

"Mmm." Gemma squeezed her hand briefly. "You know I don't mind being your one and only. But there are things Charlie can do for you that I can't."

Liv slid a look at Gemma, mildly scandalized, but Gemma was just looking at her with wide-eyed innocence. In the kitchen, the electric kettle clicked off and Gemma jumped up before she had to give an answer. She had the feeling that her friend was trying to shock her out of her complacency, and she'd succeeded. But she was also somewhat correct in her assessment. Hadn't Liv's first impulse been to want Charlie's presence? She loved Gemma like a sister, and she knew she would always be there for her, but she had responsibilities. She had a boyfriend—who, if Liv wasn't mistaken, would eventually turn into a husband—not to mention two businesses and a busy life. Taylor was her own person, as evidenced by this unpleasant surprise, and she would be going off to college. Yes, Liv had people in her life, but none of them belonged to her. Not in the way that she craved. That she missed.

Was that the wrong reason to get involved with someone?

Gemma came back with two steaming cups of English tea and set them down on coasters on the coffee table. "Maybe this all is a good thing. The job, the bookstore, even Maggie."

Liv looked at her incredulously. "How do you figure?"

"Maybe it will get you to realize that life doesn't have to go according to plan to still be good."

"Is that what you think? That I have to have everything go according to plan?"

Gemma just raised an eyebrow.

"Whatever you're thinking, it's wrong. Clearly I didn't plan for my husband to be killed in a plane crash and make me the legal guardian of a girl I'd only known for a few years."

"Right. And because that wasn't in your plan, you decided to preserve your life in amber. To never move forward. To hold your breath in case something else bad happened."

The words rocked her. Was that what Gemma really thought? And more importantly, was she right?

Sure, Liv had had plans. She followed them all the way to New York, accomplished her goals. But she hadn't planned on getting married at twenty-five and then moving back home. When she said as much, Gemma laughed.

"Oh please. Don't you remember your husband checklist? You'd meet him in your twenties in New York. He was going to be tall, dark, and handsome. Nice body but not too muscular because you didn't like muscles. Clean-shaven, obviously because beards are gross. Smart but also adventurous. Trustworthy and straightforward." Gemma drilled her with a look. "Sound familiar?"

Liv flushed. It did describe Jason rather well. "So I have a type! What's wrong with that?"

"There's something wrong with that when you're overlooking a perfectly nice guy who bends over backwards for you, who is capable and handsome, just because he has a blue-collar job and his biceps make you want to jump him every time you see him."

Liv gaped openly at her best friend. And then in unison, they both dissolved into laughter. She gasped for air, holding her stomach. "You're right," she squeezed out finally. "They really do!"

When they finally managed to catch their breath and Liv was wiping tears from her eyes, some of the tightness had eased from her middle. "I know it sounds stupid. I just hate being that predictable."

"Smart girls have needs too," Gemma said

airily, which just made Liv laugh again. "Seriously though, I'm not trying to push you toward a guy you don't like. If you're not interested, you're not interested. But I don't think he's the problem here."

Gemma was right. There was absolutely nothing wrong with Charlie. He was sweet and considerate and capable. He made her smile and feel safe. She didn't know nearly enough about him, but she was letting the raw chemistry between them keep her from actually finding out. As if admitting that a guy could curl her toes and take her breath away from across the room was a betrayal of her late husband, who had done none of those things even though she had loved him with all her heart. As if it somehow took away what she and Jason had.

"It's okay to miss Jason," Gemma said, almost as if she was reading her mind. "He would never expect you to be alone forever. And he definitely wouldn't expect you to find his clone. In fact, he'd probably be a little disturbed by the idea of you trying to replace him exactly." She smiled softly at Liv. "Is there anything so wrong with just letting yourself *see* if maybe Charlie could be something to you?"

"No," Liv said slowly. The twist in her stomach this time felt a lot more like anticipation than fear. "I don't think there's anything wrong with that."

Gemma smiled. "Then my work here is done. Eat a cookie. This is my best recipe yet, if I do say so myself."

Liv leaned forward to take a cookie, which she could agree was one of the better things she'd tasted. But her mind was elsewhere, on tomorrow.

And what a new day with Charlie might bring.

CHAPTER TWENTY-THREE

Liv met Thursday with a jumble of anxiety and anticipation in her middle. It took a few long moments to unravel the source of her feelings. The reasons for the anxiety hit first as yesterday's events flooded back to her—Taylor, Maggie, the unexpected addition to their work day today. She shoved it down ruthlessly. She couldn't show Taylor how much it bothered her. She couldn't risk her feelings toward the girl's birth mom driving her stepdaughter away. As much as she feared her getting hurt, Taylor was almost an adult and she needed to make this decision for herself. However much Liv might want to, she couldn't save her from all forms of heartbreak.

And deep down, Liv knew this situation would lead to heartbreak. She just didn't know if it would be Taylor's or hers.

Better to delve into the anticipation then, and not just the fact that they were going to be starting work on the bookshop today. Charlie would be there, and the mere thought of him gave her spirits a lift. How could she resist someone who made her happy just by thinking of him? Gemma was right. She was holding herself back from him for nothing.

That stopped today.

The flutter in her stomach drove her out of her bed and into her bathroom, where she flew through her morning routine. She twisted her hair up on top of her head and fastened it with a big claw clip, then dug through her wardrobe for something to wear. Practicality said she should throw on a pair of old jeans and a long-sleeved shirt that would protect her from whatever they might encounter in the mess. Vanity had her reaching for a pair of black compression leggings that made her butt look fantastic. She threw a long-sleeved T-shirt on over her least uni-boob sports bra and pulled down her hiking boots from the top of the closet.

She was practically a Colorado social media cliche.

Whatever. She'd be comfortable, covered, and still look cute. Because she wasn't even going to try to pretend the latter one didn't matter.

When she walked into the hallway, sounds from the bathroom told her that Taylor was already getting ready, so she went to start their coffee and rummage through the pantry for something to eat. She stilled when her fingers brushed the forgotten pink pastry box from the Broken Hearts Bakery. Not that it mattered—Gemma's croissants were almost as good the next day—but she didn't remember putting them away. They'd been out on the table when Maggie got there and then she'd been too distracted by parenting angst to wonder what happened to them.

A smile came to her lips when she remembered Charlie had been in charge of making coffee, which they had never actually managed to drink. He must have whisked them away. There was no way he was going to let Maggie eat the croissants that he'd brought for her and Taylor. The combination of sweet and petty made her smile.

She could come to love that kind of thoughtfulness.

The thought stopped her in her tracks, and her heart stuttered like an old engine trying to turn over. The metaphor wasn't too far from the truth either. The parts of her that Charlie brought to life were neglected and rusted from disuse. She'd practically forgotten what it was like to be important to someone.

Charlie treated her like she was the most precious thing in the world.

"Hey, are we going over soon?" Taylor's sleepy voice dragged her out of her reverie, and Liv spun to find the pajama-dressed teenager leaning in the hallway, her phone already in hand.

"Yeah, I thought we'd go over as soon as we eat breakfast. Maybe seven thirty?"

"Cool," Taylor said, and swiveled off, tapping on her phone as she went.

Probably telling Maggie when to meet them.

Ugh. Liv shoved down the wave of jealousy and resentment and turned back to the croissant box. She could be polite and cordial and even friendly. She could ignore the subtle ways that Maggie was trying to shift her daughter to her side, against Liv. Maggie might be coming into Taylor's life all fun and games, but Liv was the one who actually had custody. The one who actually had a life with Taylor. Nothing Maggie did was going to change that.

The edge of the pink box crumpled under the sudden clench of Liv's hands.

"Gah!" Liv reached for her own phone, opening up the messaging app. But instead of clicking on Gemma's thread, she chose Charlie's.

I need you to do one thing for me today.

Almost immediately, the dots began dancing while Charlie typed his reply. Only one?

Liv smiled. Somehow he managed to load flirtation into two simple words. Or maybe that was just her wishful thinking. For now. Keep me from strangling Maggie.

I'll do my very best. But if that fails, I've got bail money.

She chuckled and shoved the phone into the thigh pocket of her leggings, some of her frustration already ebbing. Gemma was right. She did need someone else in her corner. Liv smiled as she pulled out a croissant, set it on a plate, and then moved to get the coffee going.

By the time that Taylor emerged, dressed in baggy black cargos and an impractical black crop top with combat boots, Liv mostly had a handle on her jealousy and anxiety. "I texted Maggie to meet us at 7:30. She said she'd bring doughnuts."

"I will never turn down doughnuts," Liv said, proud of how steady and normal her voice sounded.

But Taylor still paused and looked at her anyway. "I'm sorry I didn't tell you ahead of time. I was afraid of what you might do."

Oh lord. She didn't have the energy for this conversation this morning. But Taylor was opening up to her and she wasn't going to waste that opportunity. She moved to the girl's side and squeezed her arm. "Taylor, you know that I'll love you no matter what. I'm on your side. Even when things are . . . less than convenient for me."

Something in Taylor's eyes softened. "Really?"

"Of course." Liv slipped her arms around her shoulders and pulled her close. "Just next time, give me a heads-up. You know how little I like surprises."

Taylor laughed and pulled away. "Yeah, I know. I'm sorry. So you're really okay with all this?"

Not even a little bit, but there was only one answer she could give. Liv nodded. "Of course. She's your mom. But I'm responsible for you, which means you can't get mad if I'm cautious."

"That's fair," Taylor said. "Thanks, Liv."

"You're welcome. Now get your travel mug and a croissant and let's get going."

The mood in the SUV on the way to town was

much lighter than it had been in the last twenty-four hours, and Liv let herself take her first full breath since Maggie had arrived. When they pulled up on Beacon Street, a big black dumpster was sitting directly in front of the building, Charlie's truck already parked a couple spaces down. Liv made a U-turn and parked across from their shop.

Their shop.

Liv threw a look at Taylor. "You realize we're really doing this."

Excitement sparkled in Taylor's eyes, another assurance Liv hadn't realized she needed. "We are. Couple boss ladies up in here." She made a little shoulder-dust gesture that made Liv laugh and they both reached for their door handles at the same time.

They were only partway across the street when Charlie's truck door opened and he climbed out, a bright smile aimed in their direction. "Morning, ladies. I realized once I got here that I should have asked you for the key."

Liv held up her key ring. "I'll give you a copy right now. Have you been waiting long?"

Charlie shook his head and joined them on the sidewalk in front of the building, a tool bag in one hand. "Not at all. Max just delivered the roll-off a couple of minutes ago, so it gave me some time to drink my coffee and listen to the radio."

Taylor threw him a sideways glance. "It was

country, wasn't it? You're a country-music lover. I promise I won't hold it against you."

Charlie chuckled. "Actually, it was NPR."

"Fancy," Taylor said, swiping the keys from Liv's hand and heading straight for the front door.

Charlie moved close to Liv and pitched his voice low. "She seems like she's in a good mood this morning."

"Yeah, Mom is going to be here with *dough-nuts*."

"Ah." Charlie bumped her arm with his. "And how are you doing?"

"About as well as you'd expect." She glanced at him, catching his eye. "Better now, though."

Surprise sparked in his expression and his lips tipped up in the beginning of a smile. "I was about to say the same thing."

That flutter was back, and she let herself enjoy it before she followed Taylor into the bookshop. "So what's the plan of attack?"

Charlie set down his bag in the clear spot near the front door and unzipped it. He straightened with three pairs of gloves in his hands. "Any junk that you don't want inside the building goes inside the dumpster."

Liv laughed. "That easy, huh?"

"Yeah. Save the broken bookshelves though. Last time I was here, they looked salvageable. And old. I hate to throw away good wood."

Liv and Taylor accepted their gloves and pulled them on while Charlie went back and shoved a wedge of cardboard under the front door to hold it open. They were just taking the first armload of paper out of the shop when the old dingy wall sconces flickered to life.

"And that would be the power getting turned on," Liv said. "With any luck, the water will be back on today too."

"We might not even need it." Taylor gathered up what looked like a stack of out-of-date fliers for a band that probably no longer existed. "This really isn't as bad as it looks."

And then she screamed.

Both Liv and Charlie whirled at the same time, and Liv rushed to her side. "What? What's wrong?"

Taylor pointed down at the desiccated carcass of what could only be a rat.

Liv laughed.

Taylor glared at her. "It's not funny. I almost picked it up!"

"Girl, you dress in all black and you have skulls on your pajamas. You're afraid of a dried-up rat?"

"That's an *aesthetic*. It doesn't mean I want to handle corpses."

Charlie was staying out of it, but he was still grinning. He grabbed a piece of cardboard and slid it under the shriveled body. "I'll get rid of it." He turned toward the door, holding it out in front of him.

And almost ran directly into Maggie.

She let out a little yelp, but to her credit, she just stepped aside, then moved inside with a wry smile. "Was it something I said?"

Despite herself, Liv found herself hating her a little less.

Maggie held out a pink box stamped with the name of a doughnut shop in Salida. "I brought these. But I'm thinking maybe we want to wait until we're not removing dead animals from the building?"

Taylor took the box with a bright smile and set them on the stairs, which was virtually the only clear spot in the building. "Thanks. We're just getting rid of all the junk in here."

"Okay, then." Maggie wiped her hands on her jeans and shoved up the sleeves of her shirt. "Just point me in the right direction."

"Here." Charlie reappeared with a pair of gloves. "You might want these."

"Thank you," Maggie said with surprise and slipped them on. Liv sent him a raised-eyebrow look.

Charlie brushed by her and bent to whisper in her ear. "I'm banking brownie points with Taylor."

Liv gave a little shiver at his proximity, his breath on her neck rustling the strands of hair that had fallen free of her clip. "You should be worried about getting brownie points with me," she murmured.

He pulled back to look her in the eye. "Oh, trust me. I have some ideas."

Liv barely staved off the full-body shiver his words summoned, and Charlie's little chuckle said he knew it, too. It was a good thing that they weren't alone because she'd be tempted to find out exactly what he meant by those words.

With the four of them, it took less time than Liv expected to clear out all the old paper and cardboard that had been scattered around the room. Charlie retrieved the pieces of broken bookshelves and stacked them along one brick wall, and they went to work on the stained carpet with box cutters, each strip peeled back to reveal original wood planks. By lunchtime, they could actually walk around in the space, unhindered by trash or unfortunate rodent remains.

"It's big," Taylor said, turning to take in the area. "I didn't realize how big it is."

"Yeah." Liv had been thinking the same thing, but not with the wonder that Taylor had. Before, in its cluttered state, she'd almost believed that they could fill the space with the boxes of books they already had, plus a few donations from the community. Now that she saw how many square feet there actually were to fill—not to mention clean—all she could see was dollar signs.

But that reminded her. She had been so distracted by the events of yesterday that she hadn't even thought to check their crowdfunding page. She pulled her gloves off and tucked them under her arm, then brought up the website on her phone. And gaped.

"We've already raised twelve thousand dollars," she said, holding the screen to face the others, stunned. "In only a couple of days."

"Oh, that's great," Maggie said, coming close to look at the screen. "Looks like you've gotten some corporate donations too."

Liv turned the phone back to herself, frowning. Corporate donations? She looked closely and there at the top was two thousand dollars from Tamberlane Books.

"What?" The company that had let her go had actually given a donation to her business? She opened her email and sure enough, there was an email from her old boss, who had elected to stay.

Dear Liv,

We miss you here. The division certainly isn't the same without your wit and insight. But it looks like you're living the dream back in Colorado. Tamberlane is pleased to contribute in a small way to your success (otherwise known as me breaking into the department's discretionary fund). Let me know when you're up and running. I'm sending you a copy of every book we have in the office to put on your shelves.

All the best,
Louise

Liv blinked away sudden tears. When she'd posted the information on her personal social media, she'd been thinking more in terms of letting friends and family know about their venture. But she should have known that all her old colleagues would have seen it too. Louise's donation might have seemed like a small thing, but Liv knew how carefully she guarded that discretionary fund. It paid for everything from author visits to business lunches to birthday gifts. Which meant that Louise was sacrificing something else from her department to help out Liv.

And a copy of every one of the books in the office was nothing to sneeze at either . . . they kept at least a hundred books on hand.

But that wasn't the only email. There was one from Malcolm Barry, her favorite author, pledging to send her two copies of his books, one for the bookshop and one for the library, and asking when he could plan a reading at her new place.

There was another from Adrienne Lee, a wonderful illustrator who did charming old-fashioned picture books with her sister, pledging their books as well.

And on and on.

Only then did Liv realize that Louise had done so much more than simply send her money. She had rallied Liv's authors, all the people she had found and nurtured and edited and published over the years. And they'd responded.

She didn't realize that there were tears tracking down her face until Charlie was beside her, slipping an arm around her shoulders.

"I'm fine, I'm fine," she said, waving her hands in front of her face to dry her tears. "I just . . ." She shook her head. "Let's just say there's a lot of books coming for us in the next couple of weeks."

Maggie was looking a bit confused, but she stayed at the edge of the group and didn't ask questions. Taylor came over to her and gave her a little hug.

"Everyone loves you, Liv. Of course they want to help." She threw her a sassy little look. "And they want to be part of something so fabulous, obviously."

"Obviously," Liv said with a watery laugh and gave Taylor another hug. "On that note, I think it's time to get cleaned up for lunch."

Maggie looked down at herself, her jeans and T-shirt now streaked with dirt. "Do we really want to go anywhere looking like this?"

"The Brick House Cafe will do carry-out," Liv said. "We can just pick it up and bring it back."

"Mom and I can do that now," Taylor volunteered, and just like that the spike went right back into Liv's heart.

She credited herself for managing not to flinch. "That would be great. Charlie and I can get started on the back office while you're waiting. Can you just get me a turkey sandwich with fries and an iced tea?"

"That sounds good," Charlie said. "Same here."

Maggie glanced at Taylor and smiled. "Well, let's go then." Taylor's answering smile was almost painful in its brilliance. Liv turned away until they had rounded the corner down the street before she pulled out the piece of cardboard and let the door shut.

"You know she still loves you, right?" Charlie said quietly. "You can tell. Maggie being here isn't going to change that."

"Maggie being here is going to change a lot of things." Liv brushed past him, holding up her dirty hands. "I'm going to see if the water is on yet." She continued down the hall to the single restroom, a narrow space with a pull-chain toilet and a pedestal sink, and twisted on the tap. Nothing. She turned and almost bumped directly into Charlie outside the door.

He held up a plastic canister of wipes. "I came prepared." When she didn't immediately move, he set the canister down between them and pulled a wipe from the top. Then he took one of her hands in his and gently began to wipe the dirt from her palms and fingers.

"I can do that myself," Liv said, suddenly embarrassed.

"And you can also let someone do something for you," Charlie murmured, clearly not talking just about wipes. When he was finished with her right hand, he got another square and began cleaning her left hand as well. It was so incredibly sweet and strangely intimate that she found herself standing there, frozen and transfixed by his gentle ministrations.

But this time he didn't let her hand go. His eyes met hers as he brought it up and gently brushed his lips against the back of her fingers.

Liv sucked in a breath at the contact, swaying as if gravity had shifted, as if he had suddenly developed his own irresistible celestial pull. But no, there was no suddenly about it. She'd felt it the very first time she met him, and no matter how hard she attempted to break free, he always drew her back again.

And now, staring up into his blue-gray eyes, darkened and dilated with want, she couldn't think of a good reason not to give in.

So she let herself step forward, closer to him. Her other hand came up to rest against his chest to feel the twitch of muscle beneath her fingertips, the rapid beat of his heart against her palm. He went so still that the only sound around them was the faint rasp of their breath in the close, warm hallway. She imagined that she could hear the crackle of electricity between them.

"Liv," he whispered, his voice hoarse. His eyes never left hers. "I've already made my feelings clear. You're going to have to be very specific about what you want here."

In response, she reached up and pulled his head down to hers.

The minute their lips met, every other thought fled from her mind. There was only Charlie, his hands on her waist pulling her flush against him, the soft press of his lips, the sweep of his tongue. Their breaths rasped together as they shifted and separated and met again, choreographed by instinct and desire, until her head swam and her worries fled. Here in this heated bubble, there were no problems or thoughts about the future. There was only him, his taste, his touch. Everything else seemed to recede except how he made her feel right this moment.

She loved it. Needed it. Wanted more of it.

The jingle of a bell somewhere in the background brought her back to consciousness, but it took a moment longer to realize that it was the shop's front door. Liv pulled back, her breath quick, her body flushed with desire and happiness, and twisted toward the entryway.

There stood Maggie and Taylor.

Abruptly, Charlie dropped his hands and Liv took a big step back, smoothing back her mussed hair. "Hi," she said brightly, as if they hadn't just caught her wrapped around Charlie. "Did you forget something?"

Slowly, Maggie reached over and picked up her purse where she'd left it by the front window. "Just forgot my wallet. We'll . . . go get the food now. Come on, Taylor." Liv couldn't be sure, but she thought she saw the other woman repress a smile. Slowly, Taylor stepped back and followed her mom out of the building.

Maggie might have found it funny. But the only way to describe Taylor's expression was stricken.

CHAPTER TWENTY-FOUR

Charlie knew the exact moment that he lost Liv, and it happened before his blood had even cooled from the kiss.

And what a kiss. All his imaginings had not prepared him for what she would feel like in his arms, how her taste would weaken his knees and ignite a craving he suspected would never be fulfilled. He knew he had the tendency to think the best of whoever he was dating, to paint her in a rosier light than she maybe even deserved, but there was no question that Liv was special.

And any resistance that he had to her, any chance that she wouldn't break his heart if she rejected him, disappeared.

Which was why it was so difficult to feel her withdraw when she backed away, shaking her head. "I'm sorry. That was probably a bad idea."

"I thought it was a pretty fantastic idea myself," Charlie said, "one that I'd like to repeat at our earliest convenience."

That got her. A little smile tipped up the corners of her mouth and she threw him a look. "Okay, it was a pretty good kiss."

The relief that flooded through him was completely out of proportion to the comment. At least she wasn't saying it was a mistake, that she regretted kissing him. "You know, I feel the need to remind you that *you* kissed me."

She licked her lips and her gaze went a little distant, as if she was remembering how it had come about. "Yeah. But in plain view . . . ? And Taylor . . ."

"Taylor will be fine. Taylor is almost a grown-up. Taylor is probably kissing her own boyfriend when she's not with you, you know."

Liv groaned and pressed her hand to her forehead. "Please don't talk about that. I don't want to think about Taylor doing anything with any boy."

Charlie darted a look toward the front of the shop to confirm that they were again alone, then moved up behind her and slid his arms around her waist. Almost instinctively, she relaxed against him. "It'll be okay," he whispered in her ear. "Taylor will get used to the idea. She was just startled. And probably annoyed that you didn't tell her first. Girl code and all that."

"Maybe," Liv conceded, but she didn't sound all that convinced.

In response, he moved aside a tendril of hair that had fallen from her clip and bent to press his lips to the patch of skin it exposed.

She sagged against him, a groan slipping from her lips. "Stop. You're killing me here."

Charlie grinned at her response, but he took her at her word and let her go. "Can't have that happen. Do you want to try to get a little more cleaning done before they come back?"

"No . . ." The look she shot him did good things to his ego. "But we probably should."

Which is how they passed the next twenty minutes in the small back office. There wasn't much inside, just some old paperwork in banker boxes and a lot of dust. Liv rifled through them to make sure there was nothing important and Charlie carried them out, each circling the other with exaggerated care as if they thought that a single careless touch would have them falling into each other's arms.

Which, to be fair, probably wasn't too far from the truth. Charlie had done a good job keeping his impulses in check while Liv was deciding what she wanted to do about him. But now, the heat that had kindled so quickly between them simmered beneath the surface, never cooling, just waiting to ignite again.

It was the most frustrating and delicious thing he'd experienced in a long time.

It was probably a good thing when Maggie and Taylor returned with two large paper bags. Charlie came out of the office first with a box to go to the dumpster, and Liv followed with a broom. Maggie did a passable job at pretending she hadn't seen anything—and let's face it, by the standards of a grown woman, she really *hadn't* seen anything—but Taylor kept scanning them as if she was looking for evidence that they'd continued making out after they'd gone.

Well, Taylor had him pegged, but she should know Liv better.

Maggie sat on the indentation of the windowsill and began unloading food. "A turkey sandwich, fries, and iced tea for Liv . . ."

Liv came forward and grabbed her food, then took it back to the stairs, where she perched on the second one up.

"A second turkey for Charlie." Maggie handed over Charlie's food, and Liv scooted over to make room for him on the steps. At least she wasn't trying to pretend there wasn't something going on between them when all the evidence said otherwise.

"And cheeseburgers for Taylor and me." Maggie smiled at Taylor and handed her daughter her food.

They all dug into their lunch, their silence driven mostly by hunger but at least a little by awkwardness. When they were almost done, Maggie cleared her throat. "So, I'm happy to help here for as long as you'd like, Liv. But I have reservations tonight at that restaurant on the river in Salida. I was hoping I could take Taylor? I'll have her back early."

Next to Charlie, Liv tensed and he had to prevent himself from placing a comforting hand on her knee. Now that he'd kissed her, it was going to be hard to prevent himself from touching her all the time. Instead, he settled for putting his hand on the step beside her and linking his pinky finger with hers.

She threw him a surprised glance and a little smile before she turned back to Maggie and Taylor, who were both looking at Liv hopefully. Obviously, Taylor knew this was coming, because it had the feeling of a united front.

Charlie could almost see the ease that had developed over the morning between Liv and Maggie evaporate.

"I don't see why not," Liv finally said, her voice a touch choked. "Taylor, just keep me posted on your plans, okay?"

Taylor beamed. "Thanks, Liv. We won't be back too late, I promise. I wanted to show her that little coffee shop we like to go to when we're there."

"Oh, yeah, that's a good one," she said faintly.

Bringing Maggie to one of *their* places.

Charlie couldn't help but feel bad for Liv. Teenagers weren't particularly known for their self-awareness, but it was hard to believe that after living with her for five years, Taylor couldn't pick up on how Liv was feeling about this. Or maybe she was just so desperate for her mom to like her that she didn't have room for any other thoughts.

After all, the woman had walked out on her

entire family and never even contacted Taylor when she'd heard that Jason had died. If you were going to make a big appearance in your kid's life, that would seem to be the proper time.

That alone made Charlie distrust her. He didn't know Taylor well, but he'd come to like her and her contradictory ways. He wished he had been that secure with himself in high school; maybe he would have had an easier time of it had he not been so self-conscious about his perceived shortcomings.

The silence in the room was starting to get awkward, so Charlie stood and gathered the remnants of his lunch in the bag. "We should probably get back to it. Once the sun gets low enough to come in through these windows, it's going to get too hot to work."

Liv threw him a grateful look as she handed her trash over as well. "Yeah, we really do need to talk about what we're going to do for cooling. The brick exterior only helps so much."

"We'll have to get an HVAC specialist out here to give us a quote. But I figured we should worry about what we can do ourselves first."

They cleaned up their lunch and then they got back to work, but the ease of the morning was gone. Liv opted to stay on the lower floor and finish sweeping out the office and the storage room, which was thankfully empty. Charlie went upstairs to the second and third floors to help "supervise" more trash removal. If the best thing he could do for Liv right now was run interference, then he would do it. And by the time the sun hit the front windows, which indeed heated the upper floors like a greenhouse, they were pretty much finished for the day.

Charlie went back downstairs and found Liv in the storage room, just staring into space with a broom in her hands. She started when he walked in.

"You okay?"

"I am now," she said with a soft smile.

It was all the encouragement he needed. He shut the door behind him, crossed the room, and pulled her into his arms. She lifted her face for his kiss, for which he was more than happy to oblige.

"Why don't you come over to my place for dinner tonight," he murmured in her ear. He nuzzled her neck and planted a light kiss just behind her earlobe.

She shivered. "I'm not sure that's a good idea."

He pulled back enough to smile down at her. "I promise I'll be good. But only if you want me to be."

She laughed a little breathlessly, her eyes sparkling. "How about you come over to *my* place. I'll put a couple of steaks on the grill, we can sit on the patio and watch the sunset. And then . . . we'll see."

"I like the sound of *we'll see*," he murmured, and she gave him a playful shove away.

"Behaving starts *now*," she said pointedly. But she threw a wicked little look over her shoulder before she opened the door and disappeared out of the room.

And that's when he knew the truth.

No matter how many kisses or touches or flirtatious looks he shared with this woman, it was never, ever going to be enough.

It always amazed Liv that she could feel so good and so bad at the same time.

Charlie: only good. She replayed their first kiss over and over in her mind until she was vibrating with repressed desire and found herself sweeping the same spot over and over. Even the judgmental part of her subconscious that wanted to compare him to Jason couldn't get her down. How did you resist someone who made your toes curl and your whole body vibrate when he was *across the stupid room?*

On the other hand, Maggie: unbelievably bad. Liv had woken up this morning determined that she was going to make this work, give her the benefit of the doubt. After all, the situation wasn't entirely her fault, and Taylor was her daughter. Liv could never understand what it would be like to give birth to a child, raise her for four years, and then not be sure if she was going to ever see her again. If it was anything like the pain she felt at the possibility of losing Taylor now, she couldn't blame her for wanting to get back in her life.

And yet Liv didn't trust her. Call it instinct or jealousy or well-founded caution, but there was just something off there. Something false. Vaguely manipulative. Every supposed consultation was a land mine that Liv had to navigate, and in every exchange, Maggie won. If Liv said yes, Maggie got to spend more alone time with Taylor. If Liv said no, it would inevitably push Taylor into the arms of her mother.

She had no choice but to stick it out. Maggie would only be here for another few days and then she'd be flying back to Wichita. Surely Liv could survive this annoyance until then. No doubt Taylor would be sullen and weird when she left, but Liv had navigated that before. She would grit her teeth and smile and let thoughts of Charlie and his magic touch distract her.

Still, she took a moment when everyone else was occupied to text Gemma: Anything from Andrew?

It wasn't until Liv was alone in her parked SUV—Taylor was driving back to their house with Maggie—that Gemma's reply came through. Nothing yet. I think he needs to find someone who has a fluid understanding of department rules before he asks.

Liv laughed to herself, though she felt a pang of guilt as well. She was asking someone that she didn't even really know to put his job on the line in order to dig up background dirt on her stepdaughter's mom. Then again, this was what Haven Ridge did. The new Haven Ridge, at least.

While she was mulling the ethics of what she was asking, Gemma had sent another message: How are things going?

As well as you'd expect. Taylor can't see anything but how wonderful Maggie is and I still have my doubts. I just don't trust her.

Wasn't talking about Maggie. Was talking about Charlie.

A smile came unbidden to her face, heat rising to her cheeks. Let's just say the man can kiss.

Almost immediately, a wordless reply from Gemma: !!!!!!!!!

Through her windshield, she saw Taylor climb into the rental car with Maggie. Across the street, Charlie locked up the front door of the shop and then got into his own truck. As soon as she was satisfied that everyone was safely ensconced in their cars and out of earshot, she dialed Gemma, put her on speaker, and pulled away from the sidewalk.

Gemma didn't even bother to say hello, just led with the question: "So he finally kissed you?"

"No," Liv said slowly, drawing out the suspense. "I kissed him."

Gemma let out an uncharacteristic squeal. "So, how was it?"

"It was . . . it was . . ." Her vocabulary failed her. "Oh my word."

Gemma sighed. "Oh, I miss those days . . ."

"What, Stephen is already getting a little stale?"

"No, of course not! But you know, our first kiss was something like eighteen years ago. As amazing as it is, it's just not the same as that very first time."

Liv sighed. She was right. Kissing someone only got better over time as you found your rhythm and what each of you liked and disliked and the companionship grew. But there was nothing that could compare to the sheer raw desire and anticipation leading up to that first kiss.

"Liv, you okay?"

"I'm sorry, I might have zoned out there for a second. What were we talking about?"

Gemma laughed gaily on the other end of the line. "This has been a long time in coming. What now?"

"Well, *Maggie* is taking Taylor out to dinner tonight—" she let all her feelings come out in the emphasis on that one word—"so I invited Charlie over. We're going to barbecue."

"Barbecue and hot tub?"

"I'm not so sure about that," Liv said slowly. "If any clothes come off, they're probably *all* going to come off."

Gemma gave a low whistle. "That answers that question, then. You good, Liv?"

She wasn't sure what Gemma was asking: Was she good with how intense these feelings were? Was she okay that she was fantasizing about a man who was not her late husband? Was she prepared for the practicalities if she did end up in bed with him? The very thought made her flush like she'd been out in the sun all day.

"No," she said finally, honestly. "I'm really not."

"Then tell him that. And you will find out very quickly if he's a keeper or not."

It was good advice, and no surprise since Gemma knew her better than anyone. Knew she'd been a virgin when she'd gotten married. And probably understood the calculations going on in her head right now—did it matter anymore? Neither she nor Gemma had really been raised religious like some of their friends were. And her innocence and naivete were long gone.

And yet even as she twisted it over in her mind, she knew she was a traditional girl at heart.

More than that, she knew she was falling for Charlie, fast and hard. And if she made love with him, especially this early in the relationship, she would be crushed if it didn't work out.

After all, she'd only slept with one man in her life, and she'd married him. That was a pretty high standard to live up to.

"Yeah, definitely no hot tub. Thanks, Gem."

"You're welcome. You know I love you no matter what, right? I've always got your back."

"Yeah, I know. Let me know if you hear anything from Andrew."

"I will. Just . . . try not to think about all that, okay? Make the best decisions you can. Listen to your gut. On both counts actually."

Liv laughed. "Love you."

"Yeah, love you too. Call me later. I want details."

Liv grinned and punched the button to end the call. She was almost home, and despite the fact that she was still buzzing from the topic of their discussion, she felt more settled. Who would have thought these decisions would be just as fraught at thirty-one as they'd been at sixteen or twenty-five?

She wondered idly if Taylor was talking to Maggie about Dylan and what kind of advice she was giving her.

"Enough," she told herself sternly. She was going to make herself sick with the constant whiplash of emotion. Between Charlie and Maggie and Taylor, it was a nonstop roller coaster between the highest highs and the lowest lows.

Taylor and her mom had beaten her back to the house, Maggie's car parked in Liv's spot. She rolled her eyes and climbed out, but before she got very far, Maggie pushed away from the wall near the front door.

"Hey," Liv said in surprise. "Everything okay?"

"Yeah, Taylor is taking a shower and changing. I wanted to talk to you while she was busy."

Uneasiness traced a cold path down Liv's spine. "Oh?"

Maggie reached into her pocket and pulled out a piece of paper. "That's the restaurant we're going to, and the other one is my vacation rental. And my cell phone. In case you need to find Taylor."

"Well, she has a phone and we use a tracking app," Liv said. "But thank you. I appreciate this."

"Sure." Maggie chewed her bottom lip for a second. "I wanted to thank you for being so accommodating. I know this can't be easy for you. I wanted to talk to you before I came out, but Taylor thought it might be easier for her to do it, to explain. I'm guessing that was a mistake."

"I did feel a little blindsided," Liv admitted. "But I don't want to keep Taylor from getting to know you again. I wasn't there, but I know she still harbors a lot of hurt over how you left. And later, when you relinquished your parental rights."

Maggie hung her head, swallowing hard. "I know. I regret that." She glanced up, saw the look on Liv's face. "Not because I thought I had any business being in her life back then, but because

I didn't stop to think how it would make Taylor feel. I knew she had a good life with Jason and I didn't want to mess it up. And now . . . she's all grown up and I've missed it all." She shook her head. "If I can at least let her know that there's another adult in her corner if she needs it . . . to feel like she's not alone, no matter what happens."

Liv looked at her closely. "I don't know what you think is going to happen, but Taylor is never going to be alone."

"No, of course not. I just meant . . . You're technically only her guardian until she's eighteen. So—"

"I'm her *family*," Liv said firmly. "And eighteen or twenty-eight or eighty, that's not going to change. So if you have any fears about that, I can put those to rest. Taylor will have a home with me for however long she wants it."

Maggie seemed taken aback by her vehemence, but she just nodded slowly. "I'm glad to hear it. You've done wonderful things for her, you and Jason. She's a great girl."

"Yeah," Liv said. "She is."

The door opened then and Taylor stepped out. Liv blinked at her for a long moment, barely able to process what she was seeing: she was fresh-faced, wearing only mascara and blush, her black eyeliner gone; and while she was still wearing her favorite black jeans and boots, she'd borrowed one of Liv's floral blouses.

"I hope you don't mind," she said, gesturing to the top. "I wanted something cooler for tonight. It's still pretty warm."

"I don't mind at all," Liv said, though inwardly she was screaming. "Have a good time, you two. And don't be home too late, okay? We've got another long day at the bookstore tomorrow."

"Sure." Taylor hesitated, then leaned forward and gave Liv a little hug. "Good night. Have fun."

Liv's stomach clenched as Maggie and Taylor climbed into the car and then reversed down the driveway enough to make a U-turn. There was nothing about this that she liked. The disappearance of the heavy makeup, the floral blouse, the little shy hug at the end. None of these things were Taylor. They bore the hallmarks of Maggie's influence and Taylor's desire to please her.

Liv was still standing there on the front porch when Charlie pulled up. He climbed out of his truck and slowly crossed the yard to her side. "You okay?"

"Not remotely," she said softly, then lifted her face for a kiss. "But I'm getting there."

CHAPTER TWENTY-FIVE

Liv and Charlie parted ways at the front door, going to their respective places to shower and change. Liv lingered in front of her closet for several long minutes before she pushed her usual shorts and T-shirts aside and grabbed instead a long, ruffled floral dress. It was more feminine and boho than she usually wore; in fact, it still had the tag on it from last summer. But she wanted to feel pretty tonight, and she was not going to feel any shame about it.

She blow-dried her hair and then looped a few pieces around her large curling iron to set the wave, then swiped on a little mascara and blush. She purposely left the lipstick off. She might have determined that she was not going to be sleeping with Charlie, but she fully planned to do some kissing. A *lot* of kissing.

Charlie showed up at the front door just as she was taking the steaks out of the freezer to thaw them in hot water in the sink. He too had made an effort, trading his usual T-shirt for a crisp blue button-down that made his eyes shift more to blue than gray; though he still wore jeans, they were a new-looking dark indigo pair. She smiled and stepped aside for him.

He gave her a once-over. "Wow. You look amazing."

"Thank you. You do too."

"No, I look passable. You look like a goddess."

She laughed, but rather than kissing her, he just brushed his fingertips along her bare upper arm. She gestured for him to enter. "Come on in. I'm still thawing the steaks. I forgot to take them out of the freezer when I got home. You want something to drink?"

"Uh yeah, thanks." He pushed his hands in his pockets, looking suddenly uncomfortable. He'd spent plenty of time in her house, but always as a contractor, never as a date.

Liv went to the fridge. "Water, tea, or soda?"

"Uh, whatever you're having is fine."

Liv went to the fridge and pulled out the pitcher of iced tea, holding it up for his approval. He nodded. She poured them each a glass, then went to the TV to tune it to one of the music stations. He followed more slowly and took a seat a couple of feet away from her on the sofa.

"So, what was that all about when I got home? Are you ready to talk about it?"

The pleasant glow she was feeling from Charlie's presence vanished. "I don't know. Am I being too critical of Maggie?"

"I don't know," Charlie said, setting his glass on the side table. "Is there something in particular that's bothering you?"

She blew out her breath and tipped her head back against the sofa. "I don't know. I feel like she's trying to undermine me with Taylor, but subtly. Manipulate the outcome because she knows I don't want to put my foot down and drive Taylor toward her." She lifted her head enough to look significantly at Charlie. "Taylor got rid of the eyeliner."

"Really? I can't even visualize what Taylor would look like without eyeliner. Maybe she's just trying to please her mom."

"That's what worries me. Taylor shouldn't be worried about making her mom like her. Maggie should be worried about getting back into Taylor's good graces."

"Yeah, but kids don't think like that."

Liv groaned. "This is such a mess. I'm twisted up in knots about it all the time and then I feel guilty about being twisted up in knots."

Charlie looked at her, then gestured. "Come on. Put your feet up here."

She blinked. "What?"

Smiling a little, he bent down, took her feet in his hands and swiveled them toward him so she had no choice but to turn sideways on the sofa. He pillowed them in his lap, then took one of her feet and began to knead the sole with his thumb.

"What are you doing?" Liv asked horrified. "That's gross! My feet are dirty from walking around barefoot."

He threw her an amused look. "How dirty could they be? You just got out of the shower. Besides, you have pretty feet."

"I hate feet," she said, but then he hit a particularly tight spot in her arch and all she could do was moan. "Okay, you're right. That's really nice."

He grinned at her, kneading out the sore spots with strong hands. His touch sent tingles straight up her body.

"Is this some sort of seduction thing? Like, are you really into feet?"

Charlie huffed out a laugh. "Not especially, no. I just thought you needed to relax a little bit and telling you to lie down for a back massage sounded inappropriate."

Liv flushed. "Sorry."

"Now, on the other hand, if you *want* me to seduce you . . ."

Liv stiffened and pulled her legs back. "Charlie . . ."

He suddenly looked mortified. "Hey, I'm sorry. I was just joking. I thought that's what we did."

"Yeah. But . . . I just need you to know up-front. I don't want to sleep with you."

Now he was completely taken aback. "Wow. Now that's . . . a blow to the ego. I—"

"No no." Liv groaned and buried her face in her hands. "I just mean . . . I *want* to sleep with you—"

His grin came back and she flushed hot with humiliation.

"You know, theoretically . . ."

"Oh yes, that's always what a guy wants to hear. A woman is only interested in theoretical sex."

Liv suddenly wished the ground would open up and swallow her.

But Charlie just laughed and patted her ankle. "Here. Put your feet back."

Reluctantly, she stretched out her legs into his lap, and he went back to work.

"Let me make it easy for you. You haven't slept with anyone since your husband died. Which means you haven't slept with any man other than your husband in a long time." He cocked his head and studied her closely. "Or maybe ever."

"How did you do that?"

"Lucky guess," he said wryly. He dug his thumb into that spot on her arch and she practically melted into the cushions. "I told you I was patient, Liv. So don't worry about that. Sometimes a foot rub is just a foot rub."

"It's a really good foot rub," she sighed.

He just smiled. "I'm crazy about you, you know."

The seriousness in his tone stalled her brain. "Already?"

"From the first time I saw you."

Liv swallowed. "Yeah. Me too."

"Good. So why don't you lean back and close your eyes and relax for a little bit. And then we will get up and cook steaks and watch the sunset while not having any other expectations for the night."

She smiled at him. "I'm glad you're here."

"I'm not going anywhere."

And if she hadn't completely lost her heart to Charlie before, she did right then.

He was not going to do anything to ruin this.

That was the thought that circulated over and over in Charlie's head while he sat on the sofa, massaging Liv's clean and nicely pedicured feet and trying not to listen too closely to the little sounds of pleasure she made. Just because he'd meant what he said to Liv—he *was* a patient man—didn't mean that this wasn't torture. The very best kind, but torture nonetheless.

Gradually, though, her breathing deepened and her eyes drifted shut. He stilled his hands, resting them over her insteps and just watched her for a second while she slept. She was such a strange combination of savvy and naive, and the way she'd stammered through her explanation of her expectations, he hadn't been able to resist teasing her, just to see the beautiful flush rise into her cheeks.

Somehow, in a matter of weeks, he'd fallen head over heels in love with her.

And even though she wasn't ready to say it, he thought she felt the same way.

That was okay. He was satisfied just to be near her while she figured it out. To touch her, kiss her, talk over her day. Listen to her fears. Help her finish her bookstore and accomplish a new dream with her stepdaughter. He still had plenty of details to figure out—what moving to Haven Ridge might look like, if he could actually make a living here, what it would take to work in the surrounding areas. As long as he was moving forward, making himself useful, helping people achieve their visions, it didn't much matter where he did it.

But it mattered very much who he did it with.

These were all thoughts that she wasn't ready to hear, and so he'd keep them to himself until the time was right. Until they put a name to their relationship, actually started dating for real. So far they'd been hanging out and they'd kissed a few times. He supposed he could probably call *this* their first actual date, but women didn't usually fall asleep on him.

He chuckled softly to himself and searched for the remote, then changed his mind. He didn't want to wake her up. Instead, he contorted himself to feel in the cavity of the end table for a magazine or something else to pass the time. His fingers touched a book.

Carefully he drew it out. It was a pretty hefty

volume for what appeared to be a kid's book—the cover had a boy holding his hands out with glowing light around them. Must be about magic. He shrugged, flipped it open, and began to read.

When the sun was finally starting to dip toward the horizon, Liv stirred and then sat bolt upright, her expression horrified. "Oh my gosh. I fell asleep. I'm so sorry."

"No worries. I'm reading."

"What are you reading exactly?"

"*Artemis Potter and the Illuminati*, I think."

Liv let out a laugh. "Let me see for real." She leaned forward to twist the book so she could see the cover and let out a splutter. "It's *Max Merillion and the Secret of Elia*."

"Huh," Charlie said, enjoying the charade. "So it is. Pretty good, actually."

"It's geared for nine- to twelve-year-olds."

"Then just about right, I'd say." He dropped the act and smiled at her. "Is this one of the books that you edited?"

She smiled and nodded. "Yeah. One of my favorite series. Middle grade or not, they just make me happy."

"I can see why. They're fun." He set the book aside and squeezed her foot. "So what do you say we make some steak? I'm hungry."

"I think that sounds like a very good idea." Liv swung her feet to the ground and pushed herself up, still looking languid and wobbly. She had really needed that nap.

The rest of the night was about as pleasant as any he could remember. Liv seasoned the now-thawed steaks and they went out to the patio together to cook them, then ate them with a tossed salad on the back porch as the sun went down. Liv talked a little bit about her old job as an editor, the longing clear in her voice. Charlie talked about the disaster that had lost him his business and how he was thinking of rebuilding up here where they really needed people. Liv raised an eyebrow over that but didn't press. Then they washed dishes together, picked out a movie on cable, and plopped down on the sofa, where Liv promptly fell asleep with his arm around her shoulders, and her cheek pressed to his chest.

Perfect.

She barely stirred when the keypad beeped on the front door and the door scraped open. Charlie froze, debating whether or not he should wake Liv up, but he dithered too long, because Taylor came around the corner and stopped short.

"Hey," he said softly. "Did you have fun?"

She looked between him and Liv for several seconds, then breezed past without answering his question. "Tell Liv I'm home when she wakes up."

Charlie sighed and rubbed the bridge of his nose thoughtfully. This had been a fail on his part. He'd been hoping that if she saw they were acting all normal together and not making out when she came in that maybe she would realize they were actually in a relationship. That he wasn't just some guy trying to get into her stepmom's pants. Though now to think about it, she probably would have felt better about that option. It was the long-term interest that would bother her.

As if she sensed Charlie's tension, Liv stirred and then sat up, blinking owlishly in the single light of the living room. "Did I hear someone talking?"

"Taylor came home."

Her expression shifted to horror. "Oh no. How was she?"

"She seemed fine. Not too happy to see me, I don't think."

Liv jumped up from the sofa, obviously about to go to Taylor's room, but Charlie grasped her hand to keep her there. "I'd give her a few minutes at least." He pushed himself to his feet. "I should be going anyway."

Liv stifled a yawn. "I'm sorry. I'd honestly intended to do a lot more kissing tonight."

Charlie laughed. He was sure that comment was from her sleepy, unfiltered subconscious. She'd probably be mortified tomorrow when she realized that she'd said it out loud. "You're the one who fell asleep on me. Twice."

She scrunched up her nose. "I know. I'm sorry."

She reached up on tiptoes to press a kiss to his lips. "I'll make it up to you. I promise."

"Oh?" He took her by the waist and tugged her closer, enjoyed the way she suddenly became a little more alert, her eyes widening. "When exactly?"

"I'll let you take me out on a real date this weekend. Without interruptions. How does that sound?"

"That sounds wonderful," he murmured.

This time, their kiss was slow and sweet, and she wound her arms around his neck like she didn't want to let him go. Finally he drew away and pressed one more quick kiss to the corner of her mouth. "Good night, beautiful. I'll see you tomorrow at the shop."

"Mmm," she said, following him to the door. "Good night. Thank you."

He turned to face her on the stoop. "For what?"

"For everything."

After Charlie left, Liv rapped on Taylor's door, only to get a terse "I'm sleeping" in response. She stood there in the hallway, groggy and slightly disheveled, trying to decide if she should force the conversation she knew they had to have. In the end, she chickened out and walked barefoot down the hall to her room, where she collapsed on her bed, feeling simultaneously gutted by Taylor and enthralled by Charlie.

It was one thing when she'd thought it was just nothing but chemistry, some perfect combination of pheromones that drew her to him. Another when she realized that she really truly liked him. Enjoyed his company. Appreciated that he was intelligent without being arrogant, straight-forward without being blunt. That he liked to tease her about her awkwardness when it came to sexy topics but was content to let her lead in that area. In fact, he'd barely touched her all night in more than a friendly, comforting way.

Though when she thought back to that foot massage—before he had somehow found her *off* button and knocked her out cold—it made her toes curl and shivers trace her spine.

Probably for the best. She'd been all in her head earlier, making more out of the situation than there needed to be. Just because she and Jason had moved pretty fast, getting engaged after knowing each other for a month, didn't mean that her other relationships needed to progress the same way. In fact, it was better to take things slowly. Get to know each other. And yeah, while she knew most people ended up sleeping together on the third or fourth date, she thought that Charlie wouldn't be the type to pressure her. Even if he was likely to tease her mercilessly for her awkwardness in talking about it.

She fell asleep smiling.

And woke up to a bang.

Liv sat straight up in bed, groggy and disoriented in early-morning light, until she realized that the sound was the slam of cabinets in the kitchen. Which was truly an impressive feat given that they had soft-close hinges.

Taylor was trying to make a point.

Dread crept into Liv's stomach as she pushed herself out of bed and shoved her feet into slippers, then moved down the hall. Taylor looked up with a blank look on her face when she entered. "Oh hello. Did I wake you?"

Liv leaned against the wall in Taylor's usual place and crossed her arms. "You did, just as you intended. What's going on?"

"Nothing," Taylor said innocently. "Just getting breakfast going before we head over to the shop this morning." She banged a pan down on the grates of the stove and twisted the burner under it. "I'm making eggs. You want some?"

"No. I don't want eggs." Liv pushed herself up to move closer. "What's going on? You're obviously mad about something. Is it about last night? Is it about Charlie?"

Taylor huffed out a little laugh. "No. It's not about Charlie. You can do whatever you want with your new boyfriend. It makes no difference to me."

Liv drew in a deep breath and let it out, casting her eyes skyward for patience. She was no stranger to irrationality with Taylor. As delightful as she could be, she could also flip moods on a whim, and she was extremely emotional, even if she hid it behind sarcasm and dark clothing. They'd gone through plenty of rough patches after Jason had died, when Liv had wondered why she'd ever taken on the task of raising a teen she barely knew. But always, she'd understood what was behind the moods.

Right now, she absolutely had no clue. Because if it had nothing to do with Charlie, what was it about?

"Tay," she said quietly. "Talk to me. What's going on here?"

Taylor twisted the burner off and turned to face her. "You sure changed your tune pretty quickly."

"What tune?"

"The one about not being interested in Charlie."

Okay. So it was about Charlie. "Well, Taylor . . . it just kind of happened. You're sixteen years old. You understand how these things work. You knew I wasn't going to stay single forever, right?"

Taylor rolled her eyes, the visual representation of *duh*. "It would just have been nice if you'd consulted me."

The arch affront in her tone wormed under Liv's skin. "Consulted you? Like you consulted me about having Maggie come out to visit?"

It was the wrong thing to say, and Liv knew it before the words even finished leaving her mouth. But the idea that Taylor—who had pretty much been running on selfishness and self-interest the entire week—wanted to take away the one bright spot in Liv's life chafed her already-stretched nerves raw.

"So this is payback. I shouldn't have been surprised." Taylor closed her eyes, shook her head, and then pushed away from the stove. "I'm going back to bed. I'll come over to the shop later."

Liv stared after Taylor in utter disbelief. Her first instinct was to let her go, to let her sleep off her irrational anger, figure out what lay behind it another time. But no. She was tired of letting it go, tired of tiptoeing. "Taylor," she said in a low voice, "don't walk away from me. We're not done here."

To her surprise, Taylor halted in her flight and spun, her face stony. "Okay. So talk."

Liv took a deep breath to steady herself. "I don't entirely know why you're mad, and honestly, at this very moment, I don't care. When you can tell me without arguing with me, then we can discuss it. But you are not going back to bed. You're going to go get dressed and come to the shop with me, where we are going to clean all day and get the place ready for fixtures."

"Why—"

"This was partially your idea and you're committed to it. You can't just blow it off because you're mad at me or you don't feel like working. Because however annoyed you are with me, I'd be a pretty crappy mom if I let you think that this behavior was okay."

The second the words left her mouth, Liv was bracing herself for the retort. Hoping it wouldn't come, but expecting it anyway.

Taylor let out a little laugh and let it fly. "Well. It's not like you're my real mom anyway." And when she was sure she had hit her mark, she whirled away and raced back down the hall to the safety of her room.

Liv stood there, frozen like someone who had been shot but hadn't yet realized it. Then she crumpled in on herself with the weight of the words that she'd been whispering to herself for five years, desperately fighting against. Usually she could stave them off, telling herself that imperfect or not, she was the only mom that Taylor had.

But this time, it wasn't true. This time, Taylor was right.

CHAPTER TWENTY-SIX

You're not my real mom anyway.

The words, or a hundred variations of it, dogged Liv as she dressed for the day. It was as if Taylor had looked inside her head, dragged out her deepest insecurity, and then weaponized it at the worst time possible.

Or perhaps Maggie had tipped Taylor off to her deepest insecurity and weaponized it at the most convenient time possible.

Liv shook off the thoughts. It hardly mattered whether the idea had come from Taylor or been whispered in her ear. Now that it was out there—now that there was a *real mom* in the house, though Liv would argue that a real mom wouldn't have left in the first place—she couldn't wish it away. Liv had to deal with it, face it head on. And as much as it was contrary to her desire to make Taylor like her again, she wasn't going to let her stepdaughter get away with bad behavior.

Assuming that she still had any pull with her at all.

But to her surprise and relief, when Taylor came out of her room, still sullen and unrepentant, she was dressed for work. The makeup was still conspicuously absent. Liv shook her head to herself. She might be the only parent who was concerned when her teenage daughter came out in normal clothes and not some variation on her usual goth style. She'd long since figured out that it was a theatrical choice and not a representation of some inner turmoil.

Or maybe she'd let herself think that and only now was she seeing the real Taylor.

No. She couldn't do that to herself. She'd been the only mother Taylor had had for the last five years. Liv knew the girl as well as one could actually know a teenager, and she couldn't start second-guessing everything because Taylor was dealing with some pretty serious feelings about seeing her long-lost mother. So Liv did the one thing that had always served her well: put on a pleasant, unconcerned face and pretended that there was nothing wrong.

"There's some bagels in the pantry," Liv said when she appeared, swiveling away to pour some coffee into a travel mug. The thermometer on the counter said that the outside temperature was already sixty-eight, which hinted at a hot day ahead. She didn't care. She needed her caffeine to face the day and lots of it. Besides, they would probably only get in six hours before it got too hot inside the un-air-conditioned building to work.

Taylor slipped by her for the bagels and wordlessly popped one into the toaster. Liv didn't try to make conversation or smooth things over. She stood by what she said. She wasn't going to try to make everything good between them when Taylor was the one in the wrong, but she wasn't going to give her the cold shoulder either.

Still, it made for an awkward drive into town, Taylor staring out the window while Liv fiddled with the radio to find a station that didn't make her want to scream. When she pulled up in front of the bookshop, Charlie's truck was parked at the curb and the front door was propped open.

Liv retrieved the buckets and rags she'd brought from home and headed inside without waiting for Taylor. Her heart skipped a beat, lifting immediately when she saw Charlie kneeling in the middle of the floor, hammering out bent nails from the remnants of the shelves. "Salvageable, you think?"

He sat back on his heels, his entire face lighting up. "Good morning. Yeah, I think so. The last owner didn't secure them to the wall properly, probably didn't want to screw into the brick."

"Good." Liv was going to say something else, but Taylor had finally slunk her way into the room, arms crossed over her chest.

"Morning, Taylor," Charlie said cheerfully, as if he didn't notice the rain cloud following her. "I thought maybe you could start on the third floor while it's still cool up there?"

"Sure," she mumbled. She grabbed a broom from where it sat in the corner, shoved earbuds into her ears, and started fiddling with her phone as she walked up the stairs.

Charlie waited until she was out of the room to push himself to his feet and come over to Liv. "What's that all about? Is it because of us?"

Liv winced. "No. At least I don't think so. She and I had a fight and she played the you're-not-my-real-mom card."

Instantly, his face twisted with sympathy and he slid an arm around her shoulders. "I'm sorry. You okay?"

"Not really. I mean, I was expecting it when Maggie showed up, but I still wasn't really prepared for how much it would hurt."

"You think she's involved in this somehow?"

The fact that he'd so easily jumped to the same conclusion suggested that maybe she wasn't very far off the mark. "Perhaps tangentially. If Maggie's influencing her, she's subtle. It's more likely that Taylor really wants her approval and she thinks that distancing herself from me will prove that she didn't replace her."

"Hmm." Charlie's tone didn't sound convinced. He threw a glance over his shoulder to make sure they were still alone and then pulled her against his chest, pressing his lips to the top of her head. "I missed you, you know."

She'd seen him eight hours ago. It was silly to say that he'd missed her. But she knew exactly how he felt. "Yeah. I missed you too."

"You two will get through this," he murmured into her hair. "Maggie will be gone in another couple of days. Taylor will mope a bit and then things will get back to normal. I'm not sure I believe how much Maggie actually wants to be part of her life and how much she just wanted to convince herself that she could be."

"You may be right," Liv said, but inwardly, she didn't think it was going to be that easy. Maggie coming back had shifted more than just their schedule for the week. It had messed with Taylor's head, reminded her of what she was missing. Liv wasn't sure that they'd ever fully recover from that. She blinked away the prick of tears and pulled away from Charlie. "So. Shall I get started cleaning the second floor?"

"Sure. I forgot to tell you. The water's on."

"Perfect!" Liv grabbed the bucket and wood-cleaning solution she'd brought from home and then moved into the bathroom. It took some maneuvering to figure out how to fit the bucket in the sink and then get it back out without spilling half the water, but when she'd finally filled the bucket and mixed in the cleaner, she took her tools up to the second floor and got started.

The job hadn't seemed that daunting. But when a single pass over a tiny corner of the space turned her mop water nearly black, she realized there was probably more work here than she'd thought.

Liv lost count of the number of times she went up and down the stairs to change the water. At some point, she got wise to the process and brought up three buckets, which she used in succession to keep the water that went on the floor as clean as possible. Even so, by midmorning, she'd only cleaned about a quarter of the loft.

That didn't even include all the hands-and-knees scrubbing she'd have to do on the baseboards.

"I changed my mind," she called over the balcony to where Charlie was attaching the repaired shelving units to the brick walls. "I don't want this place anymore. I quit."

Charlie paused in his work and grinned up at her. "You can't quit. I just put bolts into hundred-year-old brick. You're committed now."

"Oh, well in that case . . ." She made a face at him, then grinned when he slid her a crafty wink.

Just being here in the same building as him lifted her spirits. As if all the terrible feelings that churned inside her when she thought about Taylor and Maggie were less terrible because of his presence.

As if, maybe, finally, she wasn't completely alone.

It was silly and premature, she knew, but she also had a feeling that even if their romance didn't work out, Charlie wouldn't abandon her.

It wasn't who he was. He possessed an innate desire to help that he couldn't suppress.

But, now that she was thinking about it . . . where was Maggie? Hadn't the woman said she was going to come today? Was it too much to hope that she'd changed her mind and gone home early? Gotten called back for a heavy equipment rental emergency?

Almost as if she'd read her mind, Taylor clomped down the staircase from the top floor, flushed and dirt-smudged and holding a plastic bag of trash. "Hey," Liv said. "Is Maggie coming over today?"

"No. I told her it was probably better that she didn't." Taylor brushed by her and continued down the stairs and straight outside, where she chucked the bag into the dumpster.

She'd told Maggie not to come. Probably also told her that Liv had had a freak-out and she was afraid that she would react badly to the situation. Great. The picture Taylor painted of their actual life grew worse by the day.

But Liv couldn't do anything about that and she certainly wasn't going to let Taylor get out of work. As soon as the girl came back in, she leaned over the balcony. "Grab another mop and come up here and help me with this. It's taking forever."

Taylor scowled, but she did as she was told, appearing upstairs a moment later with a second mop. Liv explained the three-bucket process she had implemented, and the girl got to work without another word. At least she hadn't lost interest in the project itself. The way she tackled the dirty back corner, kneeling to pick debris out of the spaces between the floorboards, seemed to speak for itself.

All in all, it was the longest morning that Liv could remember spending.

And then came the voice to ruin the only bright spot in the day thus far: Maggie's cheery alto rang from downstairs. "Surprise! I brought everyone lunch!"

Taylor's face lit up. She dropped the mop and rushed downstairs, where she skidded to a stop before Maggie, who was holding three huge cardboard boxes. "Pizza?"

"Of course. You told me Mario's was good, so I figured it was the perfect excuse for a lunch break."

Liv rested her arms on the banister of the balcony, vaguely registering that she probably should have Charlie check it out more thoroughly before she put weight on it. "You didn't have to do that, Maggie."

"Of course I did. If I couldn't be here to help this morning, I might as well be able to feed you all."

Liv straightened, frowning. Wasn't able to be here this morning? That was a different story than the one that Taylor had told her. She leaned her own mop in the corner and grabbed the two dirtiest buckets to take downstairs with her, emptying them first in the bathroom before she went out to join the pizza party.

Charlie had already created a makeshift table with two buckets and a couple of boards from the last unassembled shelving unit, and Taylor was setting out two pizzas and a giant box of garlic cheese bread. Despite herself, Liv's stomach rumbled.

"Oh, I forgot some things in the car." Maggie rushed outside and then returned a minute later with a drink carrier and a stack of paper plates. She smiled at Liv and held out a Styrofoam cup for her. "Iced tea."

"Thank you." Liv took the cup, surprised that Maggie had remembered. Had she misread the woman? Misread the situation? Had Taylor just been needling her because she was mad at her? She took a paper plate, grabbed a slice from the fully loaded deluxe pizza and plopped herself down cross-legged against the wall. Charlie came to sit beside her with his own food, and predictably, Taylor joined Maggie by the window. Liv tried not to pay attention when they tipped their heads together, conversing in low tones that she couldn't catch from across the room.

"Well, now I don't know what to think," Liv muttered before she bit into her slice.

Charlie slanted her an unimpressed look. "She brought pizza. She didn't cure cancer."

Liv smiled. It had been a long time since she'd had complete, unconditional support.

They were just finishing up their food when Maggie cleared her throat. "So I wanted to ask you something."

Liv's heart plummeted instantly to her stomach. She'd known this was too good to be true. She tried to keep her voice level, unsuspecting. "Oh?"

"I was hoping you might let me take Taylor to Denver for the weekend. I have a friend who lives there and he gave me tickets to MeowWolf tomorrow. I thought she might like to go. And if we're going to drive three hours each way, might as well make a weekend of it." Maggie must have seen Liv's instant recoil because she hurried on, "I know it's a lot to ask. But I'm going back to Wichita on Monday morning and it's hard for me to get time off. I'm not sure when I'm going to make it back here."

Liv glanced at Charlie, whose cautious, doubtful expression mimicked the feeling building in her tight chest.

For the first time today, Taylor looked at Liv with something other than contempt. "Please, Liv? It's only for the weekend. After she goes home, I'll have plenty of time to work on the shop. I promise I'm not just going to dump it on you."

That's what she thought this was about? She thought Liv was worried about having to do all the work herself?

"I don't know, Taylor. You kind of sprang this on me. Again. I need to think about it."

Taylor started to protest, but Maggie stilled her with a hand on her arm. "It's okay, Taylor. She just wants what's best for you. You can give her the rest of the day to consider. We wouldn't have to leave until tomorrow morning anyway. The tickets are for the evening."

It was exactly what she should have said, exactly the right thing to say, and still Liv had to grit her teeth to keep herself from snapping. Instead, she took a deep breath and put on a smile. "Thank you. I appreciate your understanding. Are you going to stay and help clean?"

"Ah." Maggie looked down at her crisp jeans and chiffon top. "Unfortunately, I think I used up my work-suitable clothes yesterday. I only have a couple of things left to wear for the weekend."

"No problem." Liv pushed herself to her feet and started gathering the trash to put in the dumpster. "I'll have Taylor call you tonight."

"Thank you." Maggie looked down at Taylor and squeezed her shoulder. "I'll talk to you later. And don't worry, no matter what she decides, we'll have fun. The important thing is that we get to spend time together, not where we do it, right?"

Taylor smiled up at her, looking so hopeful it was heartbreaking. And in that moment, Liv's reasons for hating Maggie—for what she was taking away from Liv—shifted over to what she was doing to Taylor. Building her up right before she disappeared again. How long would it be before she was too busy to phone or visit and Taylor realized she'd been abandoned once again?

Maggie finally took her leave, and Liv looked at Taylor. "I'm still thirsty, actually. Would you mind going down to the Koffee Kabin and getting me an iced chai? Get yourself whatever you want while you're there."

Taylor looked suspicious, like it was an invented errand to get her out of the store, which it was. But Liv couldn't think of anything better in the moment, and besides . . . chai. Slowly, the teen nodded. "Use your card?"

"Yeah. Thanks."

Taylor glanced at Charlie. "You want any-thing?"

"No, thank you."

"Okay." Slowly, Taylor bent to get her purse and then walked out of the front door of the bookshop.

Liv watched as she passed in front of the large window, counted to three, and then turned to Charlie. "What the heck?"

"I know," he said. "That was a power move right there."

"So it wasn't just me."

Charlie shook his head. "Nope. I wanted to give her the benefit of the doubt, but that was next-level manipulation. Were she really concerned about being respectful, she would have asked you in private before she said anything to Taylor."

"That means I can't do anything but say yes, right? If I don't, I'm the bad guy."

"I don't know about that." Charlie crossed his arms over his chest, thinking. "If you really have reason to believe that she's dangerous to Taylor, you say no. I mean, Taylor will be mad at you until Christmas, but isn't that all a part of parenting teens?"

"I wouldn't know," Liv muttered, but Charlie grabbed her by the upper arms and turned her toward him.

"No, don't do that. You've been parenting Taylor since she was a kid, and by yourself for almost three years. Your instincts are good. Listen to them."

"My instincts say I'm losing her," she whispered, tears springing to her eyes. Charlie pulled her in for a hug and she buried her face in his chest. Inexplicably, his arms tightening around her loosened the band around her rib cage just a tiny bit.

"You are not losing her," he whispered in her ear. "She's just . . . confused. And hopeful. She'll come back to you."

"I hope you're right. Because I don't know what I would do if . . ." She couldn't put voice to the words, didn't want to think of what could happen. Yes, Taylor was only sixteen. Yes, assuming that Maggie didn't launch some sort of legal battle—which she didn't have great odds of winning anyway—Taylor would have no choice but to stay here with Liv. But that didn't mean it would be the mostly happy life she already shared with her. The idea of two years of nothing but scowls and closed doors and one-word answers made Liv's heart ache and her stomach churn.

She pulled away from Charlie reluctantly. "Why is this so hard and ugly?"

"Because this is parenting and if anyone told you the real truth about it up-front, no one would have kids?"

Liv laughed. "You don't have kids somewhere, do you? Because that sounded like experience talking."

"I have two sisters and two brothers and all of them have kids. I've heard stories over the years that would make your hair curl."

"Oh?"

"The least disturbing one is the time that Kevin—that would be my brother Eric's son— filled all their air vents with canned whipped cream. And they didn't discover it until it started to get rancid and the air conditioning turned on."

Liv cringed. "I'm glad I missed that phase."

"Or there was the time that Mira's daughter—that would be my elder sister's oldest kid—wrecked her dad's car but was afraid to come home and tell them, so she stayed out all night. We all panicked. Had the police out looking for her, called all the hospitals. It was a mess."

"That's what we call birth control," Liv quipped.

"You'd think. But even with all the drama, I think it would be worth it."

Liv shot him a sideways look. "You want kids?"

"Someday. I hope. I'm already thirty-five, so I realize the clock is kind of ticking, but yeah . . . I could see myself with a kid someday. Maybe more than one. You?"

They were actually having the *do you want kids?* conversation. The realization freaked her out a little. She swallowed. "Jason and I were trying before he died. Since then, I've been focused on Taylor. There are times I think I'll never get the opportunity."

To his credit, Charlie didn't flicker an eyelash at the mention of Jason. "Never is a long time. A lot can happen in a short period."

Tell me about it, Liv thought. But this conversation was getting serious fast and she didn't have the emotional bandwidth to deal with it.

Right now, her concern was Taylor and the decision that she had to make.

Let Taylor go against her best judgment and screaming intuition. Or tell her no and risk losing her forever.

CHAPTER TWENTY-SEVEN

Liv excused herself from Charlie and headed for the bathroom to refill the buckets. As soon as she closed the door behind her, though, she dug her phone out of her pocket and texted Gemma. Taylor wants to go to Denver with Maggie for the weekend. I need to know if it's safe. Any news from Andrew?

Almost immediately, a reply. Ouch. Let me see what I can dig up. Then right on its heels, You okay?

Not even close. Just trying to make the best decision here.

Hang in there. Love you.

Yeah, love you too.

Liv was filling the buckets when another message came in. So . . . lots of kissing? No hot tub?

How was it so little time had passed since that conversation and it had felt like a year? These had probably been the longest days of her entire life. So little kissing! I fell asleep! Twice!

While you were kissing him? It was that bad?

Liv laughed out loud and had to clap a hand over her mouth not to alert Charlie in the other room. No. Very good kisser. I was just really tired. And he had just given me the best foot rub of my life.

Foot rub? Done. Marry him.

Liv grinned, but it faded a little at the tug in her chest at those words. Gemma was right. Charlie was the marrying kind. He said he was patient—and he'd proved it thus far, though given that they'd only known each other for all of two weeks, she wasn't exactly giving him a medal yet—but his words came back to her. Thirty-five. Ticking clock. Wanted kids. He was ready to commit when he found the right woman, but the very thought sent terror into her heart. Heck, she'd barely brought herself to kiss another man, go out on a real date with him. All her desires for a companion, for someone to wake up to in the morning, had been abstract.

Those wishes, made concrete, were terrifying.

"Stop," she told herself aloud. "Don't do that to yourself." She wasn't going to sabotage something that could be really sweet and fun just because she was thinking eight steps down the line.

Almost as if she'd summoned him, Charlie rapped on the door. "Hey. You okay? I thought I heard something."

Liv opened the door. "Yeah. Sorry. That was me. Talking to myself. Can you help me with these?"

"Sure." Charlie picked up the buckets, now filled with clean water, and sidled sideways out of the door. "Second floor?"

"Yes!" She followed him up the stairs, waved vaguely toward the corner, but she hovered by the stairs, uncertainty flooding into her. "You didn't sign up for any of this, did you?"

"Carrying buckets? Kind of part of the job description."

"No. Any of this. The angst. The drama."

He frowned, coming close to her. "Angst and drama are just part of life. What's going on?"

"I just . . ." She shook her head. "I would love nothing better than just to have a normal evening, where you and I can go out to dinner and get to know each other, and not have all my stuff hanging over us."

"Okay, first of all, *stuff* is part of the deal. Any guy who doesn't realize that dating a single mom comes with *stuff* is an idiot." His voice gentled, and he reached up to brush a lock of hair away from her face. "And second of all, I don't mind stuff as long as it's *your* stuff."

His eyes held hers, sincere and unwavering, and she knew that he meant what he said. Her heart swelled with appreciation, infatuation, something that felt suspiciously like love but surely couldn't be. It was all too jumbled for words. So for the second time, she was the one who kissed him.

His lips were soft and warm and they opened beneath hers immediately, taking the kiss from sweet to heated in a split second. His hands splayed across her back, pulling her hard against his body as he deepened the kiss, sending a flush of electricity straight through her, weakening her knees. It was as if she had no defenses against him, no way of holding back. The minute he touched her, she wanted him. Every bit he gave her, she wanted more. She lost herself in his feel and his taste, reveling in how he was hard where she was soft, the way their bodies fit together. Somehow, they'd stumbled backwards until she was pressed against the wall, kissing as if they were drowning and this was their only hope of air.

And then a familiar voice. "Hey guys, I'm back. They were out of chai so I got you an iced latte. Liv?"

Liv and Charlie broke apart and it took her a long second to come back to herself, to recognize Taylor's voice. A curse slipped from her lips, but whether it was at the prospect of being caught or the fact that once again they'd been interrupted, she wasn't sure. Charlie dropped his head against the wall beside her, huffing a laugh into her ear.

Liv cleared her throat, hoping her voice didn't give her away. "Hey, Tay. That's fine, thanks. I'll be down in a minute. I just need to finish this . . . corner."

Charlie's shoulders shook in silent laughter and she smacked him in the chest. "Shut up!" she hissed, which only made him laugh harder. She ducked under his arm before he could give them away, yanked her phone out of her pocket, and flipped the camera to take stock of her appearance.

Her lips were pink and her cheeks were rosy, but with any luck, Taylor would take that as a sign she'd been mopping strenuously and not kissing her boyfriend in the corner. She shot Charlie a stern look—he just grinned, completely unrepentant—and then climbed down the stairs.

Taylor was sipping what looked like a matcha latte and she handed over Liv's order without a blink. "Have you thought about it yet?"

"Yes, I have thought about it a lot. But I have not made a decision yet." *Come on, Gemma. I need some solid data here.*

Taylor chewed her lip, a gesture that suddenly looked familiar. Maggie had the same mannerism. Liv had never realized that came from her mom. "I know you don't like her, but she's my mom. Don't I deserve the chance to get to know her?"

Liv stared at Taylor. "What gives you the idea I don't like her? I like her perfectly well, Taylor. She seems like a nice person and she also seems like she cares about you. But she's also had a lot of problems in her past, and she just suddenly showed up in your life again. Don't you understand it would be irresponsible for me to trust her completely without any proof that she's safe for you to be around?"

"She's my mom," Taylor said.

"I know, sweetie. And I don't ever want to make you unhappy. I just want to think about it some more, okay? Otherwise, I'm going to have to come along and you're not going to like that."

A tiny smile surfaced and Taylor gave a little nod. "Okay."

"Okay." Liv smiled too. "Help me finish the second floor before it gets too hot up there?"

Taylor arched an eyebrow, and Liv realized then that the girl knew *exactly* what she had been doing upstairs.

What she wouldn't give for a little alone time with Charlie right now. Just an hour—no, heck, at this point, she'd take twenty minutes—when she could be sure that they wouldn't get interrupted, wouldn't have company, could just . . . be a couple without worrying about what it looked like from the outside.

Maybe she and Taylor needed a little space from each other.

Which may have been the reason for her snap decision when Gemma's text came through.

Hate to say it, but Maggie is clean. Not so much as a speeding ticket for the past six years. Residence in Wichita, though she does have a former address in Denver.

That was weird, but maybe not all that surprising, since Maggie said she had a friend in Denver. Maybe she'd stayed there at one point. Liv took a deep breath, steeled herself for the

380

inevitable avalanche of regret and worry and guilt, and turned to Taylor. "Okay. You can go."

Taylor's face lit up and she threw her arms around Liv's neck. "Thank you, thank you!"

"Ground rules though. You keep your phone charged so I know where you are. You check in before bed. And I want you back no later than six o'clock on Sunday. Got me?"

"Yes, yes, I promise, that's all fine." Taylor looked positively gleeful as she held up her phone. "I'm going to call her now and let her know."

Liv watched her stepdaughter escape into the other room, phone already pressed against her ear. Charlie came up behind her, slipped his arms around her waist, and rested his chin on top of her head. "You okay?"

"Not at all," she said, leaning back against his warm body. "But I will be."

CHAPTER TWENTY-EIGHT

Something had shifted in their relationship.

And by that, Charlie meant that it seemed like there was a potential to actually *have* a relationship with Liv.

It wasn't that he was glad for the trouble she'd been having with Taylor; quite the opposite. But he couldn't help but be grateful that the latest conflict had seemed to drive home the point that she couldn't rely on her stepdaughter for company and emotional support. Or even her friends. As close as she seemed to be with Gemma, and to a lesser degree, Stephen, they had their own lives, their own jobs, their own problems.

This had all driven home what Charlie had known for a long time. You needed someone in your corner who had your best interests and *only* your best interests in mind. He knew he could be that for Liv, and he was starting to hope that she could be that for him.

But at the moment, Liv was jumpy bordering on manic because of her decision to let Taylor go to Denver for two days with Maggie. He couldn't blame her. Taylor wasn't even his responsibility and he felt uneasy at the idea of seeing her drive away with a woman they barely knew. But he also understood why Liv had done it. The background check had turned up no logical reason that she should refuse, and like it or not, Maggie was Taylor's biological mother. If Liv denied her this, not only was she denying her closure—or at least some little bit of healing—she would be setting herself up as the one who had held Taylor back from the thing that she thought would make her happy.

It wouldn't. Charlie knew from experience. Just because his parents had stayed married and in the same house didn't mean that either of them were actually present for their five kids. At least Taylor had the advantage of a stepmother who really truly loved her and was concerned about her. Charlie had just had to make do with the best that his older siblings could manage. The rest of the time, he'd been on his own.

Heck, he'd been closer to his high school baseball coach than his own father.

So even though he understood this situation better than Liv probably could imagine, it wasn't his mess to fix. He had to stay out of it. The only thing that he could do was support Liv and be there for her.

Well, that, and distract her from her worries. He had a number of ways planned for that.

He didn't need to ask to know that Liv wanted to spend this evening with Taylor, so when the heat pouring through the windows began to make the place unbearable at about three o'clock, he drew Liv aside in the back hallway, kissed her gently, and whispered in her ear, "I'm just across the driveway if you need me."

She twined her arms around his neck and smiled up at him. "How does a whole Saturday together sound? I can make breakfast and then we can decide what we want to do for the day."

Charlie didn't much care what they did as long as he spent it with Liv, so he nodded. "Sure. And then maybe you'll let me take you out to dinner? A new place opened in Buena Vista that looks promising."

Her smile brightened. "That sounds wonderful. I'll text you in the morning when Taylor leaves."

He kissed her again, this time longer, though he pulled away before things could get heated. "I can hardly wait."

And it was true. The minute she was out of his sight, he wanted to be with her again. Which was probably why it was good that he had a meeting with a potential client this afternoon, a request that had so thoroughly surprised him that he wasn't even sure they'd asked the right person.

Charlie had no idea when Taylor would be leaving, but he wasn't going to risk missing Liv's breakfast text, which meant he was up with the sun the next morning. Not that he could have slept in anyway. His brain was too full of worries and excitement and considerations about what a new life in Haven Ridge might mean. So he took advantage of the early awakening to do some laundry and straighten the apartment from back to front. Just in case Liv happened to come over sometime this weekend.

He needn't have worried, though. He wouldn't have been able to sleep through the grinding rattle of the gate. As he moved to the window and peered down on the property, he saw Maggie's white rental slowly move up the gravel driveway. Even before it came to a stop, Taylor was running out to meet it. He craned his neck to glimpse Liv, standing stiffly on the porch, every muscle in her body belying the smile on her face.

An ache pierced Charlie's heart. He'd meant it when he said this didn't have any long-term implications for Taylor's life with Liv. In his experience, people rarely changed: the occasional bout of interest didn't negate overall self-involvement. But he could see what it cost Liv to smile and chat with Maggie, the way she took the slip of paper the other woman offered and then crumpled it into her pocket. Taking the high road was killing her.

The minute Taylor climbed in the car and Maggie turned to drive away, Charlie was out of his apartment and across the yard, where Liv was watching the departing vehicle with a strangled look on her face. She turned anguished eyes on him. "This is worse than sending her off alone when she got her driver's license. At least then, I knew she wanted to come home."

Charlie reached for Liv's hand and squeezed it. "She wants to come home. But she also wants to prove that her mom didn't leave because she was unlovable."

Liv's expression of surprise melted into understanding, and Charlie realized he may have inadvertently given away more than he'd intended. She stepped closer and laid a palm on his cheek. "You are absolutely lovable."

"Well, I know I am," he quipped, trying to divert the suddenly serious mood. "If I recall, someone might have promised breakfast?"

Liv dropped her hand with a laugh. "Come on in then. It's almost ready. I thought I might convince Taylor to stay for breakfast, but apparently, I overestimated the draw of blueberry pancakes." She pushed the door open and led him in, enveloping them in the sweet smell of griddle cakes and its salty-savory breakfast meat counterpart.

She went straight to the kitchen and gestured to the collection of covered dishes on the island. "Grab a couple of those, will you?"

Charlie did as directed and followed her out to the patio table, already set beautifully with porcelain dishes and tulip-shaped glasses. He set down the plates where directed, and she swept off the foil coverings to reveal scrambled eggs, crispy-fried bacon, and a mound of fluffy pancakes.

"Have a seat," she said. "I need to grab the coffee and juice."

He slowly sat in one of the iron chairs, admiring the scene. Beyond the patio, the wild foliage of her property obscured the fence line, giving the impression that they were the only two people in the wide, wild landscape, even though he could faintly hear the hum of the highway just a few hundred yards north. When she came back, even the view couldn't distract him from her, long-legged and gorgeous in shorts and a tank top.

"What?" she asked suspiciously.

"You're heart-stopping," he said.

Liv flushed and glanced away, but her secretive smile said she was pleased. "Help yourself. I made way too much food."

Charlie did as she bade and piled pancakes, eggs, and bacon onto his plate, then drizzled some of her blueberry syrup—freshly made, she said with a smile—over the stack. It was delicious, of course, but he expected nothing less. Liv struck him as a person who did everything well.

When he'd made a significant dent in his meal, he put down his fork. "I wanted to talk to you about something."

Dread flashed onto her face, and he reached across the table to squeeze her hand. "It's nothing bad, I promise. But I do have a decision to make, and in a roundabout way, it involves you."

The dread gave way to caution. "Okay?"

"I met with Thomas Rivas yesterday. In his capacity as mayor, actually. Now that the town has started to get a little more traffic, and businesses like yours and Gemma's are starting to open, he's been able to convince the town council that it's time to invest in tourism and infrastructure. He wants to reopen the hot springs building in town and turn it into a rec center."

Liv blinked at him. Whatever she'd expected him to say, clearly this wasn't it. "Really? That's great! They've been closed for as long as I can remember."

"Right. And he asked me to head up the project."

Slowly, a smile spread over her face. "That means you're staying?"

"That means I'm staying. The scope of his project, his vision, will probably take several years. It's not exactly full-time from what I can tell, but it will give me the opportunity to build up my business, expand into surrounding towns. And if this is successful, from what Thomas says, there's more work to be done here."

She let out a laugh. "That's wonderful. I'm very glad to hear that. Assuming . . . you do want to take the job, don't you?"

Charlie's gaze never left her face. "As long as there's a reason for me to stay here."

He held his breath while he watched her consider what he was asking. It was early in their relationship—they'd barely just defined it as a relationship—but he had to know if she saw this going somewhere. If she thought it was worth pursuing. Slowly, she nodded.

He broke into a wide smile. "I'm so glad. That does bring me to another question. How do you feel about me being a long-term tenant? Would that be weird?"

"I don't see why it would be," she said slowly. "But don't you want your own place?"

"That is my own place," he said. "The apartment is nice. I feel better with you and Taylor being alone in the house if I'm on the property. But if this—you and I—work out, I'm kind of hoping the next place I look for will be *our* place."

Her eyes widened, and he realized he'd pushed things too far. "I'm sorry. That's too much. I didn't mean anytime soon. I just thought . . ."

"No," she said quickly, looking down at her hands. "I . . . you surprised me is all. I only just started thinking of the possibility of you and I being together. This? This is . . . a lot." She took a deep breath and folded her hands on top of the table before her. "Charlie, you're being honest with me, and I need to be honest with you."

Now it was his turn to feel dread.

"I love being with you. I want to see where this goes. But . . . my husband hasn't even been gone for three years. Just being here with you is a big step for me. Marriage . . . I'm not sure when I'll be ready for that. Someday, I'm sure. Just not . . . soon."

He let out his held breath. "As long as it's not never."

Liv looked like she was considering it, picturing it. Her eyes went distant for a moment. "No. It's not never."

He smiled and reached to squeeze her hand once more. "That's all I'm asking for. A chance."

For a meal that started out that intensely, the rest of it proceeded pleasantly, without complication. The food was good. The conversation was entertaining. Charlie could tell that she was surprised by the range of his interests, that he could talk books and politics, but he didn't take offense, even if she did tease him about only reading books with a body count. In turn, he theorized about how she probably hid the smut in her bedroom nightstand. (She reluctantly admitted that she did.)

"So what do you want to do today?" he asked finally. "I'm at your disposal."

"You like hiking?"

He liked anything that made her eyes light up with excitement like that. "Sure."

She laughed. "Why don't I actually believe you?"

"Because I haven't done much hiking in my life?"

She brought her hand to her chest in a mock expression of shock. "You're a Colorado native and you don't hike?"

"I was a city boy who spent his weekends playing baseball," he corrected her. "I didn't have much opportunity. But I'm sure if I'm with you, I'm going to love it."

"Good answer," she said, narrowing her eyes playfully. "We'll see. Has anyone told you about the hot springs?"

"The ones in town?"

"Oh no," she said, her eyes gleaming. "Our special ones."

Which is how after helping her clean up the patio table and the kitchen, he found himself dressing in his single pair of athletic shorts, a T-shirt, and a baseball cap and meeting her in front of her SUV. "Aren't we supposed to do this before it gets too hot?"

"It's a cool day," she threw back. "Only eighty-five." She thrust out a bottle of sunscreen. "Put this on."

He didn't argue. That was one thing that a native Coloradoan knew from birth—you didn't underestimate the sun. He squeezed some sunscreen into his hand and slathered it on his exposed skin. And became aware of Liv laughing at him.

"What?"

She came closer and reached up to rub the extra

cream into his skin at his temples and jaw, her touch light and feathery. He captured her hand then bent down to kiss her just as lightly on the lips, was gratified to feel her answering sigh.

"Hiking," she whispered. "Before it really does get too hot."

"I think that has nothing to do with the time of day," he quipped, and her cheeks flushed pink in answer.

But he would behave himself, if only because she looked genuinely excited about what she was going to show him. "My car or yours?"

She glanced at his work truck, nicked and scraped from hauling materials in and out, and he saw it from her perspective. He grimaced. "It's okay if you want to drive. I did own a car once. A nice one, actually. I sold it when . . . you know."

"I'll drive," she said, "but not because I'm embarrassed by your truck. Just because you have no idea where you're going."

He could give her that one. He climbed into her passenger seat and buckled in, watching her as she backed out of the driveway. There was virtually nothing she did that wasn't fascinating to him now.

When they turned onto the highway, Liv flicked him a look. "We don't really go for cars up here, you know. SUVs maybe, definitely trucks. Well, unless you're Gemma, in which case it seems perfectly reasonable to be driving around a bright red Audi in the snow."

Charlie laughed. "You two have known each other for a long time?"

"Since we were kids. We grew up together. There was a stretch of fifteen years when we lived in different places, but the three of us made it back here eventually." At his quizzical look, she added, "Stephen, Gemma's boyfriend. They were high school sweethearts."

"They're still together but they're not married?"

"They're together *again*," Liv corrected. "They moved back here within a year of each other."

"That's a big coincidence."

"Not as much as you might think."

"Am I missing something?"

Liv gave a little scrunched-nose grimace. "Let's just say that this town has a mind of its own and a history of bringing people together who need to be together."

"You have a matchmaking town?"

"No, not exactly." She laughed. "Okay, that too. But more like . . . people who need to be here find their way here *just* in the nick of time. You know Thomas? He moved back here just as his grandmother was going to have to close the cafe because she couldn't manage it anymore. And then a year later, Mallory comes into town— on her last dime, practically—falls in love with Thomas, and now they run the place together. Stephen came back because he hated his job and *just* happened to find an open literature teacher position at the high school just when he needed it, which was what he wanted to do with his life in the first place. Not eight months later, Gemma had her own career crisis, ran into Stephen, they realized they still loved each other, and the rest is history. She moved her law practice to Colorado and opened a bakery."

Charlie watched her, amused as she outlined the town's supposed machinations. So that was what was behind the oblique, knowing mentions he got at the diner. He wasn't sure he bought any of it, but it was adorable that Liv did. "And me? How do I fit into this?"

Liv took a deep breath. "I'm not sure it's any coincidence that you showed up *just* when Will needed you, which brought you to me just as I wanted to open a bookstore—and finish my kitchen." She shook her head. "That sounds crazy, doesn't it?"

Charlie started to tell her it was exactly that, coincidence, but he stopped before he could. After all, he had never figured out how Will had gotten his business card. To his knowledge, he had absolutely no connection to the elder Parker's nursing home. Had it not been for that small thing, he would never have come to Haven Ridge, would never have met Liv, wouldn't be discussing revitalization plans for the town with its mayor. It certainly hadn't taken long after his arrival for big things to start happening.

"I don't know," he said finally. "Whatever the reason, I'm glad I came."

It must have been the right thing to say, because she shot him a smirk. "I'm just glad that if the town or the universe or whatever saw fit to send me a handyman, it decided to send me a hot one."

Charlie choked on a surprised laugh. "Thank you. I guess."

She flushed again, and he laughed, feeling lighter than he could remember in years. To think that he'd thought this was just a quick detour in a little mountain town no one had ever heard of, and instead he'd found everything he'd ever wanted.

CHAPTER TWENTY-NINE

Charlie's naive enthusiasm was adorable. A Coloradoan who didn't hike! Liv hadn't thought they existed. Regardless, the path that she'd chosen—the one that she usually ran, by the secret hot spring pool—was more of a comfortable nature walk than an actual hike. She assumed that he was in good shape, but when he'd come out in running shoes instead of hiking boots, she was glad she'd decided to play it safe.

Not to mention the fact that this was just something to fill the day. If left to their own devices, they'd start the kissing now and be in bed together by sundown. Not a problem she thought she'd be having at her age. She'd always prided herself on being much more sensible and self-controlled than that, but Charlie proved to her that her earthy side was just buried, not non-existent like she'd always thought.

So hiking it was.

Liv drove to her usual parking spot on the other side of the crumbling split-rail fence and pulled over as far off the road as she could manage. She grabbed a water bottle from the console on the seat and handed it over, then found its twin for herself. "Can you grab the backpack from the back seat?"

They were just stepping through the gap in the fence to the trail when her phone buzzed. She whipped it out of the pocket in her leggings. *Missed call from Taylor Quinn.* She frowned. It hadn't even rung, which was a sure sign that the signal was weak today.

"Problem?" Charlie asked.

"I don't think so." She held her phone up, watched the little data symbol flicker on and off. "I just missed Taylor's call."

"You need to call her back?"

She considered. It was possible that it had been an accident, especially since enough time had passed to know Taylor hadn't left a message. And in that case, all she'd get was exasperated annoyance that she'd interrupted her weekend with Maggie. Instead, she texted Taylor: Hiking. You need something?

Charlie leaned against the car, waiting patiently while she held the phone, waiting for a reply. When she got none, despite showing two bars and a little download symbol, she shrugged. "I guess not. Let's go."

Despite the warm start of the day, the breeze was pleasant, and the dusty smell of piñon pine and sagebrush filled the air. Liv led the way onto the trail, lifting her face to the sun to feel its warmth on her skin. "I try to soak it up as much as possible during the summer. Winters can be long here. I'm always ready to hike by February but it's usually another couple of months until the trails are dry enough to do it regularly."

Charlie fell into step beside her. "What do you do for fun during the winter, then?"

She looked at him wryly. "Read. Bake. Hibernate like a bear."

"Ever think about trying cross-country skiing or snowshoeing?"

"Are you crazy? I only go outside when I have to if it's below fifty." She grinned at him so he would know she was kidding—okay, *partially* kidding—and scrambled up a rockfall. "Though I admit, I have considered doing something outdoorsy on sunny days."

"Well, I may not hike, but I do ski. Maybe you'll let me teach you sometime this winter."

Sometime this winter. As in, he would still be here and they would still be together this winter. Somehow, it was so far from the "take it one day at a time" approach that she'd initially intended, it felt even more serious than him talking about staying in town, maybe buying a house together someday. She threw him a smile. "For you? I'll give it a shot."

It only took a few minutes to get to the hot spring pool, over which he oohed and ahhed, and then she led him deeper into the valley. It was rocky and uneven in some places, sandy in others, but Charlie just continued on gamely, chatting with her about everything and nothing.

What he did in his spare time—he used to have a motorcycle, which he'd sold; he had both skis and snowboards, which he'd kept—how a rotator cuff injury had killed his dreams of playing pro ball, how he had gotten into construction. She wanted to know everything about him, and he answered each question honestly and openly, even the hard stuff.

"Will you miss the Springs by moving here?" she asked finally.

He gave it some thought. "I don't think so. It's close enough that I can still see my family if I want or need to, but I don't anticipate that happening often."

"You're not close to your family?"

He shook his head. "My parents were more of the type to provide for material needs and overlook emotional ones. They both passed a few years ago. I used to be closer to my brothers and sisters, but they're all busy with work and kids, we really only see each other on holidays."

"I'm sorry," she said softly, reaching for his hand.

He squeezed her fingers before dropping it again. "Thanks. I always envied those close families, who went camping together or took trips or just hung out on the weekends together. We weren't like that. But eventually, you realize that there's no point in regretting what you never could have had; it's better just to try to build it yourself in the future."

"Well, if you want people all up in your business, then Haven Ridge is the place for you." Liv grinned at him. "It's like having dozens of aunts and uncles. Which, when you're a kid and you've gotten into something you shouldn't, is really annoying. And then you move someplace anonymous and you realize you miss being around people you've known all your life. Not constantly having to explain your backstory. I don't think Taylor will know what she's given up until she leaves for college. Not that I would want to keep her here against her will," she added, "but I do hope that she comes back."

"She will," Charlie said.

"How can you be so sure?"

He smiled at her. "Because you're here. And like it or not, big complicated feelings or not, you're her home."

Her smile surfaced to match his and she nudged his arm. "Thank you. That's a nice thing to say." It faded as she thought of Maggie with Taylor now, no doubt trying to talk her into . . . she didn't know what. Taking Liv's place? If not physically, then emotionally? Liv shook off the thought. She'd made her decision to let Taylor go. She wasn't going to ruin some of the rare alone time she had with Charlie by worrying about things they couldn't control.

They stopped at the halfway point to sit on a group of boulders, drinking some of their water and eating homemade granola that Liv had brought in the backpack. The quiet was so deep here it almost had weight. You didn't realize how much background noise there was in everyday modern life—the hum of appliances, the faint strains of traffic. But out here it was just nothing: the sweep of wind through the native grasses and distant trees, the buzz of pollinators, the occasional scurrying of a small animal or a call of a raptor overhead. She liked the silence, the solitude, and Charlie seemed to understand that because he didn't try to fill it as they sat.

Then a cloud scudded across the sun, casting a deep shadow over everything and breaking the golden glow of the moment. Liv pushed herself off the rock and dusted off the back of her shorts, squinting at the clouds. What had been white and fluffy just minutes ago now carried a gray underbelly. "We should start heading back. That looks like rain."

Charlie shoved his water bottle and the granola bag back into the backpack and slipped it over his shoulders. "Lead the way. If we hurry, we'll make it back to the car. It's not far."

But almost as soon as they rejoined the trail, the first fat drop hit the ground in a little puff of dust. Then several more. At first, it was refreshing, cooling their sun-heated skin. But soon the breeze turned cooler, the raindrops colder, coming down faster and faster. Liv pulled the brim of her cap over her face and sped into the fastest walk she dared.

And then the first little chip of ice hit.

Charlie grinned at her, though she could tell he wasn't thrilled at the idea of getting caught up in a hailstorm. "Want to make a run for it?"

The chips turned into little pea-sized chunks of ice, and Liv gave a quick nod. Soon they were hurrying down the trail as fast as they could, the soft, fine dirt turning into mud beneath their feet and splattering their shoes and legs, while the soft hail stung their skin. When they neared the pool, they had to slow; Charlie went first over the slick rock falls, holding his hands up to steady her as she descended. It was unnecessary—she was as confident as a mountain goat on these trails after all the years she'd jogged them—but his concern was sweet. By the time they reached her car again, it had turned almost completely back to rain.

The damage, however, was already done. Their clothes were soaked through, their shoes and legs muddy, and her arms were a mottled red from the impact of the hail. When Liv unlocked the car, Charlie immediately popped the hatch and started rummaging through the supplies in the back. He pulled out a blanket and dragged her beneath the shelter of the lift gate, wrapping the blanket around her.

Only then did she realize she was shivering.

"Are you okay? You're freezing."

"I'm fine," she said, forcing her teeth to stop chattering. "It's just the sudden temperature drop. Plus I'm really wet." She grinned up at him. "That was fun."

He just stared at her incredulously. "Fun?"

"Yeah. It's part of hiking in Colorado. From now on, we'll always say, 'You remember the first time we went hiking and it started to hail? And we were soaked and muddy?' You wouldn't remember it nearly as well if it had been a perfect sunny day the whole time."

Charlie hauled her close to him, wrapping his arms around her and the blanket. He kissed the top of her nose, and only the warmth of his lips told her how cold she'd really gotten. "Nonsense. I would remember every minute."

She smiled up at him, accepted his light kiss, feeling happier than she could remember. He peered out from beneath the lift gate, judging the storm that had finally slowed to a light patter of rain. "What do you say we get home and get changed?"

Liv nodded and stepped back to close the rear hatch, then moved toward the driver's side. But Charlie tugged her back and took the key from her hand. "Nope. I'm driving. You still need the blanket."

And even though she would be perfectly fine—

especially once she turned on the heated seats—his concern and conviction were so sweet that she didn't argue. It was nice, for the first time in a long while, to be the one being cared for instead of the one doing the caring.

It was still early in the afternoon, but Liv and Charlie decided to part ways to get cleaned up and remove the mud from their shoes, then meet back later to go to dinner. Liv checked her phone screen as soon as she had a good signal again. Nothing. Either Taylor had butt-dialed her, or she'd resolved whatever issue it was that she had.

She wasn't exactly sorry. This was the first time in months that she'd had an entire day alone without anyone else to worry about, and she wasn't going to ruin it. She ran herself a bath and soaked in it until her fingers and toes were pruney and the chill had finally left her bones. Then she wrapped her wet hair up in a towel and curled up on her bed with a book, enjoying the luxury of lounging in a bathrobe without any chance of anyone walking in on her or needing something. And finally, when the clock started edging toward five, she put it aside—back in her dresser drawer—and began to get ready for the night.

After applying a face of light makeup and doing a simple blowout, the traces of the day's exertions were completely gone. She chose one of the only dresses in her closet: a light blue sleeveless wrap style with a deep ruffle sweeping diagonally across the front. The color was feminine and pretty but not seductive; the hint of cleavage it showed kept it from reading kindergarten teacher. She pulled out the same white sandals she'd worn the night before and swapped out her tote for a smaller, more delicate handbag.

She opened the front door to head over to Charlie's, but before she got more than a few steps, he appeared in the driveway. He was freshly groomed and looking painfully hand-some, his hair dipping a little over one eye. Like her, he'd gone casual: dark jeans and a long-sleeved button down that skimmed his body closely enough to show off his muscular frame to good advantage. He took a step forward to kiss her cheek in greeting. She grinned. "You clean up pretty nice, mister."

"I'd say you don't look so bad yourself." He looked her over with an appreciative smile. "In fact, every time I think you can't look more beautiful, you prove me wrong."

She laughed. "You are probably the smoothest talker I've ever met."

"Nope. Just honest. Speaking of which, I can drive, but if you'd rather go in yours . . ."

She glanced at his big truck and thought about climbing up into it in sandals and her silky dress. "I don't mind driving again."

Buena Vista was only about twenty minutes away, just a curve around the highway. Despite the skyrocketing prices of real estate, it somehow still displayed its rural roots. It was, therefore, one of the least likely places to find a nice restaurant, considering most of them were either cedar-clad boxes on the side of a highway or a storefront squeezed into an aging strip mall. But she followed his directions and parked on the street just down from what looked like a little blue house.

"This is it?" she asked, surprised.

"This is it." Despite the fact he wasn't driving, he hopped out of the car and circled to open her door, then closed it behind her and offered his arm. She felt a little silly, but she took it and locked her door, letting him escort her up the front steps into the tiny space.

The interior was cool and dim and still sported its original features: hardwood floors and wooden moldings, old-fashioned mullioned windows. There were only perhaps ten tables inside, more than half of them already occupied, and each of them was covered in a fresh white tablecloth with a flickering candle in the middle.

A woman in a slim black dress appeared and smiled warmly at them. "Good evening. Welcome to Alpenglow. Do you have a reservation?"

"Castro," Charlie said, and after checking her screen, the woman ushered them to a table in the corner.

"This is pretty," Liv whispered when she took her seat and the hostess draped her napkin in her lap. "How did you find it?"

"Internet. Apparently it just opened. Which is probably the only reason I got a last-minute reservation."

She looked around the space, noting the simple framed black-and-white photos on the wood-paneled walls, the rustic glass-and-iron fixtures hanging from the ceiling. It was beautiful and tasteful, even if it was much more congruent with Colorado Springs or Denver than Buena Vista.

A server came over and introduced himself as Chadwick, recited the specials, and then disappeared again, but Liv hardly heard any of it. She was studying Charlie across the table, watching his eyes flick down the length of the menu, as comfortable here as he was in her house or her bookshop. Totally unconcerned about what anyone thought of him. It was an appealing trait in an already appealing package.

"Why are you staring at me?" he asked in a sing-song voice without looking up at her.

"I'm staring at you and thinking that I really like you."

He lowered the menu and looked her straight in the face. "Be careful. I'm going to start to believe that if you say that enough."

"Good," she said. "Because it's true."

He reached for her hand and brought it to his

lips, the gesture reminding her so much of their first kiss that her cheeks immediately flushed. He clocked the reaction, a smile coming to his own lips. But before he could comment, Chadwick was back with their sparkling water, pouring it into two large goblets. "Do you need some more time to look at the menu?"

Liv hadn't bothered to look at it, so she scanned it quickly. But Charlie waved the server off. "We're in no rush," he said. "Nowhere to be, no one to get back to, remember?"

"Yeah, I do," she said wryly. "It's weird and I'm trying to distract myself."

"I'm sure she's fine. Did she ever call you back?"

"No, but from the app, it looked like they were hanging out in lower downtown today." Liv lifted the menu, forcing down the little jitter of apprehension in her gut. She'd feel better once she talked to Taylor. She wished that Charlie hadn't brought it up. Until then, she'd been doing an admirable job of pretending to be fine. "I have no idea what to order."

"Me neither. I kind of thought this was American, but this is all in French."

"We should have guessed from the name *Alpenglow*." Liv laughed. "I took French in high school and I still don't know what half of this is."

Which was the point when Chadwick, obviously waiting within hearing range, surreptitiously appeared and turned over the menu in her hand to the English side.

Liv and Charlie both dissolved into stifled laughter, feeling like kids dressed up and pretending to be adults. Liv finally ordered the trout, Charlie ordered beef, and they both got back to staring at each other with restrained mirth still in their eyes.

"Can't take us anywhere," she giggled.

"Speak for yourself," Charlie said, sipping his sparkling water. "I am a paragon of sophistication."

Liv chuckled. "Don't get me wrong. I really appreciate this. I like nice restaurants and I like eating out. I used to do it a lot in New York. But since I've been back in Haven Ridge, I would honestly rather eat ice cream out of the tub in my pajamas and fuzzy slippers."

"Talk dirty to me some more," Charlie intoned.

"Yeah, I know. It's not sexy at all."

"Hey, I wasn't joking. That's about the sexiest thing I can think of."

Liv rolled her eyes. "Right."

"No, really. I think the domestic thing is underrated. Or maybe it's just that nothing you do could fail to be sexy to me."

"Charlie . . ."

"What? Too much? I thought you wanted me to be honest, and this is what I honestly think."

She leaned forward over her arms. "No, I

do . . . it's just . . . We've known each other for two weeks and suddenly . . . Don't you think this is all a little bit intense?"

He reached for her hand again, but this time he turned it over and traced his fingertips over her palm. "Yes. I do. Trust me, this is the last thing I expected when I took a quick little job in a town I'd never heard of. But Liv . . ." He swallowed hard. "You destroy me. In all the best ways. And the only thing I can do is be honest about that. If that bothers you, if that scares you, I can back off."

"That's the problem," she whispered. "I don't want you to back off. But Charlie . . . I've spent all this time protecting myself. Grieving. Trying to be sensible about my life. And then you come along and blow that all up. What happens if it goes away just as quickly? Where does that leave me?"

He seemed to be taking her seriously, thinking over his words before he spoke them. "I can't promise you forever, Liv. It's too soon and it wouldn't be fair, and I think you'd probably leave me sitting at this table alone if I did. But you already know that I'm not playing around, and I would never intentionally hurt you. Would you rather take a risk that this could be something great or do we back off and just dance around it for another six months for propriety's sake?"

What he said made sense. It might not make

her feel any less afraid or feel any less foolish about how wholeheartedly she was diving into this relationship, but the alternative painted a picture she didn't like. Going back to just being friends, having a landlord/tenant, contractor/client relationship, pretending that he didn't make her heart skip a beat and her breath still in her chest. Seeing him and wanting to touch him, but knowing that she couldn't. Dreaming about his kiss.

That sounded like swapping potential future heartbreak for certain present misery. And while it might be the smart move, it was one she couldn't bring herself to make.

"No," she whispered. "I don't think I could pretend that my feelings are any different than they are."

Satisfaction lit in his eyes, and his hand gripped hers hard across the table. Her heart squeezed in her chest. So this was what it felt like. All in. Leaping without a parachute.

As guilty as it made her feel to compare, she'd never felt this way about Jason.

She'd loved him deeply, she'd always miss him, but she wasn't sure that she'd ever felt that panicked about the prospect of losing him.

Did she really want to ruin what she had now because she felt guilty she hadn't had it with the man she actually married?

They tried to talk about lighter topics, but the

intensity of the conversation underpinned every word and every gesture. Her stomach fluttered almost too much to eat, though she finally did, because the food was indeed very good. When they finally left the restaurant in the dark, holding hands over the console as they drove, an unanswered question lingered between them, a tension that hadn't existed even in those early days when they were denying the magnetic pull between them.

When Liv finally pulled into her driveway and parked next to Charlie's truck, she sat there for a long moment. "Come in for coffee," she murmured, and then climbed out before he could give an answer. It wasn't a question anyway.

Liv sensed rather than saw him follow a few steps behind, heard him close the front door when she moved into the kitchen, dropping her purse onto the beautiful granite of her new island. She retrieved the coffee pot and went to the sink to fill it with water. Her skin prickled with awareness as Charlie came up behind her.

But she still wasn't prepared when his lips brushed the exposed skin of her neck just above her dress. Warmth flooded her and her knees went weak, her breath leaving her in a surprised exhale. She set the coffee pot aside with shaky hands, tilting her head to expose more to his touch. Every brush of his lips turned her molten, made her heart thud in her chest.

"Is this okay?" he whispered in her ear before he kissed the edge of her earlobe. "I know how you feel about your coffee."

Liv let out a shaky laugh and turned within his grasp, the heat of his hands searing her through the thin fabric of her dress. In response, she lifted her face and parted her lips, an invitation.

She expected him to crush her, overwhelm her. Hoped for it, in fact. But his kiss was slow and assured, as if they had all the time in the world. As if he wanted nothing better than to taste her for hours, his fingertips holding her in place against him, trapping her between the cool stone and the warm solidity of his body. Her head swam, every brush of his lips making her weak and shaky until she could barely form coherent thought. His hands skimmed up the side of her ribs, leaving shivery trails of heat in their wake. This was why she'd been dying to get him alone and why it was such a very bad idea . . .

From across the room, an electronic trill broke through her pleasant fog. Liv jerked back, blinking as if she'd been released from a trance. "Oh, you've got to be kidding me!"

Charlie let out a big sigh and took a step back, releasing her so she could dig in her purse for her phone. She held it up ruefully. "Taylor. I did tell her to check in."

"Coffee," he said, and reached past her for the pot.

Liv shook her head, taking a moment to gather herself, and answered the phone. "Hey, Tay. What's up?"

But the only thing that met her on the other end was crying.

And then the line went dead.

CHAPTER THIRTY

Liv stared at the phone, her brain not working fast enough to understand what had just happened. She hit Taylor's number in her recent calls list and waited for it to dial, seeing but not really processing Charlie's concerned face in her vision.

The phone rang repeatedly and then went to Taylor's voice mail, a chirpy, cheerful message that was completely at odds with the sudden weight of dread in Liv's gut.

"What happened?" Charlie asked. "Was it Taylor?"

"She was crying. Now she's not picking up."

Charlie moved alongside her to stare at her phone. "Check her location."

Good idea. With trembling hands, she brought up the location app and looked for the little photo icon that indicated Taylor's whereabouts. There it was, in the middle of Denver just like before. She let out a little sigh of relief.

Until she saw the legend at the bottom of the screen that read *no network/out of network since 6:05 p.m.* A chill of disquiet shot through her.

"What does that mean?" Charlie asked, frowning at the screen.

"It means that she's either out of network

range, which I find very difficult to believe, or she turned off location services." Fear clogged Liv's throat. "It means I have no idea where she is."

Her legs sagged, and Charlie caught her, sliding an arm around her waist. He guided her into the living room and settled her on the end of the sofa, then knelt before her. "That doesn't mean anything, Liv. We know where she was three hours ago. And we don't know that anything is wrong. Call her again."

Liv nodded, wanting desperately to believe that he was right. She redialed, and this time, she punched the speaker button. They looked at each other while it rang and rang and rang. "Hey, you've reached Taylor. Leave a message . . ."

This time, Liv waited for the beep. "Taylor, it's Liv. Please call me immediately. I'm worried about you." She hung up and looked at Charlie, her eyes filling with tears.

A bit of concern had crept into his face as well. He shifted to sit next to her and put his arm around her. She nestled into his shoulder, taking comfort from his warmth and presence, even as fear folded her stomach into origami.

"Okay, let's look at this reasonably," Charlie said. "She's sixteen, for one thing, so she's almost a grown woman. That eliminates a lot of the scary stuff."

Liv looked at him with a raised eyebrow.

"I just mean she's not a lost child," he said, squeezing her a little closer. "She's with a responsible adult. Is it possible that you mistook what you heard? Could she have been laughing? If she's someplace noisy and she called you accidentally, she might not have any idea you're trying to reach her. Probably doesn't have any idea location services are turned off either."

It was a reasonable explanation, and one that could very well be true. And yet all Liv's doubts and concerns about sending her with Maggie rushed back in a flood. She'd *seemed* reasonable and responsible . . .

"The papers!" Liv turned to Charlie. "Maggie gave me her cell number earlier this week and then one for the hotel this morning. They're in my purse."

Charlie jumped up and went to the kitchen, then brought her whole handbag to her. She rummaged through the contents until she pulled out two sheets of paper, one folded and one crumpled from her earlier frustration. With trembling hands, she dialed Maggie's cell number, still on speaker.

The phone went directly to voice mail, no greeting, just a robotic *this subscriber is not available* message. Now the worry turned to cold panic. What if they were both out of range? What if they were on their way to Kansas right now and that's why they didn't have cell service?

There were huge stretches of I-70 that had patchy reception; they could conceivably have left the state in the course of three hours. Her breathing went ragged and the room spun around her.

"Liv." Charlie looked into her face, then grabbed her shoulders and shook her. "Liv, look at me. You have to breathe slowly. Like this. Breathe with me."

Liv focused on Charlie with difficulty, mimicking his breathing until things came back into focus. She'd been hyperventilating again. But her brain was still locked in some primal fear pattern; she couldn't think or move.

Gently, Charlie took the papers and the phone from her hand, then dialed again. "Hey, could you please connect me with a guest? Maggie Quinn." His brow furrowed and he covered the speaker with his hand. "Do you know her maiden name?"

Liv blinked but nothing came to mind. Charlie figured out she was going to be no help and went back to the call. "How about a Taylor Quinn? No? I don't suppose you remember a woman and a teenage girl checking in yesterday? Dark hair, dark eyes? The girl is a little bit goth-looking—"

That detail broke through her fog. "She was wearing a flowered blouse. Mine."

"Wearing a flowered blouse. Ah, okay. Thanks." Charlie hung up.

"So?"

He shook his head slowly. "No one registered by that name and they don't remember anyone by that description, but it would have been the day shift receptionist anyway."

"So what do I do now?" Liv looked up at Charlie. She'd had moments of worry before when Taylor hadn't been reachable. But that had been here in Haven Ridge. There were only so many places a teen girl could go, and barring car accidents on the highway, it wasn't particularly dangerous. But now she was three hours away, in a city of millions of people, and the best guess Liv had about her location was a restaurant in Denver from three hours ago.

Charlie was looking far calmer than she felt, but that furrow of concern hadn't left his forehead since he called the hotel. "What about Gemma? Wouldn't she know what to do? She deals with custodial cases as a divorce lawyer, doesn't she?"

"You're brilliant," Liv said. She took her phone back and hit Gemma's contact. Her best friend answered almost immediately, and Liv plowed over her greeting in a rush. "Gem, I need your help. I can't find Taylor."

She poured out the whole situation, including their failed attempts to call Maggie and the hotel. Gemma listened quietly until Liv stopped.

"Well," Gemma said thoughtfully, "we could always call Denver PD. Amber Alerts apply to children under seventeen, and Maggie is a noncustodial parent. But," she added before Liv could respond, "that might be a little premature. You gave Taylor permission to go with Maggie for the weekend. She's not technically missing. You just can't reach her right now. So I'm not sure how seriously they're going to take you if you call."

Liv swallowed around the lump in her throat. Gemma was probably right, but right now all she wanted to do was scream from the rooftop for anyone to help her locate her daughter. "So what do you suggest?"

"I suggest that you keep trying to call her and Maggie. And maybe call around to all the hotels in the area and see if they have a record of them. Start with ones that are near that last location you have for her. Chances are they had dinner close by."

It was good advice. "But what if Maggie's not going by Quinn?"

"Oh. Hold on." Gemma went away for a second and there was muffled conversation in the background, the rustle of papers. "Maggie's maiden name is Appleton."

"Thanks, Gemma. I'm going to do that now."

"You're welcome. Call me if you need anything else."

Liv hung up without saying goodbye, galvanized by her new plan of action. "She says to call all the hotels in the area. Maggie's maiden name is Appleton and her full name is Margaret." She remembered seeing the name on paperwork years ago.

Charlie nodded. "Let me help. You take anything starting with *A* through *M* and I'll do *N* through *Z*. That way we don't overlap."

Liv threw him a grateful look. He rose and then bent to kiss her forehead. "We'll find her. And then we'll have a good laugh about how panicked she made us because she accidentally changed her phone settings."

"And I'm never letting her leave the house again," Liv muttered, though she knew that was just fear talking. Maybe it was unreasonable fear, but she'd had a bad feeling about this trip from the beginning and she'd ignored her instincts because she didn't want Taylor to resent her. If only she'd listened to those instincts, they wouldn't be in this situation right now.

Charlie went into the kitchen to start making his calls. Liv threw Taylor's last known location into her map, enlarged it, and then clicked the button to show accommodations. Several hotels popped up in the immediate vicinity. She clicked on the closest one in her letter range and dialed.

But it only took half an hour for her renewed optimism to fade. Not a single place she called had a record of a Quinn or an Appleton, no Margaret, Maggie, or Taylor. Either the reservation wasn't under those names or they weren't staying in the immediate area.

Or they weren't staying in Denver at all.

Liv dismissed that thought immediately. While it wasn't out of the realm of possibility, she doubted that Taylor would go along with that plan. She'd never leave without saying goodbye, without telling her friends. That would mean forcible kidnapping and even in Liv's panicked state, that seemed unlikely.

Wait. Her friends. She had Taylor's friends' numbers. After trying Taylor's cell one more time—it went straight to voice mail this time and she had to fight not to read too much into it— Liv began texting all the numbers in her phone, starting with Dylan. It was all. This is Liv Quinn. Have you heard from Taylor this weekend? I haven't been able to reach her.

And then one by one, the replies trickled back, some variation of *not since she left Haven Ridge.*

Liv slowly lowered the phone and looked to Charlie, where he bent over the kitchen island on his elbows, talking on his cell phone. When he finally hung up, his eyes met hers and he shook his head slowly.

Okay. She had to look at this reasonably. She might be misunderstanding the earlier call like Charlie suggested. Taylor had only been out of contact for three—no, four—hours. Most likely there wasn't anything wrong and she was just overreacting because that's what parents did when their teenage daughters fell off the grid for any amount of time. The sensible thing was to stay put, keep calling and trust that Taylor would check in as soon as she could.

And yet the same sick, worried feeling that she should have listened to the first time persisted. Finally, Liv grabbed her purse from the couch and stood. "I'm driving to Denver." She marched straight for the door and struggled to put on her sandals while standing on one foot.

Charlie came after her. "Liv, wait—"

"No, I'm not going to wait. What if there is something wrong? I'm at least three hours away. I have to be there."

Charlie put a hand out to steady her as she stumbled sideways and bit off a curse. "I just meant to say, it's a long drive there and back and it's starting to get cool. Why don't you take a minute to change? And then I'll come with you."

Liv stopped, looked up into Charlie's earnest face. She wasn't thinking straight, and having him along was a good idea. Especially considering she was about to embark on what would be at least a six-hour round trip in a dress more suited for the hottest day of the year.

"Okay," she said. "Thanks."

She rushed back into her bedroom, where she pulled off the dress and tossed it onto the bed. Without really considering her options, she pulled on the nearest pair of jeans and a lightweight sweatshirt, then socks and a pair of jogging shoes. Ugly and functional, but at this point, she didn't care what she looked like. She only cared about finding her daughter.

Charlie was waiting for her in the living room when she returned, perched on the arm of the sofa. He straightened. "Ready to go?"

"Yeah. We'll take my car."

"But I'll drive." He held out his hand and she placed the keys in his palm without question. She wouldn't trust herself behind the wheel either.

Except that turned out to be even worse, because without the dark road ahead to focus on, it left her mind free to catastrophize. She kept dialing Taylor's and Maggie's numbers for as long as she had a cell signal, though she really wasn't surprised when they kept going to voice mail. The rest of the time, she stared silently out the window, watching the night-shrouded landscape slide by the window of the vehicle.

"Liv, she's going to be fine," Charlie said, reaching for her hand. She let him take it and squeeze it for a minute, but then she gently slid it free of his grasp.

It was unfair to him, she knew. He was only trying to comfort her and this wasn't his fault.

It was hers.

She had known something was off when Taylor had called her earlier that day on the hiking trail.

But she hadn't wanted to believe it because she didn't want to interrupt her date with Charlie. Had convinced herself that it had been an accidental call and that Taylor would have left a message or sent a text had it been important. But now she wondered if Taylor hadn't replied because she couldn't. Because there was something wrong and she didn't want whoever she was with—Maggie or someone else—to know that she was calling Liv.

The very thought made her want to throw up.

If something happened to Taylor, Liv would never forgive herself. And she would always know that she could have prevented it if she hadn't been so selfish. What had she been thinking?

No, she knew what she had been thinking. She'd been thinking that she missed her single life, before she had the responsibility of a teenager. That just for one weekend, she wanted to pretend like she only had herself to look after. That she could have a fun, sexy weekend with a fun, sexy man. Where this evening would have gone, she didn't know, but she also knew that she'd been willing to find out. Now, she was disgusted with how easily she had pushed aside her daughter's best interests for her own desires. It was just a miracle that she had gotten the call when she had. Who knew how long it would have taken for her to realize that something was wrong if she'd been otherwise occupied?

That wasn't behavior fit for a mother.

Liv chewed the inside of her cheek fitfully until she tasted blood. She welcomed the pain—it was no more than she deserved. And she wouldn't rest until Taylor was safe and sound and back home where she belonged.

In passing, Liv wished that her family was one of the religious ones who attended the many churches in Haven Ridge. It would be comforting right now to be able to pray and know that God had heard her pleas. But assuming God even existed, why would he even listen to her if she'd never acknowledged him?

Still, she couldn't help herself. Please, God, if you're up there and you actually care, please let Taylor be okay. Let us find her and bring her home safely. If you grant me my prayer, I promise I'll never be so irresponsible again. Taylor will be my priority for as long as she's with me. I will keep her as safe as I can make her.

Liv swallowed hard and blinked back tears, hoping with all her heart that she wasn't just sending words into the void. She'd heard the saying that there were no atheists in foxholes, and now she thought there were probably no atheists among the ranks of parents with missing children either.

The drive seemed to go on for eternity. At some point, Charlie had started playing music from his phone over her speakers, a mix of indie rock

426

she'd never heard before and wouldn't remember. But he didn't try to speak to her or reach for her again. So she existed in her own little cocoon of misery, squeezing her hands together in her lap and forcing herself to breathe. What they would do once they got to Denver, she didn't know. If she had to go to every place that showed on Taylor's map with a photo and ask if they'd seen her, she would do it. If she had to knock on every door between Taylor's last known location and the city limits, she'd do that too.

And if they didn't find her by dawn, she'd go to the police.

Finally, after what felt like a lifetime, the highway dumped them out onto the expressway that circumscribed the city, taking them north to the interstate and then into Denver proper. The closer they got, the more Liv shifted in her seat, the tighter her chest became.

"Liv, you need to breathe again." Charlie's calm, warm voice came from beside her, penetrated the tightening fog of anxiety. "We're almost there. We're going to find her."

Please please please.

And then, as they were exiting the interstate onto one of the north-south streets that bisected Denver, Liv's phone rang. She jolted straight up out of her seat, her heart pounding as if she were running a marathon, and it took her several tries to swipe the button to take the call.

"It's her," she choked out to Charlie before she pressed the phone to her ear. "Taylor, is that you?"

"Liv?" Taylor's voice came out just as strangled, as if she were holding back tears. "Liv, can you come get me?"

"Are you okay? Where are you?"

"I'm fine, I just . . ." There was a sniffle at the end of the line. "I want to go home."

"Okay, give me your address." She looked at Charlie and then punched the phone onto speaker so he could hear it as well.

Taylor hesitated, then recited an address that meant absolutely nothing to Liv, one she wouldn't remember. Charlie nodded at her and reached for his own phone when he stopped at a stoplight. He held up his map so she could see the ETA.

"Okay, it says we're twelve minutes away. Just stay where you are and we'll be right there."

"Okay . . . Wait. What? Twelve minutes, I don't—"

"We're in Denver, Taylor. We came when we couldn't reach you."

"We?"

Liv swallowed hard. "Yeah, Charlie drove me."

She held her breath, waiting for the reply, but Taylor just said, "Okay. Text me when you get here and I'll come outside."

"No way. I'm staying on the phone with you."

Another sniffle and a small voice that reminded Liv of when she had been a little girl. "Okay."

It was probably the longest twelve minutes of Liv's life. When they at last pulled into an older neighborhood, Taylor was waiting on the front porch of a crumbling Craftsman. She bounded down the steps toward them, her duffel bag thrown over her shoulder. Liv hung up the phone, tossed it into the seat, and burst out of the SUV to catch Taylor.

Taylor started sobbing the minute Liv's arms closed around her. "I'm so sorry," she said, over and over. "I was so mean to you, and Maggie wasn't what I thought . . ."

Even though the words lifted Liv's heart a little, she also registered the use of the given name instead of *Mom*. What on earth had happened today? And why was Taylor here in a residential neighborhood at a stranger's house instead of the hotel?

But those were questions that could be answered later. Right now, it only mattered that Taylor was back with her, and from the looks of it, no worse for the wear. Liv opened the back seat for the teen, ushered her in, and then closed the door behind her before she jumped back into the front seat.

"Hey Taylor," Charlie said softly, as if this was just a normal pick-up on a normal night.

"Hey Charlie," Taylor said in a small voice.

"I'm sorry you had to drive all the way up here to get me."

Liv turned around and reached for Taylor's hand. "I will always come get you, you hear me? Now let's go home."

Taylor gave her a watery smile. And then in that same small voice, she asked, "Can we stop for coffee first?"

CHAPTER THIRTY-ONE

Little by little, with a massive gas station cup of coffee in Taylor's hand, the story came out.

The weekend, it seemed, had gone awry from the beginning. Maggie never had been able to reach the friend with the MeowWolf tickets, if there indeed had been any tickets. They'd gone for sushi at an expensive restaurant—which Taylor had hated, but choked down to be polite—and then headed to a nice boutique hotel downtown to check in. Where Maggie's credit card had been declined. They'd ended up walking around lower downtown, eating convenience store snacks Maggie paid for with cash, and talking about the details of Taylor's life that she'd missed in the last ten years.

And then the real trouble had started. Apparently, that was *all* of the cash Maggie had on her, but she had friends in Denver—unclear if it was the same MeowWolf flake from before—so she had spent the afternoon calling around to see if there was a place they could stay for the rest of the weekend. By then, Taylor had figured out that her mother wasn't nearly what she had portrayed herself to be, thanks to bits and pieces of conversation she picked up on the phone about

431

her having "unexpectedly left" her previous job to move to Colorado.

"When in all this did you call me the first time?" Liv interrupted, trying to fit the narrative into what she'd been experiencing on her end.

"After the credit card was declined," Taylor said, wrapping her arms around her coffee cup. Now that she was safe and caffeinated, she was regaining some of her spirit, as if the ordeal hadn't taken a full five years off Liv's life. "I was going to ask if you could Venmo me some money just so we could grab dinner, have Maggie take me home early, but she came back and said she found us a place to stay and some stuff to do. So I decided to go with it."

She decided to go with it, Liv thought with a little internal scream.

"That's when we went over to that house we were just at. It belongs to this guy David and his girlfriend, Angela. They were really nice, actually. David is a photographer and Angela is a make-up artist and aesthetician. I helped her make lunch and then David and Maggie went off to talk about some work stuff. Angela gave me a facial and did my makeup and everything. She's really good." Taylor made a face. "I cried and ruined most of it later, but you should have seen it. She does a lot of the models on David's shoots and stuff."

Liv smiled and tried to see it as the adventure

432

that Taylor did. In her imagination, she'd been picturing drug paraphernalia and orgies, not a regular couple making a living doing regular, artistic sorts of things. "So, that didn't sound bad. What happened then?"

"Oh," Taylor said, leaning forward like they were finally getting to the juicy part. "So Maggie came back and announced that David was going to take her on as an assistant, and David said she could stay at the house with them while she was getting on her feet here. She said she wanted to be close to me. But Angela got pissed about that, because I guess David and Maggie used to hook up a long time ago? I don't know how that happened since I didn't think she ever lived in Colorado, but maybe it was in New York. Anyway, Angela stormed out and it was a ton of drama. David and Maggie said they were going to go out and grab dinner for us, but basically, they never came back."

Liv came to a hard mental stop. "What? They just left you there? Taylor, it was like one in the morning when we picked you up!"

"I know. I tried calling you when they didn't come back after an hour, but my charger was in Maggie's car and I was getting low on battery, so I put it on battery-saver mode—"

Liv slanted a look at Charlie. "—which explains no location services."

"—and tried to connect to WiFi but it basically

took forever, and then my phone died. So I figured I'd wait until they came back. And I kept waiting. Ate some bread and soup out of a can in the pantry for dinner. Got bored and started rummaging through all their drawers until I came up with a charger that worked. And that's when I called you." Taylor reached forward to grab Liv's hand. "I'm so sorry I made you worry. It was all a big mess and I shouldn't have gone. I just . . ."

"You just wanted to know your mom," Liv said gently. "I know." She hesitated before asking her next question. "Tay, do you think she's using again?"

Taylor shook her head. "I don't think so. She seemed completely clear and normal—well, as normal as she ever really is—the whole time. I think she's just . . . I think she's just struggling a little and she saw the fact I was in Colorado and she had friends in Colorado as like, I don't know, a sign or something."

"But she *left* you," Liv gritted out.

"Yeah." Taylor went quiet and stared down at her cup. "But I guess I should be used to that by now, right?"

The heartbreak contained in those few words shattered her heart. And once more, Liv regretted not going with her gut. She'd known that Maggie wasn't reliable, feared this kind of outcome. She hadn't thought she'd be rushing to Taylor's rescue in the middle of the night, but now she was glad that she'd thrown logic to the wind and gone after her.

"I'm sorry, Taylor," she said softly. "I wish it wasn't like that. I wish she was what you wanted her to be."

"Yeah. Me too." Taylor set her coffee in the cup holder and leaned her head against the headrest, falling silent. Liv let her be, and the next time she turned around to check, she was asleep.

"Well," Charlie whispered, "that was some story."

"I know. I wish I were surprised, but I'm really not." Liv shook her head. "Who does that? Abandons their own daughter once and then leaves when she's supposed to be spending the weekend with her?"

"Not a mother. Because a real mother drives three-and-a-half hours in the middle of the night to find her daughter." Charlie slanted her a significant look.

He was right. Liv had always tried to keep a little distance with Taylor, just because she didn't want her to think that she was trying to take her mother's place. It was why she'd always used the word *stepdaughter,* even in her own head. But the minute Liv thought she was missing, didn't know where she was, all those boundaries had been erased. Taylor was her daughter, as surely as if she'd given birth to her. And she was never going to make that mistake again.

When they finally pulled into the driveway of Liv's house at four in the morning, it looked different to her. It could have very easily been a place of sorrow, lonely and brimming with regrets that Liv would never be able to exorcise. And now it looked like what Jason had always wanted it to be—a sanctuary, a refuge, a home. Not because of the bricks and wood that formed its structure, but because of the people in it.

Liv climbed out of the car and opened the back seat to gently shake Taylor awake. "Tay, we're home."

Taylor blinked sleepily, but she grabbed her bag and half-climbed, half-fell out of the back seat. Once Liv was sure that she could make it into the house on her own, she turned back to Charlie.

He took her hand and pressed her keys into her palm. "I'm glad everything worked out."

"Me too. Thank you, Charlie. I couldn't have done this alone."

He stepped forward, every bit of his posture saying that he was going to kiss her, and before she knew what she was going to do, she had taken a step back. Hurt flashed over his face, but it vanished just as quickly. "Sleep well. We'll talk in the morning."

Inside, she heard water running in the bathroom, the sounds of Taylor brushing her teeth. She passed by and went to her own room, but she left the door open as she stripped off her own clothes and replaced them with pajamas. She wasn't surprised when Taylor appeared in the doorway, scrubbed clean in shorts and a T-shirt, looking young and vulnerable.

"Can I sleep in here tonight?" Taylor asked in a small voice.

Taylor hadn't slept with her since Jason had died, and it was an indication that she had been a lot more scared than she'd let on in the car. Liv nodded. "Climb on in."

Taylor closed the door and shut off the lights, then climbed under the covers beside Liv, on Jason's side. "I'm sorry," she whispered, her face close to Liv's on her pillow. "I thought you were trying to keep me from getting to know my mom, but now I know you were just trying to keep me from getting hurt."

Liv reached for Taylor's hand and laced their fingers together. "I was. I shouldn't have let you go, but I didn't want you to resent me. I was afraid if I held on too tight, I would lose you."

Silent tears slipped down Taylor's face, glinting in the soft spill of moonlight through the window. "I just wanted to have a mom."

The words struck Liv in the heart, took her breath away. "You do have a mom, Taylor. Me."

Taylor sniffled. "You're my stepmom. It's not the same thing."

"Then maybe we should fix that." The words were out of Liv's mouth before she even realized what she was saying, but as soon as she did, they felt right.

Taylor pushed herself up on her elbow, staring at Liv from the shadows. "What do you mean?"

They couldn't have this conversation in the dark. Liv reached over and flipped on the bedside lamp, then pushed herself upright, her legs bent beneath her. "What if we made it official? What if I adopted you?"

"Like, for real? Like, legally? Would I have to change my name?"

Liv stared at her. "Taylor, both of our last names are Quinn."

Taylor broke into embarrassed laughter. "Oh yeah."

"So what do you say? I know maybe it doesn't sound like a big deal, but legally, you would be my daughter. Not stepdaughter. No chance of Maggie coming back and trying to take you away."

Now it was Taylor's turn to give her the raised eyebrow. "Liv, no one is going to take me away. Not even Maggie. I'm smarter than that."

"Yeah. I guess you are. So what do you think? Should we make it official?" Sudden insecurity struck Liv. "Only if you want."

Taylor reached for Liv's hand again and squeezed. "I want."

Liv exhaled her relief, tears springing to her eyes. "Okay then. We'll talk to Gemma tomorrow

438

and she can start the process." She held her arms out and Taylor went into them without hesitation.

"Thank you for coming to get me," she whispered.

"I will always come get you." Liv let her go, smiling through tears, then turned off the bedside light.

They were settled back in bed for a few seconds, when Taylor whispered, "What about Charlie?"

The thought of Charlie struck equal parts of pain and longing into her middle, but she knew what she had to do. She'd made a bargain after all, and she'd already learned what happened when she put herself before the good of her daughter. She wasn't going to make that mistake again.

"Charlie isn't nearly as important to me as you are," Liv whispered.

"Okay." Taylor reached for her once more and squeezed her arm. "I love you, Liv. I mean . . . Mom."

And even though her heart had started breaking the minute she made her decision about Charlie, that single word already began to heal it.

Liv wasn't the only one with a sixth sense she didn't want to listen to. Charlie had a very good idea what was going to happen next, and he didn't like it.

He'd known it the minute that Liv pulled her hand away in the car on the way to get Taylor, had confirmed it when she stepped away from his kiss when they got home. It didn't matter that Taylor's situation wasn't Liv's fault. It didn't even matter what they'd been doing when she'd realized that Taylor was in trouble. It was that Liv would never forgive herself for allowing herself to have a moment of happiness that didn't relate to her daughter. And Charlie didn't know if there was anything he could do to overcome that.

But he was certainly going to try.

He woke up early the next morning, headed into town at first light, and joined the line outside of the Broken Hearts Bakery. Slowly, the line inched forward from the sidewalk into the warm, cinnamon-scented interior of the bakery. When he finally got up to the register, Gemma regarded him with sympathy.

"Well, you couldn't have gotten much sleep last night," she observed, confirming that he did indeed look as bad as he felt.

"Not much," he said. "I take it that Liv told you what happened?"

"She texted me when you were on the way home. I'm glad she found Taylor unharmed." Gemma fixed a look on Charlie. "And I'm glad she had you with her."

"Yeah," Charlie said flatly. "I'm not sure she feels the same way."

He expected to have to explain, but Gemma just nodded thoughtfully. "Give her time. She hasn't had it all that easy for the past few years, and this probably really threw her for a loop." She flicked a glance at the line still building behind him, or maybe she was just gauging whether the nosy townspeople were listening to their conversation. "I assume you're here for cinnamon rolls?"

"A whole tray, please."

"Coming right up." Gemma smiled again, then grabbed one of the prepackaged trays on the back counter. He went to pay, but she waved him off. "Send Liv and Taylor my love."

He smiled in thanks, not just for the cinnamon rolls, but for the reassurance. The whole way home, though, his stomach twisted. He had a bad feeling about this, and while part of him wanted to charge right in and have it out with Liv, the other part wanted to delay the inevitable for as long as possible.

Charlie figured he was going to have to wait a while before they were up, but when he got home, the kitchen light gleamed from the window. Someone was up. He moved to the front door and knocked lightly.

A minute later, Liv opened the door, wearing sweat pants and a tank top, her hair piled into a messy bun on top of her head. She looked exhausted, her eyes red-rimmed and shadowed from lack of sleep, but she was also the most beautiful human he'd ever seen. "Can I come in?" he asked, holding up the tray of cinnamon rolls. "I brought breakfast."

Liv hesitated, then stepped back for him. They walked together to the kitchen, where the fragrance of brewing coffee already suffused the air. He set the cinnamon rolls on the island. "Liv—"

"Charlie, please don't." She took a step back, not quite meeting his eye. "These past weeks have been lovely. And I appreciate all you've done for us more than you can ever know. I don't know what I would have done without you. But . . ." She finally raised her gaze and the pain in it practically bowled him over. "I have to focus on Taylor right now."

"I know you think that means that you can't have anything for yourself, Liv, but it's not true. Yes, you need to take care of Taylor, but who is going to take care of you?" He moved closer to her, cupped her cheek with his palm. She leaned into his hand, soaking up his warmth, his touch, her eyes closing briefly. And then she swallowed and took the step back he had been dreading, the one that put more distance between them than a mere foot.

"I made a promise," she said, "and I'm going to keep it. I . . . I'm adopting Taylor."

"That's wonderful. I'm truly glad to hear that. But—"

"Charlie," she whispered, her voice hoarse. "I

442

almost lost her. Because I was selfish. Because I put what I wanted above what she needed. I was so obsessed with having a fun, sexy weekend with my boyfriend that I knowingly put her in harm's way. If anything had happened to her . . .' "

"But it didn't. Liv, don't you see? You were obsessed because you haven't taken any time for yourself since Jason died. You've been so concerned with making a good life for Taylor that you haven't thought about making a good life for yourself. Taylor deserves a mom who is happy and fulfilled and models good relationships. How are you going to do that if you close yourself off to everyone who isn't her?"

But he might as well have been talking to a brick wall for all the words penetrated. She had made up her mind. He could see it in her eyes, the way that she palpably withdrew from him. He hadn't realized how much he craved that warmth, that connection with her. The way that she looked at him like he was amazing, like she couldn't believe her luck. The way that she always seemed to be straining to touch him.

And only now that she was beyond reach did he realize what he'd almost had.

"I'm sorry, Charlie," she said, her voice stronger now. "You're a wonderful man and I never meant to hurt you."

"I told you once that I could be patient," he said.

"No one is that patient." She smiled sadly. "You're welcome to stay in the apartment as long as you need, but I think it would be best if you started looking for another place to stay."

"And the bookshop?"

"I . . . we'll figure that out, I guess."

But he didn't have to guess. She'd figure it out by communicating with him via email and text, having Taylor deal with him, keeping their paths from crossing as much as possible. And all the while, he'd be dying a little inside, knowing she was that close and he couldn't have her.

Once more, he'd loved a woman who just couldn't love him back.

He closed his eyes to gather himself, then rapped his knuckles sharply on the stone countertop. The sting grounded him, kept him from doing something stupid, from humiliating himself.

"Okay," he said finally. "If that's what you want."

It wasn't what she wanted, he knew that. But she'd insist on it until she believed it, until she buried any feelings she had for him and convinced herself that she didn't need a life of her own to be happy. And he knew there was nothing to say to that.

So he turned and went, his heart breaking with each step.

CHAPTER THIRTY-TWO

The next week felt like something of a dream. Liv went through the motions, putting on a cheery face for Taylor while inwardly she felt nothing but numbness. Too much had happened in a short period of time, she told herself. This was trauma, a reaction to all that adrenaline that had been coursing through her system and now had to slowly seep out of her body. She wasn't really sure if that's how it worked, but it seemed logical.

And it wasn't like she didn't have a lot to do. Now that Taylor was back and Maggie was out of their life completely—the woman had called on Sunday morning to explain, but Taylor had refused to speak with her—Liv had thrown herself wholeheartedly into the plans for the bookshop. Every day was a parade of Taylor's friends in and out of the house as they put together fundraisers and book drives ahead of the start of school next week. She found herself cooking breakfast and lunch for a bunch of teens every day, feeling immensely glad for the opportunity. Things could have turned out horribly. Had Maggie's friends not been the decent sort—Liv shuddered to think what the outcome could have been.

The plans to move the store forward while

avoiding Charlie turned out to be easier than she expected. She worked on cleaning and scrubbing and organizing in the evenings with Taylor, leaving the space empty for him to work in the daytime. Each evening she returned to find he'd moved them one step closer to their goals: one day the floors were sanded, the next the banisters were refinished. One afternoon he texted to tell her that he was staining and finishing the floors, so stay out of the shop for forty-eight hours. Which Liv took as the perfect opportunity to take Taylor to Colorado Springs for a full day of school clothes shopping.

Whatever tension had been between her and Taylor had mostly vanished. Maybe it was the fact that they had the adoption process underway with Gemma or the realization that Liv wanted her permanently as a daughter, not just until the guardianship expired at eighteen. Or maybe it was that scary experience had made them realize that they did love each other, that they were family just as surely as if they were linked by blood. Maybe more because now they had chosen each other. Liv was by no means a perfect parent, but she loved Taylor and she would do everything she possibly could for her. Including sacrifice her own happiness.

"You're an idiot," Gemma told Liv bluntly when she came to her office to go over some paperwork. "You're miserable. I can see it, and you're dumber than I thought if you think that Taylor can't see it."

Liv just stared back at her. "Thanks. I appreciate those very kind and sensitive words."

"I've been doing kind and sensitive and it doesn't seem to be penetrating your thick skull. You miss him, Liv. And he misses you. I see him around town and it's like a light's gone out in him."

"He'll get over it."

"Yeah, he might. But will you?"

Liv frowned at Gemma. "You know why I'm doing this. Why can't you just accept it?"

"Uh, maybe because you had a perfect man who was madly in love with you and you pushed him away for no reason?"

"It wasn't *no* reason," Liv said. "I made a promise."

"To who? Taylor?"

"To . . . God."

Now Gemma's eyebrows tried to climb into her hairline. "You made a promise to God. I didn't think you believed in God."

"I didn't think I believed in God either until my daughter was missing. But I made a promise. If he brought her back to me okay, I would give up everything that distracted me from her. Including Charlie." Her cheeks burned as she remembered that night in the kitchen before Taylor had called, not from pleasure but from shame. "If I hadn't wanted to jump into bed with him so badly, I wouldn't have let Taylor go off for the weekend with a woman I knew wasn't trustworthy."

Gemma snorted.

"You don't believe me?"

"Oh, I believe that you believe what you're saying, even if it's a load of bunk." Gemma crossed her arms, getting that narrow-eyed court-room look that told Liv she was in for it. "If all you wanted was sex, he lives across the yard. You could have gone over there at any point and he probably wouldn't have turned you down."

Liv gaped at her, her flush now coming from embarrassment. "Charlie isn't—"

"He's a man," Gemma said. "One who isn't inclined to deny you anything. He practically worships the ground you walk on. My point is, you didn't need Taylor to leave if that's all you wanted. You wanted to be romanced and to feel important and to actually focus on yourself for a change without all those little worries creeping in."

"You're kind of making my case for me," Liv said. "That's exactly why I can't have him in my life."

"That's exactly why you need him in your life." Gemma reached across the table to grab one of Liv's hands. "When you were with him, you were more alive than I've seen you since high school. And now, you're like a shell of yourself. Is that the message you want to send to Taylor? That in order to be her mom, you have to be miserable?"

"That's not—"

"Isn't it? You had Charlie, you were happy. You decided to adopt Taylor, now you're miserable. You tell me what an insecure teenage girl is going to make of that."

"I've been really careful to make sure it doesn't spill over onto her."

"Taylor is not an idiot, Liv. And you're not that good of an actor."

Ouch. That was harsh. But Gemma was not known to pull punches when she thought her friends needed the hard truth. "It doesn't matter anyway. I already told Charlie I wasn't interested. He's been perfectly fine avoiding me. He even texted me the other night to say he found an apartment in town."

"All right," Gemma said, holding her hands up. "If that's the way you want it. I've done my duty as a friend and told you that you're making a mess of things. If you don't want to listen to me, that's your business."

Liv wasn't sure if she wanted to laugh or smack her. She settled on a smirk and keeping her hands to herself. "With friends like you . . ."

". . . who needs enemies? Please. You're lucky you have a friend who cares enough to call you out." Gemma winked at her. "Now get out of my office. I have work to do."

Despite herself, Liv felt a little lighter as she left the office. Not that Gemma had changed her mind. Not one little bit. But the fact that Gemma loved her enough to tell her that she was stupid and get in her face made her think she was going to be okay. You weren't mean to hopeless cases, just like you weren't cruel to terminally ill people. That meant that Gemma saw a future in which Liv didn't feel like her heart had been ripped out of her chest. There was a future in which she was just fine.

She was walking back to her SUV around the corner when a text from Taylor came through. Hey, Charlie says the floors are ready to walk on. He's going to be out of there soon. Want to meet over there at 5?

Liv checked her watch. It was already four fifteen on Friday afternoon, which meant there wasn't much point in going home just to turn around and come back. But it was enough time to walk down to the Koffee Kabin and grab a latte, wander around the town a little bit. She quickly typed out a reply to Taylor—Sure, see you there—dropped her keys back into her purse, and changed direction, walking the length of Dogwood Street toward the little coffee shack at the very end of the lane. She chatted with Gregory to kill some time, then took her iced vanilla latte across Alaska Avenue and up Beacon Street. She peered into the empty windows, imagining a future in which all these were filled. Thomas—and Charlie by extension—was determined to turn this town around. And she had no doubt they would manage it. Already there was a sense of renewal in the air, as if the opening of the new shops had nudged something alive that had long been dormant. She stopped into Granny Pearl's gift shop just long enough to say hello, then moved on up the street to the bookstore. Her bookstore.

Taylor was already there, pacing the ground floor, examining every inch of the baseboards like an inspector. Liv walked in and inhaled the leftover chemical scent of the stain and varnish, then looked at the original hundred-year-old floors beneath their feet. Where they'd once been grimy and worn, pockmarked with divots and splintered in places, now they gleamed with a warm honey sheen. She was pleased to see that Charlie hadn't sanded away all the character: The surface scratches were gone, but the old nail holes and gouges were still visible.

"He did a great job, didn't he?" Taylor said, glancing up to smile at her. "We were really lucky we found him when we did."

The words wrapped around Liv's heart and squeezed. "Yeah, we really were. Have you looked at the upstairs yet?"

"Yeah, but the floors still felt a little tacky. I wouldn't go up there."

Liv narrowed her eyes. She knew when her daughter was lying. "Tay, what's going on here?"

The door opened with a jingle of harness bells and Charlie ground to a complete halt, blinking at the two of them. "Hey. I thought . . ." His words stuttered to a stop, and the sudden look of pain and longing on his face almost took her knees out from under her. "Liv. Hi."

"Hi, Charlie." She dragged her eyes away from him and narrowed them at Taylor. "Explain yourself."

Taylor marched over between them. "I brought you two here because you're both being stupid."

"Taylor!" Liv exclaimed just as Charlie said mildly, "You really shouldn't call your mom stupid."

Taylor just looked at them both with a little smile. "I notice neither of you tried to defend *yourselves,* but anyway. Guys, I'm not blind. You two are in love. And for some reason that none of us can fathom, you've decided that you need to be apart."

"Taylor, it's more complicated than that," Liv said gently. "You know why—"

"Nope. It's really not more complicated than that." Taylor went to Liv's side and grabbed her hand. "I know you love me. You've done everything for me since Dad died. You're adopting me. I don't need you to give up someone you love to prove that to me."

She turned to Charlie. "And you. I swear to all that is holy, if you ever hurt her, I will track you down. I know you think I'm all sweet, but I wear black for a reason. If you're not good to my mom . . . I. Will. Destroy. You."

Charlie looked like he was fighting against a smile, but he gave a solemn nod.

"Now. I am going to leave. And you two are going to go upstairs and work all this out between you. And text me when you're ready to go." She dangled the old-fashioned key and gave them a wicked smile. "Because I have the only key and you're locked in here until I say so."

Charlie and Liv looked at each other, wondering which one of them should tell her. Liv finally took the lead. "Um, Taylor? There's a back door that opens from the inside."

"Oh." Taylor lowered her hand, looking a little crestfallen. She handed the key to Liv. "In that case, I'm going to take the SUV and go home. Charlie can bring you back." That smile returned and she winked at them. "Have fun, lovebirds."

Charlie and Liv watched Taylor as she marched out of the bookshop and then climbed into Liv's car.

"That girl is something else," Charlie said with a hint of admiration.

"And she's grounded for the rest of her life."

Charlie looked at her, the thread of hope in his expression almost more than she could bear. "If you want to go, we can go. I know she brought you here under false pretenses."

"Are you kidding me? I want to know what's on the second floor. She wouldn't let me go up there." Liv didn't wait for Charlie, just turned and marched up the newly varnished staircase, noting his meticulous work as she went. At the top, she stopped so abruptly that he bumped into the back of her.

Spread out in the middle of the floor was a large quilt scattered with pillows that Liv recognized from Taylor's own room. A picnic basket sat there, stuffed with all sorts of goodies: a bottle of sparkling water, strawberries, some French cheese, a sleeve of crackers, sliced baguettes. She'd swiped plates and glasses from their kitchen to set places. And the finishing touch? A dozen candles grouped together in twos and threes, bathing the whole space in a warm, flickering glow.

"Wow," Charlie said. "She really went all out."

It was romantic, for sure. "I don't know what she thinks she's doing."

Charlie smiled at her and reached for her hand. "I do. She's giving us her approval. And a not-so-subtle nudge."

"Charlie . . ."

"Don't. Just hear me out." Charlie reached for her other hand so she had no choice but to face him, to look him in the eye. "I know this is scary, Liv. I know that you've got a ton to deal with. I understand if you're unsure about dating again after Jason, and I know the adoption is a lot, even though it's a good thing. We can take this as slowly as you want. If you don't want me to touch you or kiss you or . . . whatever . . . I can be okay with that.

"But Liv, I love you. I don't care if it's too fast or it feels impossible. I know that I was brought here for a reason. Not just to help with the town, but to love you. To be your support. To give you someone to lean on as you go through all this heavy stuff. Just . . . just let me love you."

It was possibly the sweetest and kindest thing that anyone had ever said to her. Liv stared up at him, marking the sincerity in his eyes. How was it possible that she had gotten so lucky? To find a man who loved her so much that he demanded nothing in return, was willing to be as patient as she needed to navigate her feelings about moving on after such a huge loss. Who, if she was reading Taylor right, had won over her impossible-to-please daughter so much that she set up a huge and somewhat ill-advised candlelit picnic to make them work it out.

A man who was looking at her right now with incredible hope and love and sincerity, enough that it made her want to cry.

More importantly, it made her want to *try*.

Slowly, Liv nodded. His face lit up and she

pulled her hand free to hold up a finger. "Charlie, you make me happy in a way that I haven't felt in years. In a way I thought I would never experience again. And what I feel for you, it's real. But I can't say *that* word. Not yet. Not until I'm sure."

"It's okay," he murmured, taking a step forward. "Didn't I say I was patient?"

And then she was in his arms, and he was kissing her, sweetly and sincerely, until she forgot everything around them. They sank to the floor, still touching, until Liv pulled back. "I know it kind of ruins the moment, but I'm a little worried about all these candles near new varnish."

Charlie chuckled. "I think it's probably fine, but why take chances?" He leaned over and began blowing them out, one by one, sending the acrid smell of char into the air.

Liv reached for his hand and pulled him back toward her, smiling up at him as she did. "Some things are worth taking a chance on."

EPILOGUE

Two months later

The day of the grand opening of the Beacon Street Bookshop dawned bright and crisp, with a bright sun shining from a clear blue sky. The forecast was for a clear, pleasant day, but there was the unmistakable hint of autumn in the air, the promise of change to come.

It felt like the theme of Liv's life. The adoption was under way, and even though it wouldn't be finalized for a few more months, just the fact that it was in process had changed the way that she and Taylor related to each other. She hadn't realized how much uncertainty still existed in their relationship . . . and not just for Taylor. Now that Liv knew that Taylor was going to be her daughter forever, the last little bit of reservation that had bound up her heart seemed to have fallen away.

Or maybe that had something to do with Charlie. He'd decided to stay in the apartment over her garage, citing safety for her and Taylor, but mostly because they liked to see each other at random moments in the day. Despite Gemma's sarcastic words, Liv had *not* sneaked over to his place after Taylor went to bed, though she'd been tempted. Just because they were now officially together— to the delight of virtually the entire town—didn't mean that the heat between them had abated. It had just gone from a flash fire to a low simmer. Still, Taylor had taken to humming the wedding march every time Charlie left the room.

Who knew that her black-garbed teenage daughter was such a hopeless romantic?

"Are you ready?" Charlie appeared from the back office, carrying a box of bookmarks to put near the register. Liv took them from him gratefully, raising her face to accept his kiss, before she went back to arranging the counter. She could hardly believe that this day was here or that it had come together as quickly as it did. By some miracle, they'd hit their crowdfunding goals a couple of weeks ago, allowing them to begin stocking both the bookstore and the library. Donations had come pouring in—thanks to the teenagers' efforts—and the book drive that Stephen had taken over for the high school had yielded them boxes and boxes of gently used books for both spaces.

And almost as if it had been waiting to make its grand entrance, the nonprofit approval had come through yesterday.

"I'm ready," she said, taking a deep breath. "Open the doors."

Charlie winked at her and then moved to the front door, where he turned the key and pocketed it, then stood aside for the flood of townspeople waiting on the sidewalk. In minutes, the place was packed with shoppers and browsers examining books, flopping in the overstuffed armchairs in the lower bay window, oohing and ahhing over the huge gleaming crystal chandelier that scattered warm refracted light down on everyone below.

A couple of kids raced past and thundered up the stairs to the library and reading nook, where Taylor and Dylan were waiting to read picture books to a rapt group of toddlers and their parents. Almost immediately, they heard a wail and the shush of a grown-up voice. Charlie bent to whisper in her ear, "I don't think we thought this open second floor through enough."

Liv chuckled. "It'll be fine. Everyone's just excited." But more than that, she loved the energy. Book lovers were her people, the citizens of her heart's country. Before long, a couple of the town's seniors were at the counter with their purchases, and Liv rung them up with only a little falter as she searched for the right function on the point-of-sale system.

Mrs. Jensen held up her smartphone. "Can I tap to pay?"

Liv grinned at her and nodded, waving toward the card reader while she wrapped up the packages. There would be no plastic bags here; instead, she wrapped the purchases with brown paper and tied them with twine. Behind her, Charlie broke out in a hummed rendition of "My Favorite Things" from *The Sound of Music*.

And then Gemma was standing there before her, holding a new hardback thriller. "Pretty good turnout, I'd say."

Liv looked around in satisfaction. People were still coming in, murmuring their enthusiasm over the warm, beautiful space, many of them pulling books off the shelves to buy. At least she hoped they'd buy. But that wasn't the point. She'd meant to create a space where book lovers could come regardless of their budgets . . . and from the group of middle-school boys coming down the stairs clutching newly labeled copies of Malcolm Barry's books, she'd say that was already a success.

"I'm thrilled," she said finally, "beyond my wildest expectations."

"Hmm. Then I probably shouldn't show you this?" Gemma pulled out a newspaper folded back to display an article entitled "Charming bookstore and library signals new life in forgotten Colorado town."

Liv grabbed the newspaper out of Gemma's hand and gaped when she saw it. The Colorado Springs *Gazette*? It was one of the biggest newspapers in the state, and they'd somehow made the second page of the Lifestyle section? How was it she hadn't heard about this? Why had no one contacted her for a quote if they were doing an article?

And then Liv's eye fell on a familiar name. "That girl is unbelievable. Listen to this:

"Teenage co-owner and assistant store manager, Taylor Quinn, says that they want the bookstore to be more than just a place for townspeople to purchase their favorite fiction. 'We're a nonprofit, so we feel a real responsibility to the community. Books and knowledge are for everyone, regardless of their ability to pay, which is why our bookstore also includes a lending library. We hope that our example will inspire more business owners not just to expand into our wonderful town, but embrace an ethical and socially-responsible outlook on their place in the community.' "

Gemma was grinning. "That girl is going to change the world someday."

"If I don't kill her first," Liv muttered, but she was smiling. She'd said this was *their* business, not just Liv's, so she couldn't blame Taylor for taking her at her word. They'd just have to have a little talk about how business partners communicated things like newspaper interviews.

"Nah," Gemma says. "You love it. She keeps you on your toes." She smiled at Liv and pushed her purchase across the counter for her to ring it up. "I'm so, so proud of you, Liv."

"Thanks, Gemma, for everything." She swiped her best friend's card, then wrapped up her book and secured it with a pretty bow. "I wouldn't have done this if I hadn't seen you do it first. You inspired me."

Gemma's gaze flicked to Charlie and then back to Liv. "Love you. See you tonight."

It took hours before the crowd died down, not just from all the people making purchases, but also because of the steady stream of patrons applying for library cards and checking out books. At last, in early afternoon, there were just a scattering of people browsing both floors and Liv felt justified in plopping down on the stool behind the counter. Who knew that being on her feet and talking to people she knew all day would be this taxing?

Apparently, Charlie did, because as if he'd sensed her weariness, he appeared from the back room. He slid his arms around her waist from behind, pressed his lips to her hair. "So you did it, you and Taylor. How does it feel?"

Liv twisted on her seat to look up at him. "Weird. Not weird because it's strange, but weird because it isn't. Somehow, it feels like this was all inevitable."

"Books are in your blood," Charlie said with a smile. "In fact, I'm pretty sure ink flows through your veins."

Liv laughed and slid off the seat so she could slip her arms around his waist. "I don't just mean that. I mean you and me. Here, right now. I couldn't have done any of this without you, and

I wouldn't want to." She paused long enough to look him in the eye. "I love you, Charlie Castro."

Surprise lit Charlie's eyes. He'd been open about his feelings since Taylor's intervention, but always Liv had shied away from the words, even though the truth had been gradually building in her heart, just waiting to be voiced.

Now he looked at her as if he couldn't quite believe it, like she'd made a mistake. "Liv, I don't want you to be pressured. If you're not ready . . ."

Liv placed a finger on his lips to still his words. "Charlie, you are the kindest, most patient, most irresistible man I have ever met in my life. And every day I wake up feeling grateful that you're mine. I never want to be without you. If that's not love, I don't know what is."

Charlie closed his hands around her waist and pulled her tight against him, a mischievous grin on his lips. "Well, if you're sure . . ."

Liv smiled and sank into his kiss, the rightness of it all enveloping her in happiness. Only when he had thoroughly taken her breath away—along with all the strength in her knees—did she pull back to look at him.

She smiled up at him and rested a hand against his cheek, basking in the warmth and adoration radiating from his eyes. "I've never been so sure of anything in my life."

ABOUT THE AUTHOR

Carla Laureano could never decide what she wanted to be when she grew up, so she decided to become a novelist—and she must be kinda okay at it because she's won two RWA RITA® Awards. When she's not writing, she can be found cooking and trying to read through her TBR shelf, which she estimates will be finished in 2054. She currently lives in Denver, Colorado with her husband, two teen sons, and an opinionated cat named Willow. Visit her on Facebook, Instagram, Goodreads, Bookbub, or her website for more information about her books.

Center Point Large Print
600 Brooks Road / PO Box 1
Thorndike, ME 04986-0001 USA

(207) 568-3717

US & Canada:
1 800 929-9108
www.centerpointlargeprint.com